VOLTAIRE

Candide
and Other Tales

INTRODUCTION BY
H. N. BRAILSFORD

TRANSLATION BY
TOBIAS SMOLLETT
REVISED BY
J. C. THORNTON

D1632203

DENT: LONDON
EVERYMAN'S LIBRARY
DUTTON: NEW YORK

ISBN: 0 460 00936 2

CONTENTS

INTRODUCTION

ARCHITECTS do not sign their work. Nowhere in the stone of St Paul's is Wren's name graven, nor are we reminded daily when we enjoy the tolerance and humanity of a liberal civilization that we owe it in great measure to Locke, Newton and Voltaire. If this great Frenchman lives today in the gratitude of Everyman, it is because he wrote *Candide*. That is indisputably his gift to all time, for it comes to us labelled. With his name on the cover, this tale may be bought in cheap editions in every language of the civilized world. In that fact lies some measure of what this man achieved. When first this masterpiece set men laughing and thinking, it slunk into the world without its author's name, and even in Protestant Geneva it was publicly burned by that model democracy. The wit still sparkles, the satire still stabs and the prose retains its athletic grace. Like the men of the eighteenth century who snatched it fresh from the press, we bless its creator for the stimulus and entertainment of this unique invention. But we are apt to forget how much more we owe him. If we may read him freely, nay are expected for our own full development to read him, this liberty is the prize he won for us in a life of incessant combat. If we enjoy freedom of discussion, if books are nowhere burned alive today, we are the debtors of Voltaire and the pupils he inspired. If the tales in this volume were merely the exquisite work of a supreme artist, they would have title enough to survive. But they are immeasurably more than this. In them rings out, in laughter, the challenge that Voltaire and his generation hurled at intolerant authority. But the fun should not mislead us: this was not a good-natured battle. Men went to prison in Voltaire's day for their liberalism: they were sent to the galleys for heresy, and on occasion youths were beheaded for sacrilege.

Civil rights, equality before the law and liberty of discussion were won in France only by revolution. A reader who knew nothing of Voltaire and little about his century would none the less enjoy the wit, the fancy and genial wisdom of these tales. The salt in them has kept them fresh, while the vast bulk of this indefatigable writer's work interests only the professed students of his period. But they should gain much in significance, if we set them in the context of his life and thought. These irresponsible skirmishes in the long international war for freedom mean more to us than many a pitched battle, because it was an artist of genius who ran ahead of the legions with his sling.

The man who took the pen-name of Voltaire was born in Paris in 1694. The feeble infant was not expected to live; the struggle of his indomitable courage with the constant ill-health of his puny frame began in his cradle and was waged through eighty-four years of monumental industry and gay activity. His family was rising from a modest station in the middle class, but his father was a successful lawyer, who had among his clients, the noble houses of Sully and Richelieu. Little François-Marie Arouet lost his mother in infancy and drew from an elder sister such tenderness as fell to his lot, for his father was a stern man. The family inclined to the Jansenist heresy, the typical form which the Puritanism of the rising middle class assumed among French Catholics. This sect wore sober clothes, studied the Scriptures, disdained the pleasures and vanities of this world, but contrived to be 'diligent in business,' though its spiritual ideal was the monastic life. Against this creed of 'other-worldliness' the boy must have revolted at an early age. His godfather was the Abbé de Châteauneuf, a noted wit, poet and free-thinker. His Jansenist father, oddly enough, sent him to the most celebrated school of the rival Jesuit faction, the College of Louis le Grand. Here he had an excellent classical education, and his Jesuit teachers did much to foster his taste for French literature and modern history. The precocious youth played no games and consorted rather with the masters than the boys, but among them he made, none the less, friendships that he retained, with a typical constancy, throughout his long life.

While still at school he wrote some graceful verses that were admired in literary salons. Poetry called him; but his father insisted that he should follow the law. He was an idle and unwilling student, but he must have picked up some practical knowledge that served him well in after life. Equally futile was an attempt to launch him on a diplomatic career. He was attached to the embassy at the Hague, but was soon sent home in disgrace because he had formed an ardent and romantic attachment to a young lady who belonged to an exiled Huguenot family. Dodging the law, seeking refuge in the country houses of noble patrons and polishing verses, he was welcomed at the Temple, where there dined a gay society of cultured libertines, most of them nobles, many of them churchmen, all of them freethinkers. This youth was never embarrassed among the great. He rushed into the literary feuds in which this society indulged, and joined in the popular sport of lampooning the Regent. To this indiscretion, though in fact he did not write the verses attributed to him, he owed his first imprisonment under a *lettre de cachet* in the Bastille (1717). There was good company in this gloomy fortress, and the young man used his eleven months of leisure to write the first sketch of his epic, the *Henriade*, devoted to the glory of Henri IV, the one king of France who was great by tolerance. It seems to the modern reader a mediocre poem, but it was a bold thing to tell the story of the St. Bartholomew massacre with unsparing condemnation, and to applaud the policy of Queen Elizabeth. Liberated from prison, he completed his first tragedy *Oedipus*, which had an astonishing success on the stage and made him indisputably the foremost of the younger literary men of his day. Voltaire lives on, thanks to his tales and his histories, but in his own day his fame rested chiefly on his tragedies in verse, which we read without enthusiasm. He was a practised amateur actor, who knew all the tricks of classical stagecraft. His plots, too, are stirring, but to us the dialogue seems stilted, arid and monotonous. The themes, drawn chiefly from antiquity and the Middle Ages, reflect no direct emotional experience, and indeed the prefaces suggest that Voltaire sat down deliberately to write exercises in the grand manner. None the less, *Oedipus*, *Mérope*, *Mahomet*, *Zaïre* and *Tancred* were received by the taste of that day as masterpieces in which the polite genius of France had surpassed the Greek tragedians. This was a self-conscious age that measured itself uncertainly against the ancients. It is on record that these plays stirred the feelings of Parisian audiences : at one of them even a Chief of Police was seen to weep. One exception there is among them that does spring from a living emotion—*Alzire*, which deals with the sufferings of the Peruvians under their Spanish Conquerors. But Voltaire was always formidable and sincere when he lashed cruelty. Unless we realize Voltaire's fame as a tragic poet, his career will be unintelligible. He brought glory to France, and therefore he enjoyed in all his audacities a relative immunity from the more deadly forms of persecution. His books were burned, but not his person.

In the theatre one evening as the famous young poet was chatting with his intimate friend Adrienne Lecouvreur, the leading actress of the day, an aristocrat subjected him to a stupid insult, that turned on his change of name from Arouet to Voltaire. When the Chevalier de Rohan repeated his pleasantry next evening, Voltaire had his answer ready. ' The name *I* bear is not a great one but I at least know how to bring it honour.' A few days later the Chevalier lured him into the street from the supper table of the Duc de Sully, and directed his men-servants while they beat the poet unmercifully. Voltaire sought redress in vain from the police and at Court, but the influence of the Rohan family was too powerful. When he challenged his assailant to a duel, the family got him imprisoned in the Bastille. His second stay was brief, for by an act of relative mercy he was permitted to go into exile in England (1726). This incident was the turning point of his career. He now understood the humiliations that await even a man of genius in an aristocratic society. Rohan's cudgel consecrated him the thinker of the middle-class revolution.

His sojourn of nearly three years in England was stimulating and happy. He mastered our language, read widely and met all the leading men of the day. His impressions

were afterwards recorded in a lively little volume of
' Philosophical Letters,' which first familiarized Europe
with the intellectual revolution that sprang from the work
of Locke, Newton, and the Royal Society. A maturer
Voltaire emerges. He is as witty as ever and still avoids
' solemnity as a disease,' but he has left the libertine
hedonism of the Temple behind him, to become what that
age called a ' philosopher.' The new conception of the
universe as a system of effects and causes, subject to law
and mathematical measurement, dazzled him as a revela-
tion. Briefly here and afterwards at length he popularized
Newton's discoveries, and used them in the warfare against
intolerance and superstition. He drew a flattering picture
of England after the Whig Revolution, by way of rousing
the French middle-class to emulation. Here was liberty
with order : the monarchy had been checked : free debate
prevailed in public affairs and the church had been
subordinated to the secular power. Commerce throve :
the merchant was respected : a career was open to talent :
a Newton was honoured as the greatest of mankind. This
nation, moreover, taxed itself and no privileged class
escaped. There was much more, all of it vastly entertaining, about the Quakers (whom he respected), vaccination,
Shakespeare (whom he ranked as a barbarian of genius),
Dryden and Pope (whom he admired). The style is amusing, for only by disguising it as light entertainment could
one hope to pack undisturbed such a charge of intellectual
dynamite beneath the fabric of French society.

His exile ended, Voltaire faced again the realities of life
under a despotism. He was the centre of turbulent literary
quarrels, in which wit was his only weapon against adver-
saries who called on the law to crush him. His plays still
prospered, but all his other works circulated only in
smuggled editions. The English *Letters* were publicly
burned, and to avoid a harsher period of prison in an even
gloomier gaol than the Bastille, he fled (1734) to Cirey on
the borders of Lorraine.

There had now begun an intimacy that lasted for sixteen
years with one of the most remarkable women of her day.
Emily, Marquise du Châtelet, worked at physics and
astronomy and translated Newton. This ' blue-stocking '

was none the less a woman of strong passions, as jealous and possessive as Voltaire was affectionate and constant. The pair, with a complacent husband in the background, lived through most of this time in his family seat at Cirey, which Voltaire embellished. He was already a wealthy man, for apart from his literary earnings, he speculated, played sleeping partner to an army contractor, and lent money to German princes. He worked with incessant and methodical industry in this country retreat. He had always a tragedy in hand : when he was ill in bed he wrote verses, among them some of the most graceful madrigals in the French language. He kept up an active correspondence with his fellow ' philosophers ' all over Europe, and these lively and intensely human letters, copied and read aloud in salons, were soon a powerful instrument of propaganda. A part of his time he gave to experiments in chemistry and physics.

But his central task was now the writing of history. His first effort, published and suppressed before the flight to Cirey, was the life of Charles XII of Sweden, a masterly exercise in narrative : even in this first essay he is already the moralist, who strips Glory naked, and tears the glamour from war. At Cirey in his talks with Madame du Châtelet, he reached a new conception of history. Her scientific mind found all the accepted books as tedious as they were incredible. They were either mere chronicles of battles, miracles and the life of Courts, or else, like Bossuet, the writers abandoned themselves to speculations on the designs of Providence. So arose in Voltaire's mind the ambition to render history worthy of a scientific age : it should trace causes and effects : it should deal with the whole life of man, with literature, invention and commerce as well as with politics : it should be, in short, a history of the human mind, a record of the advance of civilization. This task he performed, however imperfectly, with spirit and industry, nor can one deny that this militant rationalist strove to be fair even to the enemy, even to Rome. He had thought out no consistent interpretation of the factors that cause movement in history, but there are many flashes of insight, more especially when he stresses the influence of economic motives. The first of his great histories, *The Century of Louis XIV*, still ranks as a classic of French literature, and indeed one may reckon it as the first notable essay in history since Tacitus polished his last epigram. The *Essay on the Customs and Genius of Nations*, of which he wrote the first sketch at Cirey, is a bolder and vaster work, for it is nothing less than a general history of civilization, which includes in its sweep Turkey, India, China and Japan as well as Europe. It is, with *Candide*, the greatest and most dynamic of Voltaire's books. The progress of research has rendered it hopelessly out of date, but through several generations it was a mighty influence in forming the mind of liberal Europe. The central theme that brought unity into European history from Charlemagne to his own day was for Voltaire the long struggle between the secular and the ecclesiastical power. This was a perilous simplification, but it enabled him to write against ' Theocracy ' a pamphlet, raised by its style, its sincerity and its learning to the level of great literature. What he is really doing is to call in morality to shame theology. Save where it turns aside to recount the progress of science and the arts, the narrative sweeps along describing the cruelties, the persecutions, the dissensions and wars inspired by ' fanaticism.' Its purpose is to reveal to us ' superstition ' in action.

But a more positive purpose is at work in these histories. With all the resources of his art, Voltaire uses his narrative to fix the scheme of moral values that we call liberalism. He does it partly by his judgments on men. He will tear down a Constantine or a Charlemagne from their seats, chiefly because of their cruelty, in order to exalt King Alfred, or Pope Alexander III because he freed the serfs. He will devote a whole page to an obscure colonial administrator who ' dug canals while others devastated the earth.' His outlook is cosmopolitan : he will go out of his way to praise a good prince who was an enemy of France, while he exposes with an unflinching hand the nationalist egoism of Richelieu and Louis XIV. He seeks out and canonizes the heroes of science. The century of Louis XIV was glorious because it began with the founding of the Royal Society and ended with the French *Encyclopædia*. He castigates Imperialism and war, eulogizes commerce and is sure that it makes for peace. It is characteristic of this sensitively humane man that he surpasses himself in wit and eloquence whenever he denounces cruelty, whether the victims were men or animals, Indians or Christians. Many powerful pages exposed both the arbitrary power of kings, and the stupid barbarity of the contemporary legal system in France. He holds up the British constitution as the model for imitation. Battling against every form of aristocratic privilege, he none the less set limits to the work of emancipation. He argued, with evident uneasiness, that economic inequality was essential to the well-being of society. Manual workers would have to remain poor, but they need not be miserable. He would educate the skilled artisans, but not the labourers. Here in its rationalism, its tolerance, its humanity and its restricted social vision was the enlightenment of the rising middle-class.

These books were the true life of Voltaire during this creative period at Cirey. But this versatile man was slow to understand his real place in society as the head of its militant opposition. He aspired to more conventional and comfortable positions. He could fill the theatres with enthusiastic crowds, shine at Court by his wit, charm every king save his own. Through many years he hesitated. Again and again he was reconciled to the Court of Louis XV, but always some luckless indiscretion drove him into flight. Failing at the first attempt to enter the Academy, he planned an amusing revenge. His play *Mahomet* had been withdrawn from the stage because of its supposed impiety. Thereupon, he dedicated the printed text, with some flattering Latin verses, to the Pope, who responded with a medal and a benediction. ' Covered with the stole of the Vicar of God,' he now strode triumphantly into the Academy (1746). At Court he became at last a Gentleman-in-waiting, and Historiographer-royal. Happily for literature, he was soon in exile again. All the while a singular duel went on between the Marquise, who meant him to shine at home, and Frederick of Prussia, who was trying ' to depopulate France of her great men.' Frederick also was ' a philosopher,' and a poet who modelled himself on Voltaire. There was nothing surprising in the friendship that began by correspondence between the royal pupil and his master. Three brief meetings confirmed their mutual attraction, and at length, much against the will of the jealous Marquise, Voltaire paid a visit of four months to the Prussian Court. Feasts and pageants were arranged in his honour : princes and princesses acted his plays. He failed, however, in the semi-official diplomatic mission with which the French Court had charged him.

The intimacy with the Marquise had long since cooled into a devoted friendship. During their exile at the Court of Lorraine, she fell in love with a brilliant young officer and was soon bearing his child. Voltaire, jealous only for a moment, stood by her faithfully to the tragic end. She finished her Newton a few hours before her delivery, and died ten days later. So ended (1749) a friendship that gave Voltaire sixteen happy years in the hermitage of Cirey. After a short stay in Paris he migrated to Frederick's Court (1750).

All went well for a time. He corrected the King's French verses, and took part every evening in his ' philosophic ' suppers. Gossip, however, began to separate them, and before long Voltaire was involved in one of those not infrequent public indiscretions in which he pitifully sacrificed his dignity. He had used as his agent in some far from scrupulous speculative transactions a Jewish banker named Hirsch. Voltaire accused the man of cheating him, and dragged the case into court. He won it, but the publicity disgusted Frederick, as well it might. A reconciliation followed, but soon a much sharper quarrel opened. Maupertuis, a French scientist of some talent and even greater vanity, whom Frederick had made President of his Academy, had treated one of its members, Professor König, with gross injustice. König, in a scientific treatise, while criticizing one of Maupertuis' discoveries in a perfectly courteous way, had quoted a letter by Leibnitz of which he had a copy. Because, for an excellent reason, the original could not be produced, Maupertuis drummed König out of his Academy on a charge of forgery. Voltaire, an old friend of König, told the story quietly but with deadly effect in an open letter. Frederick then supported his President in an unconvincing pamphlet printed with the royal arms. Voltaire had at last an adversary worthy of his rapier. He replied in one of the deadliest satires ever written, *The Diatribe of Dr. Akakia*. For rollicking irresistible fun there is nothing to equal it in literature, unless it be De Quincey's *Essay on Murder*. Though the fun was all at the expense of the pompous Maupertuis, Frederick chose to take offence—partly because Voltaire had the audacity to publish the thing through the royal press. The quarrel was now past mending, and after a half-reconciliation, Voltaire insisted on quitting Potsdam. On his arrival at Frankfurt, Voltaire was arrested, though the King of Prussia had no jurisdiction over this Free City, and detained with his niece in a far from honourable custody for six weeks (1753). The excuse for this gross action was that Frederick insisted on the return of a volume of his own poems which he had given to Voltaire. Many years later Voltaire resumed their correspondence when this philosopher-king was at the lowest ebb of his fortunes. The King, magnanimous in his turn, ordered a mass to be sung when the aged Voltaire died, the only honour of the kind that his memory received.

For two years after this adventure Voltaire led a wandering life in various German towns near the French frontier, hoping that his many friends at Court, Madame de Pompadour among them, would open the road to Paris. But Louis XV, a dull man who dreaded this dangerous genius, was adamant. Henceforth Voltaire turned his back on Courts. Struck with the beauty of Geneva, he settled there and bought a villa in which to pass his ' last days,' which lengthened out to three and twenty years. This period was the happiest of his life. A new man emerged in this atmosphere of freedom. He bought a barren estate at Ferney on French soil just outside Geneva (1755), and became an enthusiastic farmer. Like Candide he had finished his adventures and settled down to ' cultivate his garden.' This, he discovered, was ' the true life of man,' and virtue came to mean for him the planting of trees and the conquest of earth for the plough. He now had a near view of the miseries of the French peasantry, and set himself with his usual ardour to alleviate them, first on his own estate and then farther afield. He had some local success in getting taxes lightened, but failed in his assault on other crushing relics of feudalism. Out of this experience came *The Man with Forty Crowns* (1767), a pamphlet, half tale, half dialogue, on the exploitation of the peasants, which became the textbook of the generation that was to make the Revolution. Geneva, meanwhile, was in civil commotion, and Voltaire received on his estate a hundred refugee families from the popular party. Many of them were watchmakers. He built cottages for them, financed them, touted for them, and won them a market among his philosophic friends all over Europe. For others he planted mulberries and started the manufacture of silk, flattering himself that his stockings had no rival. The old man, still terrible by his wit, ended his days as the beloved father of a thriving colony. His niece kept house for him : an adopted daughter whom he called Belle et Bonne satisfied his affections : a stream of friends and distinguished pilgrims cheered his solitude.

Another passion, equally disinterested, filled his later years. In 1762 at Toulouse an aged French Protestant, Jean Calas, was executed with mediæval barbarity. Like the Dreyfus affair, this case was to be decisive for the relations of Church and State in France. Calas was accused of murdering his son to prevent his joining the Catholic Church. It was a popular belief that Huguenots were bound in such cases to kill their children. In fact the young man was not meditating apostasy : he hanged himself in despair, because no worthy career was open to his talents, for no Protestant could enter any of the professions. It was physically and psychologically inconceivable that the aged Calas could have hanged a young man in the prime of life. But Toulouse, which kept up an annual feast-day to celebrate the massacre of 4000 Protestants in 1562, was a focus of fanaticism : the Church buried young Calas as a martyr, and everything possible was done from her pulpits to defeat justice. After a scandalous trial, old Calas was sentenced as a murderer, tortured on the rack and by water, exposed half-naked before the Cathedral, then stretched on a wheel while his limbs were broken, strangled after two hours' exposure, and finally cast into the flames.

Through influential Protestant friends this story reached

Voltaire in Geneva. He made up his mind slowly, waited till he could question the survivors of the Calas family, and tested their statements by writing to leading Churchmen. Once convinced of the dead man's innocence, he laid aside all his other tasks and interests, and devoted three years to the business of extorting from Catholic France a verdict of rehabilitation. He spent his own money lavishly, collected more from his friends, pulled wires indefatigably in Paris though he was himself an exile who dared not approach the capital, used his own skilful pen and directed the pens of the whole philosophic party in an effort of propaganda as restrained as it was convincing. He succeeded completely : three years after the outrage, by a unanimous verdict, the King's Court of Appeal declared Jean Calas and all his family innocent.

This was not the only case of the kind that won Voltaire's advocacy. Few men, indeed, in any age have served justice with such devotion. Another innocent Protestant, named Sirven, accused under like circumstances of the same crime, was saved by him. Nor was it only the victims of fanaticism that he helped, for in an ordinary criminal case he saved the life of a certain Madame Montbailly. It was the last satisfaction of his long life that he managed to rehabilitate the gallant soldier Lally. He failed, though he made a well-conceived effort, to save Admiral Byng, the sailor whose execution Candide witnessed at Plymouth. He rescued several Protestants condemned for their faith to the galleys. But in one peculiarly painful case he failed. Three very young men were accused, without a scrap of evidence, of mutilating a crucifix at Abbeville. Though torture could extract no confession from the Chevalier de la Barre, he was publicly beheaded. With his head Voltaire's *Philosophic Dictionary* was thrown into the flames.

About this time in the letters of Voltaire and his philosophic friends there recurs continually his war-cry : Écrasez l'Infâme. What infamous thing would he crush? Was it supernatural religion, or the Catholic Church; or was it intolerance? It was the power, as cruel as it was stupid, that crushed the Huguenots, broke Calas on the wheel and tossed the head of young De la Barre into the flames, the power that burned books and drove every free mind to intolerable precautions and evasions. What Voltaire apparently meant was the coercive power of the Church. He swore to disarm Theocracy. In two books which had an immense influence and circulation, he set about this task more openly and with fewer ironical disguises than before. The first was the *Essay on Toleration* (1763); which sprang directly from the Calas affair. After a moving narrative of that case, he broadens his argument into a general plea for toleration. He exposes the folly and barbarity of the persecution of the Huguenots, and ends by outlining an attitude that became typical of lay common-sense in France. Could men but realize that dogma is of no consequence and social morality all-important, they would be ready to embrace Protestants and even Moslems as their brothers. The second of these popular books, the *Philosophic Dictionary* (1764), is a medley of brief and lively essays that deal with most of the familiar topics of theological and political controversy. It became for a century the textbook of French liberals. It boldly makes war on miracles, and dissects much of the narrative of the Hebrew Scriptures. It offers us the familiar dilemma : reason insists that these narratives are incredible, but if we accept them by an act of Faith, then the God they reveal was a monster of cruelty and injustice. Of this theme Voltaire never wearied. He would work at it with an imposing apparatus of learning in the great historical *Essay*, and he would simplify it for the average reader in the *Dictionary* and in countless pamphlets. This was an indispensable task of liberation and an incomparable service to humanity. If our generation tends to undervalue it, it is because we were born into a world from which *l'Infâme* had already been driven.

Voltaire's positive beliefs underwent some process of growth. Always he was a Deist : always he bowed to what he called " natural religion," the creed of social morality common, as he believed, to all men in all ages. The curse that dogged history was that supernatural religion " bade men believe, instead of telling them to be just." In his early writings his God is a somewhat aloof First Cause, who claims our veneration. Morality, he insists, requires no support from religion. Somewhat later he develops a theory of conscience : God has implanted in men's minds a set of instinctive moral judgments. He begins, notably after the earthquake at Lisbon, which bulks so largely in *Candide*, to recognize in the universe a mystery that he cannot penetrate. In his last years he affirms his belief in a God who is more than a Creator and First Cause, a God who is goodness itself, stands in some direct relationship to men, and rewards good and punishes evil, apparently in this life, though we do not know how. The source of this change of belief was evidently a doubt whether morality alone could sustain society without the support of a *Dieu-gendarme*.

The end came to the old man, before his mental powers had weakened, in an hour of triumph long delayed. He had one unfulfilled wish at Ferney, to see Paris again. Louis XV was dead; the road was open: so to Paris in 1778 he set out, to see his last play, *Irene*, acted. His journey was a triumphant progress. All the intellect of Paris rushed to pay him homage. In the theatre a spontaneous pageant was improvised in his honour. In the streets the crowds flocked to applaud the saviour of Calas' children and Sirven. The Freemasons received him and the Academy made him its acting president. All this was too much for an aged body accustomed to the calm of the Alps. In a final effort to finish some work for the Academy, he wore himself out and succumbed. A last frailty has to be recorded. He dreaded the end that the Church prescribed for heretics—to be buried like a dog in a ditch. That had happened to his friend Adrienne Lecouvreur, as Candide discovered, for actors were still outside the pale. He would have compromised by receiving the last sacrament, but an arrogant priest insisted on a detailed retractation of his errors. From that he recoiled, His body went unhonoured to an obscure grave in the country. Thirteen years passed, till the Revolution recognized its intellectual father. His body was then brought back to Paris and interred in the Pantheon. The two daughters of Jean Calas headed the procession, which paused on the site of the demolished Bastille, to do its prisoner honour. This man was perhaps the most accomplished artist in words of any age. To that gift he added an incomparable industry and unparalleled daring. Frailties he had many, but few saints in the calendar can rival his record of service to mankind. We may close it with the contemporary epitaph that stood on his bier beside the Bastille : ' he made us ready for freedom.'

Into this history of an eventful life let us now fit the five tales in this volume.

Zadig, to follow the order of composition, belongs (1748) to that middle period of Voltaire's life, when he still hoped to shine at Court. At Versailles, one evening, he whispered in English to the Marquise du Châtelet, as she was losing heavily at the Queen's card table, ' Come away, you're playing with cheats.' The treasonable words were understood, and Voltaire had to flee post-haste, to the castle of the Duchess of Maine. Here by candle-light in a shuttered room, he wrote *Zadig*, and read it each evening to his aged hostess, while they listened for the hoofs of the horse that might bring a *lettre de cachet*. This narrative of the misfortunes that befell a philosopher in the Court of Bagdad is, in a sense, a fantasy based on experience. Didactic oriental tales were in fashion in this century, in England as in France, but Voltaire easily surpassed his models. Lightly, with the jesting charm of a skilled narrator, he wove into the tale some of his most cherished doctrines. For in this whimsical romance are embedded the principles of toleration and natural religion. Towards the end an angel expounds a skilful parody of Leibnitz' theory of optimism. The moral lies in Zadig's monosyllabic ' But—— '

Micromegas (1752) is a scientific romance in a wholly different vein. Its theme, if we must translate its fun into solemn words, is the relativity of all things, the immensity of space and the insignificance of our planet. It took mankind several centuries to draw the inevitable conclusions from Copernicus' discovery, that our earth is not the centre of the solar system, and not all of us have drawn them yet. With the anthropocentric view of the universe were destined to perish many accepted bodies of belief. With a jest in this fairy tale with a purpose,

Voltaire gently hastened their end. The episode of the ship that dropped into the breeches pocket of the stellar giant, as he was laughing at the absurdities of the clerical animalcule, is an allusion to an exploit of Maupertuis. That scientist led an expedition to Lapland to test by measurement Newton's hypothesis of the flattened poles.

Candide (1758) ranks in its own way with *Don Quixote* and *Faust*. The tale is told in limpid prose and the horizon is that of the eighteenth century, yet it too is a parable of human life. This youth of excellent parts but great simplicity is the immortal idealist who sets out in quest of his good, meets reality on the way, and at the end finds a relative happiness in creative work. He tilted at no windmills, nor did he travel in a menagerie of Teutonic symbols. He knew exactly what he wanted—to embrace Mlle Cunegund, whom he had once kissed behind a screen. But his pursuit of her across two Continents had in it, none the less, something of man's craving for the infinite. What he met on the way were nicely assorted samples of eighteenth-century life. All this befell Everyman every day, though only in this veracious chronicle were so many misfortunes piled on a single head. None of them were in themselves impossible and many of them belong to authentic history. Young men were really kidnapped for the Prussian army as Candide was. The Inquisition did celebrate an *auto-da-fe* after the Lisbon earthquake. Admiral Byng was in fact shot at Plymouth. The six deposed kings who kept their carnival at Venice were actually contemporaries. Slaves and Huguenots were still sent to the galleys.

The force of this satire lies, indeed, in its directness and simplicity. Watch Voltaire at work. He gains his effects largely by the use of concrete words for abstract. He will not write that heretics were executed at an *auto-da-fe*. He says plainly that they were roasted alive over a slow fire. He compels us to see an act of cruelty as it happened, and then, with one swift, dexterous movement, comes the thrust of his wit. He wasted none of his strength on pity. When he met cruelty, he answered it with unsparing militancy. Given a little time, his thrusts were often mortal. Some object that this use of the intellect is negative. Every denial implies an affirmation. Between the blows that Voltaire rains on cruelty and injustice, a quick ear catches a hymn to brotherly love. This planet has changed since Candide travelled, and Voltaire helped to change it. But it is not yet the best of all possible worlds, nor has *Candide* gone out of date.

In *L'Ingénu* (1767; entitled in English *Master Simple*) Voltaire succeeded in yet another manner. It is a tale of contemporary life, which, in spite of its whimsical opening, turns to deadly earnest half-way. The wit, which only amuses us at the start, scorches and stabs as he goes on. At the end he succeeds in touching us by an effect of simple pathos. This is one of the most singular successes in literature. The characters are drawn in thin, abstract lines—and, indeed, nowhere in tales, plays, or histories did Voltaire show much sense for character. Wit is commonly fatal to emotion. And yet this elusive artist moves us. No book of this century presents a sharper picture of its corrupt and cruel society.

The Princess of Babylon (1768) is a much happier tale. It is an old man's work, hardly the equal of its predecessors in sparkle or force. There is less satire in it, and more fairy-tale. But it has a grace of invention new to him, and a happy charm. One asks whether the sketch of these pacific vegetarians contains a half-serious moral. Voltaire did once say that men could never be weaned from war, because they are carnivores. Often he expressed an impotent disgust at the idea of taking the life of animals to sustain one's own. For the rest, one may call the latter part of the tale a sequel to *Candide*. Again an ingenuous traveller circles the earth. Its Northern realms are vastly improved, for they all have philosophic kings. But France and Spain are no better than Candide found them. That judgment was premature.

H. N. BRAILSFORD.

SELECT BIBLIOGRAPHY

DRAMATIC WORKS. *Œdipe*, 1718; *Artémire*, 1720; *Mari-amne*, 1724; *Zaïre*, 1732; *Samson* (opera), 1732; *L'Enfant Prodigue*, 1736; *Mahomet, ou le Fanatisme*, 1742; *Mérope*, 1743; *Sémiramis*, 1748; *Nanine*, 1749; *Oreste*, 1750; *L'Orphe-lin de la Chine*, 1755; *Tancrède*, 1760; *L'Ecossaise*, 1760; *Le Dépositaire*, 1772; *Irène*, 1778; *Agathoclès*, 1779 (performed on the anniversary of the poet's death). Other dramas and operas.

POEMS. *La Bastille*, 1717; *La Henriade* (fraudulently published as *La Ligue*, 1723–4), 1728; *Mort de Mlle Lecouvreur*, 1730; *Temple du Goût* (prose and verse), 1733; *Le Mondain*, 1736; *Discours sur l'homme* (Epîtres sur le Bonheur, 1738–9); *Sur les Evénements de* 1744; *Fontenoi*, 1745; *Temple de la Gloire*, 1745; *La Pucelle d'Orléans*, 1755 (some of the ' Chants ' had been in circulation since 1735), in twenty Chants, 1762; a supplemental one, *La Capilotade*, appeared separately in 1760; *Sur le désastre de Lisbonne*, 1756; *Sur la Loi Naturelle*, 1756; *La Vanité, Le Pauvre Diable, Le Russe à Paris*, 1760; *Contes de Guillaume Vadé* (with prose, 1764); *La Guerre Civile de Génève* (burlesque poem), 1768; *Les Trois Empereurs en Sorbonne*, 1768; *Epître à Borleau*, 1769; *Les Systèmes, Les Cabales*, 1772; *La Tactique*, 1773; and others.

PROSE TALES. *Le Monde comme il va* (or *Babouc*), 1764; *Zadig*, 1748 (published in 1747 as *Memnon, Histoire Orien-telle*); *Memnon, ou la Sagesse Humaine*, 1749; *Micromégas*, 1750; *L'Histoire d'un Bon Bramin*, 1759; *Candide*, 1759; *Le Blanc et Le Noir*, 1764; *Jeannot et Colin*, 1764; *L'Homme aux Quarante Ecus*, 1767; *L'Ingénu*, 1767; *La Princesse de Baby-lone*, 1768; *Histoire de Jenny*, 1769; *Lettres d'Amabed*, 1769; *Le Taureau Blanc*, 1774; *Les Oreilles du Comte de Chesterfield*, 1774; and others.

HISTORICAL WORKS. *Histoire de Charles XII.*, 1731; *Siècle de Louis XIV.*, 1751; enlarged edition, 1753 (two chapters had been printed and suppressed in 1739); *Abrégé de l'Histoire Universelle*, vols. I. and II., 1753; Vol III., 1754; complete edition 1756 (fragments had appeared in 1745); *Annales de l'Empire*, 1753; *Précis du Siècle de Louis XV.*, published in part 1755 and 1763, with additional chapters, 1769; *Essai sur l'Histoire Générale et sur les Mœurs et l'Esprit des Nations depuis Charlemagne jusqu'à nos jours*, five vols., 1756, given in vol. VII of *Siècle de Louis XIV*. (some chapters had appeared in the ' Mercure ' in 1745–6); *Histoire de Russie sous Pierre le Grand*: first part, 1759; second part, 1763; *La Philosophie de l'Histoire*, 1765 (later the *Discours préliminaire* to *Essai sur les Mœurs*); *La Défense de mon Oncle* (in reply to an adverse criticism on the above work), 1767; *Le Pyrrhonism de l'Histoire*, 1768; *Fragments sur l'Histoire Générale* (Pyrrhonism and Tolerance), 1773.

WORKS ON PHILOSOPHY AND RELIGION. *Epître philosophique à Uranie*, 1732; *Lettres sur les Anglais* (twenty-four letters), 1733, 1734 (also published as ' *Lettres Philosophiques* ') *Traité de Métaphysique*, 1734; *Eléments de la Philosophie de Newton*, 1738; *Métaphysique de Newton*, 1740; Articles for the *Encyclopédie*, 1757; *Dictionnaire Philosophique Portatif*, 1764; *Catéchisme de l'Honnête Homme*, 1763; *Le Philosophe Ignorant*, 1766; *La Raison par Alphabet* (new edition of the *Dictionnaire Philosophique*), 1769; *Lettres de Memmius*, 1771; *Questions sur l'Encyclopédie par des Amateurs*, 1770–2; *Lettres Chinoises, Indiennes, et Tartares par un Bénédictin*, 1776; *Mémoires pour servir à la vie de M. Voltaire* (printed 1784); and others.

CRITICAL WORKS. *Essai sur la Poésie*, 1726; *Utile Examen des Epîtres de J. J. Rousseau*, 1736; *Lettres sur la ' Nouvelle Héloïse,'* 1761; *Appel à toutes les Nations de l'Europe des Jugements d'un écrivain Anglais* (later known as *Du Théâtre Anglais*), 1761; *Eloge de M. de Crébillon*, 1762; *Idées Républicaines* (in the *Contrat Social*), 1762; *Théâtre de Corneille* (with translation of Shakespeare's ' Julius Cæsar '), 1764; *Examen Important de Milord Bolingbroke*, 1767; *Commentaire historique sur les Œuvres de l'auteur de la Henriade*, 1776; *Eloge et Pensées de Pascal* (corrected and enlarged edition), 1776; *Commentaire sur l'Esprit des Lois de Montesquieu*, 1777; and others.

MISCELLANEOUS WRITINGS. *Epîtres aux Manes de Genonville*, 1729; *Epître des Vous et des Tu*, 1732; *Sur la Calomnie*, 1733; *Anecdotes sur Pierre le Grand*, 1748; *Mensonges Imprimés* (on Richelieu's Will), 1749; *Des Embellissements de Paris*, 1750; *Remerciement sincère à un Homme Charitable*, 1750; *Histoire du Doctor Akakia*, 1753; *Le Quand*, 1760; Writings for the rehabilitation of Jean Calas, who had been unjustly executed, 1762; *Traité sur la Tolérance à l'occasion de la Mort de Jean Calas*, 1763; *Le Sentiment des Citoyens* (attack on Rousseau), 1764; *Discours aux Welches*, 1764; *Les Anciens et les Modernes, ou la Toilette de Mme de Pompadour*, 1765; *Commentaires sur le Livre des Délits et des Peines*, 1766; *Le Cri des Nations* (against Papal domination), 1769; *De le Paix perpétuelle* (on fanaticism and tolerance), 1769; *La Méprise d'Arras* (on another judicial mistake), 1771; *Eloge de Louis XV.; de la Mort de Louis XV. et de la Fatalité*, 1774; and other works. Editions of Voltaire's works include a few works on physics and an enormous correspondence.

CHIEF GENERAL EDITIONS OF WORKS. Ed. Beaumarchais, etc., 70 vols., 8°, 1784; 92 vols., 12°, 1785–90; Beuchot, 70 vols., 1828, etc.; Ed. du Siècle, 8 vols., 1867–70; Moland, 50 vols., 1877–83; with 'Table Générale et Analytique,' by Charles Pierrot, 1885; 4 vols. of a new edition of the 'Œuvres Complètes' were published in 1930.

BIBLIOGRAPHY. G. Bengesco, 1882–90.

LIFE, ETC. Condorcet, 1787; G. Desnoiresterres, *Voltaire et la Société Française au XVIIImᵉ Siècle*, 1871–6; Longchamps et Wagnière, *Mèmoires sur Voltaire et sur ses ouvrages*, 1825; Bersot, *Études sur le XVIIImᵉ Siècle*, 1855; A. Pierron, *Voltaire et ses Maîtres*, 1866; Maynard, *Voltaire; sa vie et ses œuvres*, 1867; D. F. Strauss, 1870; J. Morley, 1872, 1886; James Paston, 2 vols. 1881; G. Maugras, *Voltaire et Jean Jacques Rousseau*, 1886; E. Faguet, 1895; E. Champion, *Voltaire: Etudes Critiques*, 1897; L. Crouslé, 1899; G. Lanson, 1907; and in Sainte-Beuve, *Causeries du Lundi*, vol. II.; Brunetière, *Etudes Critiques*, vols. I., III., IV.; S. G. Tallentyre, 1903; R. Aldington, 1925; André Maurois, Eng. trans., 1932; H. N. Brailsford, 1935; Alfred Noyes, 1936; N. L. Torrey, *The Spirit of Voltaire*, 1938; M. M. H. Barr, *Voltaire in America*, 1744–1806; I. O. Wade, *Voltaire and Mme du Châtelet*, 1941; M. T. Maestro, *Voltaire and Beccaria as Reformers of Criminal Law*, 1942; K. O'Flaherty, *Voltaire, Myth and Reality*, 1945; T. W. Russell, *Voltaire, Dryden, and Heroic Tragedy*, 1946; A Meyer, *Voltaire: Man of Justice*, 1951; C. Rowe, *Voltaire and the State*, 1956; P. Gay, *Voltaire's Politics*, 1959; E. Nixon, *Voltaire and the Calas Case*, 1961; W. Durant, *The Age of Voltaire*, 1966; R. H. Gross, *Voltaire Noncomformist*, 1968; T. Besterman, *Voltaire*, 1969.

See also S. G. Tallentyre, *Voltaire in his Letters*, 1919, and selections from the *Philosophical Dictionary*, by H. I. Woolf, 1924.

TRANSLATIONS. In addition to Smollett's edition of 1761–1765, there is an English edition of the Works by D. Williams and others, 10 vols., 1779–81. Translations of *The History of Charles XII.* (by Winifred Todhunter) and *The Age of Louis XIV.* (by M. P. Pollack) are in Everyman's Library.

The translation used in this volume is taken (with some revision on the score of accuracy) from the edition of Voltaire's Works by T. Smollett and others, 25 vols., 1761–5.

ZADIG;

OR,

FATE

AN

ORIENTAL HISTORY

APPROBATION

[*I, the underwritten, who have obtained the character of a learned, and even of an ingenious man, have read this manuscript, which, in spite of myself, I have found to be curious, entertaining, moral, philosophical, and capable of affording pleasure even to those who hate romances. I have therefore decried it; and have assured the Cadi-lesquier that it is an abominable performance.*]

EPISTLE DEDICATORY OF ZADIG TO THE
SULTANA SHERAH

By SADI

The 18th of the Month SCHEWAL, *in the 837th Year of the*
HEGIRA

DELIGHT of the eyes, torment of the heart, and light of
the mind, I kiss not the dust of thy feet, because thou
never walkest; or walkest only on the carpets of Iran, or
in paths strewn with roses. I offer thee the translation of
a book, written by an ancient sage, who, having the happiness to have nothing to do, amused himself in composing
the history of Zadig, a work which performs more than it
promises. I beseech thee to read and examine it; for,
though thou art in the spring of life, and every pleasure
courts thee to its embrace; though thou art beautiful, and
thy beauty be embellished by thy admirable talents;
though thou art praised from evening to morning, and, on
all these accounts, hast a right to be devoid of common
sense; yet thou hast a sound judgment, and a fine taste;
and I have heard thee reason with more accuracy than the
old dervishes, with their long beards and pointed bonnets.
Thou art discreet without being distrustful; gentle without
weakness; and beneficent with discernment. Thou lovest
thy friends, and makest thyself no enemies. Thy wit never
borrows its charms from the shafts of detraction; thou
neither sayest nor doest any ill, notwithstanding that both
are so much in thy power. In a word, thy soul hath
always appeared to me to be as pure and unsullied as thy
beauty. Besides, thou hast some little knowledge in
philosophy, which makes me believe that thou wilt take
more pleasure than others of thy sex in perusing the work
of this venerable sage.

3

It was originally written in the ancient Chaldee, a language which neither thou nor I understand. It was afterwards translated into the Arabic, to amuse the famous sultan Ouloug-beg, much about the time that the Arabians and the Persians began to write the *Thousand and One Nights*, the *Thousand and One Days*, &c. Ouloug was fond of reading about Zadig, but the sultanas were fonder of the *Thousand and One*.

' How can you prefer (would the wise Ouloug say to them) those stories which have neither sense nor meaning? '

' It is for that very reason (replied the sultanas) that we like them.'

I flatter myself that thou wilt not resemble these thy predecessors; but that thou wilt be a true Ouloug. I even hope that when thou art tired with those general conversations, which differ from the *Thousand and One* in nothing but in being less agreeable, I shall have the honour to entertain thee for a moment with a rational discourse. Hadst thou been Thalestris in the time of Alexander the son of Philip, hadst thou been the Queen of Sheba in the time of Solomon, these are the very kings that would have paid thee a visit.

I pray the heavenly powers that thy pleasures may be unmixed, thy beauty never fading, and thy happiness without end.

SADI.

CHAPTER I

THE BLIND OF ONE EYE

THERE lived at Babylon, in the reign of King Moabdar, a young man, named Zadig, of a good natural disposition, strengthened and improved by education. Though rich and young, he had learned to moderate his passions : he had nothing affected in his behaviour; he did not pretend to examine every action by the strict rules of reason, but was always ready to make proper allowances for the weakness of mankind. It was a matter of surprise that, notwithstanding his wit, he never exposed by his raillery those vague, incoherent, and noisy discourses, those rash censures, ignorant decisions, coarse jests, and all that empty jingle of words which at Babylon went by the name of conversation. He had learned, in the first book of Zoroaster, that self-love is a football swelled with wind, from which, when pierced, tempests issue forth. Above all, Zadig never boasted of his conquests among the women, nor affected to entertain a contemptible opinion of the fair sex. He was generous, and was never afraid of obliging the ungrateful; remembering the grand precept of Zoroaster: 'When thou eatest, give to the dogs, should they even bite thee.' He was as wise as it is possible for man to be; for he sought to live with the wise. Instructed in the sciences of the ancient Chaldeans, he understood the principles of natural philosophy, such as they were then supposed to be; and knew as much of metaphysics as hath ever been known in any age, that is, little or nothing at all. He was firmly persuaded, notwithstanding the new philosophy of the times, that the year consisted of three hundred and sixty-five days and six hours, and that the sun was in the centre of the universe. But when the principal magi told him, with a haughty and contemptuous air, that his sentiments were of a dangerous tendency, and that it was to be an enemy of the state to believe that the sun revolved round its own axis, and that the year had twelve months, he held his tongue with great modesty and meekness.

Possessed as he was of great riches, and consequently of many friends, blessed with a good constitution, a handsome figure, a mind just and moderate, and a heart noble and sincere, Zadig fondly imagined that he might easily be happy. He was going to be married to Semira, who, in point of beauty, birth, and fortune, was the first match in Babylon. He had a real and virtuous affection for this lady, and she loved him with the most passionate fondness. The happy moment that was to unite them had almost arrived, when happening to take a walk together towards one of the gates of Babylon, under the palm-trees that adorn the banks of the Euphrates, they saw some men approaching, armed with sabres and arrows. These were the attendants of young Orcan, the minister's nephew, whom his uncle's creatures had flattered into an opinion that he might do everything with impunity. He had none of the graces nor virtues of Zadig; but thinking himself a much more accomplished man, he was enraged to find that the other was preferred before him. This jealousy, which was merely the effect of his vanity, made him imagine that he was desperately in love with Semira. The ravishers seized her; in the violence of the outrage they wounded her, and made the blood flow from one, the sight of whom would have softened the tigers of Mount Imaus. She pierced the heavens with her complaints. She cried out :

' My dear husband! they tear me from the man I adore.'

Regardless of her own danger, she was only concerned for the fate of her dear Zadig, who, in the meantime, defended himself with all the strength that courage and love could inspire. Assisted only by two slaves, he put the ravishers to flight, and carried home Semira, insensible and covered with blood. On opening her eyes, she beheld her deliverer.

' O Zadig,' said she, ' I loved thee formerly as my intended husband; I now love thee as the preserver of my honour and my life.'

Never was heart more deeply moved than that of Semira. Never did a mouth more charming express more moving sentiments, in these glowing words inspired by a sense of the greatest of all favours, and by the most tender transports of a lawful passion. Her wound was slight, and was soon cured. Zadig was more dangerously wounded; an arrow had pierced him near his eye, and penetrated to a considerable depth. Semira wearied Heaven with her prayers for the recovery of her lover. Her eyes were constantly bathed in tears; she anxiously waited the happy moment when those of Zadig should be able to meet hers; but an abscess growing on the wounded eye, gave every cause for fear. A messenger was immediately dispatched to Memphis, for the great physician Hermes, who came with a numerous retinue. He visited the patient, and declared that he would lose his eye. He even foretold the day and hour when this fatal event would happen.

' Had it been the right eye,' said he, ' I could easily have cured it; but the wounds of the left eye are incurable.'

All Babylon lamented the fate of Zadig, and admired the profound knowledge of Hermes. In two days the abscess broke of its own accord, and Zadig was perfectly cured. Hermes wrote a book, to prove that it ought not to have been cured. Zadig did not read it : but, as soon as he was able to go abroad, he went to pay a visit to her in whom all his hopes of happiness were centred, and for whose sake alone he wished to have eyes. Semira had been in the country for three days past. He learned on the road that that fine lady, having openly declared that she had an unconquerable aversion to one-eyed men, had the night before given her hand to Orcan. At this news he fell speechless to the ground. His sorrows brought him almost to the brink of the grave. He was ill for a long time ; but reason at last got the better of his affliction ; and the severity of his fate served even to console him.

'Since,' said he, 'I have suffered so much from the cruel caprice of a woman educated at court, I must now think of marrying the daughter of a citizen.'

He pitched upon Azora, a lady of the greatest prudence, and of the best family in town. He married her, and lived with her for a month in all the delights of the most tender union. He only observed that she had a little levity ; and that she was too apt to find that those young men who had the most handsome persons were likewise possessed of most wit and virtue.

CHAPTER II

THE NOSE

ONE morning Azora returned from a walk in a terrible passion, and uttered the most violent exclamations.

'What aileth thee, my dear wife ? ' said he. 'What is it that canst thus have put thee out of temper ? '

'Alas,' said she, 'thou wouldest be as much enraged as I am, hadst thou seen what I have just beheld. I have been to comfort the young widow Cosrou, who, within these two days, hath raised a tomb to her young husband, near the rivulet that washes the skirts of this meadow. She vowed to heaven, in the bitterness of her grief, to remain at this tomb, while the water of the rivulet should continue to run near it.'

' Well,' said Zadig, ' she is an excellent woman, and loved her husband with the most sincere affection.'

' Ah,' replied Azora, ' didst thou but know in what she was employed when I went to wait upon her ! '

' In what, pray, beautiful Azora ? '

' She was turning the course of the rivulet.'

Azora broke out into such long invectives, and loaded the young widow with such bitter reproaches that Zadig was far from being pleased with this ostentation of virtue.

Zadig had a friend, named Cador, one of those young men in whom his wife discovered more probity and merit than in others. He made him his confidant, and secured his fidelity, as much as possible, by a considerable present. Azora, having passed two days with a friend in the country, returned home on the third. The servants told her, with tears in their eyes, that her husband had died suddenly the night before; that they were afraid to send her an account of this mournful event; and that they had just been depositing his corpse in the tomb of his ancestors, at the end of the garden. She wept, she tore her hair, and swore she would follow him to the grave. In the evening, Cador begged leave to wait upon her, and joined his tears with hers. Next day they wept less, and dined together. Cador told her that his friend had left him the greater part of his estate; and that he would think himself extremely happy in sharing his fortune with her. The lady wept, fell into a passion, and at last became more mild and gentle. They sat longer at supper than at dinner. They now talked with greater confidence. Azora praised the deceased; but owned that he had many failings from which Cador was free.

During supper, Cador complained of a violent pain in his side. The lady, greatly concerned, and eager to serve him, caused all kinds of essences to be brought, with which she anointed him, to try if some of them might not possibly ease him of his pain. She lamented that the great Hermes was not still in Babylon. She even condescended to touch the side in which Cador felt such exquisite pain.

' Art thou subject to this cruel disorder? ' said she to him with a compassionate air.

' It sometimes brings me,' replied Cador, ' to the brink of the grave; and there is but one remedy that can give me relief, and that is, to apply to my side the nose of a man who is lately dead.'

' A strange remedy, indeed ! ' said Azora.

' Not more strange,' replied he, ' than the sachels of Arnoult against the apoplexy.' *

This reason, added to the great merit of the young man, at last determined the lady.

' After all,' says she, ' when my husband shall cross the bridge Tchinavar, in his journey from the world of yesterday to the world of to-morrow, the angel Asrael will not refuse him a passage, because his nose is a little shorter in the second life than it was in the first.'

She then took a razor, went to her husband's tomb, bedewed it with her tears, and drew near to cut off the nose of Zadig, whom she found extended at full length in the tomb. Zadig arose, holding his nose with one hand, and checking the razor with the other.

' Madam,' said he, ' don't exclaim so violently against young Cosrou : the project of cutting off my nose is equal to that of turning the course of a rivulet.'

CHAPTER III

THE DOG AND THE HORSE

ZADIG found by experience that the first month of marriage, as it is written in the book of Zend, is the moon of honey, and that the second is the moon of wormwood. He was some time after obliged to repudiate Azora, who became

---

* There was at that time a Babylonian named Arnoult, who, according to his advertisements in the Gazettes, cured and prevented all kinds of apoplexies, by a little bag hung about the neck.

too difficult to live with; and he then sought for happiness in the study of nature.

'No man,' said he, 'can be happier than a philosopher, who reads in this great book which God hath placed before our eyes. The truths he discovers are his own, he nourishes and exalts his soul; he lives in peace; he fears nothing from men; and his tender spouse will not come to cut off his nose.'

Possessed of these ideas, he retired to a country-house on the banks of the Euphrates. There he did not employ himself in calculating how many inches of water flow in a second of time under the arches of a bridge, or whether there fell a cubic-line of rain in the month of the mouse more than in the month of the sheep. He never dreamed of making silk of cobwebs, or porcelain of broken bottles; but he chiefly studied the properties of plants and animals; and soon acquired a sagacity that made him discover a thousand differences where other men see nothing but uniformity.

One day, as he was walking near a little wood, he saw one of the Queen's eunuchs running towards him, followed by several officers, who appeared to be in great perplexity, and who ran to and fro like men distracted, eagerly searching for something they had lost of great value.

'Young man,' said the first eunuch, 'hast thou seen the Queen's dog?'

'It is a bitch,' replied Zadig with great modesty, 'and not a dog.'

'Thou art in the right,' returned the first eunuch.

'It is a very small she-spaniel,' added Zadig; 'she has lately whelped; she limps on the left fore-foot, and has very long ears.'

'Thou hast seen her,' said the first eunuch, quite out of breath.

'No,' replied Zadig, 'I have not seen her, nor did I so much as know that the Queen had a bitch.'

Exactly at the same time, by one of the common freaks of fortune, the finest horse in the King's stable had escaped from the groom in the plains of Babylon. The chief huntsman, and all the other officers, ran after him with as much eagerness and anxiety as the first eunuch had done after the bitch. The chief huntsman addressed Zadig, and asked him if he had not seen the King's horse passing by.

' He is the fleetest horse in the King's stable,' replied Zadig; ' he is five feet high, with very small hoofs, and a tail three feet and a half in length; the studs on his bit are gold of twenty-three carats, and his shoes are silver of eleven pennyweights.'

' What way did he take? Where is he? ' demanded the chief huntsman.

' I have not seen him,' replied Zadig, ' and never heard talk of him before.'

The chief huntsman and the first eunuch never doubted but that Zadig had stolen the King's horse and the Queen's bitch. They therefore had him conducted before the Assembly of the Grand Desterham, who condemned him to the knout, and to spend the rest of his days in Siberia. Hardly was the sentence passed when the horse and the bitch were both found. The judges were reduced to the disagreeable necessity of reversing their sentence; but they condemned Zadig to pay four hundred ounces of gold, for having said that he had not seen what he had seen. This fine he was obliged to pay; after this he was permitted to plead his cause before the Council of the Grand Desterham, when he spoke to the following effect :

' Ye stars of justice, mines of knowledge, mirrors of truth, who have the weight of lead, the hardness of iron, the splendour of the diamond, and many of the properties of gold : since I am permitted to speak before this august assembly, I swear to you by Ormuzd that I have never seen the Queen's respectable bitch, nor the sacred horse of the King of kings. The truth of the matter was as follows : I was walking towards the little wood, where I afterwards met the venerable eunuch, and the most illustrious chief huntsman. I observed on the sand the traces of an animal, and could easily perceive them to be those of a little dog. The light and long furrows impressed on little eminences of sand between the marks of the paws, plainly discovered that it was a bitch, whose dugs were hanging down, and that therefore she must have whelped a few

days before. Other traces of a different kind that always
appeared to have gently brushed the surface of the land
near the marks of the forefeet showed me that she had very
long ears; and as I remarked that there was always a
slighter impression made on the sand by one foot than by
the other three, I found that the bitch of our august Queen
was a little lame, if I may be allowed the expression.

'With regard to the horse of the King of kings, you will
be pleased to know that walking in the lanes of this wood,
I observed the marks of a horse's shoes, all at equal dis-
tances. This must be a horse, said I to myself, that
gallops excellently. The dust on the trees in a narrow
road that was but seven feet wide was a little brushed off,
at the distance of three feet and a half from the middle of
the road. This horse, said I, has a tail three feet and a
half long, which being whisked to the right and left has
swept away the dust. I observed, under the trees that
formed an arbour five feet in height, that the leaves of the
branches were newly fallen; from whence I inferred that
the horse had touched them, and that he must therefore
be five feet high. As to his bit, it must be gold of twenty-
three carats, for he had rubbed its bosses against a stone
which I knew to be a touchstone, and which I had tested.
In a word, from the marks made by his shoes on flints of
another kind, I concluded that he was shod with silver
eleven deniers fine.'

All the judges admired Zadig for his acute and profound
discernment. The news of this speech was carried even
to the King and Queen. Nothing was talked of but Zadig
in the antechambers, the chambers, and the cabinet; and
though many of the magi were of opinion that he ought to
be burnt as a sorcerer, the King ordered his officers to
restore him the four hundred ounces of gold which he had
been obliged to pay. The registrar, the attorneys, and
bailiffs went to his house, with great formality, to carry
him back his four hundred ounces. They only retained
three hundred and ninety-eight of them to defray the
expenses of justice; and their servants demanded their
fees.

Zadig saw how extremely dangerous it sometimes is to
appear too knowing, and he therefore resolved that on

the next occasion of the like nature he would not tell what he had seen.

Such an opportunity soon offered. A prisoner of state made his escape, and passed under the windows of Zadig's house. Zadig was examined and made no answer. But it was proved that he had looked at the prisoner from this window. For this crime he was condemned to pay five hundred ounces of gold; and, according to the custom of Babylon, he thanked his judges for their indulgence.

' Great God ! ' said he to himself, ' what a misfortune it is to walk in a wood through which the Queen's bitch or the King's horse has passed ! How dangerous to look out of a window ! and how difficult to be happy in this life ! '

CHAPTER IV

THE ENVIOUS MAN

ZADIG resolved to comfort himself by philosophy and friendship for the evils he had suffered from fortune. He had in the suburbs of Babylon a house elegantly furnished, in which he assembled all the arts and all the pleasures worthy the pursuit of a gentleman. In the morning, his library was open to the learned. In the evening, his table was surrounded by good company. But he soon found what very dangerous guests these men of letters are. A warm dispute arose on one of Zoroaster's laws, which forbids the eating of a griffin.

' Why,' said some of them, ' prohibit the eating of a griffin, if no such animal exists ? '

' There must necessarily be such an animal,' said the others, ' since Zoroaster forbids us to eat it.'

Zadig would fain have reconciled them by saying :

' If there are griffins, let us not eat them, and if there are no griffins, we cannot possibly eat them : and thus either way we shall obey Zoroaster.'

A learned man, who had composed thirteen volumes on the properties of the griffin, and was besides the chief theurgist, hasted away to accuse Zadig before one of the principal magi, named Yebor, the greatest blockhead, and therefore the greatest fanatic among the Chaldeans. This man would have impaled Zadig to do honour to the sun, and would then have recited the breviary of Zoroaster with greater satisfaction. The friend Cador (a friend is better than a hundred priests) went to Yebor, and said to him :

' Long live the sun and the griffins; beware of punishing Zadig; he is a saint; he has griffins in his inner court, and does not eat them; and his accuser is an heretic, who dares to maintain that rabbits have cloven feet, and are not unclean.'

' Well,' said Yebor, shaking his bald pate, ' we must impale Zadig for having thought contemptuously of griffins, and the other for having spoke disrespectfully of rabbits.'

Cador hushed up the affair by means of a maid of honour who had borne him a child, and who had great interest in the college of the magi. Nobody was impaled. This lenience occasioned a great murmuring among some of the doctors, who from this predicted the fall of Babylon.

' Upon what does happiness depend ? ' said Zadig ; ' I am persecuted by everything in the world, even by beings that have no existence.'

He cursed those men of learning, and resolved for the future to live with none but good company.

He assembled at his house the most worthy men, and the most beautiful ladies of Babylon. He gave them delicious suppers, often preceded by concerts of music, and always animated by polite conversation, from which he knew how to banish that affectation of wit, which is the surest method of preventing it entirely, thus spoiling the pleasure of the most agreeable society. Neither the choice of his friends nor that of the dishes was made by vanity ; for in everything he preferred the substance to the shadow ; and by these means he procured that real respect to which he did not aspire.

Opposite to his house lived one Arimazes, a man whose deformed countenance was but a faint picture of his still more deformed mind. He was tormented with malice, and inflated with pride, and to crown all, he was of most tedious

disposition. Having never been able to succeed in the
world, he revenged himself by cursing it. Rich as he was,
he found it difficult to procure a set of flatterers. The
rattling of the chariots that entered Zadig's court in the
evening filled him with uneasiness; the sound of his praises
enraged him still more. He sometimes went to Zadig's
house, and sat down at table without being desired; where
he spoiled all the pleasure of the company, as the harpies
are said to infect the viands they touch. It happened one
day he took it into his head to give an entertainment to
a lady, who, instead of accepting it, went to sup with Zadig.
At another time, as he was talking with Zadig at Court, a
Minister of State came up to them and invited Zadig to
supper, without inviting Arimazes. The most implacable
hatred has seldom a more solid foundation. This man,
who in Babylon was called the *Envious*, resolved to ruin
Zadig, because he was called the *Happy*.

' The opportunity of doing mischief occurs a hundred
times in a day, and that of doing good but once a year,' as
sayeth the wise Zoroaster.

The envious man went to see Zadig, who was walking
in his garden with two friends and a lady, to whom he said
many gallant things, without any other intention than that
of saying them. The conversation turned upon a war
which the King had just brought to a happy conclusion
against the Prince of Hyrcania, his vassal. Zadig, who had
signalized his courage in this short war, bestowed great
praises on the King, but greater still on the lady. He took
out his note-book, and wrote four lines extempore, which
he gave to this amiable person to read. His friends begged
they might see them; but modesty, or rather a well-
regulated self-love, would not allow him to grant their
request. He knew that extemporary verses are never
approved by any but the person in whose honour they
are written. He therefore tore in two the leaf on which he
had wrote them, and threw both the pieces into a thicket
of rose-bushes where the rest of the company sought for
them in vain. A slight shower falling soon after obliged
them to return to the house. The envious man, who stayed
in the garden, continued to search, till at last he found a
piece of the leaf. It had been torn in such a manner, that

each half of a line made sense, and even a verse of a shorter measure; but what was still more surprising, these short verses were found to contain the most injurious reflections on the King; they ran thus:

> to flagrant Crimes;
> his Crown he owes;
> to peaceful Times,
> the worst of Foes.

The envious man was now happy for the first time of his life. He had it in his power to ruin a person of virtue and merit. Filled with this fiend-like joy, he found means to convey to the King the satire written by the hand of Zadig, who, together with the lady and his two friends, was thrown into prison.

His trial was soon finished, without his being permitted to speak for himself. As he was going to receive his sentence, the envious man threw himself in his way, and told him with a loud voice that his verses were good for nothing. Zadig did not value himself on being a good poet; but it filled him with inexpressible concern to find that he was condemned for high treason; and that the fair lady and his two friends were confined in prison for a crime of which they were not guilty. He was not allowed to speak because his writing spoke for him. Such was the law of Babylon. Accordingly he was conducted to the place of execution, through an immense crowd of spectators, who dared not venture to express their pity for him, but who carefully examined his countenance to see if he died with a good grace. His relations alone were inconsolable; for they could not succeed to his estate. Three-fourths of his wealth were confiscated into the King's treasury, and the other fourth was given to the envious man.

Just as he was preparing for death, the King's parrot flew from its cage, and alighted on a rose-bush in Zadig's garden. A peach had been driven thither by the wind from a neighbouring tree, and had fallen on a piece of the written leaf of the note-book to which it stuck. The bird carried off the peach and the paper, and laid them on the King's knee. The King took up the paper with great eagerness, and read the words, which formed no sense, and seemed to be the endings of verses. He loved poetry; and there is always some mercy to be expected from a prince of that disposition. The adventure of the parrot set him thinking.

The Queen, who remembered what had been written on the piece of Zadig's note-book, caused it to be brought. They compared the two pieces together, and found them to tally exactly: they then read the verses as Zadig had wrote them.

> *Tyrants are prone to flagrant Crimes;*
> *To Clemency his Crown he owes;*
> *To Concord and to peaceful Times,*
> *Love only is the worst of Foes.*

The King gave immediate orders that Zadig should be brought before him, and that his two friends and the lady should be set at liberty. Zadig fell prostrate on the ground before the King and Queen; humbly begged their pardon for having made such bad verses, and spoke with so much propriety, wit, and good sense, that their Majesties desired they might see him again. He did himself that honour, and insinuated himself still further into their good graces. They gave him all the wealth of the envious man; but Zadig restored him back the whole of it; and this instance of generosity gave no other pleasure to the envious man than that of having preserved his estate. The King's esteem for Zadig increased every day. He admitted him into all his parties of pleasure, and consulted him in all affairs of state. From that time the Queen began to regard him with a tenderness that might one day prove dangerous to herself, to the King her august consort, to Zadig, and to the kingdom in general. Zadig now began to think that happiness was not so unattainable as he had formerly imagined.

CHAPTER V

THE GENEROUS

THE time was now arrived for celebrating a grand festival, which returned every five years. It was a custom in

Babylon solemnly to declare, at the end of every five years, which of the citizens had performed the most generous action. The grandees and the magi were the judges. The first satrap, who was charged with the government of the city, published the most noble actions that had passed under his administration. The competition was decided by votes; and the King pronounced the sentence. People came to this ceremony from the ends of the earth. The conqueror received from the monarch's hands a golden cup adorned with precious stones, his Majesty at the same time making him this compliment :

'Receive this reward of thy generosity, and may the gods grant me many subjects like to thee.'

This memorable day being come, the King appeared on his throne, surrounded by the grandees, the magi, and the deputies of all the nations that came to these games, where glory was acquired not by the swiftness of horses, nor by strength of body, but by virtue. The first satrap recited, with an audible voice, such actions as might entitle the authors of them to this invaluable prize. He did not mention the greatness of soul with which Zadig had restored the envious man his fortune, because it was not judged to be an action worthy of disputing the prize.

He first presented a judge, who having made a citizen lose a considerable cause by a mistake, for which, after all, he was not accountable, had given him the whole of his own estate, which was just equal to what the other had lost.

He next produced a young man, who being desperately in love with a lady whom he was going to marry, had yielded her up to his friend, whose passion for her had almost brought him to the brink of the grave, and at the same time had given him the lady's fortune.

He afterwards produced a soldier, who in the Hyrcanian war had given a still more noble instance of generosity. A party of the enemy having seized his mistress, he was fighting in her defence. At that very instant he was informed that another party, at the distance of a few paces, were carrying off his mother; he therefore left his mistress with tears in his eyes, and flew to the assistance of his mother. At last, he returned to the dear object of his love, and found her expiring. He was just going to plunge his sword in his own bosom; but his mother remonstrating against such a desperate deed, and telling him that he was the only support of her life, he had the courage to endure to live.

The judges were inclined to give the prize to the soldier. But the King took up the discourse and said :

'The action of the soldier and that of the other two are doubtless very great, but they have nothing surprising in them. Yesterday Zadig performed an action that filled me with wonder. I had a few days before disgraced Coreb, my minister and favourite. I complained of him in the most violent and bitter terms; all my courtiers assured me that I was too gentle, and seemed to vie with each other in speaking ill of Coreb. I asked Zadig what he thought of him, and he had the courage to commend him. I have read in our histories of many people who have atoned for an error by the surrender of their fortune; who have resigned a mistress; or preferred a mother to the object of their affection; but never before did I hear of a courtier who spoke favourably of a disgraced minister that laboured under the displeasure of his sovereign. I give to each of those whose generous actions have been now recited, twenty thousand pieces of gold; but the cup I give to Zadig.'

'May it please your Majesty,' said Zadig, ' thyself alone deservest the cup; thou hast performed an action of all others the most uncommon and meritorious, since, notwithstanding thy being a powerful King, thou wast not offended at thy slave, when he presumed to oppose thy passion.'

The King and Zadig were equally the object of admiration. The judge who had given his estate to his client; the lover who had resigned his mistress to his friend; and the soldier, who had preferred the safety of his mother to that of his mistress, received the King's presents, and saw their names enrolled in the catalogue of generous men. Zadig had the cup, and the King acquired the reputation of a good prince, which he did not long enjoy. The day was celebrated by feasts that lasted longer than the law enjoined; and the memory of it is still preserved in Asia. Zadig said :

' Now I am happy at last.' But he found himself fatally deceived.

CHAPTER VI

THE MINISTER

THE King had lost his first minister, and chose Zadig to supply his place. All the ladies in Babylon applauded the choice; for since the foundation of the empire there had never been such a young minister. But all the courtiers were filled with jealousy and vexation. The envious man, in particular, was troubled with a spitting of blood, and a prodigious inflammation in his nose. Zadig having thanked the King and Queen for their goodness, went likewise to thank the parrot.

' Beautiful bird,' said he, ' 'tis thou that hast saved my life, and made me first minister. The Queen's bitch and the King's horse did me a great deal of mischief; but thou hast done me much good. Upon such slender threads as these do the fates of mortals hang! but this happiness perhaps will vanish very soon.'

' Soon,' replied the parrot.

Zadig was somewhat startled at this word. But as he was a good natural philosopher, and did not believe parrots to be prophets, he quickly recovered his spirits, and resolved to execute his duty to the best of his power.

He made every one feel the sacred authority of the laws, but no one felt the weight of his dignity. He never checked the deliberations of the divan; and every vizier might give his opinion without the fear of incurring the minister's displeasure. When he gave judgment, it was not he that gave it, it was the law; the rigour of which, however, whenever it was too severe, he always took care to soften; and when laws were wanting, the equity of his decisions was such as might easily have made them pass for those of Zoroaster.

It is to him that the nations are indebted for this great principle, to wit, that it is better to run the risk of sparing the guilty than to condemn the innocent. He imagined that laws were made to secure the people from the suffering of injuries as well as to restrain them from committing crimes. His chief talent consisted in discovering the truth, which all men seek to obscure. This great talent he put into practice from the very beginning of his administration. A famous merchant of Babylon, who died in the Indies, had divided his estate equally between his two sons, after having disposed of their sister in marriage, and left a present of thirty thousand pieces of gold to that son who should be found to have loved him best. The eldest raised a tomb to his memory; the youngest increased his sister's portion by giving her a part of his inheritance. Every one said that the eldest son loved his father best, and the youngest his sister; and that the thirty thousand pieces belonged to the eldest.

Zadig sent for both of them, the one after the other. To the elder he said:

' Thy father is not dead; he is recovered of his last illness, and is returning to Babylon.'

' God be praised,' replied the young man, ' but his tomb cost me a considerable sum.'

Zadig afterwards said the same thing to the younger.

' God be praised,' said he, ' I will go and restore to my father all that I have; but I could wish that he would leave my sister what I have given her.'

' Thou shalt restore nothing,' replied Zadig, ' and thou shalt have the thirty thousand pieces, for thou art the son who loves his father best.'

A young lady possessed of a handsome fortune had given a promise of marriage to two magi; and after having, for some months, received the instructions of both, she proved with child. They were both desirous of marrying her.

' I will take for my husband,' said she, ' the man who has put me in a condition to give a subject to the state.'

' I am the man that has done the work,' said the one.

' I am the man that has done it,' said the other.

' Well,' replied the lady, ' I will acknowledge for the infant's father him that can give it the best education.'

The lady was delivered of a son. The two magi contended who should bring him up, and the cause was carried before Zadig. Zadig summoned the two magi to attend him.

' What will you teach your pupil ? ' said he to the first.

' I will teach him,' said the doctor, ' the eight parts of speech, logic, astrology, demonology, what is meant by substance and accident, abstract and concrete, the doctrine of the monads, and the pre-established harmony.'

' For my part,' said the second, ' I will endeavour to give him a sense of justice, and to make him worthy the friendship of good men.'

Zadig then cried :

' Whether thou art his father or not, thou shalt marry his mother.'

Every day complaints reached the Court about the satrap of Media, called Irax, a lord of noble birth, not bad at heart, but corrupted by vanity and a love of pleasure. Seldom did he suffer any man to address him, and none to dare to contradict him. Peacocks are not more vain, doves more given to the pursuit of delights, nor tortoises less idle. His soul was bent only upon vain glory and idle pleasures. This man Zadig undertook to correct.

He sent to him, as though at the King's behest, a conductor of music, with a choir of twelve and four and twenty fiddlers, and a butler with six chefs, and four chamberlains who were charged not to let him out of their sight. The King's orders enjoined that the following ceremonies should be observed without alteration, and thus did matters turn out.

The first day, directly the voluptuous Irax was awakened, the conductor of music entered, followed by the singers and the fiddlers. They sang a cantata which lasted for two hours, and every three minutes, the refrain was :

> Que son mérite est extrême !
> Que de grâces ! que de grandeur !
> Ah ! combien monseigneur
> Doit être content de lui-même ! *

After the performance of the cantata, a chamberlain delivered him a discourse lasting for three-quarters of an hour, praising especially in him all those qualities which he lacked. The discourse ended, Irax was conducted to

* '' How boundless is his worth ! What graces, what majesty ! Ah, how pleased my lord should be with himself.''

his meal to the sound of instruments. Dinner lasted three hours. Directly he opened his mouth to speak, the first chamberlain said, ' He will be right.' Scarce had he uttered four words than the second chamberlain cried, ' He is right.' The other two chamberlains burst into roars of laughter at the witty sayings which Irax had uttered, or ought to have uttered. After dinner the cantata was repeated.

The first day transported him with joy; he thought that the King of kings was bestowing upon him the honour which was his due. The second seemed less pleasant, the third was irritating, the fourth unbearable, the fifth a torture. At last, exasperated at the constant refrain ι

> Ah! combien monseigneur
> Doit être content de lui-même!

enraged at hearing it constantly said that he was right, and at having a discourse delivered to him every day at the same hour, he wrote a letter to the Court, begging the King to condescend to recall his chamberlains, his musicians, and his butler. He promised that henceforward he would be less conceited and more diligent. He sought flattery less, held fewer banquets, and became happier; for as the Sadder * says : ' Constant pleasure ceases to be pleasure.'

CHAPTER VII

THE DISPUTES AND THE AUDIENCES

In this manner he daily showed the subtlety of his mind and the goodness of his heart. The people at once admired and loved him. He passed for the happiest man in the world. The whole empire resounded with his name. All the ladies ogled him. All the men praised him for his justice. The learned regarded him as an oracle; and even the priests confessed that he knew more than the old Arch-magus Yebor. They were now so far from prosecuting him

* Abridgement of the Zend-Avesta.

on account of the griffins that they believed nothing but what he thought credible.

There had continued in Babylon, for the space of fifteen hundred years, a violent contention that had divided the empire into two sects. The one pretended that they ought to enter the temple of Mithras with the left foot foremost; the other held this custom in detestation, and always entered with the right foot first. The people waited with great impatience for the day on which the solemn Feast of the Sacred Fire was to be celebrated, to see which sect Zadig would favour. All the world had their eyes fixed on his two feet, and the whole city was in the utmost suspense and perturbation. Zadig jumped into the temple with his feet joined together; and afterwards proved, in an eloquent discourse, that the God of heaven and earth, who accepteth not the persons of men, makes no distinction between the right and the left foot. The envious man and his wife alleged that his discourse was not figurative enough, and that he did not make the rocks and mountains dance with sufficient agility.

' He is dry,' said they, ' and void of genius : he does not make the sea fly, and the stars fall, nor the sun melt like wax : he has not the true oriental style.'

Zadig contented himself with having the style of reason. All the world favoured him, not because he was on the right road, or followed the dictates of reason, or was a man of real merit, but because he was grand vizier.

He terminated with the same happy address the great controversy between the white and the black magi. The former maintained that it was the height of impiety to pray to God with the face turned towards the east in winter; the latter asserted that God abhorred the prayers of those who turned towards the west in summer. Zadig decreed that every man should be allowed to turn as he pleased.

He also found out the happy secret of finishing all affairs, whether of a private or public nature, in the morning. The rest of the day he employed in the enhancement of Babylon. He exhibited tragedies that drew tears from the eyes of the spectators, and comedies that shook their sides with laughter; a custom which had long been

disused, and which his good taste now induced him to
revive. He never affected to be more knowing than the
artists themselves; he encouraged them by rewards
and honours, and was never secretly jealous of their
talents. In the evening the King was highly entertained
with his conversation, and the Queen still more.

'A great minister!' said the King.

'A charming minister!' said the Queen.

Both of them added that it would have been a great
pity, had such a man been hanged.

Never was man in power obliged to give so many audiences
to the ladies. Most of them came to consult him about
no business at all, that so they might have some business
with him. The wife of the envious man was among the
first. She swore to him by Mithras, by the Zend-Avesta,
and by the Sacred Fire that she detested her husband's
conduct : she then told him in confidence that he was a
jealous brutal wretch; and gave him to understand that
heaven punished him for his crimes, by refusing him the
precious effects of the Sacred Fire, by which alone man can
be rendered like the immortals. At last she concluded by
dropping her garter. Zadig took it up with his usual
politeness, but did not tie it about the lady's leg; and this
slight fault, if it may be called a fault, was the cause of
the most terrible misfortunes. Zadig never thought
of it more; but the lady thought of it with great attention.

Never a day passed without several visits from the
ladies. The secret annals of Babylon pretend that he once
yielded to temptation, but that he was surprised to find
that he enjoyed his mistress without pleasure, and embraced her absent-mindedly. The lady to whom he gave,
almost without being sensible of it, these marks of his favour
was a maid of honour to Queen Astarte. This tender
Babylonian said to herself by way of comfort :

'This man must have his head filled with a prodigious
heap of business, since even in making love he cannot
avoid thinking on public affairs.'

Zadig happened, at the very instant when most people
say nothing at all, and others only pronounce a few sacred
words, to cry out : 'The Queen!' The Babylonian
thought that he was at last happily come to himself,

and that he said : ' My queen.' But Zadig, still absent-minded, pronounced the name of Astarte. The lady, who in this happy situation interpreted everything in her own favour, imagined that he meant to say : ' Thou art more beautiful than Queen Astarte.' After receiving some handsome presents, she left the seraglio of Zadig, and went to relate her adventure to the envious woman, who was her intimate friend, and who was greatly piqued at the preference given to the other.

' He would not so much as deign,' said she, ' to tie this garter about my leg, and I am therefore resolved never to wear it more.'

' Oh,' said the happy lady to the envious one, ' your garters are the same as the Queen's ! Do you buy them from the same weaver ? '

This hint set the envious lady thinking ; she made no reply, but went to consult her envious husband.

Meanwhile Zadig perceived that his thoughts were always distracted, as well when he gave audience as when he sat in judgment. He did not know to what to attribute this absence of mind ; and that was his only sorrow.

He had a dream, in which he imagined that he laid himself down upon a heap of dry herbs, among which there were many prickly ones that gave him great uneasiness, and that he afterwards reposed himself on a soft bed of roses, from which there sprang a serpent that wounded him to the heart with its sharp and venomed tongue.

' Alas ! ' said he, ' I have long lain on these dry and prickly herbs ; I am now on the bed of roses ; but what shall be the serpent ? '

CHAPTER VIII

JEALOUSY

ZADIG's calamities sprang even from his happiness, and especially from his merit. Every day he conversed with the King, and Astarte his august consort. The charms of his conversation were greatly heightened by that desire of pleasing, which is to the mind what dress is to beauty. His youth and graceful appearance insensibly made an impression on Astarte, which she did not at first perceive. Her passion grew and flourished in the bosom of innocence. Without fear or scruple, she indulged the pleasing satisfaction of seeing and hearing a man who was so dear to her husband, and to the empire in general. She was continually praising him to the King. She talked of him to her women, who were always sure to improve on her praises. And thus everything contributed to thrust deeper into her heart a passion, of which she did not seem to be sensible. She made several presents to Zadig, which discovered a greater spirit of gallantry than she imagined. She intended to speak to him only as a queen satisfied with his services; and sometimes her expressions were those of a woman in love.

Astarte was much more beautiful than that Semira who had such a strong aversion to one-eyed men, or that other woman who had resolved to cut off her husband's nose. Her familiarity, her tender expressions, at which she began to blush, and her eyes, which, though she endeavoured to divert them to other objects, were always fixed upon his, inspired Zadig with a passion that filled him with astonishment. He struggled hard. He called to his aid the precepts of philosophy, which had always stood him in good stead; but he derived only the light of knowledge, and received no solace. Duty, gratitude, and violated majesty presented themselves to his mind as so many avenging gods. He struggled; he conquered; but this victory, which he was obliged to purchase afresh every moment, cost him many sighs and tears. He no longer dared to speak to the Queen with that sweet and charming familiarity which had been so agreeable to them both. His countenance was covered with a cloud. His conversation was constrained and incoherent. His eyes were fixed on the ground; and when, in spite of all his endeavours to the contrary, they encountered those of the Queen, they found them bathed in tears, and darting arrows of flame. They seemed to say:

' We adore each other, and yet are afraid to love: we both burn with a fire which we condemn.'

Zadig left the royal presence full of perplexity and despair,
and having his heart oppressed with a burden which he
was no longer able to bear.   In the violence of his perturbation he involuntarily betrayed the secret to his friend
Cador, in the same manner as a man who, having long
supported the fits of a cruel disease, discovers his pain by a
cry extorted from him by a more severe fit, and by the
cold sweat that covers his brow.

' I have already discovered,' said Cador, ' the sentiments
which thou wouldst fain conceal from thyself.   The
symptoms by which the passions show themselves are
certain and infallible.   Judge, my dear Zadig, since I
have read thy heart, whether the King will not discover
something in it that may give him offence.   He has no
other fault but that of being the most jealous man in the
world.   Thou canst resist the violence of thy passion
with greater fortitude than the Queen, because thou art a
philosopher, and because thou art Zadig.   Astarte is a
woman :   she suffers her eyes to speak with so much the
more imprudence, as she does not as yet think herself
guilty.   Conscious of her own innocence, she unhappily
neglects those external appearances which are so necessary.
I shall tremble for her so long as she has nothing wherewithal to reproach herself.   Were ye both of one mind, ye
might easily deceive the whole world.   A growing passion
which we endeavour to suppress, discovers itself in spite
of all our efforts to the contrary ;   but love when gratified
is easily concealed.'

Zadig trembled at the proposal of betraying the King,
his benefactor ;   and never was he more faithful to his
prince than when guilty of an involuntary crime against
him.   Meanwhile, the Queen mentioned the name of Zadig
so frequently, and with such a blushing and downcast
look ;   she was sometimes so lively, and sometimes so
perplexed, when she spoke to him in the King's presence,
and was seized with such a deep thoughtfulness at his going
away, that the King began to be troubled.   He believed
all that he saw, and imagined all that he did not see.
He particularly remarked, that his wife's shoes were blue,
and that Zadig's shoes were blue ;   that his wife's ribbons
were yellow ;   and that Zadig's bonnet was yellow ;   and

these were terrible symptoms to a prince of so much delicacy. In his jealous mind suspicions were turned into certainty.

All the slaves of kings and queens are so many spies over their hearts. They soon observed that Astarte was tender, and that Moabdar was jealous. The envious man persuaded his wife to send the King her garter, which resembled those of the Queen; and to complete the misfortune, this garter was blue. The monarch now thought of nothing but in what manner he might best execute his vengeance. He one night resolved to poison the Queen, and in the morning to put Zadig to death by the bowstring. The orders were given to a merciless eunuch, who commonly executed his acts of vengeance. There happened at that time to be in the King's chamber a little dwarf, who, though dumb, was not deaf. He was allowed to go wherever he pleased; and, as a domestic animal, was a witness of what passed in the most profound secrecy. This little mute was strongly attached to the Queen and to Zadig. With equal horror and surprise he heard the order given for their death. But how prevent the fatal sentence that in a few hours was to be carried into execution? He could not write, but he could paint; and excelled particularly in drawing a striking resemblance. He employed a part of the night in sketching out with his pencil what he meant to impart to the Queen. The piece represented the King in one corner, boiling with rage, and giving orders to the eunuch; a blue bowstring, and a bowl on a table, with blue garters and yellow ribbons; the Queen in the middle of the picture, expiring in the arms of her woman, and Zadig strangled at her feet. The horizon represented a rising sun, to express that this shocking execution was to be performed in the morning. As soon as he had finished the picture, he ran to one of Astarte's women, waked her, and made her understand that she must immediately carry it to the Queen.

At midnight a messenger knocked at Zadig's door, awakened him, and gave him a note from the Queen. He wondered whether it was a dream; and opened the letter with a trembling hand. But how great was his surprise! and who can express the consternation and despair into which he was thrown upon reading these words :

' Fly, this instant, or thou art a dead man. Fly, Zadig, I conjure thee by our mutual love and my yellow ribbons. I have not been guilty, but I find that I must die like a criminal.'

Zadig was hardly able to speak. He sent for Cador, and, without uttering a word, gave him the note. Cador forced him to obey, and forthwith to take the road to Memphis.

' Shouldst thou dare,' said he, ' to go in search of the Queen, thou wilt hasten her death. Shouldst thou speak to the King, thou wilt infallibly ruin her. I will take upon me the charge of her destiny; follow thy own. I will spread a report that thou hast taken the road to India. I will soon follow thee, and inform thee of all that shall have passed in Babylon.'

At that instant, Cador caused two of the swiftest drome-daries to be brought to a private gate of the palace. Upon one of these he mounted Zadig, whom he was obliged to carry to the door, and who was ready to expire with grief. He was accompanied by a single domestic; and Cador, plunged in sorrow and astonishment, soon lost sight of his friend.

This illustrious fugitive arriving on the side of a hill, from whence he could take a view of Babylon, turned his eyes towards the Queen's palace, and fainted away at the sight; nor did he recover his senses but to shed a torrent of tears, and to wish for death. At length, after his thoughts had been long engrossed in lamenting the unhappy fate of the loveliest woman and the greatest queen in the world, he for a moment turned his views on himself, and cried :

' What then is human life? O virtue, how hast thou served me ! Two women have basely deceived me; and now a third, who is innocent and more beautiful than both the others, is going to be put to death ! Whatever good I have done hath been to me a continual source of calamity and affliction; and I have only been raised to the height of grandeur, to be tumbled down the most horrid precipice of misfortune.'

Filled with these gloomy reflections, his eyes overspread with the veil of grief, his countenance covered with the

paleness of death, and his soul plunged in an abyss of the
blackest despair, he continued his journey towards Egypt.

CHAPTER IX

THE WOMAN BEATEN

ZADIG directed his course by the stars. The constellation
of Orion and the bright star of Sirius guided his steps
towards the pole of Canopæa. He admired those vast
globes of light, which appear to our eyes but as so many
little sparks, while the earth, which in reality is only an
imperceptible point in nature, appears to our fond imagination as something so grand and noble. He then represented
to himself the human species as it really is, a parcel of
insects devouring one another on a little atom of clay.
This true image seemed to annihilate his misfortunes, by
making him sensible of the nothingness of his own being,
and of that of Babylon. His soul launched out into
infinity, and detached from the senses, contemplated the
immutable order of the universe. But when afterwards,
returning to himself, and entering into his own heart, he
considered that Astarte had perhaps died for him, the
universe vanished from his sight, and he beheld nothing
in the whole compass of nature but Astarte dying, and
Zadig unhappy. While he thus alternately gave up his
mind to this flux and reflux of sublime philosophy and
intolerable grief, he advanced towards the frontiers of
Egypt; and his faithful domestic was already in the first
village, in search of a lodging. Meanwhile, as Zadig was
walking towards the gardens that skirted the village, he
saw, at a small distance from the highway, a woman
bathed in tears, and calling heaven and earth to her assistance, and a man in a furious passion, pursuing her. The
man had already overtaken the woman, who embraced his
knees, notwithstanding which he loaded her with blows
and reproaches. Zadig judged by the frantic behaviour
of the Egyptian, and by the repeated pardons which the
lady asked him, that the one was jealous and the other

unfaithful. But when he surveyed the woman more
narrowly, and found her to be a lady of exquisite beauty,
and to have some resemblance to the unhappy Astarte,
he felt himself inspired with compassion for her, and horror
towards the Egyptian.

'Assist me,' cried she to Zadig with the deepest sighs,
'deliver me from the hands of the most barbarous man in
the world; save my life.'

Moved by these pitiful cries, Zadig ran and threw himself
between her and the barbarian. As he had some knowledge
of the Egyptian language, he addressed him in that tongue:

'If,' said he, 'thou hast any humanity, I conjure thee to
pay some regard to her beauty and weakness. How canst
thou behave in this outrageous manner to one of the master-
pieces of nature, who lies at thy feet, and has no defence,
but her tears?'

'Ah, ha!' replied the madman, 'thou art likewise in
love with her; I must be revenged on thee too.'

So saying, he left the lady, whom he had hitherto held
with his hand twisted in her hair, and taking his lance,
attempted to stab the stranger. Zadig, whose blood was
cool, easily eluded the blow aimed by the frantic Egyptian.
He seized the lance near the iron with which it was armed.
The Egyptian strove to draw it back; Zadig to wrest it
from the Egyptian; and in the struggle it was broken
in two. The Egyptian drew his sword; Zadig did the same.
They attacked each other. The former gave a hundred
blows at random; the latter warded them off with dexterity.
The lady, seated on a turf, readjusted her head-dress, and
looked at the combatants. The Egyptian excelled in
strength; Zadig in address. The one fought like a man
whose arm was directed by his judgment; the other like
a madman, whose blind rage made him deal his blows
at random. Zadig closed with him, and disarmed him;
and while the Egyptian, now become more furious, endeavoured to throw himself upon him, he seized him,
pressed him close, and threw him down; and then holding
his sword to his breast, offered him his life. The Egyptian,
frantic with rage, drew his dagger, and wounded Zadig
at the very instant that the conqueror was granting him
mercy. Zadig, outraged, plunged his sword in the bosom

of the Egyptian, who, giving a horrible shriek, expired struggling. Zadig then approached the lady, and said to her in a gentle tone :

' He forced me to kill him; I have avenged thy cause; thou art now delivered from the most violent man I ever saw; what further, madam, wouldst thou have me do for thee ? '

' Die, villain,' replied she, ' die; thou hast killed my lover; O that I were able to tear out thy heart ! '

' Why truly, madam,' said Zadig, ' thou hadst a strange kind of a man for a lover; he beat thee with all his might, and would have killed me, because thou didst entreat me to give thee assistance.'

' I wish he were beating me still,' replied the lady, with tears and lamentation, ' I well deserved it; for I had given him cause to be jealous. Would to heaven that he was now beating me, and that thou wast in his place.'

Zadig, struck with surprise, and inflamed with a higher degree of resentment than he had ever felt before, said :

' Beautiful as thou art, madam, thou deservest that I should beat thee in my turn, so perverse art thou; but I shall not give myself the trouble.'

So saying, he remounted his camel, and advanced towards the town. He had proceeded but a few steps, when he turned back at the noise of four Babylonian couriers, who came riding at full gallop. One of them, upon seeing the woman, cried :

' It is the very same; she resembles the description that was given us.'

They gave themselves no concern about the dead Egyptian, but instantly seized the lady. She called out to Zadig :

' Help me once more, generous stranger; I ask pardon for having complained of thy conduct; deliver me again, and I will be thine for ever.'

Zadig was no longer in the humour of fighting for her.

' Apply to another,' said he; ' thou shalt not again ensnare me by thy wiles.'

Besides, he was wounded; his blood was still flowing, and he himself had need of assistance : and the sight of four Babylonians, probably sent by King Moabdar, filled him with apprehension. He therefore hastened towards the village, unable to comprehend why four Babylonian couriers should come to seize this Egyptian woman, but still more astonished at the lady's behaviour.

CHAPTER X

SLAVERY

As he entered the Egyptian village, he saw himself surrounded by the people. Every one cried out :

' This is the man that carried off the beautiful Missouf, and assassinated Cletosis.'

' Gentlemen,' said he, ' God preserve me from carrying off your beautiful Missouf; she is too capricious for me : and with regard to Cletosis, I did not assassinate him; I only fought with him in my own defence. He endeavoured to kill me, because I humbly interceded for the beautiful Missouf, whom he beat most unmercifully. I am a stranger, come to seek refuge in Egypt; and it is not likely that in coming to implore your protection, I should begin by carrying off a woman, and assassinating a man.'

The Egyptians were at that time just and humane. The people conducted Zadig to the court-house. They first of all ordered his wound to be dressed, and then examined him and his servant apart, in order to discover the truth. They found that Zadig was not an assassin; but as he was guilty of having killed a man, the law condemned him to be a slave. His two camels were sold for the benefit of the town : all the gold he had brought with him was distributed among the inhabitants; and his person, as well as that of the companion of his journey, was exposed to sale in the market-place. An Arabian merchant, named Setoc, made the purchase; but as the servant was fitter for labour than the master, he was sold at a higher price. There was no comparison between the two men. Thus Zadig became a slave subordinate to his own servant. They were linked together by a chain fastened to their feet, and in this condition they followed the Arabian mer-

chant to his house. By the way Zadig comforted his
servant, and exhorted him to patience; but he could not
help making, according to his usual custom, some reflections on human life.

' I see,' said he, ' that the unhappiness of my fate hath
an influence on thine. Hitherto everything has turned out
for me in a most unaccountable manner. I have been
condemned to pay a fine for having seen the marks of a
bitch's feet. I thought that I should once have been
impaled on account of a griffin. I have been sent to execution for having made some verses in praise of the King.
I have been upon the point of being strangled because the
Queen had yellow ribbons; and now I am a slave with
thee because a brutal wretch beat his mistress. Come, let
us keep a good heart; all this perhaps will have an end.
The Arabian merchants must necessarily have slaves; and
why not me as well as another, since, as well as another,
I am a man? This merchant will not be cruel; he must
treat his slaves well, if he expects any advantage from
them.'

But while he spoke thus, his heart was entirely engrossed
by the fate of the Queen of Babylon.

Two days after, the merchant Setoc set out for Arabia
Deserta, with his slaves and his camels. His tribe dwelt
near the desert of Horeb. The journey was long and painful. Setoc set a much greater value on the servant than
the master, because the former was more expert in loading
the camels; and all the little marks of distinction were
shown to him. A camel having died within two days'
journey of Horeb, his burden was divided and laid on the
backs of the servants; and Zadig had his share among the
rest. Setoc laughed to see all his slaves walking with their
bodies inclined. Zadig took the liberty to explain to him
the cause, and inform him of the laws of the balance.
The merchant was astonished, and began to regard him
with other eyes. Zadig, finding he had raised his curiosity,
increased it still further by acquainting him with many
things that related to his commerce; the specific gravity
of metals and commodities under an equal bulk; the
properties of several useful animals; and the means of
rendering those useful that are not naturally so. At last

Setoc began to consider Zadig as a sage, and preferred him
to his companion, whom he had formerly so much esteemed.
He treated him well, and had no cause to repent of his
kindness.

As soon as Setoc arrived among his own tribe, he demanded the payment of five hundred ounces of silver,
which he had lent to a Jew in presence of two witnesses;
but as the witnesses were dead, and the debt could not
be proved, the Hebrew appropriated the merchant's money
to himself, and piously thanked God for putting it in his
power to cheat an Arabian. Setoc imparted this troublesome affair to Zadig, who was now become his adviser.

'In what place,' said Zadig, 'didst thou lend the five
hundred ounces to this infidel?'

'Upon a large stone,' replied the merchant, 'that lies
near Mount Horeb.'

'What is the character of thy debtor?' said Zadig.

'That of a knave,' returned Setoc.

'But I ask thee, whether he is hasty or phlegmatic,
cautious or imprudent?'

'He is, of all bad payers,' said Setoc, 'the most hasty
fellow I ever knew.'

'Well,' resumed Zadig, 'allow me to plead thy cause.'

In effect, Zadig having summoned the Jew to the tribunal,
addressed the judge in the following terms:

'Pillow of the throne of equity, I come to demand of
this man, in the name of my master, five hundred ounces of
silver, which he refuses to repay.'

'Hast thou any witnesses?' said the judge.

'No, they are dead; but there remains a large stone
upon which the money was counted; and if it please thy
grandeur to order the stone to be sought for, I hope that
it will bear witness. The Hebrew and I will tarry here
till the stone arrives: I will send for it at my master's
expense.'

'With all my heart,' replied the judge, and immediately
applied himself to the discussion of other affairs.

When the court was going to break up, the judge said
to Zadig:

'Well, friend, is not thy stone come yet?'

The Hebrew replied with a smile :

'Thy grandeur may stay here till the morrow, and after all not see the stone. It is more than six miles from hence; and it would require fifteen men to move it.'

'Well,' cried Zadig, 'did not I say that the stone would bear witness? Since this man knows where it is, he thereby confesses that it was upon it that the money was counted.'

The Hebrew was disconcerted, and was soon after obliged to confess the truth. The judge ordered him to be fastened to the stone, without meat or drink, till he should restore the five hundred ounces, which were soon after paid.

The slave Zadig and the stone were held in great repute in Arabia.

CHAPTER XI

THE FUNERAL PILE

SETOC was so delighted that he made his slave his intimate friend. He had now conceived as great an esteem for him as ever the King of Babylon had done; and Zadig was glad that Setoc had no wife. He discovered in his master a good natural disposition, much probity of heart, and a great share of good sense; but he was sorry to see that, according to the ancient custom of Arabia, he adored the host of heaven; that is, the sun, moon, and stars. He sometimes spoke to him on this subject with great prudence and discretion. At last he told him that these bodies were like all other bodies in the universe, and no more deserving of our homage than a tree or a rock.

'But,' said Setoc, 'they are eternal beings; and it is from them we derive all we enjoy. They animate nature; they regulate the seasons; and, besides, are removed at such an immense distance from us, that we cannot help revering them.'

'Thou receivest more advantage,' replied Zadig, 'from the waters of the Red Sea, which carry thy merchandise to the Indies. Why may not it be as ancient as the stars?

And if thou adorest what is placed at a distance from thee, thou shouldst adore the land of the Gangarides, which lies at the extremity of the earth.'

'No,' said Setoc, 'the brightness of the stars commands our adoration.'

At night Zadig lighted up a great number of candles in the tent where he was to sup with Setoc; and the moment his patron appeared, he fell on his knees before these lighted tapers, and said:

'Eternal and shining luminaries! be ye always propitious to me.'

Having thus said, he sat down at the table, without taking the least notice of Setoc.

'What art thou doing?' said Setoc to him in amazement.

'I act like thee,' replied Zadig, 'I adore these candles, and neglect their master and mine.'

Setoc comprehended the profound sense of this apologue. The wisdom of his slave sank deep into his soul; he no longer offered incense to the creatures, but adored the Eternal Being who made them.

There prevailed at that time in Arabia a shocking custom, sprung originally from Scythia, and which, being established in the Indies by the authority of the Brahmans, threatened to overrun all the East. When a married man died, and his beloved wife aspired to the character of a saint, she burned herself publicly on the body of her husband. This was a solemn feast, and was called the Funeral Pile of Widowhood; and that tribe in which most women had been burned was the most respected. An Arabian of Setoc's tribe being dead, his widow, whose name was Almona, and who was very devout, published the day and hour when she intended to throw herself into the fire, amidst the sound of drums and trumpets. Zadig remonstrated against this horrible custom; he showed Setoc how inconsistent it was with the happiness of mankind to suffer young widows to burn themselves every other day, widows who were capable of giving children to the state, or at least of educating those they already had; and he convinced him that it was his duty to do all that lay in his power to abolish such a barbarous practice.

'The women,' said Setoc, 'have possessed the right of

burning themselves for more than a thousand years; and who shall dare to abrogate a law which time has rendered sacred? Is there anything more respectable than ancient abuses?'

'Reason is more ancient,' replied Zadig; 'meanwhile, speak thou to the chiefs of the tribes, and I will go to wait on the young widow.'

Accordingly he was introduced to her; and, after having insinuated himself into her good graces by some compliments on her beauty, and told her what a pity it was to commit so many charms to the flames, he at last praised her for her constancy and courage.

'Thou must surely have loved thy husband,' said he to her, 'with the most passionate fondness.'

'Who, I?' replied the lady, 'I loved him not at all. He was a brutal, jealous, insupportable wretch; but I am firmly resolved to throw myself on his funeral pile.'

'It would appear then,' said Zadig, 'that there must be a very delicious pleasure in being burnt alive.'

'Oh! it makes Nature shudder,' replied the lady, 'but that must be overlooked. I am a devotee; I should lose my reputation; and all the world would depise me, if I did not burn myself.'

Having made her acknowledge that she was going to burn herself to gain the good opinion of others, and to gratify her own vanity, Zadig entertained her with a long discourse, calculated to make her a little in love with life, and even went so far as to inspire her with some degree of good will for the person who spoke to her. . . .

'And what wilt thou do at last,' said he, 'if the vanity of burning thyself should not continue?'

'Alas!' said the lady, 'I believe I should desire thee to marry me.'

Zadig's mind was too much engrossed with the idea of Astarte not to elude this declaration; but he instantly went to the chiefs of the tribes, told them what had passed, and advised them to make a law, by which a widow should not be permitted to burn herself, till she had conversed privately with a young man for the space of an hour. Since that time not a single woman hath burned herself in Arabia. They were indebted to Zadig alone for destroying in one day a cruel custom, that had lasted for so many ages; and thus he became the benefactor of Arabia.

CHAPTER XII

THE SUPPER

SETOC, who could not separate himself from this man in whom dwelt wisdom, took him to the great fair of Bassora, whither the richest merchants in the earth resorted. Zadig was highly pleased to see so many men of different countries united in the same place. He considered the whole universe as one large family assembled at Bassora. The second day he sat at table with an Egyptian, an Indian, an inhabitant of Cathay, a Greek, a Celt, and several other strangers, who, in their frequent voyages to the Arabian Gulf, had learned enough Arabic to make themselves understood. The Egyptian seemed to be in a violent passion.

'What an abominable country is Bassora!' said he, 'they refuse me a thousand ounces of gold on the best security in the world.'

'How!' said Setoc, 'on what security have they refused thee this sum?'

'On the body of my aunt,' replied the Egyptian, 'she was the most notable woman in Egypt; she always accompanied me in my journeys; she died on the road! I have converted her into one of the finest mummies in the world; and, in my own country, I could have as much as I please by giving her as a pledge. It is very strange that they will not here lend me so much as a thousand ounces of gold on such a solid security.'

Angry as he was, he was going to help himself to a bit of excellent boiled fowl, when the Indian, taking him by the hand, cried out in a sorrowful tone:

'Ah! what art thou going to do?'

'To eat a bit of this fowl,' replied the man who owned the mummy.

'Take care that thou dost not,' replied the Indian. 'It is possible that the soul of the deceased may have passed into this fowl; and thou wouldst not, surely, expose thyself to the danger of eating thy aunt? To boil fowls is a manifest outrage on nature.'

'What dost thou mean by thy nature and thy fowl?' replied the choleric Egyptian. 'We adore a bull, and yet we eat heartily of beef.'

'You adore a bull! is it possible?' said the man from the Ganges.

'Nothing is more possible,' returned the other; 'we have done so for these hundred and thirty-five thousand years; and nobody amongst us has ever found fault with it.'

'A hundred and thirty-five thousand years!' said the Indian. 'This account is a little exaggerated; it is but eighty thousand years since India was first peopled, and we are surely more ancient than you: Brahma prohibited our eating of ox-flesh before you thought of putting it on your spits or altars.'

'This Brahma of yours,' said the Egyptian, 'is a pleasant sort of an animal truly to compare with our Apis; what great things hath your Brahma performed?'

'It was he,' replied the Brahmin, 'that taught mankind to read and write, and to whom the world is indebted for the game of chess.'

'Thou art mistaken,' said a Chaldean who sat near him, 'it is to the fish Oannes that we owe these great advantages; and it is just that we should render homage to none but him. All the world will tell thee that he is a divine being, with a golden tail and a beautiful human head, and that for three hours every day he left the water to preach on dry land. He had several children who were kings, as every one knows. I have a picture of him at home, which I worship with becoming reverence. We may eat as much beef as we please; but it is surely a great sin to dress fish for the table. Besides, you are both of an origin too recent and ignoble to dispute with me. The Egyptians reckon only a hundred and thirty-five thousand years, and the Indians but eighty thousand, while we have almanacks of four thousand ages. Believe me; renounce your follies; and I will give to each of you a beautiful picture of Oannes.'

The man of Cathay took up the discourse, and said:

'I have a great respect for the Egyptians, the Chaldeans, the Greeks, the Celtics, Brahma, the bull Apis, and the beautiful fish Oannes; but I could think that Li, or Tien, as he is commonly called, is superior to all the bulls on the earth, and all the fish in the sea. I shall say nothing of my native country; it is as large as Egypt, Chaldea, and the Indies put together. Neither shall I dispute about the antiquity of our nation, because it is of little consequence whether we are ancient or not; it is enough if we are happy; but, were it necessary to speak of almanacks, I could say that all Asia takes ours, and that we had very good ones before arithmetic was known in Chaldea.'

'Ignorant men, as ye all are,' said the Greek; 'do you not know that Chaos is the father of all; and that form and matter have put the world into its present condition?'

The Greek spoke for a long time, but was at last interrupted by the Celt, who, having drunk pretty deeply while the rest were disputing, imagined he was now more knowing than all the others, and said with an oath, that there were none but Teutat and the mistletoe of the oak that were worth the trouble of a dispute; that, for his own part, he had always some mistletoe in his pocket; and that the Scythians, his ancestors, were the only men of merit that had ever appeared in the world; that it was true they had sometimes eaten human flesh, but that, notwithstanding that circumstance, his nation deserved to be held in great esteem; and that, in fine, if any one spoke ill of Teutat, he would teach him better manners. The quarrel was now become warm; and Setoc saw the table was going to be stained with blood. Zadig, who had been silent during the whole dispute, arose at last. He first addressed himself to the Celt, as the most furious of all the disputants; he told him that he had reason on his side, and begged a few mistletoes. He then praised the Greek for his eloquence; and softened all their exasperated spirits. He said but little to the man of Cathay, because he had been the most reasonable of them all. At last he said:

'You were going, my friends, to quarrel about nothing, for you are all of one mind.'

At this word they all cried out together.

' Is it not true,' said he to the Celt, ' that you adore not this mistletoe, but him that made both the mistletoe and the oak ? '

' Most undoubtedly,' replied the Celt.

' And thou, Mr. Egyptian, dost not thou revere, in a certain bull, him who gave the bulls ? '

' Yes,' said the Egyptian.

' The fish Oannes,' continued he, ' must yield to him who made the sea and the fishes.'

' True,' said the Chaldean.

' The Indian and the Chinaman,' added he, ' acknowledge, like you, a first principle. I did not fully comprehend the admirable things that were said by the Greek; but I am sure he will admit a superior being, on whom form and matter depend.'

The Greek, whom they all admired, said that Zadig had exactly taken his meaning.

' You are all then,' replied Zadig, ' of one opinion, and have no cause to quarrel.'

All the company embraced him.

Setoc, after having sold his commodities at a very high price, returned to his own tribe with his friend Zadig; and the latter learned, upon his arrival, that he had been tried in his absence, and was now going to be burned by a slow fire.

CHAPTER XIII

THE RENDEZ-VOUS

DURING his journey to Bassora, the priests of the stars had resolved to punish him. The precious stones and ornaments of the young widows whom they sent to the funeral pile belonged to them by right; and the least they could now do, was to burn Zadig for the ill office he had done them. Accordingly they accused him of entertaining erroneous sentiments of the heavenly host. They gave testimony against him, and swore that they had heard him say that the stars did not set in the sea. This horrid blasphemy made the judges tremble; they were ready to tear their garments upon hearing these impious words; and they would certainly have torn them, had Zadig had wherewithal to pay them for new ones. But, in the excess of their zeal and indignation, they contented themselves with condemning him to be burnt by a slow fire.

Setoc, filled with despair at this unhappy event, employed all his influence to save his friend, but in vain; he was soon obliged to hold his peace. The young widow Almona, who had now conceived a great fondness for life, for which she was obliged to Zadig, resolved to deliver him from the funeral pile, of the abuse of which he had fully convinced her. She revolved the scheme in her own mind, without imparting it to any person whatever. Zadig was to be executed the next day: if she could save him at all, she must do it that very night; and the method taken by this charitable and prudent lady was as follows.

She perfumed herself, she heightened her beauty by the richest and gayest apparel, and she went to demand a private audience of the chief priest of the stars. As soon as she was introduced to the venerable old man, she addressed him in these terms:

'Eldest son of the Great Bear; brother of the Bull; and cousin of the Great Dog' (such were the titles of this pontiff), 'I come to confide in thee my scruples. I am much afraid that I have committed a heinous crime in not burning myself on the funeral pile of my dear husband; for, indeed, what had I worth preserving? Perishable flesh, thou seest, that is already entirely withered.'

So saying, she drew up her long sleeves of silk, and showed her naked arms, which were of an elegant shape and a dazzling whiteness.

'Thou seest,' said she, 'that these are of little worth.'

The priest found in his heart that they were worth a great deal; his eyes said so, and his mouth confirmed it: he swore that he had never in his life seen such beautiful arms.

'Alas!' said the widow, 'my arms, perhaps, are not so bad as the rest; but thou wilt confess that my neck is not worthy of the least regard.'

She then revealed the most charming bosom that Nature had ever formed. Compared with it, a rosebud on an apple of ivory would have appeared like madder on the box-tree, and the whiteness of new-washed lambs would have seemed of a dusky yellow. Her neck; her large black eyes, languishing with the gentle lustre of a tender fire; her cheeks animated with the finest purple, mixed with the whiteness of the purest milk; her nose, which had no resemblance to the tower of Mount Lebanon; her lips, like two borders of coral, inclosing the finest pearls in the Arabian Sea; all conspired to make the old man believe that he was but twenty years of age. Stammering, he made a tender avowal, Almona, seeing him enflamed, entreated him to pardon Zadig.

' Alas! ' said he, ' my charming lady, should I grant thee his pardon, it would be of no service, as it must necessarily be signed by three others, my brethren.'

' Sign it, nevertheless,' said Almona.

' With all my heart,' said the priest, ' on condition that thy favours shall be the price of my ready compliance.'

' Thou doest me too much honour,' said Almona; ' be pleased only to come to my chamber after sunset, and when the bright star of Sheat shall appear in the horizon, thou wilt find me on a rose-coloured sofa; and thou mayest then use thy servant as thou art able.'

So saying, she departed with the signature, and left the old man full of love and distrust of his own abilities. He employed the rest of the day in bathing; he drank a liquor composed of the cinnamon of Ceylon, and of the precious spices of Tidor and Ternate; and waited with impatience till the star Sheat should make its appearance.

Meanwhile, Almona went to the second pontiff. He assured her that the sun, the moon, and all the luminaries of heaven, were but will-o'-the-wisps in comparison with her charms. She asked the same favour of him; and he proposed to grant it on the same terms. She suffered herself to be overcome; and appointed the second pontiff to meet her at the rising of the star Algenib. From thence she went to the third and fourth priest, each time taking a signature, and making an assignation from star to star. She then sent a message to the judges, entreating them to come to her house, on an affair of great importance. They obeyed her summons. She showed them the four names, and told them at what price the priests had sold the pardon of Zadig.

Each of them arrived at the hour appointed. Each was surprised at finding his brethren there, but still more at seeing the judges, before whom their shame was now manifest. Zadig was saved; and Setoc was so charmed with the ingenuity and address of Almona that he made her his wife.

CHAPTER XIV

THE DANCE

SETOC had to visit the island of Serendib on business, but the first month of marriage which is, as every one knows, the honeymoon, made him incapable either of leaving his wife or of imagining that he ever could leave her; so he begged his friend Zadig to make the journey for him.

' Alas,' said Zadig, ' must I set an even greater distance between the beautiful Astarte and myself? But to serve my benefactor is a duty.'

He consented, wept, and took his departure.

He had not long been in the island of Serendib before he was looked upon as a person of extraordinary character. He became arbiter of all the disputes that arose between merchants, the friend of sages and the adviser of that small number of people who accept advice. The King desired to see and hear him; he soon learned Zadig's worth; he grew to have confidence in him and made him his friend. The King's friendship and esteem for him caused a feeling of apprehension in Zadig. Day and night he was filled with memories of the unhappiness which Moabdar's favour had brought upon him.

' The King takes pleasure in me,' he would say. ' Shall I not be ruined? '

Yet he could not free himself of his Majesty's marks of affection; for it must be admitted that Nabussan, King of Serendib, son of Nussanab, son of Nabassun, son of Sanbunas, was one of the noblest princes in Asia, and when one spoke with him, it was difficult not to love him.

This great prince was constantly fawned upon, cheated, and robbed. He was a prey to all who would plunder his treasury. The receiver-general of the island of Serendib set this example as a matter of course, and the others followed it faithfully. The King knew of it; he had changed his treasurer frequently, but he had been unable to alter the established custom of dividing the king's revenues into unequal parts, of which the smaller was always rendered to his Majesty, and the larger to the ministers.

King Nabussan confided his distress to the wise Zadig.

' You who know so many excellent things,' he said, ' could you not invent a means of finding me a treasurer who would not rob me? '

' Certainly,' replied Zadig, ' I know an infallible way of finding a man with clean hands.'

The King, overjoyed, embraced him and asked how it could be put into effect.

' You have only,' replied Zadig, ' to make all who present themselves for the office of treasurer dance, and the one who dances most lightly will indubitably be the most honest man.'

' You are jesting,' said the king. ' That is a fine way of choosing the receiver of my monies. What? You claim that the man who cuts the best caper will be the most honest and cleverest financier? '

' I do not claim that he will be the cleverest,' replied Zadig, ' but I assure you that he will infallibly be the most honest.'

Zadig spoke with such confidence that the King thought he had some supernatural secret for divining financiers.

' I dislike the supernatural,' said Zadig, ' I have never found any enjoyment among people and books with a tendency to the prodigious. If your Majesty will grant me leave to make the trial I suggest, you will be quite convinced that my secret is the most simple and easiest affair.'

Nabussan, King of Serendib, was much more astounded at hearing that the secret was simple than if it had been presented to him as a miracle.

' Very well,' he said, ' do as you propose.'

' Leave me to carry it out,' said Zadig, ' and you will gain more than you think by this trial.'

That very day, he had it publicly announced that all who sought the office of lord high receiver of the revenues of his gracious Majesty Nabussan, son of Nussanab, should present themselves in garments of light silk on the first day of the moon of the Crocodile, in the King's anteroom. They presented themselves to the number of sixty-four. Violinists had been summoned into a room nearby. All was prepared for the dance. But the door of the room was closed, and to enter it, they had to pass along a rather dark little gallery. A hussar came to fetch and introduce each candidate, one after another, by means of this passage, where he was left alone for a few minutes. The King, who had been informed beforehand, had spread out all his treasure in the gallery. When all the claimants had arrived in the chamber, his Majesty commanded that they should dance. Never did men dance more heavily and with less grace. All held their heads down, their backs bent, their hands glued to their sides.

' What scoundrels,' said Zadig in a whisper.

Only one of them performed his steps with agility, his head high, his glance bold, his arms outstretched, his body upright, his legs straight.

' Ah, an honest man, a fine fellow,' said Zadig.

The King embraced the excellent dancer, and declared him treasurer, and all the rest were chastised and fined with the greatest justice in the world, for each, during the time that he had been in the gallery, had filled his pockets and could scarcely walk. The King was distressed at human nature, since among sixty-four dancers there were sixty-three thieves. The dark gallery was named the ' Passage of Temptation.' In Persia, those sixty-three gentlemen would have been impaled. In other countries, a court of justice would have been inaugurated which would have demanded as restitution three times as much money as was stolen. In another kingdom, they would have been fully justified and the agile dancer dishonoured. In Serendib, they were condemned merely to make a contribution to the public treasury, for Nabussan was very indulgent.

He was also ready to recognize merit. He gave Zadig a sum of money considerably larger than any treasurer had ever stolen from the king his master.

Zadig employed it to send couriers to Babylon, who were to inform him of the fate of Astarte. His voice trembled as he gave the command, the blood ebbed back to his heart, his eyes were veiled with darkness, and his soul was ready to leave him. The courier departed, Zadig saw him set out on his way, re-entered the presence of the King, and seeing no one, thought he was in his own room and uttered the word ' love.'

' Ah, love,' said the King. ' That is exactly the question. You have divined the root of my sorrow. How great a man you are. I hope you will teach me how to recognize a wife who is completely trustworthy, even as you have found me an honest treasurer.'

Zadig, recovering his senses, promised to serve him in love as in finance, although the matter appeared to him even more difficult.

CHAPTER XV

THE BLUE EYES

' THE body and heart . . .' said the King to Zadig.

At these words, the Babylonian could not forbear from interrupting his Majesty.

' How glad I am,' he said, ' that thou didst not say " The heart and soul "; for in conversation at Babylon one hears nought but these words. There are no books to be seen save those which deal with the heart and the soul, composed by men who possess neither the one nor the other. But pardon me, sire, pray proceed.'

Nabussan continued thus :

' The body and heart are in me destined to love. The former of these two masters has every opportunity of satisfaction. I have in my palace one hundred women at my will, all beautiful, obliging, willing to please, voluptuous even, or pretending to be so when they are with me. But my heart is very far from being in so happy a position. I have proved only too well that they shower caresses upon the King of Serendib, but have only too little thought for Nabussan. It is not that I believe my wives to be faithless, but I would wish to find a soul which would be my own.

For such a treasure, I would give the hundred beauties whose charms I do possess. See if among the hundred sultanas you can find me one of whose love I may be assured.'

Zadig replied as he had done in the matter of the financiers.

' Sire, give me leave to act; but grant first that I may make use of the treasures you displayed in the Passage of Temptation. I will render you a good account of them and you will lose nothing by it.'

The King gave him absolute control. He chose out, in Serendib, thirty-three little hunchbacks, the ugliest he could find, thirty-three of the handsomest pages, and thirty-three of the most eloquent and vigorous priests. He gave them absolute freedom to enter the chamber of the sultanas; each little hunchback had four thousand gold pieces to bestow, and all the hunchbacks were successful the very first day. The pages who had nothing but themselves to bestow gained no conquest till the end of two or three days. The priests had a little more trouble, but at last thrity-three pious ladies yielded to them. The King saw, and marvelled at all these proofs of affection, through blinds which gave a view into each chamber. Of his hundred wives, ninety-nine yielded before his very eyes. There remained one, very young, very new, whom his Majesty had never approached. One, two, three hunchbacks were sent to her, who offered her up to twenty thousand gold pieces. She was incorruptible and could not restrain her laughter at the idea that the hunchbacks thought themselves more attractive by the possession of money. The two most goodly pages were presented to her. She said that she found the King more handsome. The most eloquent of the priests was despatched to her, and then the boldest. The first she found a blusterer, and as for the second, she did not even deign to suspect him of merit.

' The heart accomplishes all,' she said, ' I will never yield to a hunchback's gold, nor to the charms of a young man, nor to the seductions of a priest. I shall love Nabussan, son of Nussanab alone, and I shall wait until he deigns to love me.'

The King was beside himself with joy, amazement, and tenderness. He took back all the money which had brought about the success of the hunchbacks, and presented it to the beautiful Falide : for such was the name of the maiden. He gave her his heart, which she well deserved. Never was the flower of youth so brilliant, never the charms of beauty so enchanting. Historical veracity cannot allow me to suppress the fact that her curtseys lacked grace, but she danced like the fairies, sang like the Sirens and talked like the Graces. She was as accomplished as she was virtuous.

Nabussan, knowing himself loved, adored her in turn. But she had blue eyes, and this was the source of great unhappinesses. An ancient law forbade kings to bestow their affection upon one of these women, whom the Greeks have since given the name βοῶπις. The chief priest five thousand years before that time had made this ordinance; and it was in order to have for himself the mistress of the first king of Serendib that the high priest had caused the denunciation of blue eyes to pass into the laws of the land.

All ranks throughout the kingdom came to expostulate with Nabussan. In public, men said that the last days of the kingdom had come, horror was at its zenith, and all nature was threatened with sinister events; in one word, Nabussan, son of Nussanab, loved two large blue eyes. The hunchbacks, the financiers, the priests, and the brunettes filled the realm with their lamentations.

Barbaric tribes dwelling to the north of Serendib took advantage of this general discontent. They invaded the territory of the good King Nabussan. He demanded subsidies from his subjects. The priests who owned half the revenue of the state were content to lift their hands to Heaven and refused to put them into their coffers to help the King. They uttered beautiful prayers to the strains of music and left the state a prey to the barbarians.

' O, my dear Zadig, can you save me yet again from this most dreadful situation ? ' cried Nabussan in grief.

' Willingly,' replied Zadig. ' You will have as much money from the priests as you wish. Only abandon the defence of those territories in which their castles are situated and defend only your own.'

Nabussan did not fail to carry this into effect. The priests came and flung themselves at the King's feet and begged his aid. The King answered them with beautiful strains of

music accompanied by the singing of prayers to Heaven for
the preservation of their lands. At last, the priests gave him
money and the King concluded the war successfully. Thus
Zadig, by his wise and fitting counsel and by his great
services, was drawn into an irreconcilable hostility with the
most powerful men in the State. The priests and the women
with brown eyes vowed to bring about his downfall. The
financiers and the hunchbacks gave him no respite. They
even succeeded in making the good Nabussan suspect him.
' Services rendered oft remain in the anteroom; suspicions
enter even to the closet,' as Zoroaster says. Every day
came fresh accusations; the first is parried, the second
grazes, the third wounds, the fourth kills !

Zadig became alarmed, and having successfully completed his friend Setoc's business and despatched his money
to him safely, he thought only of leaving the island, and
resolved himself to go and seek news of Astarte.

' For,' said he to himself, ' if I stay in Serendib, the priests
will have me impaled. But whither ? In Egypt I shall be
enslaved; in Arabia, burned by all appearances; in Babylon,
strangled. Yet I must learn the fate of Astarte. Let us
go, and we shall see what my sad destiny still holds in store
for me.'

CHAPTER XVI

THE ROBBER

ARRIVING on the frontiers which divide Arabia Petræa
from Syria, he passed by a pretty strong castle, from which
a party of armed Arabians sallied forth. They instantly
surrounded him, and cried, ' All thou hast belongs to us,
and thy person is the property of our master.'

Zadig replied by drawing his sword; his servant, who
was a man of courage, did the same. They killed the first
Arabians that presumed to lay hands on them; and,
though the number was redoubled, they were not dismayed,
but resolved to perish in the conflict. Two men defended
themselves against a multitude; and such a combat could

not last long. The master of the castle, whose name was
Arbogad, having observed from a window the prodigies of
valour performed by Zadig, conceived a high esteem for
this heroic stranger. He descended in haste, and went in
person to call off his men, and deliver the two travellers.

' All that passes over my lands,' said he, ' belongs to me,
as well as what I find upon the lands of others; but thou
seemest to be a man of such undaunted courage that I will
exempt thee from the common law.'

He then conducted Zadig to his castle, ordering his men
to treat him well; and in the evening Arbogad supped with
him. The lord of the castle was one of those Arabians
who are commonly called robbers; but he now and then
performed some good actions amidst a multitude of bad
ones. He robbed with a furious rapacity, and granted
favours with great generosity; intrepid in action; affable
in company; a debauchee at table, but gay in his debauchery; and particularly remarkable for his frank and
open behaviour. He was highly pleased with Zadig, whose
lively conversation lengthened the repast. At last Arbogad
said to him :

' I advise thee to enroll thyself under me; thou canst not
do better; this is not a bad trade; and thou mayest one
day become what I am at present.'

' May I take the liberty of asking thee,' said Zadig,
' how long thou hast followed this noble profession?'

' From my most tender youth,' replied the lord. ' I
was servant to a pretty good-natured Arabian, but could
not endure the hardships of my situation. I was vexed to
find that fate had given me no share of the earth, which
equally belongs to all men. I imparted the cause of my
uneasiness to an old Arabian, who said to me : " My son,
do not despair; there was once a grain of sand that lamented
that it was no more than a neglected atom in the deserts; at
the end of a few years it became a diamond; and it is now the
brightest ornament in the crown of the King of the Indies."
This discourse made a deep impression on my mind; I
was the grain of sand, and I resolved to become the diamond.
I began by stealing two horses; I soon got a party of companions; I put myself in a condition to rob small caravans;
and thus, by degrees, I destroyed the difference which had

formerly subsisted between me and other men. I had my
share of the good things of this world; and was even
recompensed with interest. I was greatly respected, and
became the captain of a band of robbers. I seized this
castle by force. The satrap of Syria had a mind to dis-
possess me of it; but I was already too rich to have anything to fear. I gave the satrap a handsome present, by
which means I preserved my castle, and increased my
possessions. He even appointed me treasurer of the tributes
which Arabia Petræa pays to the King of kings. I perform
my office of receiver; but dispense with that of paymaster.
The Grand Desterham of Babylon sent hither a petty
satrap in the name of King Moabdar, to have me strangled.
This man arrived with his orders: I was apprised of all;
I caused to be strangled in his presence the four persons he
had brought with him to draw the noose; after which I
asked him how much his commission of strangling me might
be worth. He replied that his fees would amount to above
three hundred pieces of gold. I then convinced him that he
might gain more by staying with me. I made him an
inferior robber; and he is now one of my best and richest
officers. If thou wilt take my advice, thy success may be
equal to his; never was there a better season for plunder,
since King Moabdar is killed, and all Babylon thrown into
confusion.'

'Moabdar killed!' said Zadig, 'and what is become of
Queen Astarte?'

'I know not,' replied Arbogad. 'All I know is that Moabdar lost his senses, and was killed; that Babylon is a scene
of disorder and bloodshed; that all the empire is desolated;
that there are some fine strokes to be struck yet; and that,
for my own part, I have struck some that are admirable.'

'But the Queen,' said Zadig; 'for heaven's sake, knowest thou nothing of the Queen's fate?'

'Yes,' replied he, 'I have heard something of a prince of
Hyrcania; if she was not killed in the tumult, she is
probably his concubine, but I am more curious about
booty than news. I have taken several women in my
excursions; but I keep none of them: I sell them at a high
price, when they are beautiful, without inquiring who they
are. In commodities of this kind rank makes no difference,

and a queen that is ugly will never find a merchant. Perhaps I may have sold Queen Astarte; perhaps she is dead; but, be it as it may, it is of little consequence to me, and I should imagine of as little to thee.'

So saying, he drank a large draught, which threw all his ideas into such confusion that Zadig could obtain no further information.

Zadig remained for some time without speech, sense, or motion. Arbogad continued drinking; told stories; constantly repeated that he was the happiest man in the world; and exhorted Zadig to put himself in the same condition. At last the soporiferous fumes of the wine lulled him into a gentle repose. Zadig passed the night in the most violent perturbation.

' What ! ' said he, ' did the king lose his senses? and is he killed? I cannot help lamenting his fate. The empire is rent in pieces : and this robber is happy. O fortune ! O destiny ! A robber is happy, and the most beautiful of Nature's works hath perhaps perished in a barbarous manner, or lives in a state worse than death. O Astarte ! what is become of thee? '

At daybreak, he questioned all those he met in the castle; but they were all busy, and he received no answer. During the night they had made a new capture, and they were now employed in dividing the spoil. All he could obtain in this hurry and confusion was an opportunity of departing, which he immediately embraced, plunged deeper than ever in the most gloomy and mournful reflections.

Zadig proceeded on his journey with a mind full of disquiet and perplexity, and wholly employed on the unhappy Astarte, on the King of Babylon, on his faithful friend Cador, on the happy robber Arbogad, on that capricious woman whom the Babylonians had seized on the frontiers of Egypt ; in a word, on all the misfortunes and disappointments he had hitherto suffered.

CHAPTER XVII

THE FISHERMAN

AT a few leagues distance from Arbogad's castle, he came to the banks of a small river, still deploring his fate, and considering himself as the most wretched of mankind. He saw a fisherman lying on the brink of the river, scarcely holding, in his weak and feeble hand, a net which he seemed ready to drop, and lifting up his eyes to Heaven.

' I am certainly,' said the fisherman, ' the most unhappy man in the world. I have been, as all the world admitted, the most famous dealer in cream cheese in Babylon, and yet I am ruined. I had the most handsome wife that any man in my station could have; and by her I have been betrayed. I had still left a paltry house, and that I have seen pillaged and destroyed. At last I took refuge in this cottage, where I have no other resource than fishing, and yet I cannot catch a single fish. Oh, my net ! no more will I throw thee into the water; I will throw myself in thy place.'

So saying he arose and advanced, in the attitude of a man ready to throw himself into the river, and thus to finish his life.

' What ! ' said Zadig to himself; ' are there men as wretched as I ? '

His eagerness to save the fisherman's life was as sudden as this reflection. He ran to him, stopped him, and spoke to him with a tender and compassionate air. It is commonly supposed that we are less miserable when we have companions in our misery. This, according to Zoroaster, does not proceed from malice, but necessity. We feel ourselves insensibly drawn to an unhappy person as to one like ourselves. The joy of the happy would be an insult; but two men in distress are like two slender trees, which mutually supporting each other, fortify themselves against the storm.

' Why,' said Zadig to the fisherman, ' dost thou sink under thy misfortunes ? '

' Because,' replied he, ' I see no means of relief. I was the most considerable man in the village of Derlback, near

Babylon, and with the assistance of my wife I made the best cream cheese in the empire. Queen Astarte and the famous minister Zadig were extremely fond of them. I had sent them six hundred cheeses, and one day went to the city to receive my money; but, on my arrival at Babylon, was informed that the Queen and Zadig had disappeared. I ran to the house of the Lord Zadig, whom I had never seen; but found there the inferior officers of the Grand Desterham, who being furnished with a royal licence were plundering it with great loyalty and order. From thence I flew to the Queen's kitchen, some of the lords of which told me that the Queen was dead; some said she was in prison; and others pretended that she had made her escape; but they all agreed in assuring me that I would not be paid for my cheese. I went with my wife to the house of the Lord Orcan, who was one of my customers, and begged his protection in my present distress. He granted it to my wife, but refused it to me. She was whiter than the cream cheeses that began my misfortune; and the lustre of the Tyrian purple was not more bright than the carnation which animated this whiteness. For this reason Orcan detained her, and drove me from his house. In my despair I wrote a letter to my dear wife. She said to the bearer: "Oh! Ah! Yes! I know the writer of this a little; I have heard his name mentioned; they say he makes excellent cream cheese; desire him to send me some, and he shall be paid."

' In my distress I resolved to apply to justice. I had still six ounces of gold remaining : I was obliged to give two to the lawyer whom I consulted, two to the procurator who undertook my cause, and two to the secretary of the first judge. When all this was done, my business was not begun; and I had already expended more money than my cheese and my wife were worth. I returned to my own village with the intention of selling my house, in order to enable me to recover my wife.

' My house was well worth sixty ounces of gold; but as my neighbours saw that I was poor, and obliged to sell it, the first to whom I applied offered me thirty ounces, the second twenty, and the third ten. Bad as these offers were, I was so blind that I was going to strike a bargain, when a prince of Hyrcania came to Babylon, and ravaged all in his way. My house was first sacked and then burnt.

'Having thus lost my money, my wife, and my house, I retired into this country, where thou now seest me. I have endeavoured to gain a subsistence by fishing; but the fish make a mock of me as well as the men. I catch none; I die with hunger; and had it not been for thee, august comforter, I should have perished in the river.'

The fisherman was not allowed to give this long account without interruption; at every moment Zadig in his great emotion would say:

' What! knowest thou nothing of the Queen's fate? '

' No, my lord,' replied the fisherman; ' but I know that neither the Queen nor Zadig have paid me for my cream cheeses; that I have lost my wife, and am now reduced to despair.'

' I flatter myself,' said Zadig, ' that thou wilt not lose all thy money. I have heard of this Zadig; he is an honest man; and if he return to Babylon, as he expects, he will give thee more than he owes thee: but with regard to thy wife, who is not so honest, I advise thee not to seek to recover her. Believe me, go to Babylon; I shall be there before thee, because I am on horseback, and thou art on foot. Apply to the illustrious Cador; tell him thou hast met his friend; wait for me at his house: go, perhaps thou wilt not always be unhappy.'

' O mighty Ormuzd! ' continued he, ' thou employest me to comfort this man; whom wilt thou employ to give me consolation? '

So saying, he gave the fisherman half the money he had brought from Arabia. The fisherman, struck with surprise, and ravished with joy, kissed the feet of the friend of Cador, and said:

' Thou art surely an angel sent from heaven to save me! '

Meanwhile Zadig continued to make fresh inquiries, and to shed tears.

' What! my lord! ' cried the fisherman, ' art thou then so unhappy, thou who bestowest favours? '

' A hundred times more unhappy than thee,' replied Zadig.

'But how is it possible,' said the good man, 'that the giver can be more wretched than the receiver?'

'Because,' replied Zadig, 'thy greatest misery arose from poverty, and mine is seated in the heart.'

'Did Orcan take thy wife from thee?' said the fisherman. This word recalled to Zadig's mind the whole of his adventures. He repeated the catalogue of his misfortunes, beginning with the Queen's bitch, and ending with his arrival at the castle of the robber Arbogad.

'Ah!' said he to the fisherman; 'Orcan deserves to be punished: but it is commonly such men as those that are the favourites of fortune. However, go thou to the house of the lord Cador, and there wait my arrival.'

They then parted: the fisherman walked, thanking Heaven for the happiness of his condition; and Zadig rode, accusing fortune for the hardness of his lot.

CHAPTER XVIII

THE BASILISK

ARRIVING in a beautiful meadow, he there saw several women, who were searching for something intently. He took the liberty to approach one of them, and to ask if he might have the honour to assist them in the search.

'Take care that thou dost not,' replied the Syrian; 'what we are searching for can be touched only by women.'

'Strange,' said Zadig, 'may I presume to ask thee what it is that women only are permitted to touch?'

'It is a basilisk,' said she.

'A basilisk, madam! and for what purpose, pray, dost thou seek for a basilisk?'

'It is for our lord and master Ogul, whose castle thou seest on the bank of that river, at the end of the meadow. We are his most humble slaves. The lord Ogul is sick. His physician hath ordered him to eat a basilisk, stewed in rose-water; and as it is a very rare animal, and can only be taken by women, the lord Ogul hath promised to choose for his well-beloved wife the woman that shall bring him a

basilisk; let me go on in my search; for thou seest what I
shall lose if my companions are before me.'

Zadig left her and the other Syrians to search for their
basilisk, and continued to walk in the meadow; when
coming to the brink of a small rivulet, he found another
lady lying on the grass, but she was not searching for anything. Her person seemed to be majestic; but her face
was covered with a veil. She was leaning over the
rivulet, and profound sighs proceeded from her mouth.
In her hand she held a small rod with which she was tracing
characters on the fine sand that lay between the turf and
the brook. Zadig had the curiosity to examine what this
woman was writing. He drew near; he saw the letter Z,
then an A; he was astonished: then appeared a D; he
started. But never was surprise equal to his, when he
saw the two last letters of his name. He stood for some
time immovable. At last breaking silence with a faltering
voice, he said:

' O generous lady! pardon a stranger, an unfortunate
man, for presuming to ask thee by what surprising adventure
I here find the name of Zadig traced out by thy divine
hand.'

At this voice, and these words, the lady lifted up the veil
with a trembling hand, looked at Zadig, uttered a cry of
tenderness, surprise, and joy, and sinking under the various
emotions which at once assaulted her soul, fell speechless
into his arms. It was Astarte herself; it was the Queen of
Babylon; it was she whom Zadig adored, and whom he
had reproached himself for adoring; it was she whose
misfortunes he had so deeply lamented, and for whose fate
he had been so anxiously concerned. He was for a moment
deprived of the use of his senses; then when he looked into
Astarte's eyes, which now began to open again with a
languor mixed with confusion and tenderness, he cried:

' O ye immortal powers, who preside over the fates of
weak mortals, do ye indeed restore Astarte to me! at what
a time, in what a place, and in what a condition do I again
behold her? '

He fell on his knees before Astarte, and laid his face in
the dust of her feet. The Queen of Babylon raised him up,
and made him sit by her side on the brink of the rivulet.

She frequently wiped her eyes, from which the tears continued to flow afresh : she twenty times resumed her discourse, which her sighs as often interrupted : she asked by what strange accident they were brought together; and suddenly prevented his answers by other questions : she began the account of her own misfortunes, and desired to be told of those of Zadig. At last, both of them having a little composed the tumult of their souls, Zadig acquainted her in a few words by what adventure he was brought into that meadow.

'But, O unhappy and honourable queen ! by what means do I find thee in this lonely place, clothed in the habit of a slave, and accompanied by other female slaves, who are searching for a basilisk, which, by order of the physician, is to be stewed in rose-water ? '

'While they are searching for their basilisk,' said the fair Astarte, 'I will inform thee of all I have suffered, for which heaven has sufficiently recompensed me, by restoring thee to my sight. Thou knowest that the King, my husband, was vexed to see thee the most amiable of mankind; and that for this reason he one night resolved to strangle thee and poison me. Thou knowest how Heaven permitted my little mute to inform me of the orders of his sublime Majesty. Hardly had the faithful Cador obliged thee to depart, in obedience to my command, when he ventured to enter my apartment at midnight by a secret passage. He carried me off, and conducted me to the temple of Ormuzd, where the magus his brother shut me up in that huge statue, whose base reaches to the foundation of the temple, and whose top rises to the summit of the dome. I was there buried in a manner; but was served by the magus, and supplied with all the necessaries of life. At break of day his Majesty's apothecary entered my chamber with a potion composed of a mixture of henbane, opium, hemlock, black hellebore, and aconite; and another officer went to thine with a bowstring of blue silk. Neither of us were to be found. Cador, the better to deceive the King, pretended to come and accuse us both. He said that thou hadst taken the road to the Indies, and I that to Memphis; on which the King's guards were immediately dispatched in pursuit of us both.

' The couriers who pursued me did not know me. I had hardly ever shown my face to any but thee, and to thee only in the presence and by the order of my husband. They conducted themselves in the pursuit by the description that had been given them of my person. On the frontiers of Egypt they met with a woman of the same stature as I, and possessed perhaps of greater charms. She was weeping and wandering. They made no doubt but that this woman was the Queen of Babylon, and accordingly brought her to Moabdar. Their mistake at first threw the King into a violent passion; but having viewed this woman more attentively, he found her extremely handsome, and was comforted. She was called Missouf. I have since been informed, that this name in the Egyptian language signifies *the capricious fair one.* She was so in reality; but she had as much cunning as caprice. She pleased Moabdar, and gained such an ascendency over him as to make him choose her for his wife. Her character then began to appear in its true colours. She gave herself up, without scruple, to all the freaks of a wanton imagination. She would have obliged the chief of the magi, who was old and gouty, to dance before her; and on his refusal, she persecuted him with the most unrelenting cruelty. She ordered her master of the horse to make her a pie of sweetmeats. In vain did he represent that he was not a pastry-cook; he was obliged to make it, and lost his place, because it was baked a little too hard. The post of master of the horse she gave to her dwarf, and that of chancellor to her page. In this manner did she govern Babylon. Everybody regretted the loss of me. The King, who till the moment of his resolving to poison me and strangle thee, had been a tolerably good kind of man, seemed now to have drowned all his virtues in his immoderate fondness for this capricious fair one. He came to the temple on the great day of the feast held in honour of the Sacred Fire. I saw him implore the gods in behalf of Missouf, at the feet of the statue in which I was enclosed. I raised my voice, I cried out: " The gods reject the prayers of a king who is now become a tyrant, and who attempted to murder a reasonable wife, in order to marry a woman remarkable for nothing but her folly and extravagance."

'At these words Moabdar was confounded, and his head became disordered. The oracle I had pronounced and the tyranny of Missouf conspired to deprive him of his judgment, and in a few days his reason entirely forsook him.

'His madness, which seemed to be the judgment of Heaven, was the signal for a revolt. The people rose, and ran to arms; and Babylon, which had been so long immersed in idleness and effeminacy, became the theatre of a bloody civil war. I was taken from the heart of my statue, and placed at the head of a party. Cador flew to Memphis to bring thee back to Babylon. The Prince of Hyrcania, informed of these fatal events, returned with his army and made a third party in Chaldea. He attacked the King, who fled before him with his capricious Egyptian. Moabdar died pierced with wounds. Missouf fell into the hands of the conqueror. I myself had the misfortune to be taken by a party of Hyrcanians, who conducted me to their prince's tent, at the very moment that Missouf was brought before him. Thou wilt doubtless be pleased to hear that the prince thought me more beautiful than the Egyptian; but thou wilt be sorry to be informed that he designed me for his seraglio. He told me, with a blunt and resolute air, that as soon as he had finished a military expedition, which he was just going to undertake, he would come to me. Judge how great must have been my grief. My ties with Moabdar were already dissolved; I might have been the wife of Zadig; and I was fallen into the hands of a barbarian. I answered him with all the pride which my high rank and noble sentiment could inspire. I had always heard it affirmed that heaven stamped on persons of my condition a mark of grandeur, which, with a single word or glance, could reduce to the lowliness of the most profound respect, those rash and forward persons who presume to deviate from the rules of politeness. I spoke like a queen, but was treated like a maid-servant. The Hyrcanian, without even deigning to speak to me, told his black eunuch that I was impertinent, but that he thought me handsome. He ordered him to take care of me, and to put me under the regimen of favourites that, my complexion being improved, I might be the more worthy of his

favours, when he should be at leisure to honour me with
them. I told him that I would put an end to my life. He
replied with a smile that women, he believed, were not so
bloodthirsty, and that he was accustomed to such violent
expressions; and then left me with the air of a man who
had just put another parrot into his aviary. What a state for
the first queen of the universe, and, I will say more, for a
heart devoted to Zadig ! '

At these words Zadig threw himself at her feet, and
bathed them with his tears. Astarte raised him with great
tenderness, and thus continued her story.

' I now saw myself in the power of a barbarian, and rival
to the foolish woman with whom I was confined. She
gave me an account of her adventures in Egypt. From the
description she gave of your person, from the time, from the
dromedary on which thou wert mounted, and from every
other circumstance, I inferred that Zadig was the man who
had fought for her. I doubted not but that thou wert at
Memphis, and therefore resolved to repair thither. " Beautiful Missouf," said I, " thou art more handsome than I, and
will please the Prince of Hyrcania much better. Assist me
in contriving the means of my escape; thou wilt then reign
alone; thou wilt at once make me happy, and rid thyself
of a rival." Missouf concerted with me the means of my
flight; and I departed secretly with an Egyptian slave-
woman.

' As I approached the frontiers of Arabia, a famous
robber, named Arbogad, seized me, and sold me to some
merchants, who brought me to this castle, where the lord
Ogul resides. He bought me without knowing who I was.
He is a voluptuary, ambitious of nothing but good living,
and thinks that God sent him into the world for no other
purpose than to sit at table. He is so extremely corpulent
that he is always in danger of suffocation. His physician,
who has but little credit with him when he has a good
digestion, governs him with a despotic sway when he has
eaten too much. He has persuaded him that a basilisk
stewed in rose-water will effect a complete cure. The lord
Ogul hath promised his hand to the female slave that
brings him a basilisk. Thou seest that I leave them
to vie with each other in meriting this honour; and never

was I less desirous of finding the basilisk than since Heaven hath restored thee to my sight.'

This account was succeeded by a long conversation between Astarte and Zadig, consisting of everything that their long-suppressed sentiments, their great sufferings, and their mutual love could inspire in hearts most noble and tender; and the genii who preside over love carried their words to the sphere of Venus.

The women returned to Ogul without having found the basilisk. Zadig was introduced to this mighty lord, and spoke to him in the following terms:

' May immortal health descend from heaven to bless all thy days! I am a physician: at the first report of thy indisposition I flew to thy castle, and have now brought thee a basilisk stewed in rose-water. Not that I pretend to marry thee. All I ask is the liberty of a Babylonian slave, who hath been in thy possession for a few days; and, if I should not be so happy as to cure thee, magnificent lord Ogul, I consent to remain a slave in her place.'

The proposal was accepted. Astarte set out for Babylon with Zadig's servant, promising to send couriers constantly to inform him of all that happened. Their parting was as tender as their meeting. The moment of meeting and that of parting are the two greatest epochs of life, as sayeth the great book of Zend. Zadig loved the Queen with as much ardour as he professed; and the Queen loved Zadig more than she acknowledged.

Meanwhile Zadig spoke thus to Ogul:

' My lord, my basilisk is not to be eaten; all its virtue must enter through thy pores. I have enclosed it in a little ball, blown up and covered with a fine skin. Thou must strike this ball with all thy might, and I must strike it back for a considerable time; and by observing this regimen for a few days, thou wilt see the effects of my art.'

The first day Ogul was out of breath, and thought he would have died with fatigue. The second, he was less fatigued, and slept better. In eight days he recovered all the strength, all the health, all the agility and cheerfulness of his most agreeable years.

' Thou hast played at ball, and hast been temperate,' said Zadig; ' know that there is no such thing in Nature as a basilisk; that temperance and exercise are the two great preservatives of health; and that the art of reconciling intemperance and health is as chimerical as the philosopher's stone, judicial astrology, or the theology of the magi.'

Ogul's first physician, observing how dangerous this man might prove to the medical art, formed a design, in conjunction with the apothecary, to send Zadig to search for a basilisk in the other world. Thus, after having suffered such a long train of calamities on account of his good actions, he was now upon the point of losing his life for curing a gluttonous lord. He was invited to an excellent dinner, and was to have been poisoned in the second course; but, during the first, he happily received a courier from the fair Astarte. He rose from the table and departed.

' When a man is beloved by a beautiful woman,' says the great Zoroaster, ' he hath always the good fortune to extricate himself out of every kind of difficulty.'

CHAPTER XIX

THE TOURNAMENT

THE Queen was received at Babylon with all those transports of joy which are ever felt on the return of a beautiful princess who hath been involved in calamities. Babylon was now in greater tranquillity. The Prince of Hyrcania had been killed in battle. The victorious Babylonians declared that the Queen should marry the man whom they should choose for their sovereign. They were resolved that the first place in the world, that of being husband to Astarte and King of Babylon, should not depend on cabals and intrigues. They swore to acknowledge for King the man who possessed the greatest valour and the greatest wisdom. Accordingly, at the distance of a few leagues from the city, a spacious place was marked out for the lists surrounded with magnificent amphitheatres. Thither the combatants were to repair in complete armour. Each of them had a separate apartment behind the amphitheatres, where they were neither to be seen nor known by any one. Each was to encounter four knights; and those that were so happy as to conquer four, were then to engage with one another; so that he who remained the last master of the field, would be proclaimed conqueror at the games. Four days after, he was to return with the same arms, and to explain the enigmas proposed by the magi. If he did not explain the enigmas, he was not king; and the running at the lances was to begin afresh, till a man should be found who was conqueror in both these combats; for they were absolutely determined to have a king possessed of the greatest wisdom and the most invincible courage. The Queen was all the while to be strictly guarded : she was only allowed to be present at the games, and even there she was to be covered with a veil; but was not permitted to speak to any of the competitors that they might neither receive favour, nor suffer injustice.

These particulars Astarte communicated to her lover, hoping that, in order to obtain her, he would show himself possessed of greater courage and wisdom than any other person. Zadig arrived on the banks of the Euphrates on the eve of this great day. He caused his device to be inscribed among those of the combatants, concealing his face and his name, as the law ordained; and then went to rest himself in the apartment that fell to him by lot. His friend Cador, who, after the fruitless search he had made for him in Egypt, had now returned to Babylon, sent to his tent a complete suit of armour, which was a present from the Queen; as also from himself the finest horse in Persia. Zadig perceived that these presents were sent by Astarte; and from this his courage and his love derived new strength and new hope.

The next day, the Queen being seated under a canopy of jewels, and the amphitheatres filled with all the gentlemen and ladies of rank in Babylon, the combatants appeared in the arena. Each of them came and laid his device at the feet of the Grand Magus. They drew their devices by lot; and that of Zadig was the last. The first who advanced was a certain lord, named Itobad, very rich and very vain, but possessed of little courage, of less address, and of hardly any judgment at all. His servants had persuaded

him that such a man as he ought to be king; he had said
in reply, ' Such a man as I ought to reign' ; and thus they
had armed him *cap-à-pie*. He wore an armour of gold
enamelled with green, a plume of green feathers, and a
lance adorned with green ribbons. It was instantly perceived by the manner in which Itobad managed his horse
that it was not for such a man as he that Heaven reserved the
sceptre of Babylon. The first knight that ran against him
threw him out of his saddle; the second laid him flat on his
horse's buttocks, with his legs in the air, and his arms
extended. Itobad recovered himself, but with so bad a
grace, that the whole amphitheatre burst out laughing.
The third knight disdained to make use of his lance; but,
making a pass at him, took him by the right leg, and
wheeling him half-round, laid him prostrate on the sand.
The squires of the games ran to him laughing, and replaced
him in his saddle. The fourth combatant took him by the
left leg, and tumbled him down on the other side. He
was conducted back with scornful shouts to his tent, where,
according to the law, he was to pass the night; and as he
limped along, with great difficulty, he said : ' What an
experience for such a man as I ! '

The other knights acquitted themselves with greater
ability and success. Some of them conquered two combatants; a few of them vanquished three; but none but
Prince Otamus conquered four. At last Zadig fought in
his turn. He successively threw four knights off their
saddles, with all the grace imaginable. It then remained
to be seen who should be conqueror, Otamus or Zadig.
The arms of the former were gold and blue, with a plume
of the same colour; those of Zadig were white. The wishes
of all the spectators were divided between the knight in
blue and the knight in white. The Queen, whose heart
was in a violent palpitation, offered prayers to Heaven for
the success of the white colour.

The two champions made their passes and vaults with
so much agility, they mutually gave and received such
dexterous blows with their lances, and sat so firmly in their
saddles that everybody but the Queen wished there might
be two kings in Babylon. At length, their horses being
tired, and their lances broken, Zadig had recourse to this

stratagem: he passed behind the blue prince; sprang upon the buttocks of his horse; seized him by the middle; threw him on the earth; placed himself in the saddle; and wheeled around Otamus as he lay extended on the ground. All the amphitheatre cried out, ' Victory to the white knight ! ' Otamus rose in a violent passion, and drew his sword; Zadig leaped from his horse with his sabre in his hand. Both of them were now on the ground, engaged in a new combat, where strength and agility triumphed by turns. The plumes of their helmets, the studs of their bracelets, and the rings of their armour, were driven to a great distance by the violence of a thousand furious blows. They struck with the point and the edge; to the right, to the left; on the head, on the breast; they retreated; they advanced; they measured swords; they closed; they seized each other; they bent like serpents; they attacked like lions; and the fire every moment flashed from their blows. At last Zadig, having recovered his spirits, stopped; made a feint; leaped upon Otamus; threw him on the ground and disarmed him; and Otamus cried out :

' It is thou alone, O white knight, who shouldst reign over Babylon ! '

The Queen was now at the height of her joy. The knight in blue armour, and the knight in white, were conducted each to his own apartment, as well as all the others, according to the intention of the law. Mutes came to wait upon them, and to serve them at table. It may be easily supposed that the Queen's little mute waited upon Zadig. They were then left to themselves to sleep till next morning, at which time the conqueror was to bring his device to the Grand Magus, to compare it with that which he had left, and make himself known.

Zadig, though deeply in love, was so much fatigued that he could not help sleeping. Itobad, who lay near him, never closed his eyes. He arose in the night, entered Zadig's apartment, took the white arms and the device, and put his own green armour in their place. At break of day, he went boldly to the Grand Magus to declare that so great a man as he was conqueror. This was little expected; however, he was proclaimed while Zadig was still asleep.

Astarte, surprised and filled with despair, returned to
Babylon. The amphitheatre was almost empty when
Zadig awoke; he sought for his arms, but could find none
but the green armour. With this he was obliged to cover
himself, having nothing else near him. Astonished and
enraged, he put it on in a furious passion, and advanced in
this guise.

The people that still remained in the amphitheatre and
the arena received him with hoots and hisses. They
surrounded him, and insulted him to his face. Never did
man suffer such cruel mortifications. He lost his patience;
with his sabre he dispersed such of the populace as dared to
affront him; but he knew not what course to take. He could
not see the Queen; he could not claim the white armour
she had sent him, without exposing her; and thus,
while she was plunged in grief, he was filled with fury and
distraction. He walked on the banks of the Euphrates,
fully persuaded that his star had destined him to inevitable
misery; and revolving in his mind all his misfortunes, from
the adventure of the woman who hated one-eyed men, to
that of his armour.

' This,' said he, ' is the consequence of my having slept
too long. Had I slept less, I should now have been King
of Babylon, and in possession of Astarte. Knowledge,
virtue, and courage have hitherto served only to make me
miserable.'

He then let fall some secret murmurings against Providence, and was tempted to believe that the world was
governed by a cruel destiny, which oppressed the good, and
prospered knights in green armour. One of his greatest
mortifications was his being obliged to wear that green
armour which had exposed him to such contumelious
treatment. A merchant happening to pass by, he sold it
to him for a trifle, and bought a gown and a long bonnet.
In this garb he proceeded along the banks of the Euphrates,
filled with despair, and secretly accusing Providence, which
thus continued to persecute him.

CHAPTER XX

THE HERMIT

WHILE he was thus sauntering, he met a hermit, whose white and venerable beard hung down to his girdle. He held a book in his hand, which he read with great attention. Zadig stopped, and made him a profound obeisance. The hermit returned the compliment with such a noble and engaging air that Zadig had the curiosity to enter into conversation with him. He asked him what book it was that he had been reading.

'It is the book of destinies,' said the hermit; 'wouldst thou choose to look into it?'

He put the book into the hands of Zadig, who, thoroughly versed as he was in several languages, could not decipher a single character of it. This only redoubled his curosity.

'Thou seemest,' said this good father, 'to be in great distress.'

'Alas!' replied Zadig, 'I have but too much reason.'

'If thou wilt permit me to accompany thee,' resumed the old man, 'perhaps I may be of some service to thee. I have often poured the balm of consolation into the heart of the unhappy.'

Zadig felt himself inspired with respect for the hermit's mien, his beard, and his book. He found, in the course of the conversation, that he was possessed of superior degrees of knowledge. The hermit talked of fate, of justice, of morals, of the chief good, of human weakness, and of virtue and vice, with such a spirited and moving eloquence that Zadig felt himself drawn towards him by an irresistible charm. He earnestly entreated the favour of his company till their return to Babylon.

'I ask the same favour of thee,' said the old man; 'swear to me by Ormuzd that whatever I do, thou wilt not leave me for some days.'

Zadig swore, and they set out together.

In the evening, the two travellers arrived at a superb castle. The hermit entreated a hospitable reception for himself and the young man who accompanied him. The porter, whom one might have easily mistaken for a great

lord, introduced them with a kind of disdainful civility.   He
presented them to a principal domestic, who showed them
his master's magnificent apartments.   They were admitted
to the lower end of the table, without being honoured with
the least mark of regard by the lord of the castle; but they
were served, like the rest, with delicacy and profusion.
They were then presented with water to wash their hands,
in a golden basin adorned with emeralds and rubies.   At
last they were conducted to bed in a beautiful apartment;
and, in the morning, a domestic brought each of them a
piece of gold, after which they took their leave and departed.

 ' The master of the house,' said Zadig, as they were
proceeding on the journey, ' appears to be a generous man,
though somewhat too proud : he nobly performs the duties
of hospitality.'

 At that instant he observed that a kind of large pocket,
which the hermit had, was filled and distended : and upon
looking more narrowly, he found that it contained the
golden basin adorned with precious stones, which the hermit
had stolen.   He durst not then take any notice of it ; but
he was filled with a strange surprise.

 About noon, the hermit came to the door of a paltry
house, inhabited by a rich miser, and begged the favour of
a hospitable reception for a few hours.   An old servant, in
a tattered garb, received them with a blunt and rude air, and
led them into the stable, where he gave them some rotten
olives, mouldy bread, and sour beer.   The hermit ate and
drank with as much seeming satisfaction as he had done the
evening before ; and then addressing himself to the old
servant, who watched them both, to prevent their stealing
anything, and rudely pressed them to depart, he gave him
the two pieces of gold he had received in the morning, and
thanked him for his great civility.

 ' Pray,' added he, ' allow me to speak to thy master.'

 The servant, filled with astonishment, introduced the two
travellers.

 ' Magnificent lord ! ' said the hermit ; ' I cannot but return
thee my most humble thanks for the noble manner in
which thou hast entertained us.   Be pleased to accept of this
golden basin as a small mark of my gratitude.'

 The miser started, and was ready to fall backwards;

but the hermit, without giving him time to recover from his surprise, instantly departed with his young fellow-traveller.

'Father,' said Zadig, 'what is the meaning of all this? Thou seemest to me to be entirely different from other men; thou stealest a golden basin adorned with precious stones, from a lord who received thee magnificently, and givest it to a miser who treats thee with indignity.'

'Son,' replied the old man, 'this magnificent lord, who receives strangers only from vanity and ostentation, will hereby be rendered more wise; and the miser will learn to practise the duties of hospitality. Be surprised at nothing, but follow me.'

Zadig knew not as yet whether he was in company with the most foolish or the most prudent of mankind; but the hermit spoke with such an ascendancy that Zadig, who was moreover bound by his oath, could not refuse to follow him.

In the evening, they arrived at a house built with equal elegance and simplicity, where nothing savoured either of prodigality or avarice. The master of it was a philosopher, who had retired from the world, and who cultivated virtue and wisdom in peace, and yet did not lack humanity. He had chosen to build this country house in which he received strangers with a generosity free from ostentation. He went himself to meet the two travellers, whom he led into a commodious apartment, where he desired them to rest themselves a little. Soon after he came and invited them to a decent and well ordered repast, during which he spoke with great judgment of the last revolutions in Babylon. He seemed to be strongly attached to the Queen, and wished that Zadig had appeared in the lists to dispute the crown.

'But the people,' added he, 'do not deserve to have such a king as Zadig.'

Zadig blushed, and felt his griefs redoubled. They agreed, in the course of the conversation, that the things of this world were not always in accord with the wishes of the wise. The hermit still maintained that the ways of Providence were inscrutable; and that men were in the wrong to judge of a whole, of which they understood but the smallest part.

They talked of the passions. 'Ah,' said Zadig, 'how fatal are their effects!'

' They are the winds,' replied the hermit, ' that swell the
sails of the ship : it is true, they sometimes sink her, but
without them she could not sail at all. The bile makes us
sick and choleric ; but without the bile we could not live.
Everything in this world is dangerous, and yet everything in
it is necessary.'

The conversation turned on pleasure ; and the hermit
proved that it was a present bestowed by the deity.

' For,' said he, ' man cannot give himself either sensations
or ideas : he receives all ; and pain and pleasure proceed
from a foreign cause as well as his being.'

Zadig was surprised to see a man, who had been guilty of
such extravagant actions, capable of reasoning with so
much judgment and propriety. At last, after a conversation equally entertaining and instructive, the host led back
his two guests to their apartment, blessing heaven for
having sent him two men possessed of so much wisdom and
virtue. He offered them money, with such an easy and
noble air as could not possibly give any offence. The hermit
refused it, and said that he must now take his leave of him,
as he proposed to set out for Babylon before it was light.
Their parting was tender ; Zadig especially felt himself
filled with esteem and affection for a man of such an
amiable character.

When he and the hermit were alone in their apartment,
they spent a long time in praising their host. At break of
day, the old man awakened his companion.

' We must now depart,' said he ; ' but while all the family
are still asleep, I will leave this man a mark of my esteem
and affection.'

So saying, he took a candle and set fire to the house.
Zadig, struck with horror, cried aloud, and endeavoured to
hinder him from committing such a barbarous action ; but
the hermit drew him away by force, and the house was soon
in flames. The hermit, who, with his companion, was
already at a considerable distance, looked back to the con-
flagration with great tranquillity.

' Thanks be to God,' said he, ' the house of my dear host
is entirely destroyed ! Happy man ! '

At these words Zadig was at once tempted to burst out
laughing, to reproach the reverend father, to beat him, and

to run away. But he did none of these things; for still subdued by the powerful ascendancy of the hermit, he followed him, in spite of himself, to the last stage.

This was at the house of a charitable and virtuous widow, who had a nephew fourteen years of age, full of charm, and her only hope. She performed the honours of her house as well as she could. The next day, she ordered her nephew to accompany the strangers to a bridge, which being lately broken down, was become extremely dangerous in passing. The young man walked before them with great alacrity. As they were crossing the bridge, the hermit said to the youth:

'Come, I must show my gratitude to thy aunt.'

He then took him by the hair, and plunged him into the river. The boy sank, appeared again on the surface of the water, and was swallowed up by the current.

'O monster! O thou most wicked of mankind!' cried Zadig.

'Thou didst promise to behave with greater patience,' said the hermit, interrupting him. 'Know that under the ruins of the house which Providence hath set on fire, the master hath found an immense treasure: know that this young man, whose life Providence hath shortened, would have assassinated his aunt in the space of a year, and thee in that of two.'

'Who told thee so, barbarian?' cried Zadig; 'and though thou hadst read this event in thy book of destinies, art thou permitted to drown a youth who never did thee any harm?'

While the Babylonian was thus exclaiming, he observed that the old man had no longer a beard, and that his countenance assumed the features and complexion of youth. The hermit's habit disappeared, and four beautiful wings covered a majestic body resplendent with light.

'O sent of heaven! O divine angel!' cried Zadig, humbly prostrating himself on the ground, 'hast thou then descended from the Empyrean, to teach a weak mortal to submit to the eternal decrees of Providence?'

'Men,' said the angel Jesrad, 'judge of all things without knowing anything; and, of all men, thou best deservest to be enlightened.'

Zadig begged to be permitted to speak.

' I distrust myself,' said he, ' but may I presume to ask a favour of thee to clear up one doubt that still remains in my mind ?   Would it not have been better to have corrected this youth, and made him virtuous, than to have drowned him ? '

' Had he been virtuous,' replied Jesrad, ' and enjoyed a longer life, it would have been his fate to be assassinated himself, together with the wife he would have married, and the child he would have had by her.'

' But why,' said Zadig, ' is it necessary that there should be crimes and misfortunes, and that these misfortunes should fall on the good ? '

' The wicked,' replied Jesrad, ' are always unhappy : they serve to prove and try the small number of the just that are scattered throughout the earth; and there is no evil that is not productive of some good.'

' But,' said Zadig, ' suppose there were nothing but good and no evil at all.'

' Then,' replied Jesrad, ' this earth would be another earth : the chain of events would be ranged in another order and directed by wisdom; but this other order, which would be perfect, can exist only in the eternal abode of the Supreme Being, to which no evil can approach.   The Deity hath created millions of worlds, among which there is not one that resembles another.   This immense variety is the attribute of His immense power.   There are not two leaves among the trees of the earth, nor two globes in the unlimited expanse of heaven, that are exactly similar; and all that thou seest on the little atom in which thou art born, ought to be in its proper time and place, according to the immutable decrees of Him who comprehends all. Men think that this child who hath just perished is fallen into the water by chance; and that it is by the same chance that this house is burnt : but there is no such thing as chance; all is either trial, or punishment, or reward, or foresight.   Remember the fisherman, who thought himself the most wretched of mankind.   Ormuzd sent thee to change his fate.   Cease then, frail mortal, to dispute against what thou oughtest to adore.'

' But . . .' said Zadig.

As he pronounced the word ' but,' the angel took his flight towards the tenth sphere. Zadig on his knees adored Providence, and submitted. The angel cried to him from on high :

' Direct thy course towards Babylon.'

CHAPTER XXI

THE ENIGMAS

ZADIG, as it were entranced, and like a man about whose head the thunder had burst, walked at random. He entered Babylon on the very day when those who had fought at the tournaments were assembled in the grand vestibule of the palace, to explain the enigmas, and to answer the questions of the Grand Magus. All the knights were already arrived, except the knight in green armour. As soon as Zadig appeared in the city, the people crowded round him ; every eye was fixed on him, every mouth blessed him, and every heart wished him the empire. The envious man saw him pass ; he trembled and turned aside ; the people conducted him to the place where the assembly was held. The Queen, who was informed of his arrival, became a prey to the most violent agitations of hope and fear. She was devoured with apprehension. She could not comprehend why Zadig was without arms, nor why Itobad wore the white armour. A confused murmur arose at the sight of Zadig. They were equally surprised and charmed to see him ; but none but the knights who had fought were permitted to appear in the assembly.

' I have fought as well as the other knights,' said Zadig, ' but another here wears my arms ; and while I wait for the honour of proving the truth of my assertion I demand the liberty of presenting myself to explain the enigmas.'

The question was put to the vote, and his reputation for probity was still so deeply impressed in their minds that they admitted him without scruple.

The first question proposed by the Grand Magus was :

' What of all things in the world is the longest and the

shortest, the swiftest, and the slowest, the most divisible and the most extended, the most neglected and the most regretted, without which nothing can be done, which devours all that is little, and enlivens all that is great? '

Itobad was to speak. He replied that so great a man as he did not understand enigmas, and that it was sufficient for him to have conquered by his strength and valour. Some said that the meaning of the enigma was fortune; some, the earth; and others the light. Zadig said that it was time.

' Nothing,' added he, ' is longer, since it is the measure of eternity; nothing is shorter, since it is insufficient for the accomplishment of our projects; nothing more slow to him that expects, nothing more rapid to him that enjoys; in greatness it extends to infinity, in smallness it is infinitely divisible; all men neglect it, all regret the loss of it; nothing can be done without it; it consigns to oblivion whatever is unworthy of being transmitted to posterity, and it immortalizes such actions as are truly great.'

The assembly acknowledged that Zadig was right.

The next question was : ' What is the thing which we receive without thanks, which we enjoy without knowing how, which we give to others when we know not where we are, and which we lose without perceiving it? '

Every one gave his own explanation. Zadig alone guessed that it was life, and explained all the other enigmas with the same facility. Itobad always said that nothing was more easy, and that he could have answered them with the same readiness, had he chosen to have given himself the trouble. Questions were then proposed on justice, on the sovereign good, and on the art of government. Zadig's answers were judged to be the most solid.

' What a pity is it,' said they, ' that such a great genius should be so bad a knight ! '

' Illustrious lords,' said Zadig, ' I have had the honour of conquering in the tournaments. It is to me that the white armour belongs. The lord Itobad took possession of it during my sleep. He probably thought that it would fit him better than the green. I am now ready to prove in your presence, with my gown and sword, against all that beautiful white armour which he took from me, that it is I who have had the honour of conquering the brave Otamus.'

Itobad accepted the challenge with the greatest confidence. He never doubted but that, armed as he was with a helmet, a cuirass, and brassarts, he would obtain an easy victory over a champion in a cap and a night-gown. Zadig drew his sword, saluting the Queen, who looked at him with a mixture of fear and joy. Itobad drew his without saluting any one. He rushed upon Zadig, like a man who had nothing to fear; he was ready to cleave him in two. Zadig knew how to ward off the blows, opposing the strongest part of his sword to the weakest of that of his adversary, in such a manner that Itobad's sword was broken. Upon which Zadig, seizing his enemy by the waist, threw him on the ground; and fixing the point of his sword at the extremity of his breast-plate, he said:

'Suffer thyself to be disarmed, or thou art a dead man.'

Itobad, always surprised at the disgraces that happened to such a man as he, was obliged to yield to Zadig, who took from him with great composure his magnificent helmet, his superb cuirass, his fine brassarts, his shining cuisses; clothed himself with them, and in this dress ran to throw himself at the feet of Astarte. Cador easily proved that the armour belonged to Zadig. He was acknowledged king by the unanimous consent of the whole nation, and especially by that of Astarte, who, after so many calamities, now tasted the exquisite pleasure of seeing her lover worthy, in the eyes of all the world, to be her husband. Itobad went home to be called lord in his own house. Zadig was king, and was happy; he recollected what the angel Jesrad had said to him; he even remembered the grain of sand that became a diamond. The Queen and Zadig adored Providence. He left the capricious beauty Missouf to run through the world. He sent in search of the robber Arbogad, to whom he gave an honourable post in his army, promising to advance him to the highest dignities, if he behaved like a true warrior, and threatening to hang him, if he followed the profession of a robber.

Setoc, with the fair Almona, was called from the heart of Arabia, and placed at the head of the commerce of Babylon. Cador was preferred and distinguished according to his great services. He was the friend of the King; and the King was then the only monarch on earth that had a friend. The little mute was not forgotten. A fine house was given to the fisherman; and Orcan was condemned to pay him a large sum of money, and to restore him his wife; but the fisherman, who had now become wise, took only the money.

But neither could the beautiful Semira be comforted for having believed that Zadig would be blind of an eye; nor did Azora cease to lament her having attempted to cut off his nose : their griefs, however, he softened by his presents. The envious man died of rage and shame. The empire enjoyed peace, glory, and plenty. This was the happiest age of the earth; it was governed by love and justice. The people blessed Zadig, and Zadig blessed Heaven.

[Here ends the manuscript in which the story of Zadig was discovered. It is known that he experienced many other adventures which have been faithfully recorded. Students of oriental languages are asked, if they come across any such records, to make them known.]

MICROMEGAS :

A PHILOSOPHICAL TALE

CHAPTER I

In one of the planets that revolve round the star known
by the name of Sirius was a certain young gentleman of
promising parts, whom I had the honour to be acquainted
with, in his last voyage to this our little ant-hill. His name
was Micromegas, a name admirably suited to all great men,
and his stature amounted to eight leagues in height, that is,
four and twenty thousand geometrical paces, five feet in
each.

Some of your mathematicians, a set of people always
useful to the public, will perhaps instantly seize the pen,
and calculate that Mr. Micromegas, inhabitant of the
country of Sirius, being from head to foot four and twenty
thousand paces in length, making one hundred and twenty
thousand royal feet; that we, denizens of this earth, being
at a medium little more than five feet high, and our globe
nine thousand leagues in circumference; these things being
premised, I say, they will conclude that the periphery of the
globe which produced him must be exactly one and twenty
millions six hundred thousand times greater than that of
this our tiny ball. Nothing in nature is more simple and
common. The dominions of some sovereigns of Germany
or Italy, which may be compassed in half an hour, when
compared with the empires of Ottoman, Muscovy, or China,
are no other than faint instances of the prodigious difference
which nature hath made in the scale of beings.

The stature of his Excellency being of these extraordinary
dimensions, all our painters and statuaries will easily agree
that the round of his belly might amount to fifty thousand
royal feet: a very agreeable and just proportion. His
nose being equal in length to one third of his face, and his

jolly countenance engrossing one seventh part of his height, it must be owned that the nose of this same Sirian was six thousand three hundred and thirty-three royal feet and a fraction long; which was to be demonstrated.

With regard to his understanding, it was one of the best cultivated I have known; he was perfectly well acquainted with abundance of things, some of which were of his own invention : for when he was still not 250 years old, and was studying, as the custom was, at the Jesuit College on his planet, he, by dint of genius, found out upwards of fifty propositions of Euclid, having the advantage, by more than eighteen, of Blaise Paschal, who (as we are told by his own sister) after demonstrating two and thirty for his amusement, became in after life a moderate geometrician and an extremely poor metaphysician. About the four hundred and fiftieth year of his age, or latter end of his childhood, he dissected a great number of small insects not more than one hundred feet in diameter, which are not discernible by an ordinary microscope, of which he composed a very curious treatise, which involved him in some trouble. The mufti of the nation, though very old and very ignorant, made shift to discover in his book certain lemmas that were suspicious, unseemly, rash, heretic, and unsound; and prosecuted him with great animosity; for the subject of the author's inquiry was whether, in the world of Sirius, there was any difference between the substantial forms of a flea and a snail.

Micromegas defended his philosophy with such spirit as made all the female sex his proselytes; and the process lasted two hundred and twenty years. In the end, in consequence of the mufti's interest, the book was condemned by judges who had never read it, and the author expelled from court for the term of eight hundred years.

Not much afflicted at his banishment from a court that teemed with nothing but turmoils and trifles, he made a very humorous song upon the mufti, who did not trouble himself about the matter, and set out on his travels from planet to planet in order (as the saying is) to improve his mind and finish his education. Those who never travel but in a post-chaise or berlin will doubtless be astonished at the equipages used above : for we that strut upon this little mud-heap are at a loss to conceive anything that surpasses our own customs. But our traveller was a wonderful adept in the laws of gravitation, together with the whole force of attraction and repulsion; and he made such seasonable use of his knowledge that sometimes, by the help of a sunbeam, and sometimes by the convenience of a comet, he and his retinue glided from sphere to sphere as a bird hops from one bough to another. He in a very little time posted through the milky way; and I am obliged to own that he did not see, between the stars with which it is set, that fair empyrean, which the illustrious Doctor Derham brags of having observed through his telescope. Not that I pretend to say the doctor was mistaken. God forbid! but Micromegas was upon the spot, an exceedingly good observer, and I have no mind to contradict any man. Be that as it may, after many windings and turnings, he arrived at the planet Saturn; and, accustomed as he was to the sight of novelties, he could not for his life repress that supercilious and conceited smile which often escapes the wisest philosopher, when he perceived the smallness of that globe, and the diminutive size of its inhabitants : for really Saturn is but about nine hundred times larger than this our earth, and the people of that country mere dwarfs, about a thousand fathoms high. In short, he at first derided those poor pigmies, just as an Italian fiddler, when he comes to France, laughs at the music of Lully; but as this Sirian was a person of good sense, he soon perceived that a thinking being may not be altogether ridiculous for being only six thousand feet high; and therefore he became familiar with them, after he had ceased to amaze them. In particular, he contracted an intimate friendship with the secretary of the Academy of Saturn, a man of good understanding, who, though in truth he had invented nothing of his own, gave a very good account of the inventions of others, and enjoyed a passable reputation as a little poet and a great calculator. And here, for the edification of the reader, I will repeat a very singular conversation that one day passed between Mr. Secretary and Micromegas.

CHAPTER II

THE CONVERSATION BETWEEN THE INHABITANTS OF SIRIUS AND SATURN

His Excellency laid himself down, and the secretary approached his nose.

'It must be confessed,' said Micromegas, 'that nature is full of variety.'

'Yes,' replied the Saturian, 'nature is like a parterre whose flowers——'

'Pshaw!' cried the other, 'a truce with your parterres.'

'It is,' resumed the secretary, 'like an assembly of fair and brown women whose dresses——'

'What a plague have I to do with your brunettes?' said the other.

'Then it is like a gallery of pictures, the strokes of which——'

'Not at all,' answered the traveller, 'I tell you once for all, nature is like nature. Why seek comparison?'

'Well, to please you,' said the secretary.

'I won't be pleased,' replied the traveller; 'I want to be instructed : begin therefore, without further preamble, and tell me how many senses the people of this world enjoy.'

'We have seventy and two,' said the academician, 'but we are daily complaining of the small number. Our imagination transcends our wants; for, with these seventy-two senses, our five moons and ring, we find ourselves very much restricted; and notwithstanding all our curiosity, and the no small number of passions that result from our seventy-two senses, we have still time enough to be tired of idleness.'

'I sincerely believe what you say,' cried Micromegas, 'for we in our world have near a thousand senses, and there still remains a certain vague desire, an unaccountable uneasiness, incessantly advertising us of our own un-importance, and giving us to understand that there are other beings who are much our superiors in point of perfection. I have travelled a little, and seen mortals both far inferior and far superior to ourselves : but I have met with none who did not have more desire than necessity and more want than gratification; perhaps I shall one day arrive in some country where nought is wanting; but, hitherto I have had no certain information of such a happy land.'

The Saturnian and the Sirian exhausted themselves in conjectures upon this subject, and after abundance of argumentation equally ingenious and uncertain, were obliged to return to matters of fact.

' To what age do you commonly live? ' said the Sirian.

' Lack-a-day ! a mere trifle,' replied the little gentleman.

' It is the very same case with us,' resumed the other; ' the shortness of life is our daily complaint, so that this must be a universal law in nature.'

' Alas ! ' cried the Saturnian, ' few, very few on this globe, outlive five hundred great revolutions of the sun.' [These, according to our way of reckoning, amount to about fifteen thousand years.] ' So, you see, we in a manner begin to die the very moment we are born : our existence is no more than a point, our duration an instant, and our globe an atom. Scarce do we begin to learn a little, when death intervenes before we can profit by experience : for my own part, I am deterred from laying any schemes. I consider myself as a single drop in an immense ocean. I am particularly ashamed, in your presence, of the ridiculous figure I make among my fellow creatures.'

To this declaration, Micromegas replied :

' If you were not a philosopher, I should be afraid of mortifying your pride by telling you that the term of our lives is seven hundred times longer than yours : but you are very well aware that when the texture of the body is resolved into the elements in order to reanimate nature in another form, which is what we call death : when that moment of change arrives, there is not the least difference between having lived a whole eternity, or a single day. I have been in some countries where the people live a thousand times longer than we do, and yet they murmured at the shortness of their time; but one will find everywhere some few persons of good sense who know how to make the best of their portion, and render thanks to the author of nature. There is a profusion of variety scattered throughout the universe, and yet there is an admirable vein of uniformity that runs through the whole : for example, all thinking

beings are different among themselves, though at bottom
they resemble one another, in the powers and passions of
the soul : matter, though interminable, hath different
properties in every sphere.   How many principal attributes
do you reckon in the matter of this world? '

' If you mean those properties,' said the Saturnian,
' without which we believe this our globe could not subsist
in its present form, we reckon in all three hundred, such as
extent, impenetrability, motion, gravitation, divisibility, and
so on.'

' That small number,' replied the traveller, ' probably
answers the purpose of the creator on this your narrow
sphere.   I admire his wisdom in all his works.   I see
infinite variety, but everywhere proportion.   Your globe
is small; so are the inhabitants : you have few sensations;
your matter is endued with few properties : these are the
works of unerring Providence.   Of what colour does your
sun appear when accurately examined? '

' Of a yellowish white,' answered the Saturnian; ' and in
separating one of his rays, we find it contains seven colours.'

' Our sun,' saith the Sirian, ' is of a reddish hue, and we
have no less than thirty-nine original colours.   Among all
the suns I have seen, there is no sort of resemblance, just
as in this sphere of yours, there is not one face like another.'

After divers questions of this nature, he asked how many
substances, essentially different, they counted in the world
of Saturn ; and understood that they numbered but thirty :
such as God, space, matter, beings endued with sense and
extension, beings that have extension, sense, and reflection,
thinking beings who have no extension, those that are
penetrable, those that are impenetrable, and the rest.   But
this Saturnian philosopher was prodigiously astonished,
when the Sirian told him that they had no less than three
hundred, and that he himself had discovered three thousand
more in the course of his travels.   In short, after having
communicated to each other a little of what they knew, and
a good deal of what they did not know, and argued during a
complete revolution of the sun, they resolved to set out
together on a short philosophical tour.

CHAPTER III

THE VOYAGE OF THE INHABITANTS OF SIRIUS AND SATURN

OUR two philosophers were just ready to embark for the atmosphere of Saturn, being prettily provided with mathematical instruments, when the Saturnian's mistress, having got an inkling of their design, came all in tears to make her remonstrances. She was a little handsome brunette, not above six hundred and threescore fathoms high; but her agreeable attractions made amends for the smallness of her stature.

' Ah ! cruel man,' cried she, ' after a resistance of fifteen hundred years, when at length I was about to surrender, and scarce have passed a hundred in thy embrace, to leave me thus, and go wandering with a giant of another world ! Go, go, thou art a mere virtuoso, thou hast never loved ! If thou wert a true Saturnian, thou wouldst be faithful. Ah ! whither art thou going? What is thy design? Our five moons are not so inconstant, nor our ring so changeable as thee ! But see, all is over, henceforth I ne'er shall love another man.'

The philosopher embraced her and wept over her, notwithstanding his philosophy; and the lady, after having swooned, went to console herself with the conversation of a certain beau.

Meanwhile, our two virtuosi set out, and at one jump leaped upon the ring, which they found pretty flat, according to the ingenious guess of an illustrious inhabitant of this our little earth : from thence they easily slipped from moon to moon; and a comet chancing to pass near the last one they sprung upon it with all their servants and apparatus. Thus carried about one hundred and fifty millions of leagues, they met with the satellites of Jupiter, and arrived upon the body of the planet itself, where they continued a whole year; during which they learned some very curious secrets, which would actually be sent to the press, were it not for fear of the gentleman inquisitors, who have found among them some corollaries very hard of digestion. Nevertheless, I have read the manuscript in the library of the illustrious Archbishop of ——, who has granted me permission to peruse his books with that generosity and goodness which can never be enough commended; wherefore I promise he shall have a long article in the next edition of Moreri, where I shall not forget the young gentlemen his sons, who give us such pleasing hopes of seeing perpetuated the race of their illustrious father.   But to return to our travellers.   When they took leave of Jupiter, they traversed a space of about one hundred millions of leagues, and, coasting along the planet Mars, which is well known to be five times smaller than our little earth, they descried two moons subservient to that orb, which have escaped the observation of our astronomers.   I know Father Castel will write, and that pleasantly enough, against the existence of these two moons; but I entirely refer myself to those who reason by analogy.   Those worthy philosophers are very sensible that Mars, which is at such a distance from the sun, must be in a very uncomfortable situation, without the benefit of a couple of moons : be that as it may, our gentlemen found the planet so small that they were afraid they would not find room to take a little repose; so they pursued their journey like two travellers who despise the paltry accommodation of a village, and push forward to the next town.   But the Sirian and his companion soon repented; for they journeyed a long time without finding a resting place, till at length they discerned a small speck, which was the Earth.   Coming from Jupiter, they could not but be moved with compassion.   However, they resolved to land, lest they should be a second time disappointed.   They accordingly moved towards the tail of the comet, where, finding an Aurora Borealis at hand, they embarked, and arrived on the northern coast of the Baltic on the fifth day of July, according to the new calendar, in the year 1737.

CHAPTER IV

WHAT BEFELL THEM UPON THIS OUR GLOBE

HAVING taken some repose, they ate for their breakfast two mountains which their servants cooked very excellently for them, and being desirous of reconnoitring the narrow field in which they were, they traversed it at once from north to south. Every step of the Sirian and his attendants measured about thirty thousand imperial feet : whereas, the dwarf of Saturn, whose stature did not exceed a thousand fathoms, followed at a distance quite out of breath, because for every single stride of his companion he was obliged to make twelve good steps at least. The reader may figure to himself (if we are allowed to make such comparisions) a very small lap-dog dodging after a captain of the King of Prussia's grenadiers.

As those strangers walked at a good pace, they compassed the globe in six and thirty hours; the sun, it is true, or rather the earth, describes the same space in the course of one day; but it must be observed that it is much easier to turn upon an axis than to walk on foot. Behold them then returned to the spot from whence they had set out, after having discovered that almost imperceptible sea, which is called the Mediterranean; and the other narrow pond that surrounds this mole-hill, under the denomination of the great Ocean. In wading through this the dwarf had never wet more than half his leg, while the other scarce moistened his heel. In going and coming through both hemispheres, they did all that lay in their power to discover whether or not the globe was inhabited. They stooped, they lay down, they groped in every corner; but their eyes and hands were not at all proportioned to the small beings that crawl upon this earth; and therefore they could not find the smallest reason to suspect that we and our fellow citizens of this globe had the honour to exist.

The dwarf, who sometimes judged too hastily, concluded at once that there was no living creature upon earth; and his chief reason was that he had seen nobody. But Micromegas, in a polite manner, made him sensible of the unjust conclusion.

'For,' said he, ' with your diminutive eyes you cannot see certain stars of the fiftieth magnitude, which I distinctly perceive; and do you take it for granted that no such stars exist ? '

'But I have groped with great care,' replied the dwarf.

'Then your sense of feeling must be bad,' resumed the
other.

'But this globe,' said the dwarf, 'is ill contrived; and
so irregular in its form as to be quite ridiculous. The
whole together looks like chaos. Do but observe these little
rivulets; not one of them runs in a straight line; and these
ponds which are neither round, square, nor oval, nor indeed
of any regular figure; together with those little sharp
pebbles' [meaning the mountains] 'that roughen the whole
surface of the globe, and have tore all the skin from my
feet. Besides, pray take notice of the shape of the whole,
how it flattens at the poles, and turns round the sun in an
awkward oblique manner, so that the polar circles cannot
possibly be cultivated. Truly, what makes me believe
there is no inhabitant on this sphere is a full persuasion that
no sensible being would live in such a disagreeable place.'

'What then?' said Micromegas. 'Perhaps the beings
that inhabit it come not under that denomination; but in
all appearance it was not made for nothing. Everything
here seems to you irregular, because in Jupiter or Saturn
everything is laid out by rule and line. Perhaps this is the
very reason of the confusion here; have not I told you that
in the course of my travels I have always met with variety?'

The Saturnian replied to all these arguments; and
perhaps the dispute would have known no end, if Micromegas in the heat of the contest had not luckily broke the
string of his diamond necklace, so that the jewels fell to the
ground, consisting of pretty, unequal stones, of small size,
the largest of which weighed four hundred pounds, and the
smallest fifty. The dwarf, in helping to pick them up,
perceived, as they approached his eye, that every single
diamond was cut in such a manner as to answer the purpose
of an excellent microscope. He therefore took up a small
one, about one hundred and sixty feet in diameter, and
applied it to his eye, while Micromegas chose another of two
thousand five hundred; though they were of excellent
powers, the observers could at first perceive nothing by
their assistance, so that they had to adjust them. At
length the inhabitant of Saturn discerned something almost
imperceptible moving between two waves in the Baltic:
this was no other than a whale, which, in a dexterous

manner, he caught with his little finger; and, placing it on the nail of his thumb, he showed it to the Sirian, who laughed heartily at the excessive smallness peculiar to the inhabitants of our globe. The Saturnian, by this time convinced that our world was inhabited, began to imagine we had no other animals than whales; and being a mighty arguer, he forthwith set about investigating the origin of this small atom's motion, curious to know whether or not it was furnished with ideas, judgment, and free will. Micromegas was very much perplexed upon this subject; he examined the animal with the most patient attention, and the result of his inquiry was that he could see no reason to believe a soul was lodged in such a body. The two travellers were actually inclined to think there was no such thing as mind in this our habitation, when by the help of their microscope they perceived something as large as a whale floating upon the surface of the sea. It is well known that at this period a flight of philosophers were upon their return from the polar circle, where they had been making observations, for which nobody has hitherto been the wiser. The gazettes record that their vessel ran ashore on the coast of Bothnia, and that they with great difficulty saved their lives; but in this world one can never dive to the bottom of things: for my own part, I will honestly relate what took place, just as it happened, without any addition of my own; and this is no small effort for a modern historian.

CHAPTER V

EXPERIENCES AND CONCLUSIONS OF THE TWO TRAVELLERS

MICROMEGAS stretched out his hand gently towards the place where the object appeared, and advanced two fingers, which he instantly pulled back, for fear of being disappointed, then opening softly and shutting them, he very dexterously seized the ship that contained those gentlemen, and placed it on his nail, avoiding too much pressure, which might have crushed the whole in pieces.

' This,' said the Saturnian dwarf, ' is a creature very different from the former.'

The Sirian placed the supposed animal in the hollow of his hand. The passengers and crew, who believed themselves thrown by a hurricane upon some rock, began to put themselves in motion. The sailors having hoisted out some casks of wine, jumped after them into the hand of Micromegas : the mathematicians having secured their quadrants, sectors, and Lapland mistresses, went overboard at a different place, and made such a bustle in their descent, that the Sirian at length felt his fingers tickled by something that seemed to move. An iron pole chanced to penetrate about a foot deep into his forefinger; and from this prick he concluded that something had issued from the little animal he held in his hand; but at first he suspected nothing more : for the microscope, which scarcely rendered a whale and a ship visible, had no effect upon an object so imperceptible as man. I do not intend to shock the vanity of any person whatever; but here I am obliged to beg your people of importance to consider a small remark of my own. Supposing the stature of a man to be about five feet, we mortals make just such a figure upon the earth, as an animal the sixty thousandth part of a foot in height would exhibit upon a bowl ten feet in circumference. When you reflect upon a being who could hold this whole earth in the palm of his hand, and is endued with organs proportioned to those we possess, you will easily conceive that there must be a great variety of created substances;——and pray, what must such beings think of those battles which have brought us two villages which we have had to surrender again ?

I do not at all doubt that if some captain of grenadiers should chance to read this work, he would add two large feet at least to the caps of his company : but I assure him his labour will be in vain; for, do what he will, he and his soldiers will never be other than infinitely diminutive and inconsiderable.

What wonderful skill must have been inherent in our Sirian philosopher that enabled him to perceive those atoms of which we have been speaking. When Leuwenhoek and Hartsoeker observed the first rudiments of which we are formed, they did not make such an astonishing discovery.

What pleasure, therefore, did Micromegas experience in observing the motion of those little machines, in examining all their pranks, and pursuing them in all their operations! How he exclaimed! With what joy did he put his microscope into his companion's hand; and with what transport did they both at once cry out:

'I see them distinctly,—don't you perceive them carrying burdens, lying down and rising up again?'

While they were speaking, their hands shook with pleasure at seeing such uncommon objects and with fear at possibly losing them.—The Saturnian, making a sudden transition from the most cautious distrust to the most excessive credulity, imagined he saw them in the very work of propagation, and cried aloud:

'I have surprised nature in the very act.'

Nevertheless, he was deceived by appearances: a case too common, whether we do or do not make use of microscopes.

CHAPTER VI

WHAT HAPPENED IN THEIR INTERCOURSE WITH MEN

MICROMEGAS, being a much better observer than the dwarf, perceived distinctly that those atoms spoke; and remarked on this to his companion, who was so much ashamed of being mistaken on the subject of generation that he would not believe such a puny species could possibly communicate their ideas: for, though he had the gift of tongues, as well as his companion, he could not hear those particles speak; and he therefore supposed they had no language: besides, how should such imperceptible beings have the organs of speech? And what in the name of God can they say to one another? In order to speak, they must have something like thought, and if they think, they must surely have something equivalent to a soul: now, to attribute anything like a soul to such an insect species, appears a mere absurdity.

'But just now,' replied the Sirian, 'you believed they made love to each other; and do you think this could be done without thinking, without using some sort of language, or at least some way of making themselves understood? Or do you suppose it is more difficult to advance an argument than to produce a child? For my own part, I look upon both these faculties as equally mysterious.'

'I will no longer venture to believe or deny,' answered the dwarf : 'in short I have no opinion at all. Let us endeavour to examine these insects, and we will reason upon them afterwards.'

'With all my heart,' said Micromegas, who taking out a pair of scissors which he kept for paring his nails, cut off a paring from his thumb-nail, of which he immediately formed a kind of large speaking trumpet, like a vast funnel, and clapped the pipe to his ear : as the circumference of this funnel included the ship and all the crew, the most feeble voice was conveyed along the circular fibres of the nail; so that, thanks to his industry, the philosopher could distinctly hear the buzzing of our insects that were below; in a few hours he distinguished articulate sounds, and at last plainly understood the French language. The dwarf heard the same, though with more difficulty.

The astonishment of our travellers increased every instant. They heard a nest of mites talk in a pretty sensible strain : and that jest of Nature seemed to them inexplicable. You need not doubt that the Sirian and his dwarf glowed with impatience to enter into conversation with such atoms. The dwarf being afraid that his voice of thunder, and worse still, that of Micromegas, would deafen and confound the mites, without being understood by them, saw the necessity of diminishing the sound; each, therefore, put into his mouth a sort of small tooth-pick, the slender end of which reached to the vessel. The Sirian setting the dwarf upon his knees, and the ship and crew upon his nail, held down his head and spoke softly. In fine, having taken these and a great many more precautions, he addressed himself to them in these words.

'O ye invisible insects, whom the hand of the Creator hath deigned to produce in the abyss of infinite littleness, I give praise to His goodness, in that He hath been pleased to disclose unto me those secrets that seemed to be impenetrable; perhaps the court of Sirius will not disdain to behold you with admiration : for my own part, I despise no creature, and therefore offer you my protection.'

If ever there was such a thing as astonishment, it seized upon the people who heard this address, and who could not conceive from where it proceeded. The chaplain of the ship repeated exorcisms, the sailors swore, and the philosophers formed a system : but, notwithstanding all their systems, they could not divine who the person was that spoke to them. Then the dwarf of Saturn, whose voice was softer than that of Micromegas, gave them briefly to understand what species of beings they had to do with. He related the particulars of their voyage from Saturn, made them acquainted with the rank and quality of Mr. Micromegas; and after having pitied their smallness, he asked if they had always been in that miserable state, so near akin to annihilation; and what their business was upon that globe which seemed to be the property of whales; he also desired to know if they were happy in their situation, if they propagated their species, if they were inspired with souls. And he put a hundred questions of the like nature.

A certain mathematician on board, more courageous than the rest, and shocked to hear his soul called in question, planted his quadrant and took two observations of this interlocutor.

' You believe then, Mr. What-d'ye-callum,' said he, ' that because you measure from head to foot a thousand fathoms——'

' A thousand fathoms ! ' cried the dwarf. ' Good heavens ! How should he know the height of my stature? A thousand fathoms ! My very dimensions to a hair. What, measured by a mite ! this atom, forsooth, is a geometrician, and knows exactly how tall I am : while I, who can scarce perceive him through a microscope, am utterly ignorant of his extent ! '

' Yes, I have taken your measure,' answered the philosopher, ' and I will now do the same by your tall companion.'

The proposal was embraced; his Excellency lay down at full length : for, had he stood upright, his head would have reached too far above the clouds. Our mathematicians planted a tall tree in a certain part of him which Doctor

Swift would have mentioned without hesitation, but which I forbear to call by its name out of my inviolable respect for the ladies; then, by a series of triangles joined together, they discovered that the object of their observation was a strapping youth, exactly one hundred and twenty thousand imperial feet in length.

In consequence of this calculation, Micromegas uttered these words:

' I am now more than ever convinced that we ought to judge of nothing by its external magnitude. O God, who hast bestowed understanding upon such seemingly contemptible beings, Thou canst with equal ease produce that which is infinitely small, as that which is incredibly great : and if it be possible that among Thy works there are beings still more diminutive than these, they may nevertheless, be endued with understanding superior to the intelligence of those stupendous animals I have seen in Heaven, a single foot of whom is larger than this whole globe on which I have alighted.'

One of the philosophers bade him be assured that there were intelligent beings much smaller than man, and recounted not only Virgil's whole fable of the bees, but also described all that Swammerdam hath discovered, and Réaumur dissected. In a word, he informed him that there are animals which bear the same proportion to bees as bees bear to man; the same as the Sirian himself was to those vast beings whom he had mentioned; and as those huge animals were to other substances before whom they would appear like so many particles of dust. Here the conversation became very interesting, and Micromegas proceeded in these words.

CHAPTER VII

THE CONVERSATION WITH MEN

' O ye intelligent atoms, in whom the Supreme Being hath been pleased to manifest His omniscience and power, without all doubt your joys on this earth must be pure and exquisite : for being unencumbered with matter, and, to all appearance, little else than soul, you must spend your lives in the delights of love and reflection, which are the true enjoyments of a perfect spirit. True happiness I have nowhere found; but certainly here it dwells.'

At this harangue, all the philosophers shook their heads, and one among the rest, more candid than his brethren, frankly owned that, excepting a very small number of inhabitants, who were very little esteemed by their fellows, all the rest were a parcel of knaves, fools, and miserable wretches.

'We have matter enough,' said he, 'to do abundance of mischief, if mischief comes of matter; and too much understanding, if evil flows from understanding. You must know, for example, that at this very moment, while I am speaking, there are one hundred thousand animals of our own species, covered with hats, slaying an equal number of fellow-creatures who wear turbans; or else are slain by them; and this hath been nearly the case all over the earth from time immemorial.'

The Sirian, shuddering at this information, begged to know the cause of those horrible quarrels among such a puny race.

'The dispute is about a mud-heap, no bigger than your heel,' said the philosopher. 'It is not that any one of those millions who cut one another's throats pretends to have the least claim to that clod; the question is to know, whether it shall belong to a certain person who is known by the name of Sultan, or to another whom (for what reason I know not) they dignify with the appellation of Cæsar. Neither the one nor the other has ever seen, or ever will see, the pitiful corner in question; and scarcely one of those wretches who slay one another hath ever beheld the animal on whose account they are mutually slain !'

'Ah, miscreants !' cried the indignant Sirian, 'such excess of desperate rage is beyond conception. I have a good mind to take two or three steps, and trample the whole nest of such ridiculous assassins under my feet.'

'Don't give yourself the trouble,' replied the philosopher, 'they are industrious enough in procuring their own destruction; at the end of ten years the hundredth part of those wretches will be no more : for you must know that though they should not draw a sword in the cause they have espoused, famine, fatigue, and intemperance would sweep almost all of them from the face of the earth. Besides, the punishment should not be inflicted upon them, but upon those sedentary and slothful barbarians, who, from their close-stools, give orders for murdering a million of men, and then solemnly thank God for their success.'

Our traveller was moved with compassion for the little human race, in which he discovered such astonishing contrasts.

' Since you are of the small number of the wise,' said he, ' and in all likelihood do not engage yourselves in the trade of murder for hire, be so good as to tell me your occupation.'

' We anatomize flies,' replied the philosopher, ' we measure lines, we make calculations, we agree upon two or three points which we understand, and dispute upon two or three thousand that are beyond our comprehension.'

Then the strangers were seized with the whim of interrogating those thinking atoms, upon the subjects about which they were agreed.

' How far,' said the Sirian, ' do you reckon the distance between the great star of the constellation Gemini, and that called Caniculus? '

To this question all of them answered with one voice : ' Thirty-two degrees and a half.'

' And what is the distance from here to the moon? '

' Sixty semi-diameters of the earth.'

He then thought to puzzle them by asking the weight of the air; but they answered distinctly that common air is about nine hundred times specifically lighter than an equal column of the lightest water, and nineteen hundred times lighter than current gold. The little dwarf of Saturn, astonished at their answers, was now tempted to believe those very people sorcerers whom, but a quarter of an hour before, he would not allow to be inspired with souls.

' Well,' said Micromegas, ' since you know so well what is outside you, doubtless you are still more perfectly acquainted with that which is within; tell me what is the soul, and how your ideas are framed? '

Here the philosophers spoke all together as before; but each was of a different opinion. The eldest quoted Aristotle; another pronounced the name of Descartes; a third mentioned Malebranche; a fourth Leibnitz; and a fifth Locke. An old Peripatetic lifting up his voice exclaimed with an air of confidence :

' The soul is an absolute, and is reason by which it has power to be such as it is : as Aristotle expressly declares on page 633 of the Louvre edition :

Εντελεχέια τις ἔστι καί λόγος τοῦ δυνάμιν ἔχοντος τοιοῦδι ἔιται.'

' I am not very well versed in Greek,' said the giant.

' Nor I either,' replied the philosophical mite.

' Why then do you quote that same Aristotle in Greek ? ' resumed the Sirian.

' Because,' answered the other, ' it is but reasonable we should quote what we do not comprehend in a language we do not understand.'

Here the Cartesian interposed.

' The soul,' said he, ' is a pure spirit or intelligence, which hath received in the mother's womb all the metaphysical ideas; but, upon leaving that prison, is obliged to go to school, and learn anew that knowledge which it hath lost, and will never more attain.'

' So it was necessary,' replied the animal of eight leagues, ' that thy soul should be learned in thy mother's womb in order to be so ignorant when thou hast got a beard upon thy chin : but what dost thou understand by spirit ? '

' To what purpose do you ask me that question ? ' said the philosopher. ' I have no idea : indeed it is supposed to be immaterial.'

' At least, thou knowest what matter is ? ' resumed the Sirian.

' Perfectly well,' answered the other. ' For example, that stone is grey, is of a certain shape, has three dimensions, specific weight, and divisibility.'

' Right,' said the giant, ' I want to know what that object is which, according to thy observation, hath a grey colour, weight, and divisibility. Thou seest a few qualities, but dost thou know the nature of the thing itself ? '

' Not I truly,' answered the Cartesian.

E 936

'Then you do not know what matter is.'

Then addressing himself to another sage who was standing on his thumb, he asked what was the soul and what were her functions.

'Nothing at all,' replied this disciple of Malebranche; 'God hath made everything for my convenience; in Him I see everything, by Him I act; He is the universal Agent, and I never meddle in His work.'

'That is being a nonentity indeed,' said the Sirian sage; and, turning to a follower of Leibnitz, he added, 'Hark ye, friend, what is thy opinion of the soul?'

'In my opinion,' answered this metaphysician, 'the soul is the hand that points to the hour, while my body does the office of a clock; or, if you please, the soul is the clock, and the body is the pointer; or again, my soul is the mirror of the universe, and my body the frame. All this is clear and uncontrovertible.'

A little partizan of Locke, who chanced to be present, being asked his opinion on the same subject, said :

'I do not know by what power I think; but well I know that I should never have thought without the assistance of my senses : that there are immaterial and intelligent substances, I do not at all doubt; but that it is impossible for God to communicate the faculty of thinking to matter, I doubt very much. I revere the Eternal Power, to which it would ill become me to prescribe bounds : I affirm nothing, and am content to believe that many more things are possible than are usually thought so.'

The Sirian smiled at this declaration, and did not look upon the author as the least sagacious of the company : and as for the dwarf of Saturn, he would have embraced this adherent of Locke, had it not been for the extreme disparity between their respective sizes. But unluckily there was another animalcule in a square cap, who, silencing all his philosophical brethren, affirmed that he knew the whole secret which was contained in the *Summa* of St. Thomas Aquinas : he surveyed the two celestial strangers from top to toe, and maintained to their faces that their persons, their fashions, their suns and their stars were created solely for the use of man. At this wild assertion our two travellers tumbled over each other, seized with a fit of that inextinguishable laughter, which (according to Homer) is the portion of the immortal gods; their bellies quivered, their shoulders rose and fell, and, during these convulsions, the vessel fell from the Sirian's nail into a pocket of the Saturnian's trousers, where these worthy people searched for it a long time with great diligence. At length, having found the ship and set everything to rights again, the Sirian resumed the discourse with these diminutive mites, and spoke to them again with great kindness, though he was, at the bottom of his heart, rather annoyed that beings so infinitely small had such infinitely great pride. He promised, however, to compose for them a choice book of philosophy, written very small for their use, in which they would discover the purpose of existence. Accordingly, before his departure, he made them a present of the book, which was brought to the Academy of Sciences at Paris; but when the old secretary came to open it, he saw nothing but blank paper.

' Ay, ay,' said he, ' this is just what I expected.'

CANDIDE;

OR, THE

OPTIMIST

Translated from the German of DOCTOR RALPH

With the additions which were found in the Doctor's pocket
when he died at Minden, in the year of grace 1759.

CHAPTER I

In the country of Westphalia, in the castle of the most noble Baron of Thunder-ten-tronckh, lived a youth whom nature had endowed with a most sweet disposition. His face was the true index of his mind. He had a solid judgment joined to the most unaffected simplicity; and hence, I presume, he had his name of Candide. The old servants of the house suspected him to have been the son of the Baron's sister, by a mighty good sort of a gentleman of the neighbourhood, whom that young lady refused to marry, because he could produce no more than threescore and eleven quarterings in his arms; the rest of the genealogical tree belonging to the family having been lost through the injuries of time.

The Baron was one of the most powerful lords in Westphalia; for his castle had not only a gate, but even windows; and his great hall was hung with tapestry. He used to hunt with his mastiffs and spaniels instead of greyhounds; his groom served him for huntsman; and the parson of the parish officiated as grand almoner. He was called 'My Lord' by all his people, and he never told a story but every one laughed at it.

My lady Baroness weighed three hundred and fifty pounds, consequently was a person of no small consideration; and then she did the honours of the house with a dignity that commanded universal respect. Her daughter Cunegund was about seventeen years of age, fresh coloured, comely, plump, and desirable. The Baron's son seemed to be a youth in every respect worthy of his father. Pangloss the preceptor was the oracle of the family, and little Candide listened to his instructions with all the simplicity natural to his age and disposition.

Master Pangloss taught the metaphysico-theologo-cosmolo-nigology. He could prove to admiration that there is no effect without a cause; and that, in this best of all possible worlds, the Baron's castle was the most magnificent of all castles, and my lady the best of all possible baronesses.

'It is demonstrable,' said he, 'that things cannot be otherwise than they are; for as all things have been created for some end, they must necessarily be created for the best end. Observe, for instance, the nose is formed for spectacles, therefore we wear spectacles. The legs are visibly designed for stockings, accordingly we wear stockings. Stones were made to be hewn, and to construct castles, therefore my lord has a magnificent castle; for the greatest baron in the province ought to be the best lodged. Swine were intended to be eaten; therefore we eat pork all the year round: and they who assert that everything is right do not express themselves correctly; they should say, that everything is best.'

Candide listened attentively, and believed implicitly; for he thought Miss Cunegund excessively handsome, though he never had the courage to tell her so. He concluded that next to the happiness of being Baron of Thunder-ten-tronckh, the next was that of being Miss Cunegund, the next that of seeing her every day, and the last that of hearing the doctrine of Master Pangloss, the greatest philosopher of the whole province, and consequently of the whole world.

One day, when Miss Cunegund went to take a walk in a little neighbouring wood, which was called a park, she saw, through the bushes, the sage Doctor Pangloss giving a lecture in experimental physics to her mother's chambermaid, a little brown wench, very pretty, and very tractable. As Miss Cunegund had a great disposition for the sciences, she observed with the utmost attention the experiments which were repeated before her eyes; she perfectly well understood the force of the doctor's reasoning upon causes and effects. She retired greatly flurried, quite pensive, and filled with the desire of knowledge, imagining that she might be a sufficing reason for young Candide, and he for her.

On her way back she happened to meet Candide; she blushed, he blushed also : she wished him a good morning in a faltering tone; he returned the salute, without knowing what he said. The next day, as they were rising from dinner, Cunegund and Candide slipped behind the screen; She dropped her handkerchief, the young man picked it up. She innocently took hold of his hand, and he as innocently kissed hers with a warmth, a sensibility, a grace—all very extraordinary; their lips met; their eyes sparkled; their knees trembled; their hands strayed. The Baron of Thunder-ten-tronckh chanced to come by; he beheld the cause and effect, and, without hesitation, saluted Candide with some notable kicks on the breech, and drove him out of doors. Miss Cunegund fainted away, and, as soon as she came to herself, the Baroness boxed her ears. Thus a general consternation was spread over this most magnificent and most agreeable of all possible castles.

CHAPTER II

WHAT BEFELL CANDIDE AMONG THE BULGARIANS

CANDIDE, thus driven out of this terrestrial paradise, wandered a long time, without knowing where he went; sometimes he raised his eyes, all bedewed with tears, towards heaven, and sometimes he cast a melancholy look towards the magnificent castle where dwelt the fairest of young baronesses. He laid himself down to sleep in a furrow, heartbroken and supperless. The snow fell in great flakes, and, in the morning when he awoke, he was almost frozen to death; however, he made shift to crawl to the next town, which was called Waldberghoff-trarbk-dikdorff, without a penny in his pocket, and half dead with hunger and fatigue. He took up his stand at the door of an inn. He had not been long there, before two men dressed in blue fixed their eyes steadfastly upon him.

' Faith, comrade,' said one of them to the other, ' yonder is a well-made young fellow, and of the right size.'

Thereupon they made up to Candide, and with the greatest civility and politeness invited him to dine with them.

' Gentlemen,' replied Candide, with a most engaging modesty, ' you do me much honour, but, upon my word, I have no money.'

' Money, Sir ! ' said one of the men in blue to him, ' young persons of your appearance and merit never pay anything; why, are not you five feet five inches high? '

' Yes, gentlemen, that is really my size,' replied he, with a low bow.

' Come then, Sir, sit down along with us; we will not only pay your reckoning, but will never suffer such a clever young fellow as you to want money. Mankind were born to assist one another.'

' You are perfectly right, gentlemen,' said Candide; ' that is precisely the doctrine of Master Pangloss; and I am convinced that everything is for the best.'

His generous companions next entreated him to accept of a few crowns, which he readily complied with, at the same time offering them his note for the payment, which they refused, and sat down to table.

' Have you not a great affection for——'

' O yes ! ' he replied, ' I have a great affection for the lovely Miss Cunegund.'

' May be so,' replied one of the men, ' but that is not the question ! We are asking you whether you have not a great affection for the King of the Bulgarians? '

' For the King of the Bulgarians? ' said Candide. ' Not at all. Why, I never saw him in my life.'

' Is it possible ! Oh, he is a most charming king ! Come, we must drink his health.'

' With all my heart, gentlemen,' Candide said, and he tossed off his glass.

' Bravo ! ' cried the blues; ' you are now the support, the defender, the hero of the Bulgarians; your fortune is made; you are on the high road to glory.'

So saying, they put him in irons, and carried him away to the regiment. There he was made to wheel about to the right, to the left, to draw his ramrod, to return his ramrod, to present, to fire, to march, and they gave him thirty blows with a cane; the next day he performed his exercise a little

better, and they gave him but twenty; the day following
he came off with ten, and was looked upon as a young
fellow of surprising genius by all his comrades.

Candide was struck with amazement, and could not for
the soul of him conceive how he came to be a hero. One
fine spring morning, he took it into his head to take a walk,
and he marched straight forward, conceiving it to be a
privilege of the human species, as well as of the brute
creation, to make use of their legs how and when they
pleased. He had not gone above two leagues when he was
overtaken by four other heroes, six feet high, who bound
him neck and heels, and carried him to a dungeon. A
court-martial sat upon him, and he was asked which he
liked best, either to run the gauntlet six and thirty times
through the whole regiment, or to have his brains blown
out with a dozen musket-balls. In vain did he remonstrate
to them that the human will is free, and that he chose
neither; they obliged him to make a choice, and he determined, in virtue of that divine gift called free will, to run
the gauntlet six and thirty times. He had gone through
his discipline twice, and the regiment being composed of
two thousand men, they composed for him exactly four
thousand strokes, which laid bare all his muscles and
nerves, from the nape of his neck to his rump. As they
were preparing to make him set out the third time, our
young hero, unable to support it any longer, begged as a
favour they would be so obliging as to shoot him through
the head. The favour being granted, a bandage was tied
over his eyes, and he was made to kneel down. At that
very instant, his Bulgarian Majesty, happening to pass by,
inquired into the delinquent's crime, and being a prince of
great penetration, he found, from what he heard of Candide,
that he was a young metaphysician, entirely ignorant of
the world; and therefore, out of his great clemency, he
condescended to pardon him, for which his name will be
celebrated in every journal, and in every age. A skilful
surgeon made a cure of Candide in three weeks, by means
of emollient unguents prescribed by Dioscorides. His
sores were now skinned over, and he was able to march,
when the King of the Bulgarians gave battle to the King of
the Abares.

CHAPTER III

NEVER was anything so gallant, so well accoutred, so brilliant, and so finely disposed as the two armies. The trumpets, fifes, hautboys, drums, and cannon, made such harmony as never was heard in hell itself. The entertainment began by a discharge of cannon, which, in the twinkling of an eye, laid flat about six thousand men on each side. The musket bullets swept away, out of the best of all possible worlds, nine or ten thousand scoundrels that infested its surface. The bayonet was next the sufficient reason for the deaths of several thousands. The whole might amount to thirty thousand souls. Candide trembled like a philosopher, and concealed himself as well as he could during this heroic butchery.

At length, while the two kings were causing *Te Deum* to be sung in each of their camps, Candide took a resolution to go and reason somewhere else upon causes and effects. After passing over heaps of dead or dying men, the first place he came to was a neighbouring village, in the Abarian territories, which had been burnt to the ground by the Bulgarians in accordance with international law. Here lay a number of old men covered with wounds, who beheld their wives dying with their throats cut, and hugging their children to their breasts all stained with blood. There several young virgins, whose bellies had been ripped open after they had satisfied the natural necessities of the Bulgarian heroes, breathed their last; while others, half burnt in the flames, begged to be dispatched out of the world. The ground about them was covered with the brains, arms, and legs of dead men.

Candide made all the haste he could to another village, which belonged to the Bulgarians, and there he found that the heroic Abares had enacted the same tragedy. From thence continuing to walk over palpitating limbs, or through ruined buildings, at length he arrived beyond the theatre of war, with a little provision in his pouch, and Miss Cune-

gund's image in his heart. When he arrived in Holland
his provisions failed him; but having heard that the
inhabitants of that country were all rich and Christians, he
made himself sure of being treated by them in the same
manner as at the Baron's castle, before he had been driven
from thence through the power of Miss Cunegund's bright
eyes.

He asked charity of several grave-looking people, who
one and all answered him that if he continued to follow this
trade, they would have him sent to the house of correction,
where he should be taught to earn his bread.

He next addressed himself to a person who had just
been haranguing a numerous assembly for a whole hour
on the subject of charity. The orator, squinting at him
under his broad-brimmed hat, asked him sternly, what
brought him thither? and whether he was for the good
cause?

' Sir,' said Candide, in a submissive manner, ' I conceive
there can be no effect with a cause; everything is necessarily
concatenated and arranged for the best. It was necessary
that I should be banished the presence of Miss Cunegund;
that I should afterwards run the gauntlet; and it is necessary I should beg my bread, till I am able to earn it : all
this could not have been otherwise.'

' Hark ye, friend,' said the orator, ' do you hold the
Pope to be Antichrist?'

' Truly, I never heard anything about it,' said Candide;
' but whether he is or not, I am in want of something to
eat.'

' Thou deservest not to eat or to drink,' replied the orator,
' wretch, monster that thou art! hence! avoid my sight,
nor ever come near me again while thou livest.'

The orator's wife happened to put her head out of the
window at that instant, when, seeing a man who doubted
whether the Pope was Antichrist, she discharged upon his
head a chamber-pot full of ——. Good heavens, to what
excess does religious zeal transport the female kind!

A man who had never been christened, an honest Anabaptist, named James, was witness to the cruel and
ignominious treatment showed to one of his brethren, to a
rational, two-footed, unfledged being. Moved with pity,

he carried him to his own house, cleaned him up, gave him meat and drink, and made him a present of two florins, at the same time proposing to instruct him in his own trade of weaving Persian silks which are fabricated in Holland. Candide threw himself at his feet, crying :

' Now I am convinced that Master Pangloss told me truth, when he said that everything was for the best in this world; for I am infinitely more affected by your extraordinary generosity than by the inhumanity of that gentleman in the black cloak and his wife.'

The next day, as Candide was walking out, he met a beggar all covered with scabs, his eyes were sunk in his head, the end of his nose was eaten off, his mouth drawn on one side, his teeth as black as coal, snuffling and coughing most violently, and every time he attempted to spit, out dropped a tooth.

CHAPTER IV

HOW CANDIDE FOUND HIS OLD MASTER IN PHILOSOPHY, DR. PANGLOSS, AGAIN, AND WHAT HAPPENED TO THEM

CANDIDE, divided between compassion and horror, but giving way to the former, bestowed on this shocking figure the two florins which the honest Anabaptist James had just before given to him. The spectre looked at him very earnestly, shed tears, and threw his arms about his neck. Candide started back aghast.

' Alas ! ' said the one wretch to the other, ' don't you know your dear Pangloss? '

' What do I hear? Is it you, my dear master ! you I behold in this piteous plight? What dreadful misfortune has befallen you? What has made you leave the most magnificent and delightful of all castles? What is become of Miss Cunegund, the mirror of young ladies, and nature's masterpiece? '

' Oh Lord ! ' cried Pangloss, ' I am so weak I cannot stand.'

Thereupon Candide instantly led him to the Anabaptist's

stable, and procured him something to eat. As soon as Pangloss had a little refreshed himself, Candide began to repeat his inquiries concerning Miss Cunegund.

' She is dead,' replied the other.

Candide immediately fainted away : his friend recovered him by the help of a little bad vinegar which he found by chance in the stable. Candide opened his eyes.

' Dead ! Miss Cunegund dead ! ' he said. ' Ah, where is the best of worlds now? But of what illness did she die? Was it for grief upon seeing her father kick me out of his magnificent castle? '

' No,' replied Pangloss; ' her belly was ripped open by the Bulgarian soldiers, after they had ravished her as much as it was possible for damsel to be ravished : they knocked the Baron her father on the head for attempting to defend her; my lady her mother was cut in pieces; my poor pupil was served just in the same manner as his sister; and as for the castle, they have not left one stone upon another; they have destroyed all the ducks, and the sheep, the barns, and the trees : but we have had our revenge, for the Abares have done the very same thing in a neighbouring barony, which belonged to a Bulgarian lord.'

At hearing this, Candide fainted away a second time; but, having come to himself again, he said all that it became him to say; he inquired into the cause and effect, as well as into the sufficing reason, that had reduced Pangloss to so miserable a condition.

' Alas ! ' replied the other, ' it was love : love, the comfort of the human species; love, the preserver of the universe, the soul of all sensible beings; love ! tender love ! '

' Alas,' replied Candide, ' I have had some knowledge of love myself, this sovereign of hearts, this soul of souls; yet it never cost me more than a kiss, and twenty kicks on the backside. But how could this beautiful cause produce in you so hideous an effect? '

Pangloss made answer in these terms : ' O my dear Candide, you must remember Pacquette, that pretty wench, who waited on our noble Baroness; in her arms I tasted the pleasures of paradise, which produced these hell-torments with which you see me devoured. She was infected with the disease, and perhaps is since dead of it;

she received this present of a learned cordelier, who derived it from the fountain-head; he was indebted for it to an old countess, who had it of a captain of horse, who had it of a marchioness, who had it of a page; the page had it of a Jesuit, who, during his novitiate, had it in a direct line from one of the fellow-adventurers of Christopher Columbus; for my part I shall give it to nobody, I am a dying man.'

' O Pangloss,' cried Candide, ' what a strange genealogy is this ! Is not the devil the root of it ? '

' Not at all,' replied the great man, ' it was a thing unavoidable, a necessary ingredient in the best of worlds; for if Columbus had not, in an island of America, caught this disease, which contaminates the source of generation, and frequently impedes propagation itself, and is evidently opposite to the great end of nature, we should have had neither chocolate nor cochineal. It is also to be observed that, even to the present time, in this continent of ours, this malady, like our religious controversies, is peculiar to ourselves. The Turks, the Indians, the Persians, the Chinese, the Siamese, and the Japanese are entirely unacquainted with it; but there is a sufficing reason for them to know it in a few centuries. In the meantime, it is making prodigious progress among us, especially in those armies composed of well-disciplined hirelings, who determine the fate of nations; for we may safely affirm that, when an army of thirty thousand men fights another equal in number, there are about twenty thousand of them poxed on each side.'

' Very surprising, indeed,' said Candide, ' but you must get cured.'

' How can I ? ' said Pangloss : ' my dear friend, I have not a penny in the world; and you know one cannot be bled, or have a clyster, without a fee.'

This last speech had its effect on Candide; he flew to the charitable Anabaptist James, he flung himself at his feet, and gave him so touching a picture of the miserable situation of his friend, that the good man, without any further hesitation, agreed to take Dr. Pangloss into his house, and to pay for his cure. The cure was effected with only the loss of one eye and an ear. As he wrote a good hand and understood accounts tolerably well, the Anabaptist made him his book-keeper. At the expiration of two months, being obliged to go to Lisbon, about some mercantile affairs, he took the two philosophers with him in the same ship; Pangloss, during the voyage, explained to him how everything was so constituted that it could not be better. James did not quite agree with him on this point.

'Mankind,' said he, 'must, in some things, have deviated from their original innocence; for they were not born wolves, and yet they worry one another like those beasts of prey. God never gave them twenty-four pounders nor bayonets, and yet they have made cannon and bayonets to destroy one another. To this account I might add, not only bankruptcies, but the law, which seizes on the effects of bankrupts, only to cheat the creditors.'

'All this was indispensably necessary,' replied the one-eyed doctor; 'for private misfortunes are public benefits; so that the more private misfortunes there are, the greater is the general good.'

While he was arguing in this manner, the sky was overcast, the winds blew from the four quarters of the compass, and the ship was assailed by a most terrible tempest, within sight of the port of Lisbon.

CHAPTER V

A TEMPEST, A SHIPWRECK, AN EARTHQUAKE; AND WHAT ELSE BEFELL DR. PANGLOSS, CANDIDE, AND JAMES THE ANABAPTIST

ONE half of the passengers, weakened and half dead with the inconceivable anguish which the rolling of a vessel at sea occasions to the nerves and all the humours of the body, tossed about in opposite directions, were lost to all sense of the danger that surrounded them. The other made loud outcries, or betook themselves to their prayers; the sails were blown into shivers, and the masts were brought by the board. The vessel leaked. Every one was busily employed, but nobody could be either heard or obeyed.

The Anabaptist, being upon deck, lent a helping hand as well as the rest, when a brutish sailor gave him a blow, and laid him speechless; but, with the violence of the blow, the tar himself tumbled head foremost overboard, and fell upon a piece of the broken mast, which he immediately grasped. Honest James flew to his assistance, and hauled him in again, but, in the attempt, was thrown overboard himself in sight of the sailor, who left him to perish without taking the least notice of him. Candide, who beheld all that passed, and saw his benefactor one moment rising above water, and the next swallowed up by the merciless waves, was preparing to jump after him; but was prevented by the philosopher Pangloss, who demonstrated to him that the coast of Lisbon had been made on purpose for the Anabaptist to be drowned there. While he was proving his argument *à priori*, the ship foundered, and the whole crew perished, except Pangloss, Candide, and the brute of a sailor who had been the means of drowning the good Anabaptist. The villain swam ashore; but Pangloss and Candide got to land upon a plank.

As soon as they had recovered a little, they walked towards Lisbon; with what little money they had left they thought to save themselves from starving after having escaped drowning.

Scarce had they done lamenting the loss of their benefactor and set foot in the city, when they perceived the earth to tremble under their feet, and the sea, swelling and foaming in the harbour, dash in pieces the vessels that were riding at anchor. Large sheets of flames and cinders covered the streets and public places; the houses tottered, and were tumbled topsy-turvy, even to their foundations, which were themselves destroyed, and thirty thousand inhabitants of both sexes, young and old, were buried beneath the ruins.

The sailor, whistling and swearing, cried, 'Damn it, there's something to be got here.'

'What can be the sufficing reason of this phenomenon?' said Pangloss.

'It is certainly the day of judgment,' said Candide.

The sailor, defying death in the pursuit of plunder, rushed into the midst of the ruin, where he found some money, with which he got drunk, and after he had slept himself sober, he purchased the favours of the first good-natured wench that came his way, amidst the ruins of demolished houses, and the groans of half-buried and expiring persons. Pangloss pulled him by the sleeve.

'Friend,' said he, 'this is not right, you trespass against the universal reason, and have mistaken your time.'

'Death and zounds!' answered the other, 'I am a sailor, and born at Batavia, and have trampled four times upon the crucifix in as many voyages to Japan: you are come to a good hand with your universal reason.'

Candide, who had been wounded by some pieces of stone that fell from the houses, lay stretched in the street, almost covered with rubbish.

'For God's sake,' said he to Pangloss, 'get me a little wine and oil. I am dying.'

'This concussion of the earth is no new thing,' replied Pangloss, 'the city of Lima, in America, experienced the same last year; the same cause, the same effects: there is certainly a train of sulphur all the way under ground from Lima to Lisbon.'

'Nothing more probable,' said Candide; 'but, for the love of God, a little oil and wine.'

'Probable!' replied the philosopher, 'I maintain that the thing is demonstrable.'

Candide fainted away, and Pangloss fetched him some water from a neighbouring spring.

The next day, in searching among the ruins, they found some eatables with which they repaired their exhausted strength. After this, they assisted the inhabitants in relieving the distressed and wounded. Some, whom they had humanely assisted, gave them as good a dinner as could be expected under such terrible circumstances. The repast, indeed, was mournful, and the company moistened their bread with their tears; but Pangloss endeavoured to comfort them under this affliction by affirming that things could not be otherwise than they were.

'For,' said he, 'all this is for the very best end; for if there is a volcano at Lisbon, it could be on no other spot; for it is impossible for things not to be as they are, for everything is for the best.'

By his side sat a little man dressed in black, who was one of the familiars of the Inquisition. This person, taking him up with great politeness, said, ' Possibly, my good Sir, you do not believe in original sin; for if everything is best, there could have been no such thing as the fall or punishment of man.'

' I humbly ask your Excellency's pardon,' answered Pangloss, still more politely; ' for the fall of man, and the curse consequent thereupon necessarily entered into the system of the best of worlds.'

' That is as much as to say, Sir,' rejoined the familiar, ' you do not believe in free will.'

' Your Excellency will be so good as to excuse me,' said Pangloss; ' free will is consistent with absolute necessity; for it was necessary we should be free, for in that the will——'

Pangloss was in the midst of his proposition, when the familiar made a sign to the attendant who was helping him to a glass of port wine.

CHAPTER VI

HOW THE PORTUGUESE MADE A SUBERB AUTO-DA-FÉ TO PREVENT ANY FUTURE EARTHQUAKES, AND HOW CANDIDE UNDERWENT PUBLIC FLAGELLATION

AFTER the earthquake which had destroyed three-quarters of the city of Lisbon, the sages of that country could think of no means more effectual to preserve the kingdom from utter ruin, than to entertain the people with an *auto-da-fé*, it having been decided by the University of Coimbra that burning a few people alive by a slow fire, and with great ceremony, is an infallible secret to prevent earthquakes.

In consequence thereof they had seized on a Biscayan for marrying his godmother, and on two Portuguese for taking out the bacon of a larded pullet they were eating. After dinner, they came and secured Dr. Pangloss, and his pupil Candide; the one for speaking his mind, and the other for seeming to approve what he had said. They were conducted to separate apartments, extremely cool, where they were never incommoded with the sun. Eight days afterwards they were each dressed in a *fanbenito*,* and their heads were adorned with paper mitres. The mitre and *fanbenito* worn by Candide were painted with flames reversed, and with devils that had neither tails nor claws; but Dr. Pangloss's devils had both tails and claws, and his flames were upright. In these habits they marched in procession, and heard a very pathetic sermon, which was followed by a chant, beautifully intoned. Candide was flogged in regular cadence, while the chant was being sung; the Biscayan, and the two men who would not eat bacon, were burnt, and Pangloss was hanged, although this is not a common custom at these solemnities. The same day there was another earthquake, which made most dreadful havoc.

Candide, amazed, terrified, confounded, astonished, and trembling from head to foot, said to himself, ' If this is the best of all possible worlds, what are the others? If I had only been whipped, I could have put up with it, as I did among the Bulgarians; but, O my dear Pangloss! thou greatest of philosophers! that ever I should live to see thee hanged, without knowing for what! O my dear Anabaptist, thou best of men, that it should be thy fate to be drowned in the very harbour! O Miss Cunegund, you mirror of young ladies! that it should be your fate to have your belly ripped open.'

He was making the best of his way from the place where he had been preached to, whipped, absolved, and received benediction, when he was accosted by an old woman, who said to him, ' Take courage, my son, and follow me.'

* A kind of garment worn by the criminals of the inquisition.

CHAPTER VII

HOW THE OLD WOMAN TOOK CARE OF CANDIDE, AND HOW HE FOUND THE OBJECT OF HIS LOVE

CANDIDE followed the old woman, though without taking courage, to a decayed house where she gave him a pot of pomatum to anoint his sores, showed him a very neat bed, with a suit of clothes hanging up by it; and set victuals and drink before him.

'There,' said she, 'eat, drink, and sleep, and may our blessed Lady of Atocha, and the great St. Anthony of Padua, and the illustrious St. James of Compostella, take you under their protection. I shall be back to-morrow.'

Candide, struck with amazement at what he had seen, at what he had suffered, and still more with the charity of the old woman, would have shown his acknowledgment by kissing her hand.

'It is not my hand you ought to kiss,' said the old woman, 'I shall be back to-morrow. Anoint your back, eat, and take your rest.'

Candide, notwithstanding so many disasters, ate and slept. The next morning, the old woman brought him his breakfast; examined his back, and rubbed it herself with another ointment. She returned at the proper time, and brought him his dinner; and at night she visited him again with his supper. The next day she observed the same ceremonies.

'Who are you?' said Candide to her. 'What god has inspired you with so much goodness? What return can I ever make you?'

The good old beldame kept a profound silence. In the evening she returned, but without his supper.

'Come along with me,' said she, 'but do not speak a word.'

She took him by the arm, and walked with him about a quarter of a mile into the country, till they came to a lonely house surrounded with moats and gardens. The old woman knocked at a little door, which was immediately opened, and she showed him up a pair of back stairs into a small, but richly furnished apartment. There she made him sit down on a brocaded sofa, shut the door upon him, and left him. Candide thought himself in a trance; he looked upon his whole life hitherto as a frightful dream, and the present moment as a very agreeable one.

The old woman soon returned, supporting with great difficulty a young lady, who appeared scarce able to stand. She was of a majestic mien and stature; her dress was rich, and glittering with diamonds, and her face was covered with a veil.

'Take off that veil,' said the old woman to Candide.

The young man approached, and, with a trembling hand, took off her veil. What a happy moment! What surprise! He thought he beheld Miss Cunegund; he did behold her, it was she herself. His strength failed him, he could not utter a word, he fell at her feet. Cunegund fainted upon the sofa. The old woman bedewed them with spirits; they recovered; they began to speak. At first they could express themselves only in broken accents; their questions and answers were alternately interrupted with sighs, tears, and exclamations. The old woman desired them to make less noise; and left them together.

'Good heavens!' cried Candide, 'is it you? Is it Miss Cunegund I behold, and alive? Do I find you again in Portugal? Then you have not been ravished? They did not rip open your belly, as the philosopher Pangloss informed me?'

'Indeed but they did,' replied Miss Cunegund; 'but these two accidents do not always prove mortal.'

'But were your father and mother killed?'

'Alas!' answered she, 'it is but too true!' and she wept.

'And your brother?'

'And my brother also.'

'And how did you come to Portugal? And how did you know of my being here? And by what strange adventure did you contrive to have me brought into this house?'

'I will tell you all,' replied the lady, 'but first you must acquaint me with all that has befallen you since the innocent kiss you gave me, and the rude kicking you received.'

Candide, with the greatest submission, obeyed her, and though he was still wrapped in amazement, though his voice was low and tremulous, though his back pained him, yet he gave her a most ingenuous account of everything that had befallen him since the moment of their separation. Cunegund, with her eyes uplifted to heaven, shed tears when he related the death of the good Anabaptist James, and of Pangloss; after which, she thus related her adventures to Candide, who lost not one syllable she uttered, and seemed to devour her with his eyes all the time she was speaking.

CHAPTER VIII

THE HISTORY OF CUNEGUND

' I was in bed and fast asleep, when it pleased heaven to send the Bulgarians to our delightful castle of Thunderten-tronckh, where they murdered my father and brother, and cut my mother in pieces. A tall Bulgarian soldier, six feet high, perceiving that I had fainted away at this sight, attempted to ravish me; the operation brought me to my senses. I cried, I struggled, I bit, I scratched, I would have torn the tall Bulgarian's eyes out, not knowing that what had happened at my father's castle was a customary thing. The brutal soldier gave me a cut in the left groin with his hanger, the mark of which I still carry.'

' I hope I shall see it,' said Candide, with all imaginable simplicity.

' You shall,' said Cunegund; ' but let me proceed.'

' Pray do,' replied Candide.

She continued. ' A Bulgarian captain came in and saw me weltering in my blood, and the soldier still as busy as if no one had been present. The officer, enraged at the fellow's want of respect to him, killed him with one stroke of his sabre as he lay upon me. This captain took care of me, had me cured, and carried me prisoner of war to his quarters. I washed what little linen he was master of, and dressed his victuals: he thought me very pretty, it must be confessed; neither can I deny that he was well made, and had a white soft skin, but he was very stupid, and knew nothing of philosophy : it might plainly be perceived that he had not been educated under Doctor Pangloss. In three months' time, having gamed away all his money, and being grown tired of me, he sold me to a Jew, named Don Issachar, who traded in Holland and Portugal, and was passionately fond of women. This Jew showed me great kindness in hopes to gain my favours ; but he never could prevail on me. A modest woman may be once ravished ; but her virtue is greatly strengthened thereby. In order to make sure of me, he brought me to this country house you now see. I had hitherto believed that nothing could equal the beauty of the castle of Thunder-ten-tronckh ; but I found I was mistaken.

' The Grand Inquisitor saw me one day at mass, ogled me all the time of service, and, when it was over, sent to let me know he wanted to speak with me about some private business. I was conducted to his palace, where I told him of my parentage : he represented to me how much it was beneath a person of my birth to belong to an Israelite. He caused a proposal to be made to Don Issachar that he should resign me to his lordship. Don Issachar, being the court banker, and a man of credit, was not easily to be prevailed upon. His lordship threatened him with an *auto-da-fé* ; in short, my Jew was frightened into a compromise, and it was agreed between them that the house and myself should belong to both in common ; that the Jew should have Monday, Wednesday, and the Sabbath to himself ; and the Inquisitor the other days of the week. This agreement has lasted almost six months ; but not without several disputes, whether the space from Saturday night to Sunday morning belonged to the old or the new law. For my part, I have hitherto withstood them both, and truly I believe this is the very reason why they both still love me.

' At length, to turn aside the scourge of earthquakes, and to intimidate Don Issachar, my lord Inquisitor was pleased to celebrate an *auto-da-fé*. He did me the honour to invite me to the ceremony. I had a very good seat ; and refreshments were offered the ladies between mass and the execution. I was dreadfully shocked at the burning of the two Jews, and the honest Biscayan who married his godmother; but how great was my surprise, my consternation, and concern, when I beheld a figure so like Pangloss, dressed in a *sanbenito* and mitre! I rubbed my eyes, I looked at him attentively. I saw him hanged, and I fainted away : scarce had I recovered my senses, when I beheld you stark naked; this was the height of horror, grief, and despair. I must confess to you for a truth, that your skin is far whiter and more blooming than that of the Bulgarian captain. This spectacle worked me up to a pitch of distraction. I screamed out, and would have said, " Hold, barbarians! " but my voice failed me; and indeed my cries would have been useless. After you had been severely whipped I said to myself, " How is it possible that the lovely Candide and the sage Pangloss should be at Lisbon, the one to receive a hundred lashes, and the other to be hanged by order of my lord Inquisitor, of whom I am so great a favourite? Pangloss deceived me most cruelly, in saying that everything is fittest and best."

' Thus agitated and perplexed, now distracted and lost, now half dead with grief, I revolved in my mind the murder of my father, mother, and brother; the insolence of the rascally Bulgarian soldier; the wound he gave me in the groin; my servitude; my being a cook wench to my Bulgarian captain; my subjection to the villainous Don Issachar, and my cruel Inquisitor; the hanging of Doctor Pangloss; the *Miserere* sung while you were whipped; and particularly the kiss I gave you behind the screen the last day I ever beheld you. I returned thanks to God for having brought you to the place where I was, after so many trials. I charged the old woman who attends me to bring you hither, as soon as possible. She has carried out my orders well, and I now enjoy the inexpressible satisfaction of seeing you, hearing you, and speaking to you. But you must certainly be half dead with hunger; I myself have got a good appetite, and so let us sit down to supper.'

Upon this the two lovers immediately placed themselves at table, and, after having supped, they returned to seat themselves again on the magnificent sofa already mentioned ; they were there when Signor Don Issachar, one of the masters of the house, entered unexpectedly; it was the

Sabbath day, and he came to enjoy his privilege, and sigh forth his tender passion.

CHAPTER IX

WHAT HAPPENED TO CUNEGUND, CANDIDE, THE GRAND INQUISITOR, AND THE JEW

THIS same Issachar was the most choleric little Hebrew that had ever been in Israel since the captivity in Babylon.

' What,' said he, ' you Galilean bitch, my lord Inquisitor was not enough for thee, but this rascal must come in for a share with me? '

Uttering these words, he drew out a long poniard which he always carried about him, and never dreaming that his adversary had any arms, he attacked him most furiously; but our honest Westphalian had received a handsome sword from the old woman with the suit of clothes. Candide drew his rapier; and though he was the most gentle, sweet-tempered young man breathing, he whipped it into the Israelite and laid him sprawling on the floor at the fair Cunegund's feet.

' Holy Virgin ! ' cried she, ' what will become of us? A man killed in my apartment ! If the peace-officers come, we are undone.'

' Had not Pangloss been hanged,' replied Candide, ' he would have given us most excellent advice in this emergency, for he was a profound philosopher. But, since he is not here, let us consult the old woman.'

She was very intelligent, and was beginning to give her advice when another door opened suddenly. It was now one o'clock in the morning, and of course the beginning of Sunday, which, by agreement, fell to the lot of my lord Inquisitor. Entering, he discovered the flagellated Candide with his drawn sword in his hand, a dead body stretched on the floor, Cunegund frightened out of her wits, and the old woman giving advice.

At that very moment a sudden thought came into Candide's head.

' If this holy man,' thought he, ' should call assistance, I shall most undoubtedly be consigned to the flames, and Miss Cunegund may perhaps meet with no better treatment; besides, he was the cause of my being so cruelly whipped; he is my rival; and I have now begun to dip my hands in blood; there is no time to hesitate.'

This whole train of reasoning was clear and instantaneous; so that, without giving time to the inquisitor to recover from his surprise, he ran him through the body, and laid him by the side of the Jew.

' Good God ! ' cried Cunegund, ' here's another fine piece of work ! now there can be no mercy for us, we are excommunicated; our last hour is come. But how in the name of wonder could you, who are of so mild a temper, dispatch a Jew and a prelate in two minutes' time ? '

' Beautiful lady,' answered Candide, ' when a man is in love, is jealous, and has been flogged by the Inquisition, he becomes lost to all reflection.'

The old woman then put in her word.

' There are three Andalusian horses in the stable,' said she, ' with as many bridles and saddles; let the brave Candide get them ready; madam has moidores and jewels; let us mount immediately, though I have only one buttock to sit upon; let us set out for Cadiz; it is the finest weather in the world, and there is great pleasure in travelling in the cool of the night.'

Candide, without any further hesitation, saddled the three horses; and Miss Cunegund, the old woman, and he set out, and travelled thirty miles without once stopping. While they were making the best of their way, the Holy Brotherhood entered the house. My Lord the Inquisitor was interred in a magnificent manner, and Issachar's body was thrown upon a dunghill.

Candide, Cunegund, and the old woman had, by this time, reached the little town of Aracena, in the midst of the mountains of Sierra Morena, and were engaged in the following conversation in an inn.

CHAPTER X

IN WHAT DISTRESS CANDIDE, CUNEGUND, AND THE OLD WOMAN ARRIVE AT CADIZ; AND OF THEIR EMBARKATION

' Who could it be who has robbed me of my moidores and jewels? ' exclaimed Miss Cunegund, all bathed in tears. ' How shall we live? What shall we do? Where shall I find Inquisitors and Jews who can give me more? '

' Alas! ' said the old woman, ' I have a shrewd suspicion of a reverend father cordelier, who lay last night in the same inn with us at Badajoz: God forbid I should condemn any one wrongfully, but he came into our room twice, and he set off in the morning long before us.'

' Alas! ' said Candide, ' Pangloss has often demonstrated to me that the goods of this world are common to all men, and that every one has an equal right to the enjoyment of them; but, according to these principles, the cordelier ought to have left us enough to carry us to the end of our journey. Have you nothing at all left, my beautiful Cunegund? '

' Not a sou,' replied she.

' What is to be done then? ' said Candide.

' Sell one of the horses,' replied the old woman, ' I will get behind my young lady though I have only one buttock to ride on, and we shall reach Cadiz, never fear.'

In the same inn there was a Benedictine prior who bought the horse very cheap. Candide, Cunegund, and the old woman, after passing through Lucena, Chellas, and Lebrija, arrived at length at Cadiz. A fleet was then getting ready, and troops were assembling in order to reduce the reverend fathers, the Jesuits of Paraguay, who were accused of having excited one of the Indian tribes, in the neighbourhood of the town of the Holy Sacrament, to revolt against the Kings of Spain and Portugal. Candide, having been in the Bulgarian service, performed the military exercise of that nation before the general of this little army with so intrepid an air, and with such agility and expedition that he gave him the command of a company of foot.

Being now made a captain, he embarked with Miss Cunegund, the old woman, two valets, and the two Andalusian horses which had belonged to the Grand Inquisitor of Portugal.

During their voyage they amused themselves with many profound reasonings on poor Pangloss's philosophy.

'We are now going into another world,' said Candide, 'and surely it must be there that everything is best; for I must confess that we have had some little reason to complain of what passes in ours, both as to the physical and moral part.'

'Though I have a sincere love for you,' said Miss Cunegund, 'yet I still shudder at the reflection of what I have seen and experienced.'

'All will be well,' replied Candide, 'the sea of this new world is already better than our European seas: it is smoother, and the winds blow more regularly.'

'God grant it,' said Cunegund; 'but I have met with such terrible treatment in this that I have almost lost all hopes of a better.'

'What murmuring and complaining is here indeed!' cried the old woman. 'If you had suffered half what I have done, there might be some reason for it.'

Miss Cunegund could scarcely refrain from laughing at the good old woman, and thought it droll enough to pretend to a greater share of misfortunes than herself.

'Alas! my good dame,' said she, 'unless you have been ravished by two Bulgarians, have received two deep wounds in your belly, have seen two of your own castles demolished, and beheld two fathers and two mothers barbarously murdered before your eyes, and, to sum up all, have had two lovers whipped at an *auto-da-fé*, I cannot see how you could be more unfortunate than me. Add to this, though born a baroness and bearing seventy-two quarterings, I have been reduced to a cook-wench.'

'Miss,' replied the old woman, 'you do not know my family as yet; but if I were to show you my backside, you would not talk in this manner, but suspend your judgment.'

This speech raised a high curiosity in Candide and Cunegund; and the old woman continued as follows.

CHAPTER XI

THE HISTORY OF THE OLD WOMAN

'I HAVE not always been blear-eyed. My nose did not always touch my chin, nor was I always a servant. You must know that I am the daughter of Pope Urban X, and of the Princess of Palestrina. Up to the age of fourteen I was brought up in a castle, compared with which all the castles of the German barons would not have been fit for stabling, and one of my robes would have bought half the province of Westphalia. I grew in beauty, in wit, and in every graceful accomplishment, in the midst of pleasures, homage, and the highest expectations. I already began to inspire the men with love : my breast began to take its right form; and such a breast! white, firm, and formed like that of Venus of Medici : my eyebrows were as black as jet; and as for my eyes, they darted flames, and eclipsed the lustre of the stars, as I was told by the poets of our part of the world. My maids, when they dressed and undressed me, used to fall into an ecstasy in viewing me before and behind : and all the men longed to be in their places.

' I was contracted to a sovereign prince of Massa-Carrara. Such a prince ! as handsome as myself, sweet-tempered, agreeable, of brilliant wit, and in love with me over head and ears. I loved him too, as our sex generally do for the first time, with transport and idolatry. The nuptials were prepared with surprising pomp and magnificence; the ceremony was attended with a succession of feasts, carousals, and burlesques : all Italy composed sonnets in my praise, though not one of them was tolerable. I was on the point of reaching the summit of bliss, when an old marchioness who had been mistress to the Prince my husband invited him to drink chocolate. In less than two hours after he returned from the visit he died of most terrible convulsions : but this is a mere trifle. My mother, in despair, and yet less afflicted than me, determined to absent herself for some time from so fatal a place. As she had a very fine estate in the neighbourhood of Gaeta, we embarked on board a galley which was gilded like the high

altar of St. Peter's at Rome. In our passage we were
boarded by a Sallee corsair. Our men defended themselves
like true Pope's soldiers; they flung themselves upon their
knees, laid down their arms and begged the corsair to give
them absolution *in articulo mortis.*

' The Moors presently stripped us as bare as monkeys.
My mother, my maids of honour, and myself, were served
all in the same manner. It is amazing how quick these
gentry are at undressing people. But what surprised me
most was that they thrust their fingers into that part of our
bodies where we women seldom permit anything but enemas
to enter. I thought it a very strange kind of ceremony;
for thus we are generally apt to judge of things when we
have not seen the world. I afterwards learnt that it was
to discover if we had any diamonds concealed. This practice has been established since time immemorial among those
civilized nations that scour the seas. I was informed that
the religious Knights of Malta never fail to make this
search, whenever any Moors of either sex fall into their
hands. It is a part of the law of nations from which they
never deviate.

' I need not tell you how great a hardship it was for a
young princess and her mother to be made slaves and carried
to Morocco. You may easily imagine what we must have
suffered on board a corsair. My mother was still extremely
handsome, our maids of honour, and even our common
waiting-women, had more charms than were to be found
in all Africa. As to myself, I was enchanting; I was
beauty itself, and then I had my virginity. But, alas! I
did not retain it long; this precious flower, which was
reserved for the lovely Prince of Massa-Carrara, was
cropped by the captain of the Moorish vessel, who was a
hideous negro, and thought he did me infinite honour.
Indeed, both the Princess of Palestrina and myself must
have had very strong constitutions to undergo all the
hardships and violences we suffered till our arrival at
Morocco. But I will not detain you any longer with such
common things; they are hardly worth mentioning.

' Upon our arrival at Morocco, we found that kingdom
bathed in blood. Fifty sons of the Emperor Muley Ishmael
were each at the head of a party. This produced fifty civil

wars of blacks against blacks, of blacks against tawnies, of tawnies against tawnies, and of mulattoes against mulattoes. In short, the whole empire was one continual scene of carnage.

'No sooner were we landed than a party of blacks, of a contrary faction to that of my captain, came to rob him of his booty. Next to the money and jewels, we were the most valuable things he had. I was witness on this occasion to such a battle as you never beheld in your cold European climates. The northern nations have not that fermentation in their blood, nor that raging lust for women that is so common in Africa. The natives of Europe seem to have their veins filled with milk only; but fire and vitriol circulate in those of the inhabitants of Mount Atlas and the neighbouring provinces. They fought with the fury of the lions, tigers, and serpents of their country, to know who should have us. A Moor seized my mother by the right arm, while my captain's lieutenant held her by the left; another Moor laid hold of her by one leg, and one of our corsairs held her by the other. In this manner were almost every one of our women dragged between soldiers. My captain kept me concealed behind him, and with his drawn scimitar cut down every one who opposed him; at length I saw all our Italian women and my mother mangled and torn in pieces by the monsters who contended for them. The captives, my companions, the Moors who had taken them, the soldiers, the sailors, the blacks, the tawnies, the whites, the mulattoes, and lastly my captain himself, were all slain, and I remained alone expiring upon a heap of dead bodies. The like barbarous scenes were enacted every day over the whole country, which is an extent of three hundred leagues, and yet they never missed the five stated times of prayer enjoined by their prophet Mahomet.

'I disentangled myself with great difficulty from such a heap of slaughtered bodies, and made shift to crawl to a large orange tree that stood on the bank of a neighbouring rivulet, where I fell down exhausted with terror, and overwhelmed with horror, despair, and hunger. My senses being overpowered, I fell asleep, or rather seemed to be in a trance. Thus I lay in a state of weakness and insensibility between life and death, when I felt myself pressed by something that moved up and down upon my body. This brought me to myself; I opened my eyes, and saw a pretty fair-faced man, who sighed and muttered these words between his teeth, " *O che sciagura d'essere senza coglioni !* " '

CHAPTER XII

THE ADVENTURES OF THE OLD WOMAN CONTINUED

' ASTONISHED and delighted to hear my native language, and no less surprised at the young man's words, I told him that there were far greater misfortunes in the world than what he complained of. And to convince him of it, I gave him a short history of the horrible disasters that had befallen me; and again fell into a swoon. He carried me in his arms to a neighbouring cottage, where he had me put to bed, procured me something to eat, waited on me, comforted me, caressed me, told me that he had never seen anything so perfectly beautiful as myself, and that he had never so much regretted the loss of what no one could restore to him.

' " I was born at Naples," said he, " where they caponize two or three thousand children every year : several die of the operation; some acquire voices far beyond the most tuneful of your ladies; and others are sent to govern states and empires. I underwent this operation very happily, and was one of the singers in the Princess of Palestrina's chapel."

' " How," cried I, " in my mother's chapel ! "

' " The Princess of Palestrina, your mother ! " cried he, bursting into a flood of tears, " is it possible you should be the beautiful young princess whom I had the care of bringing up till she was six years old, and who, at that tender age, promised to be as fair as I now behold you ? "

' " I am the same," I replied. " My mother lies about a hundred yards from here, cut in pieces, and buried under a heap of dead bodies."

' I then related to him all that had befallen me, and he in return acquainted me with all his adventures, and how he had been sent to the court of the King of Morocco by a Christian prince to conclude a treaty with that monarch; in consequence of which he was to be furnished with military stores, and ships to enable him to destroy the commerce of other Christian governments.

' " I have executed my commission," said the eunuch; " I am going to take shipping at Ceuta, and I'll take you along with me to Italy. *Ma che sciagura d'essere senza coglioni !* "

' I thanked him with tears of joy; but, instead of taking me with him into Italy, he carried me to Algiers, and sold me to the dey of that province. I had not been long a slave when the plague, which had made the tour of Africa, Asia, and Europe, broke out at Algiers with redoubled fury. You have seen an earthquake; but tell me, miss, had you ever the plague? '

' Never,' answered the young Baroness.

' If you ever had,' continued the old woman, ' you would own an earthquake was a trifle to it. It is very common in Africa; I was seized with it. Figure to yourself the situation of the daughter of a pope, only fifteen years old, and who in less than three months had felt the miseries of poverty and slavery; had been ravished almost every day; had beheld her mother cut into four quarters; had experienced the scourges of famine and war, and was now dying of the plague at Algiers. I did not, however, die of it; but my eunuch, and the dey, and almost the whole seraglio of Algiers, were swept off.

' As soon as the first fury of this dreadful pestilence was over, a sale was made of the dey's slaves. I was purchased by a merchant, who carried me to Tunis. This man sold me to another merchant, who sold me again to another at Tripoli; from Tripoli I was sold to Alexandria, from Alexandria to Smyrna, and from Smyrna to Constantinople. After many changes, I at length became the property of an aga of the janissaries, who, soon after I came into his possession, was ordered away to the defence of Azov, then besieged by the Russians.

' The aga being fond of women, took his whole seraglio with him, and lodged us in a small fort on Lake Maeotis, with two black eunuchs and twenty soldiers for our guard.

Our army made a great slaughter among the Russians, but they soon returned us the compliment. Azov was taken by storm, and the enemy spared neither age nor sex, but put all to the sword, and laid the city in ashes. Our little fort alone held out; they resolved to reduce us by famine. The twenty janissaries had bound themselves by an oath never to surrender the place. Being reduced to the extremity of famine, they found themselves obliged to eat two eunuchs rather than violate their oath. After a few days they determined to devour the women.

' We had a very pious and humane imam, who made them a most excellent sermon on this occasion, exhorting them not to kill us all at once.

' " Only cut off one of the buttocks of each of those ladies," said he, " and you will fare extremely well; if ye are still under the necessity of having recourse to the same expedient again, ye will find the like supply a few days hence. Heaven will approve of so charitable an action, and work your deliverance."

' By the force of this eloquence he easily persuaded them, and all underwent the operation. The imam applied the same balsam as they do to children after circumcision. We were all ready to give up the ghost.

' The janissaries had scarcely time to finish the repast with which we had supplied them, when the Russians attacked the place by means of flat-bottomed boats, and not a single janissary escaped. The Russians paid no regard to the condition we were in; but as there are French surgeons in all parts of the world, a skilful operator took us under his care, and made a cure of us; and I shall never forget, while I live, that as soon as my wounds were perfectly healed, he made me certain proposals. In general, he desired us all to have a good heart, assuring us that the like had happened in many sieges; and that it was the law of war.

' As soon as my companions were in a condition to walk, they were sent to Moscow. As for me, I fell to the lot of a boyard, who put me to work in his garden, and gave me twenty lashes a-day. But this nobleman having, in about two years afterwards, been broken alive upon the wheel, with about thirty others, for some court intrigues, I took advantage of the event, and made my escape. I travelled over a great part of Russia. I was a long time an inn-keeper's servant at Riga, then at Rostock, Wismar, Leipsic, Cassel, Utrecht, Leyden, The Hague, and Rotterdam: I have grown old in misery and disgrace, living with only one buttock, and in the perpetual remembrance that I was a pope's daughter. I have been an hundred times upon the point of killing myself, but still was fond of life. This ridiculous weakness is, perhaps, one of the dangerous prin-ciples implanted in our nature. For what can be more absurd than to persist in carrying a burden of which we wish to be eased? to detest, and yet to strive to preserve our existence? In a word, to caress the serpent that devours us, and hug him close to our bosoms till he has gnawed into our hearts?

' In the different countries which it has been my fate to traverse, and the many inns where I have been a servant, I have observed a prodigious number of people who held their existence in abhorrence, and yet I never knew more than twelve who voluntarily put an end to their misery; namely, three negroes, four Englishmen, as many Genoese, and a German professor named Robek. My last place was with the Jew, Don Issachar, who placed me near your person, my fair lady; to your fortunes I have attached myself, and have been more affected by your adventures than my own. I should never have even mentioned the latter to you, had you not a little piqued me on the head of sufferings; and if it were not customary to tell stories on board a ship in order to pass away the time. In short, my dear miss, I have a great deal of knowledge and ex-perience of the world, therefore take my advice; divert yourself, and prevail upon each passenger to tell his story, and if there is one of them all that has not cursed his existence many times, and said to himself over and over again, that he was the most wretched of mortals, I give you leave to throw me headforemost into the sea.'

CHAPTER XIII

HOW CANDIDE WAS OBLIGED TO LEAVE THE FAIR CUNEGUND AND THE OLD WOMAN

THE fair Cunegund, being thus made acquainted with the history of the old woman's life and adventures, paid her all the respect and civility due to a person of her rank and merit. She very readily came into her proposal of engaging every one of the passengers to relate their adventures in their turns, and was at length, as well as Candide, compelled to acknowledge that the old woman was in the right.

'It is a thousand pities,' said Candide, 'that the sage Pangloss should have been hanged contrary to the custom of an *auto-da-fé*, for he would have read us a most admirable lecture on the moral and physical evil which overspreads the earth and sea; and I think I should have courage enough to presume to offer (with all due respect) some few objections.'

While everyone was reciting his adventures, the ship continued her way, and at length arrived at Buenos Ayres, where Cunegund, Captain Candide, and the old woman, landed and went to wait upon the Governor Don Fernando d'Ibaraa y Figueora y Mascarenas y Lampourdos y Souza. This nobleman carried himself with a haughtiness suitable to a person who bore so many names. He spoke with the most noble disdain to every one, carried his nose so high, strained his voice to such a pitch, assumed so imperious an air, and stalked with so much loftiness and pride, that everyone who had the honour of conversing with him was violently tempted to bastinade his Excellency. He was immoderately fond of women, and Cunegund appeared in his eyes a paragon of beauty. The first thing he did was to ask her if she was the captain's wife. The air with which he made this demand alarmed Candide; he did not dare to say he was married to her, because, indeed, he was not; neither durst he say she was his sister, because she was not that either: and though a lie of this nature proved of great service to one of the ancients, and might possibly be useful to some of the moderns, yet the purity of his heart would not permit him to violate the truth.

' Miss Cunegund,' replied he, ' is to do me the honour of marrying me, and we humbly beseech your Excellency to condescend to grace the ceremony with your presence.'

Don Fernando d'Ibaraa y Figueora y Mascarenas y Lampourdos y Souza, twirling his mustachio, and putting on a sarcastic smile, ordered Captain Candide to go and review his company. Candide obeyed, and the Governor was left with Miss Cunegund. He made her a strong declaration of love, protesting that he was ready on the morrow to give her his hand in the face of the Church, or otherwise, as should appear most agreeable to a young lady of her prodigious beauty. Cunegund desired leave to retire a quarter of an hour to consult the old woman, and determine how she should proceed.

The old woman gave her the following counsel : ' Miss, you have seventy-two quarterings in your arms, it is true, but you have not a penny to bless yourself with : it is your own fault if you are not wife to one of the greatest noblemen in South America, with an exceeding fine mustachio. What business have you to pride yourself upon an unshaken constancy? You have been ravished by a Bulgarian soldier; a Jew and an Inquisitor have both tasted of your favours. People take advantage of misfortunes. I must confess, were I in your place, I should, without the least scruple, give my hand to the Governor, and thereby make the fortune of the brave Captain Candide.'

While the old woman was thus haranguing, with all the prudence that old age and experience furnish, a small bark entered the harbour, in which was a magistrate and his alguazils. Matters had fallen out as follows.

The old woman rightly guessed that the cordelier with the long sleeves was the person who had taken Cunegund's money and jewels while they and Candide were at Badajoz, in their hasty flight from Lisbon. This same friar attempted to sell some of the diamonds to a jeweller, who at once knew them to have belonged to the Grand Inquisitor. The cordelier, before he was hanged, confessed that he had stolen them, and described the persons, and the road they had taken. The flight of Cunegund and Candide was already the town-talk. They sent in pursuit of them to Cadiz; and the vessel which had been sent, to make the greater dispatch, had now reached the port of Buenos Ayres. A report was spread that a magistrate was going to land, and that he was in pursuit of the murderers of my lord the Grand Inquisitor. The wise old woman immediately saw what was to be done.

'You cannot run away,' said she to Cunegund; 'but you have nothing to fear; it was not you who killed my lord Inquisitor: besides, as the Governor is in love with you, he will not suffer you to be ill-treated; therefore stand your ground.'

Then hurrying away to Candide, 'Be gone,' said she, 'from hence this instant, or you will be burnt alive.'

Candide found there was no time to be lost; but how could he part from Cunegund, and whither must he fly for shelter?

CHAPTER XIV

THE RECEPTION CANDIDE AND CACAMBO MET WITH AMONG THE JESUITS IN PARAGUAY

CANDIDE had brought with him from Cadiz such a footman as one often meets with on the coasts of Spain and in the colonies. He was the fourth part of a Spaniard, of a mongrel breed, and born in Tucuman. He had successively gone through the profession of a choirboy, sexton, sailor, monk, pedlar, soldier, and lackey. His name was Cacambo; he had a great affection for his master because his master was a mighty good man. He immediately saddled the two Andalusian horses.

'Come, my good master,' he said, 'let us follow the old woman's advice, and make all the haste we can from this place, without staying to look behind us.'

Candide burst into a flood of tears.

'O my dear Cunegund, must I then be compelled to quit you, just as the Governor was going to honour us with his presence at our wedding! Cunegund, so long lost, and found again, what will become of you?'

' Lord ! ' said Cacambo, ' she must do as well as she can ; women are never at a loss. God takes care of them, and so let us make the best of our way.'

' But whither wilt thou carry me? Where can we go? What can we do without Cunegund? ' cried the disconsolate Candide.

' By St. James of Compostella,' said Cacambo, ' you were going to fight against the Jesuits of Paraguay; now, let us go and fight for them : I know the road perfectly well; I'll conduct you to their kingdom; they will be delighted with a captain that understands the Bulgarian exercise; you will certainly make a prodigious fortune. If we cannot find our account in one world, we may in another. It is a great pleasure to see new objects, and perform new exploits.'

' Then you have been in Paraguay? ' said Candide.

' Ay, marry, have I,' replied Cacambo : ' I was a scout in the College of the Assumption, and I am as well acquainted with the new government of Los Padres as I am with the streets of Cadiz. Oh, it is an admirable government, that is most certain ! The kingdom is at present upwards of three hundred leagues in diameter, and divided into thirty provinces; the fathers are there masters of everything, and the people have no money at all; this is the masterpiece of justice and reason. For my part, I see nothing so divine as the good fathers, who wage war in this part of the world against the King of Spain and the King of Portugal, at the same time that they hear the confessions of those very princes in Europe; who kill Spaniards in America, and send them to Heaven in Madrid. This pleases me exceedingly, but let us push forward; you are going to be most fortunate of all mortals. How charmed will those fathers be to hear that a captain who understands the Bulgarian exercise is coming among them ! '

As soon as they reached the first barrier, Cacambo called to the advance guard, and told them that a captain wanted to speak to my Lord the General. Notice was given to the main guard, and immediately a Paraguayan officer ran to throw himself at the feet of the Commandant to impart this news to him. Candide and Cacambo were immediately disarmed, and their two Andalusian horses were seized.

The two strangers were now conducted between two files of
musketeers, the Commandant was at the farther end with
a three-cornered cap on his head, his gown tucked up, a
sword by his side, and a half-pike in his hand; he made
a sign, and instantly four-and-twenty soldiers drew up
round the newcomers. A sergeant told them that they
must wait, the Commandant could not speak to them;
and that the Reverend Father Provincial did not suffer
any Spaniard to open his mouth but in his presence, or
to stay above three hours in the province.

'And where is the Reverend Father Provincial?' said
Cacambo.

'He is just come from mass, and is at the parade,'
replied the sergeant, 'and in about three hours' time,
you may possibly have the honour to kiss his spurs.'

'But,' said Cacambo, 'the captain, who, as well as myself,
is perishing with hunger, is no Spaniard, but a German;
therefore, pray, might we not be permitted to break our
fast till we can be introduced to his Reverence?'

The sergeant immediately went, and acquainted the
Commandant with what he heard.

'God be praised,' said the Reverend Commandant,
'since he is a German, I will hear what he has to say;
let him be brought to my arbour.'

Immediately they conducted Candide to a beautiful
pavilion, adorned with a colonnade of green and gold
marble, and with trellises of vines, which served as a kind
of cage for parrots, humming-birds, fly-birds, guinea-hens,
and all other curious kinds of birds. An excellent breakfast was provided in vessels of gold; and while the Paraguayans were eating coarse Indian corn out of wooden
dishes in the open air, and exposed to the burning heat
of the sun, the Reverend Father Commandant retired to
his cool arbour.

He was a very handsome young man, round-faced, fair,
and fresh-coloured, his eyebrows were finely arched, he had
a piercing eye, the tips of his ears were red, his lips ver-
milion, and he had a bold and commanding air; but such
a boldness as neither resembled that of a Spaniard nor of a
Jesuit. He ordered Candide and Cacambo to have their
arms restored to them, together with their two Andalusian

horses. Cacambo gave the poor beasts some oats to eat close by the arbour, keeping a strict eye upon them all the while for fear of surprise.

Candide having kissed the hem of the Commandant's robe, they sat down to table.

' It seems you are a German ? ' said the Jesuit to him in that language.

' Yes, Reverend Father,' answered Candide.

As they pronounced these words, they looked at each other with great amazement, and with an emotion that neither could conceal.

' From what part of Germany do you come ? ' said the Jesuit.

' From the dirty province of Westphalia,' answered Candide : ' I was born in the castle of Thunder-ten-tronckh.'

' Oh heavens ! is it possible ? ' said the Commandant.

' What a miracle ! ' cried Candide.

' Can it be you ? ' said the Commandant.

On this they both retired a few steps backwards, then embraced, and let fall a shower of tears.

' Is it you then, Reverend Father ? You are the brother of the fair Cunegund ? you who were slain by the Bulgarians! you the Baron's son ! you a Jesuit in Paraguay ! I must confess this is a strange world we live in. O Pangloss ! Pangloss ! what joy would this have given you, if you had not been hanged.'

The Commandant dismissed the negro slaves, and the Paraguayans who were presenting them with liquor in crystal goblets. He returned thanks to God and St. Ignatius a thousand times ; he clasped Candide in his arms, and both their faces were bathed in tears.

' You will be more surprised, more affected, more transported,' said Candide, ' when I tell you that Miss Cunegund, your sister, whose belly was supposed to have been ripped open, is in perfect health.'

' Where ? '

' In your neighbourhood, with the Governor of Buenos Ayres ; and I myself was going to fight against you.'

Every word they uttered during this long conversation was productive of some new matter of astonishment.

Their souls fluttered on their tongues, listened in their ears, and sparkled in their eyes. Like true Germans, they continued a long time at table, waiting for the Reverend Father Provincial; and the Commandant spoke to his dear Candide as follows:

CHAPTER XV

HOW CANDIDE KILLED THE BROTHER OF HIS DEAR CUNEGUND

' NEVER while I live shall I lose the remembrance of that horrible day on which I saw my father and mother barbarously butchered before my eyes, and my sister ravished. When the Bulgarians retired, we found no sign of my dear sister; but the bodies of my father, mother, and myself, with two servant maids, and three little boys with their throats cut, were thrown into a cart, to be buried in a chapel belonging to the Jesuits, within two leagues of our family seat. A Jesuit sprinkled us with some holy water, which was confoundedly salt, and a few drops of it went into my eyes: the father perceived that my eyelids stirred a little; he put his hand on my breast, and felt my heart beat; upon which he gave me proper assistance, and at the end of three weeks I was perfectly recovered. You know, my dear Candide, I was very handsome; I became still more so, and the Reverend Father Croust, Superior of the House, took a great fancy to me; he gave me a novice's habit, and some years afterwards I was sent to Rome. Our general stood in need of new levies of young German Jesuits. The sovereigns of Paraguay admit as few Spanish Jesuits as possible; they prefer those of other nations, as being more obedient to command. The Reverend Father General looked upon me as a proper person to work in that vineyard. I set out in company with a Pole and a Tyrolese. Upon my arrival, I was honoured with a subdeaconship and a lieutenancy. Now I am colonel and priest. We shall give a warm reception to the King of Spain's troops; I can assure you, they will be well excommunicated and beaten. Providence has sent you hither to assist us. But is it true that my dear sister

Cunegund is in the neighbourhood with the Governor of Buenos Ayres?'

Candide swore that nothing could be more true; and the tears began again to trickle down their cheeks.

The Baron knew no end of embracing Candide: he called him his brother, his deliverer.

'Perhaps,' said he, 'my dear Candide, we shall be fortunate enough to enter the town sword in hand, and rescue my sister Cunegund.'

'Ah! that would crown my wishes,' replied Candide, 'for I intended to marry her; and I hope I shall still be able to do so.'

'Insolent fellow!' replied the Baron. 'You! you have the impudence to marry my sister, who bears seventy-two quarterings! I think you have an insufferable degree of assurance to dare so much as to mention such an audacious design to me.'

Candide, thunder-struck at the oddness of this speech, answered, 'Reverend Father, all the quarterings in the world are of no significance. I have delivered your sister from a Jew and an Inquisitor; she is under many obligations to me, and she is resolved to give me her hand. Master Pangloss always told me that mankind are by nature equal. Therefore, you may depend upon it, that I will marry your sister.'

'We shall see about that, villain!' said the Jesuit Baron of Thunder-ten-Tronckh, and struck him across the face with the flat side of his sword.

Candide, in an instant, drew his rapier, and plunged it up to the hilt in the Jesuit's body; but, in pulling it out reeking hot, he burst into tears.

'Good God!' cried he, 'I have killed my old master, my friend, my brother-in-law; I am the mildest man in the world, and yet I have already killed three men; and of these three two were priests.'

Cacambo, standing sentry near the door of the arbour, instantly ran up.

'Nothing remains,' said his master, 'but to sell our lives as dearly as possible; they will undoubtedly look into the arbour; we must die sword in hand.'

Cacambo, who had seen many of these kind of adventures,

was not discouraged! He stripped the Baron of his Jesuit's habit, and put it upon Candide, then gave him the dead man's three-cornered cap, and made him mount on horse-back. All this was done as quick as thought.

' Gallop, master,' cried Cacambo; ' everybody will take you for a Jesuit going to give orders; and we shall have passed the frontiers before they are able to overtake us.'

He flew as he spoke these words, crying out aloud in Spanish, ' Make way, make way for the Reverend Father Colonel.'

CHAPTER XVI

WHAT HAPPENED TO OUR TWO TRAVELLERS WITH TWO GIRLS, TWO MONKEYS, AND THE SAVAGES, CALLED OREILLONS

CANDIDE and his servant had already passed the frontiers before it was known that the German Jesuit was dead. The wary Cacambo had taken care to fill his wallet with bread, chocolate, ham, fruit, and a few bottles of wine. They penetrated with their Andalusian horses into a strange country where they could discover no beaten path. At length, a beautiful meadow, intersected with streams, opened to their view. Our two travellers allowed their steeds to graze. Cacambo urged his master to take some food, and he set him an example.

' How can you desire me to eat ham, when I have killed the son of my Lord the Baron, and am doomed never more to see the beautiful Cunegund? What will it avail me to prolong a wretched life that might be spent far from her in remorse and despair; and then, what will the *Journal of Trevoux* say? ' *

While he was making these reflections, he still continued eating. The sun was now on the point of setting, when the ears of our two wanderers were assailed with cries which seemed to be uttered by a female voice. They could not

* A periodical critique on the works of the learned, executed by Jesuits.

tell whether these were cries of grief or joy : however, they instantly started up, full of that uneasiness and apprehension which a strange place inspires. The cries proceeded from two young women who were tripping stark naked on the edge of the prairie, while two monkeys followed close at their heels biting their buttocks. Candide was touched with compassion; he had learned to shoot while he was among the Bulgarians, and he could hit a filbert in a hedge without touching a leaf. Accordingly, he took up his double-barrelled Spanish musket, pulled the trigger, and laid the two monkeys lifeless on the ground.

'God be praised, my dear Cacambo, I have rescued two poor girls from a most perilous situation : if I have committed a sin in killing an Inquisitor and a Jesuit, I made ample amends by saving the lives of these two girls. Who knows but they may be young ladies of a good family, and that this assistance I have been so happy to give them may procure us great advantage in this country.'

He was about to continue, when he felt himself struck speechless at seeing the two girls embracing the dead bodies of the monkeys in the tenderest manner, bathing their wounds with their tears, and rending the air with the most doleful lamentations.

'Really,' said he to Cacambo, 'I should not have expected to see such a prodigious share of good nature.'

'Master,' replied Cacambo, 'you have made a precious piece of work of it; do you know that you have killed the lovers of these two ladies ! '

'Their lovers ! Cacambo, you are jesting ! it cannot be ! I can never believe it.'

'Dear Sir,' replied Cacambo, 'you are surprised at everything; why should you think it so strange that there should be a country where monkeys insinuate themselves into the good graces of the ladies? They are the fourth part of a man as I am the fourth part of a Spaniard.'

'Alas ! ' replied Candide, 'I remember to have heard Master Pangloss say that such accidents as these frequently came to pass in former times, and that these commixtures are productive of centaurs, fauns, and satyrs; and that

many of the ancients had seen such monsters : but I looked
upon the whole as fabulous.'

'Now you are convinced,' said Cacambo, 'that it is very
true, and you see what use is made of those creatures
by persons who have not had a proper education : all
I am afraid of is that these same ladies will play us some
ugly trick.'

These judicious reflections operated so far on Candide,
as to make him quit the meadow and strike into a thicket.
There he and Cacambo supped, and after heartily cursing
the Grand Inquisitor, the Governor of Buenos Ayres,
and the Baron, they fell asleep on the ground. When they
awoke, they were surprised to find that they could not
move; the reason was that the Oreillons who inhabit that
country, and to whom the two girls had denounced them,
had bound them with cords made of the bark of trees.
They were surrounded by fifty naked Oreillons armed with
bows and arrows, clubs, and hatchets of flint; some were
making a fire under a large cauldron; and others were
preparing spits, crying out one and all, 'A Jesuit ! a
Jesuit ! We shall be revenged; we shall have excellent
cheer; let us eat this Jesuit; let us eat him up.'

'I told you, master,' cried Cacambo mournfully, 'that
those two wenches would play us some scurvy trick.'

Candide seeing the cauldron and the spits, cried out,
'I suppose they are going either to boil or roast us. Ah !
what would Master Pangloss say if he were to see how pure
nature is formed ! Everything is right : it may be so :
but I must confess it is something hard to be bereft of
Miss Cunegund, and to be spitted by these Oreillons.'

Cacambo, who never lost his presence of mind in distress,
said to the disconsolate Candide, 'Do not despair; I
understand a little of the jargon of these people; I will
speak to them.'

'Ay, pray do,' said Candide, 'and be sure you make them
sensible of the horrid barbarity of boiling and roasting
human creatures, and how little of Christianity there is in
such practices.'

'Gentlemen,' said Cacambo, 'you think perhaps you
are going to feast upon a Jesuit; if so, it is mighty well;
nothing can be more agreeable to justice than thus to treat

your enemies. Indeed, the law of nature teaches us to kill
our neighbour, and accordingly we find this practised all
over the world; and if we do not indulge ourselves in
eating human flesh, it is because we have much better
fare; but you have not such resources as we have; it is
certainly much better judged to feast upon your enemies
than to abandon to the fowls of the air the fruits of your
victory. But surely, gentlemen, you would not choose
to eat your friends. You imagine you are going to roast
a Jesuit, whereas my master is your friend, your defender,
and you are going to spit the very man who has been destroying your enemies: as to myself, I am your countryman; this gentleman is my master, and so far from being
a Jesuit, he has very lately killed one of that order, whose
spoils he now wears, and which have probably occasioned
your mistake. To convince you of the truth of what I say,
take the habit he now has on, and carry it to the first
barrier of the Jesuits' kingdom, and inquire whether my
master did not kill one of their officers. There will be little
or no time lost by this, and you may still reserve our
bodies in your power to feast on, if you should find what we
have told you to be false. But, on the contrary, if you
find it to be true, I am persuaded you are too well acquainted
with the principles of the laws of society, humanity, and
justice, not to use us courteously.'

This speech appeared very reasonable to the Oreillons;
they deputed two of their people with all expedition to
inquire into the truth of this affair. The two delegates
acquitted themselves of their commission like men of sense,
and soon returned with good tidings. Upon this the
Oreillons released their two prisoners, showed them all
sorts of civilities, offered them girls, gave them refreshments,
and reconducted them to the confines of their country,
crying before them all the way, in token of joy, ' He is no
Jesuit, he is no Jesuit.'

Candide could not help admiring the cause of his deliverance.

' What men ! what manners ! ' cried he : ' if I had not
fortunately run my sword up to the hilt in the body of
Miss Cunegund's brother, I should have infallibly been
eaten alive. But, after all, pure nature is an excellent

thing; since these people, instead of eating me, showed me a thousand civilities, as soon as they knew I was not a Jesuit.'

CHAPTER XVII

CANDIDE AND HIS SERVANT ARRIVE IN THE COUNTRY OF EL DORADO. WHAT THEY SAW THERE

WHEN they got to the frontiers of the Oreillons, Cacambo said to Candide, ' You see, this hemisphere is no better than the other : take my advice, and let us return to Europe by the shortest way possible.'

' But how can we get back ? ' said Candide; ' and whither shall we go? To my own country? the Bulgarians and the Abares are laying that waste with fire and sword. Or shall we go to Portugal? there I shall be burnt; and if we abide here, we are every moment in danger of being spitted. But how can I bring myself to quit that part of the world where Miss Cunegund has her residence ? '

' Let us turn towards Cayenne,' said Cacambo; ' there we shall meet with some Frenchmen; for you know those gentry ramble all over the world; perhaps they will assist us, and God will look with pity on our distress.'

It was not so easy to get to Cayenne. They knew pretty nearly whereabouts it lay; but the mountains, rivers, precipices, robbers, savages, were dreadful obstacles in the way. Their horses died with fatigue, and their provisions were at an end. They subsisted a whole month upon wild fruit, till at length they came to a little river bordered with cocoa-nut palms, the sight of which at once sustained life and hope.

Cacambo, who was always giving as good advice as the old woman herself, said to Candide, ' You see there is no holding out any longer; we have travelled enough on foot. I see an empty canoe near the river-side; let us fill it with cocoa-nuts, get into it, and go down with the stream; a river always leads to some inhabited place. If we do not meet with agreeable things, we shall at least meet with something new.'

' Agreed,' replied Candide; ' let us recommend ourselves to Providence.'

They rowed a few leagues down the river, the banks of which were in some places covered with flowers; in others barren; in some parts smooth and level, and in others steep and rugged. The stream widened as they went further on, till at length it passed under one of the frightful rocks whose summits seemed to reach the clouds. Here our two travellers had the courage to commit themselves to the stream beneath this vault, which, contracting in this part, hurried them along with a dreadful noise and rapidity. At the end of four-and-twenty hours, they saw daylight again; but their canoe was dashed to pieces against the rocks. They were obliged to creep along, from rock to rock, for the space of a league, till at last a spacious plain presented itself to their sight, bound by inaccessible mountains. The country appeared cultivated equally for pleasure, and to produce the necessaries of life. The useful and agreeable were here equally blended. The roads were covered, or rather adorned, with carriages formed of glittering materials, in which were men and women of a surprising beauty, drawn with great rapidity by red sheep of a very large size, which far surpassed in speed the finest coursers of Andalusia, Tetuan, or Mequinez.

' Here is a country, however,' said Candide, ' preferable to Westphalia.'

He and Cacambo landed near the first village they saw, at the entrance of which they perceived some children covered with tattered garments of the richest brocade, playing at quoits. Our two inhabitants of the other hemisphere amused themselves greatly with what they saw. The quoits were large round pieces, yellow, red, and green, which cast a most glorious lustre. Our travellers picked some of them up, and they proved to be gold, emeralds, rubies, and diamonds, the least of which would have been the greatest ornament to the superb throne of the great Mogul.

' Without doubt,' said Cacambo, ' those children must be the king's sons, that are playing at quoits.'

As he was uttering those words, the schoolmaster of the village appeared, who came to call them to school.

' There,' said Candide, ' is the preceptor of the royal family.'

The little ragamuffins immediately quitted their game, leaving the quoits on the ground with all their other playthings. Candide gathered them up, ran to the schoolmaster, and, with a most respectful bow, presented them to him, giving him to understand by signs that their Royal Highnesses had forgotten their gold and precious stones. The schoolmaster, with a smile, flung them upon the ground, then having examined Candide from head to foot with an air of great surprise, went on his way.

Our travellers took care, however, to gather up the gold, the rubies, and the emeralds.

' Where are we? ' cried Candide. ' The king's children in this country must have an excellent education, since they are taught to show such a contempt for gold and precious stones.'

Cacambo was as much surprised as his master.

They at length drew near the first house in the village, which was built after the manner of a European palace. There was a crowd of people round the door, and a still greater number in the house. The sound of the most delightful musical instruments was heard, and the most agreeable smell came from the kitchen. Cacambo went up to the door, and heard those within talking in the Peruvian language, which was his mother tongue; for every one knows that Cacambo was born in a village of Tucuman where no other language is spoken.

' I will be your interpreter here,' said he to Candide, ' let us go in; this is an eating-house.'

Immediately two waiters, and two servant-girls, dressed in cloth of gold, and their hair braided with ribbons of tissue, accosted the strangers, and invited them to sit down to the ordinary. Their dinner consisted of four dishes of different soups, each garnished with two young paroquets, a large dish of bouille that weighed two hundredweight, two roasted monkeys of a delicious flavour, three hundred humming-birds in one dish, and six hundred fly-birds in another; some excellent ragouts, delicate tarts, and the whole served up in dishes of rock-crystal. Several sorts of liquors, extracted from the sugar-cane, were handed about by the servants who attended.

Most of the company were chapmen and wagoners, all extremely polite : they asked Cacambo a few questions, with the utmost discretion and circumspection; and replied to his in a most obliging and satisfactory manner.

As soon as dinner was over, both Candide and Cacambo thought they would pay very handsomely for their entertainment by laying down two of those large gold pieces which they had picked off the ground; but the landlord and landlady burst into a fit of laughing and held their sides for some time before they were able to speak.

'Gentlemen,' said the landlord, 'I plainly perceive you are strangers, and such we are not accustomed to see; pardon us, therefore, for laughing when you offered us the common pebbles of our highways for payment of your reckoning. To be sure, you have none of the coin of this kingdom; but there is no necessity to have any money at all to dine in this house. All the inns, which are established for the convenience of those who carry on the trade of this nation, are maintained by the government. You have found but very indifferent entertainment here, because this is only a poor village; but in almost every other of these public houses you will meet with a reception worthy of persons of your merit.'

Cacambo explained the whole of this speech of the landlord to Candide, who listened to it with the same astonishment with which his friend communicated it.

'What sort of a country is this,' said the one to the other, 'that is unknown to all the world, and in which Nature had everywhere so different an appearance from what she has in ours? Possibly this is that part of the globe where everything is right, for there must certainly be some such place; and, for all that Master Pangloss could say, I often perceived that things went very ill in Westphalia.'

CHAPTER XVIII

WHAT THEY SAW IN THE COUNTRY OF EL DORADO

CACAMBO vented all his curiosity upon the landlord by a thousand different questions.

The honest man answered him thus : ' I am very ignorant, Sir, but I am contented with my ignorance ; however, we have in this neighbourhood an old man retired from court, who is the most learned and communicative person in the whole kingdom.'

He then directed Cacambo to the old man; Candide acted now only a second character, and attended his servant. They entered a quite plain house, for the door was nothing but silver, and the ceiling was only of beaten gold, but wrought in so elegant a taste as to vie with the richest. The antechamber, indeed, was only incrusted with rubies and emeralds ; but the order in which everything was disposed made amends for this great simplicity.

The old man received the strangers on a sofa, which was stuffed with humming-birds' feathers ; and ordered his servants to present them with liquors in golden goblets, after which he satisfied their curiosity in the following terms :

' I am now one hundred and seventy-two years old; and I learnt of my late father who was equerry to the king the amazing revolutions of Peru, to which he had been an eye-witness. This kingdom is the ancient patrimony of the Incas, who very imprudently quitted it to conquer another part of the world, and were at length conquered and destroyed themselves by the Spaniards.

' Those princes of their family who remained in their native country acted more wisely. They ordained, with the consent of their whole nation, that none of the inhabitants of our little kingdom should ever quit it ; and to this wise ordinance we owe the preservation of our innocence and happiness. The Spaniards had some confused notion of this country, to which they gave the name of El Dorado ; and Sir Walter Raleigh, an Englishman, actually came very near it, about a hundred years ago : but the inaccessible rocks and precipices with which our country is surrounded on all sides have hitherto secured us from the rapacious fury of the people of Europe, who have an unaccountable fondness for the pebbles and dirt of our land, for the sake of which they would murder us all to the very last man.'

The conversation lasted some time and turned chiefly on the form of government, the customs, the women, the public diversions, and the arts. At length, Candide, who had always had a taste for metaphysics, asked whether the people of that country had any religion.

The old man reddened a little at this question.

' Can you doubt it? ' said he. ' Do you take us for wretches lost to all sense of gratitude? '

Cacambo asked in a respectful manner what was the established religion of El Dorado. The old man blushed again.

' Can there be two religions then? ' he said. ' Ours, I apprehend, is the religion of the whole world; we worship God from morning till night.'

' Do you worship but one God? ' said Cacambo, who still acted as the interpreter of Candide's doubts.

' Certainly,' said the old man; ' there are not two, nor three, nor four Gods. I must confess the people of your world ask very extraordinary questions.'

However, Candide could not refrain from making many more inquiries of the old man; he wanted to know in what manner they prayed to God in El Dorado.

' We do not pray to him at all,' said the reverend sage; ' we have nothing to ask of him, he has given us all we want, and we give him thanks incessantly.'

Candide had a curiosity to see some of their priests, and desired Cacambo to ask the old man where they were.

At this he, smiling, said, ' My friends, we are all of us priests; the King and all the heads of families sing solemn hymns of thanksgiving every morning, accompanied by five or six thousand musicians.'

' What! ' said Cacambo, ' have you no monks among you, to dispute, to govern, to intrigue, and to burn people who are not of the same opinion with themselves? '

' Do you take us for fools? ' said the old man. ' Here

we are all of one opinion, and know not what you mean by
your monks.'

During the whole of this discourse Candide was in raptures, and he said to himself:

'What a prodigious difference is there between this
place and Westphalia, and this house and the Baron's
castle! If our friend Pangloss had seen El Dorado, he
would no longer have said that the castle of Thunder-ten-
Tronckh was the finest of all possible edifices: there is
nothing like seeing the world, that's certain.'

This long conversation being ended, the old man ordered
six sheep to be harnessed, and put to the coach, and sent
twelve of his servants to escort the travellers to Court.

'Excuse me,' said he, ' for not waiting on you in person;
my age deprives me of that honour. The King will receive
you in such a manner that you will have no reason to
complain; and doubtless you will make a proper allowance
for the customs of the country, if they should not happen
altogether to please you.'

Candide and Cacambo got into the coach, the six sheep
flew, and in less than a quarter of an hour they arrived at
the King's palace, which was situated at the further end
of the capital. At the entrance was a portal two hundred
and twenty feet high, and one hundred wide; but it is
impossible for words to express the materials of which it
was built. The reader, however, will readily conceive they
must have a prodigious superiority over the pebbles and
sand which we call gold and precious stones.

Twenty beautiful young virgins-in-waiting received
Candide and Cacambo at their alighting from the coach,
conducted them to the bath, and clad them in robes woven
of the down of humming-birds; after this they were
introduced by the great officers of the crown of both sexes
to the King's apartment, between two files of musicians,
each file consisting of a thousand, according to the custom
of the country. When they drew near to the presence
chamber, Cacambo asked one of the officers in what manner
they were to pay their obeisance to his Majesty: whether
it was the custom to fall upon their knees, or to prostrate
themselves upon the ground? whether they were to put
their hands upon their heads, or behind their backs?

whether they were to lick the dust off the floor? in short, what was the ceremony usual on such occasions?

'The custom,' said the great officer, 'is to embrace the King, and kiss him on each cheek.'

Candide and Cacambo accordingly threw their arms round his Majesty's neck; and he received them in the most gracious manner imaginable, and very politely asked them to sup with him.

While supper was preparing, orders were given to show them the city, where they saw public structures that reared their lofty heads to the clouds; the market-places decorated with a thousand columns; fountains of spring water, besides others of rose water, and of liquors drawn from the sugar-cane, incessantly flowing in the great squares; these were paved with a kind of precious stone that emitted an odour like that of cloves and cinnamon. Candide asked to see the high court of justice, the parliament; but was answered that they have none in that country, being utter strangers to lawsuits. He then inquired, if they had any prisons; they replied, 'None.' But what gave him at once the greatest surprise and pleasure was the Palace of Sciences, where he saw a gallery two thousand feet long, filled with the various apparatus of mathematics and natural philosophy.

After having spent the whole afternoon in seeing only about the thousandth part of the city, they were brought back to the King's palace. Candide sat down at the table with his Majesty, his servant Cacambo, and several ladies of the Court. Never was entertainment more elegant, nor could any one possibly show more wit than his Majesty displayed while they were at supper. Cacambo explained all the King's *bons mots* to Candide, and although they were translated they still appeared to be *bons mots*. Of all the things that surprised Candide, this was not the least. They spent a whole month in this hospitable place, during which time Candide was continually saying to Cacambo:

'I own, my friend, once more, that the castle where I was born is a mere nothing in comparison with the place where we now are; but still Miss Cunegund is not here, and you yourself have doubtless some mistress in Europe. If we remain here, we shall only be as others are: whereas, if we return to our own world with only a dozen of El Dorado sheep, loaded with the pebbles of this country, we shall be richer than all the kings in Europe; we shall no longer need to stand in awe of the Inquisitors; and we may easily recover Miss Cunegund.'

This speech pleased Cacambo. A fondness for roving, for making a figure in their own country, and for boasting of what they had seen in their travels, was so strong in our two wanderers that they resolved to be no longer happy; and demanded permission of his Majesty to quit the country.

'You are about to do a rash and silly action,' said the King; 'I am sensible my kingdom is an inconsiderable spot; but when people are tolerably at their ease in any place, I should think it would be their interest to remain there. Most assuredly, I have no right to detain you or any strangers against your wills; this is an act of tyranny to which our manners and our laws are equally repugnant: all men are free; you have an undoubted liberty to depart whenever you please, but you will have many difficulties in passing the frontiers. It is impossible to ascend that rapid river which runs under high and vaulted rocks, and by which you were conveyed hither by a miracle. The mountains by which my kingdom is hemmed in on all sides are ten thousand feet high, and perfectly perpendicular; they are above ten leagues over each, and the descent from them is one continued precipice. However, since you are determined to leave us, I will immediately give orders to the superintendent of machines to cause one to be made that will convey you safely. When they have conducted you to the back of the mountains, nobody can attend you further; for my subjects have made a vow never to quit the kingdom, and they are too prudent to break it. Ask me whatever else you please.'

'All we shall ask of your Majesty,' said Cacambo, 'is a few sheep laden with provisions, pebbles, and the clay of your country.'

The King smiled at the request, and said, 'I cannot imagine what pleasure you Europeans find in our yellow clay; but take away as much of it as you will, and much good may it do you.'

He immediately gave orders to his engineers to make a

machine to hoist these two extraordinary men out of the kingdom. Three thousand good mathematicians went to work and finished it in about fifteen days; and it did not cost more than twenty millions sterling of that country's money. Candide and Cacambo were placed on this machine, and they took with them two large red sheep, bridled and saddled, to ride upon when they got on the other side of the mountains ; twenty others to serve as pack-horses for carrying provisions; thirty laden with presents of whatever was most curious in the country ; and fifty with gold, diamonds, and other precious stones. The King embraced the two wanderers with the greatest cordiality.

It was a curious sight to behold the manner of their setting off, and the ingenious method by which they and their sheep were hoisted to the top of the mountains. The mathematicians and engineers took leave of them as soon as they had conveyed them to a place of safety, and Candide was wholly occupied with the thoughts of presenting his sheep to Miss Cunegund.

' Now,' said he, ' thanks to heaven, we have more than sufficient to pay the Governor of Buenos Ayres for Miss Cunegund, if she is redeemable. Let us make the best of our way to Cayenne, where we will take ship, and then we may at leisure think of what kingdom we shall purchase.'

CHAPTER XIX

WHAT HAPPENED TO THEM AT SURINAM, AND HOW CANDIDE BECAME ACQUAINTED WITH MARTIN

OUR travellers' first day's journey was very pleasant; they were elated with the prospect of possessing more riches than were to be found in Europe, Asia, and Africa together. Candide, in amorous transports, cut the name of Miss Cunegund on the trees. The second day, two of their sheep sank into a morass, and were swallowed up with their loads; two more died of fatigue some few days afterwards ; seven or eight perished with hunger in a desert, and others, at different times, tumbled down precipices; so that, after travelling about a hundred days, they had only two sheep left.

Said Candide to Cacambo, ' You see, my dear friend, how perishable the riches of this world are; there is nothing solid but virtue and the joy of seeing Miss Cunegund again.'

' Very true,' said Cacambo; ' but we have still two sheep remaining, with more treasure than ever the King of Spain will be possessed of; and I espy a town at a distance, which I take to be Surinam, a town belonging to the Dutch. We are now at the end of our troubles, and at the beginning of happiness.'

As they drew near the town, they saw a negro stretched on the ground with only one half of his habit, which was a pair of blue cotton drawers; for the poor man had lost his left leg, and his right hand.

' Good God,' said Candide in Dutch, ' what dost thou here, friend, in this deplorable condition? '

' I am waiting for my master Mynheer Vanderdendur, the famous trader,' answered the negro.

' Was it Mynheer Vanderdendur that used you in this cruel manner? '

' Yes, Sir,' said the negro; ' it is the custom here. They give a pair of cotton drawers twice a year, and that is all our covering. When we labour in the sugar-works, and the mill happens to snatch hold of a finger, they instantly chop off our hand; and when we attempt to run away, they cut off a leg. Both these cases have happened to me, and it is at this expense that you eat sugar in Europe; and yet when my mother sold me for ten pattacoons on the coast of Guinea, she said to me, " My dear child, bless our fetishes; adore them for ever; they will make thee live happy; thou hast the honour to be a slave to our lords the whites, by which thou wilt make the fortune of us thy parents." Alas! I know not whether I have made their fortunes; but they have not made mine: dogs, monkeys, and parrots, are a thousand times less wretched than me. The Dutch fetishes who converted me tell me every Sunday that, blacks and whites, we are all children of Adam. As for me, I do not understand any thing of genealogies; but if what these preachers say is true, we are all second cousins; and you must allow, that it is impossible to be worse treated by our relations than we are.'

' O Pangloss ! ' cried out Candide, ' such horrid doings never entered thy imagination. Here is an end of the matter; I find myself, after all, obliged to renounce thy Optimism.'

' Optimism ! ' said Cacambo, ' what is that ? '

' Alas ! ' replied Candide, ' it is the obstinacy of maintaining that everything is best when it is worst ' : and so saying, he turned his eyes towards the poor negro, and shed a flood of tears; and in this weeping mood he entered the town of Surinam.

Immediately upon their arrival, our travellers inquired if there was any vessel in the harbour which they might send to Buenos Ayres. The person they addressed themselves to happened to be the master of a Spanish bark, who offered to agree with them on moderate terms, and appointed them a meeting at a public-house. Thither Candide and his faithful Cacambo went to wait for him, taking with them their two sheep.

Candide, who was all frankness and sincerity, made an ingenuous recital of his adventures to the Spaniard, declaring to him at the same time his resolution of carrying off Miss Cunegund.

' In that case,' said the shipmaster, ' I'll take good care not to take you to Buenos Ayres. It would prove a hanging matter to us all. The fair Cunegund is the Governor's favourite mistress.'

These words were like a clap of thunder to Candide; he wept bitterly for a long time, and, taking Cacambo aside, he said to him :

' I'll tell you, my dear friend, what you must do. We have each of us in our pockets to the value of five or six millions in diamonds; you are cleverer at these matters than I; you must go to Buenos Ayres and bring off Miss Cunegund. If the Governor makes any difficulty, give him a million; if he holds out, give him two; as you have not killed an Inquisitor, they will have no suspicion of you : I'll fit out another ship and go to Venice, where I will wait for you : Venice is a free country, where we shall have nothing to fear from Bulgarians, Abares, Jews, or Inquisitors.'

Cacambo greatly applauded this wise resolution. He was inconsolable at the thought of parting with so good a master, who treated him more like an intimate friend than a servant; but the pleasure of being able to do him a service soon got the better of his sorrow. They embraced each other with a flood of tears. Candide charged him not to forget the old woman. Cacambo set out the same day. This Cacambo was a very honest fellow.

Candide continued some days longer at Surinam, waiting for any captain to carry him and his two remaining sheep to Italy. He hired domestics and purchased many things necessary for a long voyage; at length, Mynheer Vanderdendur, skipper of a large Dutch vessel, came and offered his service.

'What will you take,' said Candide, 'to carry me, my servants, my baggage, and these two sheep you see here, direct to Venice?'

The skipper asked ten thousand piastres; and Candide agreed to his demand without hesitation.

'Oh, ho!' said the cunning Vanderdendur to himself, 'this stranger must be very rich; he agrees to give me ten thousand piastres without hesitation.'

Returning a little while after, he told Candide that upon second consideration he could not undertake the voyage for less than twenty thousand.

'Very well, you shall have them,' said Candide.

'Zounds!' said the skipper to himself, 'this man agrees to pay twenty thousand piastres with as much ease as ten.'

Accordingly he went back again, and told him roundly that he would not carry him to Venice for less than thirty thousand piastres.

'Then you shall have thirty thousand,' said Candide.

'Odso!' said the Dutchman once more to himself, 'thirty thousand piastres seem a trifle to this man. Those sheep must certainly be laden with an immense treasure. I'll stop here and ask no more; but make him pay down the thirty thousand piastres, and then we shall see.'

Candide sold two small diamonds, the least of which was worth more than all the skipper asked. He paid him before-hand, and the two sheep were put on board, and Candide followed in a small boat to join the vessel in the road. The skipper took his opportunity, hoisted his sails, and put out to sea with a favourable wind. Candide, confounded and amazed, soon lost sight of the ship.

' Alas ! ' said he, ' this is a trick like those in our old world ! '

He returned back to the shore overwhelmed with grief; and, indeed, he had lost what would have been the fortune of twenty monarchs.

Immediately upon his landing, he applied to the Dutch magistrate : being transported with passion, he thundered at the door; which being opened, he went in, told his case, and talked a little louder than was necessary. The magistrate began with fining him ten thousand piastres for his petulance, and then listened very patiently to what he had to say, promised to examine into the affair at the skipper's return, and ordered him to pay ten thousand piastres more for the fees of the court.

This treatment put Candide out of all patience : it is true, he had suffered misfortunes a thousand times more grievous; but the cool insolence of the judge and of the skipper who robbed him raised his choler and threw him into a deep melancholy. The villainy of mankind presented itself to his mind in all its deformity, and his soul was a prey to the most gloomy ideas. After some time, hearing that the captain of a French ship was ready to set sail for Bordeaux, as he had no more sheep loaded with diamonds to put on board, he hired the cabin at the usual price; and made it known in the town that he would pay the passage and board of any honest man who would give him his company during the voyage; besides making him a present of ten thousand piastres, on condition that such person was the most dissatisfied with his condition and the most unfortunate in the whole province.

Upon this there appeared such a crowd of candidates that a large fleet could not have contained them. Candide, willing to choose from among those who appeared most likely to answer his intention, selected twenty, who seemed to him the most sociable, and who all pretended to merit the preference. He invited them to his inn, and promised to treat them with a supper, on condition that every man should bind himself by an oath to relate his own history. He declared at the same time that he would make choice of that person who should appear to him the most deserving of compassion, and the most justly dissatisfied with his condition of life; and that he would make a present to the rest.

This extraordinary assembly continued sitting till four in the morning. Candide, while he was listening to their adventures, called to mind what the old woman had said to him on their voyage to Buenos Ayres, and the wager she had laid that there was not a person on board the ship but had met with some great misfortune. Every story he heard put him in mind of Pangloss.

' My old master,' said he, ' would be confoundedly put to it to demonstrate his favourite system. Would he were here! Certainly if everything is for the best, it is in El Dorado, and not in the other parts of the world.'

At length he determined in favour of a poor scholar who had laboured ten years for the booksellers at Amsterdam, being of opinion that no employment could be more detestable.

This scholar, who was in fact a very honest man, had been robbed by his wife, beaten by his son, and forsaken by his daughter, who had run away with a Portuguese. He had been likewise deprived of a small employment on which he subsisted, and he was persecuted by the clergy of Surinam, who took him for a Socinian. It must be acknowledged that the other competitors were, at least, as wretched as he; but Candide was in hopes that the company of a man of letters would relieve the tediousness of the voyage. All the other candidates complained that Candide had done them great injustice; but he stopped their mouths by a present of a hundred piastres to each.

CHAPTER XX

WHAT BEFELL CANDIDE AND MARTIN ON THEIR VOYAGE

THE old scholar, whose name was Martin, took shipping with Candide for Bordeaux. They both had seen and suffered a great deal; and if the ship had been destined to sail from Surinam to Japan round the Cape of Good Hope, they could have found sufficient entertainment for each other during the whole voyage in discoursing upon moral and natural evil.

Candide, however, had one advantage over Martin : he lived in the pleasing hopes of seeing Miss Cunegund once more; whereas the poor philosopher had nothing to hope for. Besides, Candide had money and jewels, and, notwithstanding he had lost a hundred red sheep, laden with the greatest treasure on the earth, and though he still smarted from the reflection of the Dutch skipper's knavery, yet when he considered what he had still left, and repeated the name of Cunegund, especially after meal-times, he inclined to Pangloss's doctrine.

' And pray,' said he to Martin, ' what is your opinion of the whole of this system? What notion have you of moral and natural evil ? '

' Sir,' replied Martin, ' our priests accused me of being a Socinian; but the real truth is, I am a Manichæan.'

' Nay, now you are jesting,' said Candide; ' there are no Manichæans existing at present in the world.'

' And yet I am one,' said Martin; ' but I cannot help it; I cannot for the soul of me think otherwise.'

' Surely the devil must be in you,' said Candide.

' He concerns himself so much,' replied Martin, ' in the affairs of this world that it is very probable he may be in me as well as everywhere else; but I must confess, when I cast my eye on this globe, or rather globule, I cannot help thinking that God has abandoned it to some malignant being. I always except El Dorado. I scarce ever knew a city that did not wish the destruction of its neighbouring city; nor a family that did not desire to exterminate some other family. The poor, in all parts of the world, bear an inveterate hatred to the rich, even while they creep and cringe to them; and the rich treat the poor like sheep, whose wool and flesh they barter for money : a million of regimented assassins traverse Europe from one end to the other to get their bread by regular depredation and murder, because it is the most gentleman-like profession. Even in those cities which seem to enjoy the blessings of peace, and where the arts flourish, the inhabitants are devoured with envy, care, and anxiety, which are greater plagues than any experienced in a town besieged. Private chagrins are still more dreadful than public calamities. In a word, I have seen and suffered so much, that I am a Manichæan.'

' And yet there is some good in the world,' replied Candide.

' May be,' said Martin, ' but it has escaped my knowledge.'

While they were deeply engaged in this dispute they heard the report of cannon, which redoubled every moment. Each took out his glass, and they espied two ships warmly engaged at the distance of about three miles. The wind brought them both so near the French ship that those on board her had the pleasure of seeing the fight with great ease. At last one of the two vessels gave the other a shot between wind and water, which sank her outright. Then could Candide and Martin plainly perceive a hundred men on the deck of the vessel which was sinking, who, with hands uplifted to heaven, sent forth piercing cries, and were in a moment swallowed up by the waves.

' Well,' said Martin, ' you now see in what manner mankind treat each other.'

' It is certain,' said Candide, ' that there is something diabolical in this affair.'

As he was speaking thus, he saw something of a shining red hue, which swam close to the vessel. The boat was hoisted out to see what it might be, when it proved to be one of his sheep. Candide felt more joy at the recovery of this one animal than he did grief when he lost the other hundred, though laden with the large diamonds of El Dorado.

The French captain quickly perceived that the victorious ship belonged to the crown of Spain ; that the other which sank was a Dutch pirate, and the very same captain who had robbed Candide. The immense riches which this villain had amassed were buried with him in the deep, and only this one sheep saved out of the whole.

'You see,' said Candide to Martin, 'that vice is sometimes punished : this villain, the Dutch skipper, has met with the fate he deserved.'

'Very true,' said Martin; 'but why should the passengers be doomed also to destruction? God has punished the knave, and the devil has drowned the rest.'

The French and Spanish ships continued their cruise, and Candide and Martin their conversation. They disputed fourteen days successively, at the end of which they were just as far advanced as the first moment they began. However, they had the satisfaction of disputing, of communicating their ideas, and of mutually comforting each other. Candide embraced his sheep.

'Since I have found thee again,' said he, ' I may possibly find my Cunegund once more.'

CHAPTER XXI

CANDIDE AND MARTIN, WHILE THUS REASONING WITH EACH
OTHER, DRAW NEAR TO THE COAST OF FRANCE

At length they sighted the coast of France.

'Pray, Mr. Martin,' said Candide, 'have you ever been in France?'

'Yes, Sir,' said Martin, 'I have been in several provinces of that kingdom. In some, one half of the people are madmen; in some, they are too artful; in others, again, they are in general either very good-natured or very brutal; while in others, they affect to be witty, and in all, their ruling passion is love, the next is slander, and the last is to talk nonsense.'

'But pray, Mr. Martin, were you ever in Paris?'

'Yes, Sir, I have been in that city, and it is a place that contains the several species just described; it is a chaos, a confused multitude, where everyone seeks for pleasure without being able to find it; at least, as far as I have observed during my short stay in that city. At my arrival, I was robbed of all I had in the world by pickpockets and sharpers, at the fair of St. Germain. I was taken up myself for a robber, and confined in prison a whole week; after that I hired myself as corrector to a press in order to get a little money towards defraying my expenses back to Holland on foot. I knew the whole tribe of scribblers, malcontents, and religious convulsionaries. It is said the people of that city are very polite; I believe they may be so.'

'For my part, I have no curiosity to see France,' said Candide, 'you may easily conceive, my friend, that, after spending a month at El Dorado, I can desire to behold nothing upon earth but Miss Cunegund; I am going to wait for her at Venice; I intend to pass through France on my way to Italy; will you not bear me company?'

'With all my heart,' said Martin: 'they say Venice is agreeable to none but noble Venetians; but that, nevertheless, strangers are well received there when they have plenty of money; now I have none, but you have, therefore I will attend you wherever you please.'

'Now we are upon this subject,' said Candide, 'do you think that the earth was originally sea, as we read in that great book which belongs to the captain of the ship?'

'I believe nothing of it,' replied Martin, 'any more than I do of the many other chimeras which have been related to us for some time past.'

'But then, to what end,' said Candide, 'was the world formed?'

'To make us mad,' said Martin.

'Are you not surprised,' continued Candide, 'at the love which the two girls in the country of the Oreillons had for those two monkeys?—You know I have told you the story.'

'Surprised!' replied Martin, 'not in the least; I see nothing strange in this passion. I have seen so many extraordinary things, that there is nothing extraordinary to me now.'

'Do you think,' said Candide, 'that mankind always massacred each other as they do now? Were they always guilty of lies, fraud, treachery, ingratitude, inconstancy, envy, ambition, and cruelty? Were they always thieves, fools, cowards, gluttons, drunkards, misers, calumniators, debauchees, fanatics, and hypocrites?'

'Do you believe,' said Martin, 'that hawks have always been accustomed to eat pigeons when they came in their way?'

'Doubtless,' said Candide.

'Well then,' replied Martin, 'if hawks have always had the same nature, why should you pretend that mankind change theirs?'

'Oh!' said Candide, 'there is a great deal of difference, for free will . . .'

Reasoning thus, they arrived at Bordeaux.

CHAPTER XXII

WHAT HAPPENED TO CANDIDE AND MARTIN IN FRANCE

CANDIDE stayed no longer at Bordeaux than was necessary to dispose of a few of the pebbles he had brought from El Dorado, and to provide himself with a post-chaise for two persons, for he could no longer stir a step without his philosopher Martin. The only thing that gave him concern was the being obliged to leave his sheep behind him, which he entrusted to the care of the Academy of Sciences at Bordeaux. The academicians proposed, as a prize-subject for the year, to prove why the wool of this sheep was red; and the prize was adjudged to a northern sage, who demonstrated by A plus B, minus C, divided by Z, that the sheep must necessarily be red, and die of the rot.

In the meantime, all the travellers whom Candide met with in the inns, or on the road, told him to a man that they were going to Paris. This general eagerness gave him likewise a great desire to see this capital, and it was not much out of his way to Venice.

He entered the city by the suburbs of St. Marceau, and thought himself in one of the vilest hamlets in all Westphalia.

Candide had not been long at his inn before he was seized with a slight disorder owing to the fatigue he had undergone. As he wore a diamond of an enormous size on his finger, and had, among the rest of his equipage, a strong box that seemed very weighty, he soon found himself between two physicians whom he had not sent for, a number of intimate friends whom he had never seen, and who would not quit his bedside, and two female devotees who warmed his soup for him.

' I remember,' said Martin to him, ' that the first time I came to Paris I was likewise taken ill; I was very poor, and, accordingly, I had neither friends, nurses, nor physicians, and yet I did very well.'

However, by dint of purging and bleeding Candide's disorder became very serious. The priest of the parish came with all imaginable politeness to desire a note of him, payable to the bearer in the other world. Candide refused to comply with his request; but the two devotees assured him that it was a new fashion. Candide replied that he was not one that followed the fashion. Martin was for throwing the priest out of the window. The clerk swore Candide should not have Christian burial. Martin swore in his turn that he would bury the clerk alive, if he continued to plague them any longer. The dispute grew warm; Martin took him by the shoulders, and turned him out of the room, which gave great scandal, and occasioned a lawsuit.

Candide recovered; and, till he was in a condition to go abroad, had a great deal of very good company to pass the evenings with him in his chamber. They played deep. Candide was surprised to find he could never turn a trick; and Martin was not at all surprised at the matter.

Among those who did him the honours of the place, was a little spruce Abbé from Périgord, one of those insinuating, busy, fawning, impudent, accommodating fellows, that lie in wait for strangers at their arrival, tell them all the scandal of the town, and offer to minister to their pleasures at various prices. This man conducted Candide and Martin to the playhouse: they were acting a new tragedy. Candide found himself placed near a cluster of wits: this, however, did not prevent him from shedding tears at some scenes which were perfectly acted. One of these talkers said to him between the acts:

'You are greatly to blame in shedding tears; that actress plays horribly, and the man that plays with her still worse, and the piece itself is still more execrable than the representation. The author does not understand a word of Arabic, and yet he has laid his scene in Arabia; and what is more, he is a fellow who does not believe in innate ideas. To-morrow I will bring you a score of pamphlets that have been written against him.'

'Pray, Sir,' said Candide to the Abbé, 'how many theatrical pieces have you in France?'

'Five or six thousand,' replied the other.

'Indeed! that is a great number,' said Candide: 'but how many good ones may there be?'

'About fifteen or sixteen.'

'Oh! that is a great number,' said Martin.

Candide was greatly taken with an actress who performed the part of Queen Elizabeth in a dull kind of tragedy that is played sometimes.

'That actress,' said he to Martin, 'pleases me greatly; she has some sort of resemblance to Miss Cunegund. I should be very glad to pay my respects to her.'

The Abbé of Périgord offered his services to introduce him to her at her own house. Candide, who was brought up in Germany, desired to know what might be the ceremonial used on those occasions, and how a Queen of England was treated in France.

'There is a necessary distinction to be observed in these matters,' said the Abbé. 'In a country town we take them to a tavern; here in Paris, they are treated with great respect during their lifetime, provided they are handsome, and when they die, we throw their bodies upon a dunghill.'

'How,' said Candide, 'throw a queen's body upon a dunghill!'

'The gentleman is quite right,' said Martin; 'he tells you nothing but the truth. I happened to be in Paris when Mlle. Monime made her exit, as one may say, out of this world into another. She was refused what they call here the rights of sepulture; that is to say, she was denied the privilege of rotting in a churchyard by the side of all the beggars in the parish. She was buried alone by her troupe at the corner of Burgundy Street, which must certainly have shocked her extremely, as she had very exalted notions of things.'

'This is acting very impolitely,' said Candide.

'Lord!' said Martin, 'what can be said to it? It is the way of these people. Figure to yourself all the contradictions, all the inconsistencies possible, and you may meet with them in the government, the courts of justice, the churches, and the public spectacles of this odd nation.'

'Is it true,' said Candide, 'that the people of Paris are always laughing?'

'Yes,' replied the Abbé, 'but it is with anger in their hearts; they express all their complaints by loud bursts of laughter, and commit the most detestable crimes with a smile on their faces.'

'Who was that great overgrown beast,' said Candide, 'who spoke so ill to me of the piece with which I was so much affected, and of the players who gave me so much pleasure?'

'A good-for-nothing sort of a man,' answered the Abbé, 'one who gets his livelihood by abusing every new book and play; he abominates to see anyone meet with success, like eunuchs, who detest every one that possesses those powers they are deprived of; he is one of those vipers in literature who nourish themselves with their own venom; a pamphlet-monger.'

'A pamphlet-monger!' said Candide, 'what is that?'

'Why, a pamphlet-monger,' replied the Abbé, 'is a writer of pamphlets, a Fréron.'

Candide, Martin, and the Abbé of Périgord argued thus on the staircase, while they stood to see people go out of the playhouse.

'Though I am very earnest to see Miss Cunegund again,' said Candide, 'yet I have a great inclination to sup with Mlle. Clairon, for I am really much taken with her.'

The Abbé was not a person to show his face at this lady's house, which was frequented by none but the best company.

'She is engaged this evening,' said he; 'but I will do myself the honour of introducing you to a lady of quality of my acquaintance, at whose house you will see as much of the manners of Paris as if you had lived here for four years.'

Candide, who was naturally curious, suffered himself to

be conducted to this lady's house, which was in the suburb of St. Honoré. The company were engaged at faro; twelve melancholy punters held each in his hand a small pack of cards, the corners of which doubled down were so many registers of their ill fortune. A profound silence reigned throughout the assembly, a pallid dread was in the countenances of the punters, and restless anxiety in the face of him who kept the bank; and the lady of the house, who was seated next to him, observed pitilessly with lynx's eyes every parole, and sept-et-le-va as they were going, as likewise those who tallied, and made them un-double their cards with a severe exactness, though mixed with a politeness which she thought necessary not to frighten away her customers. This lady assumed the title of Marchioness of Parolignac. Her daughter, a girl of about fifteen years of age, was one of the punters, and took care to give her mamma an item, by signs, when any one of them attempted to repair the rigour of their ill fortune by a little innocent deception. The company were thus occupied, when Candide, Martin, and the Abbé made their entrance : not a creature rose to salute them, or indeed took the least notice of them, being wholly intent upon the business in hand.

' Ah ! ' said Candide, ' my lady Baroness of Thunder-ten-tronckh would have behaved more civilly.'

However, the Abbé whispered in the ear of the marchioness, who half rose, and honoured Candide with a gracious smile and Martin with a dignified inclination of her head. She then ordered a seat for Candide and a hand of cards. He lost fifty thousand francs in two rounds. After that, they supped very elegantly, and every one was astounded that Candide was not disturbed at his loss. The servants said to each other in their servants' language :

' This must be some English lord ! '

Supper was like most others of this kind in Paris; at first there was silence, then there was an indistinguishable babel of words, then jokes, most of them insipid, false reports, bad reasonings, a little political talk, and much scandal. They spoke also of new books.

' Have you seen,' said the Abbé of Périgord, ' the romance written by Monsieur Gauchat, the doctor of theology ? '

*G 936

' Yes,' replied one of the guests, ' but I had not the patience to go through it. We have a throng of impertinent writers, but all of them together do not approach Gauchat, the doctor of theology, in impertinence. I am so sated with reading these piles of vile stuff that flood upon us that I even resolved to come here and make a party at faro.'

' But what say you to Archdeacon Trublet's miscellanies ?' said the Abbé.

' Oh,' cried the Marchioness of Parolignac, ' tedious creature. What pains he is at to tell one things that all the world knows. How he labours an argument that is hardly worth the slightest consideration ! How absurdly he makes use of other people's wit ! How he mangles what he pilfers from them ! How he disgusts me ! But he will disgust me no more. It is enough to have read a few pages of the Archdeacon.'

There was at the table a person of learning and taste, who supported what the Marchioness had advanced. They next began to talk of tragedies. The lady desired to know how it came about that there were several tragedies which still continued to be played, but which were unreadable. The man of taste explained very clearly how a piece may be in some manner interesting, without having a grain of merit. He showed, in a few words, that it is not sufficient to throw together a few incidents that are to be met with in every romance, and that dazzle the spectator ; the thoughts should be new without being far-fetched ; frequently sublime, but always natural ; the author should have a thorough knowledge of the human heart and make it speak properly. He should be a complete poet, without showing an affectation of it in any of the characters of his piece ; he should be a perfect master of his language, speak it with all its purity, and with the utmost harmony, and yet not so as to make the sense a slave to the rhyme.

' Whoever,' added he, ' neglects any of these rules, though he may write two or three tragedies with tolerable success, will never be reckoned in the number of good authors. There are a few good tragedies, some are idylls, in well-written and harmonious dialogue, and others a chain of political reasonings that send one to sleep, or else pompous and high-flown amplifications that disgust rather than please. Others again are the ravings of a madman, in an uncouth style, with unmeaning flights, or long apostrophes, to the deities, for want of knowing how to address mankind; in a word, a collection of false maxims and dull commonplaces."

Candide listened to this discourse with great attention, and conceived a high opinion for the person who delivered it; and as the Marchioness had taken care to place him at her side, he took the liberty to whisper softly in her ear and ask who this person was who spoke so well.

' It is a man of letters,' replied her ladyship, ' who never plays and whom the Abbé brings with him to my house sometimes to spend an evening. He is a great judge of writing, especially in tragedy; he has composed one himself which was damned, and has written a book which was never seen out of his bookseller's shop, excepting only one copy, which he sent me with a dedication.'

' What a great man,' cried Candide, ' he is a second Pangloss.'

Then, turning towards him, ' Sir,' said he, ' you are doubtless of opinion that everything is for the best in the physical and moral world and that nothing could be otherwise than it is? '

" I, Sir,' replied the man of letters, ' I think no such thing, I assure you. I find that all in this world is set the wrong end uppermost. No one knows what is his rank, his office, nor what he does, nor what he should do; and that except for our evenings which we generally pass tolerably merrily, the rest of our time is spent in idle disputes and quarrels, Jansenists against Molinists, the Parliament against the Church, men of letters against men of letters, countries against countries, financiers against the people, wives against husbands, relations against relations. In short, there is eternal warfare.'

' Yes,' said Candide, ' and I have seen worse than all that; and yet a learned man, who had the misfortune to be hanged, taught me that everything was marvellously well, and that these evils you are speaking of were only so many shadows in a beautiful picture.'

' Your hempen sage,' said Martin, ' laughed at you. These shadows as you call them are most horrible blemishes.'

'It is men who make these blemishes,' rejoined Candide, 'and they cannot do otherwise.'

'Then it is not their fault,' added Martin.

The greater part of the gamesters, who did not understand a syllable of this discourse, continued to drink, while Martin reasoned with the learned gentleman, and Candide recounted some of his adventures to the lady of the house.

After supper, the Marchioness conducted Candide into her dressing-room, and made him sit down on a sofa.

'Well,' said she, 'are you still so violently fond of Miss Cunegund of Thunder-ten-tronckh?'

'Yes, Madam,' replied Candide.

The Marchioness said to him with a tender smile, 'You answer like a young man from Westphalia. A Frenchman would have said, "It is true, Madam, I had a great passion for Miss Cunegund, but since I have seen you, I fear I can no longer love her as I did."'

'Alas! Madam,' replied Candide, 'I'll make you what answer you please.'

'You fell in love with her, I find, in picking up her handkerchief. You shall pick up my garter.'

'With all my heart,' said Candide.

'But you must tie it on,' said the lady; and Candide tied it on.

'Look you,' said the lady, 'you are a stranger. I make some of my lovers here in Paris languish for me a fortnight, but I surrender to you the first night, because I am willing to do the honours of my country to a young Westphalian.'

The fair one having cast her eye on two large diamonds on the young stranger's finger, praised them in so earnest a manner that they passed from Candide's fingers to those of the Marchioness.

As Candide was going home with the Abbé, he felt some qualms of conscience for having been guilty of infidelity to Miss Cunegund. The Abbé shared with him in his uneasiness; he had but an inconsiderable share in the fifty thousand francs that Candide had lost at play, and in the value of the two jewels, half given, half extorted from him. His plan was to profit as much as he could from the advantages which his acquaintance with Candide could procure for him. He spoke to him much of Miss Cunegund, and Candide assured him that he would heartily ask pardon of that fair one for his infidelity to her, when he saw her at Venice.

The Abbé redoubled his civilities and seemed to interest himself warmly in everything that Candide said, did, or seemed inclined to do.

' And so, Sir, you have a *rendez-vous* at Venice ? '

' Yes, Monsieur l'Abbé,' answered Candide. ' I must indeed go and find Miss Cunegund.'

Then the pleasure he took in talking about the object he loved led him insensibly to relate, according to custom, part of his adventures with the illustrious Westphalian beauty.

' I fancy,' said the Abbé, ' Miss Cunegund has a great deal of wit, and that her letters must be very entertaining.'

' I never received any from her,' said Candide, ' for you are to consider that being kicked out of the castle on her account, I could not write to her; especially as, soon after my departure, I heard she was dead; that though I found her again, I lost her, and that I have sent a messenger to her two thousand five hundred leagues from here, and I wait here for his return with an answer from her.'

The Abbé listened attentively—and seemed a little thoughtful. He soon took leave of the two strangers, after having embraced them tenderly. The next day, immediately on waking, Candide received a letter couched in these terms :

' My dearest lover, I have been ill in this city these eight days. I have heard of your arrival and should fly to your arms, were I able to move a limb of me. I was informed of your procedure at Bordeaux. I left there the faithful Cacambo and the old woman who will soon follow me. The Governor of Buenos Ayres has taken everything from me; but I still have your heart. Come. Your presence will restore me to life or will make me die with pleasure.'

At the receipt of this charming, this unexpected letter, Candide felt the utmost joy, though the malady of his beloved Cunegund overwhelmed him with grief. Distracted between these two passions, he took his gold and his diamonds and procured a person to direct him with Martin to the house where Miss Cunegund lodged. He entered, trembling with emotion, his heart fluttered, his tongue faltered. He attempted to draw the curtain apart, and called for a light to the bedside.

'Take care,' said the servant, 'the light is unbearable to her'; and immediately she closed the curtains again.

'My beloved,' said Candide, weeping, 'how are you? If you cannot see me, at least speak to me.'

'She cannot speak,' said the servant. The lady then put from the bed a plump hand which Candide bathed with his tears; then filled with diamonds, leaving a purse full of gold on the arm-chair.

In the midst of his transports there arrived an officer, followed by the Abbé of Périgord and a file of musketeers.

'There,' said he, 'are the two suspected foreigners.'

He had them seized forthwith and bade the soldiers carry them off to prison.

'Travellers are not treated in this manner in El Dorado,' said Candide.

'I am more of a Manichæan now than ever,'' said Martin.

'But pray, good Sir, where are you taking us?' asked Candide.

'To a dungeon,' said the officer.

Martin having recovered his calm judged that the lady who pretended to be Cunegund was a cheat, that the Abbé of Périgord was a sharper, who had imposed upon Candide's simplicity so quickly as he could, and the officer another knave whom they might easily get rid of.

Candide, following the advice of his friend Martin, and burning with impatience to see the real Cunegund, rather than be obliged to appear at a court of justice, proposed to the officer to make him a present of three small diamonds, each of them worth three thousand pistoles.

'Ah, Sir,' said this understrapper of justice, 'had you committed ever so much villainy, this would render you the honestest man living in my eyes. Three diamonds, worth three thousand pistoles. Why, my dear Sir, so far from leading you to jail, I would lose my life to serve you. There are orders to arrest all strangers, but leave it to me. I have a brother at Dieppe in Normandy. I myself will conduct you thither, and if you have a diamond left to give him, he will take as much care of you as I myself should.'

' But why,' said Candide, ' do they arrest all strangers ? '

The Abbé of Périgord answered that it was because a poor devil of the province of Atrébatie heard somebody tell foolish stories, and this induced him to commit a parricide; not such a one as that in the month of May, 1610, but such as that in the month of December in the year 1594, and such as many that have been perpetrated in other months and years by other poor devils who had heard foolish stories.

The officer then explained to them what the Abbé meant.

' Monsters,' exclaimed Candide. ' Is it possible that such horrors should pass among a people who are continually singing and dancing? Is there no immediate means of flying this abominable country, where monkeys provoke tigers ? I have seen bears in my country, but men I have beheld nowhere but in El Dorado. In the name of God, Sir,' said he to the officer, ' do me the kindness to conduct me to Venice, where I am to wait upon Miss Cunegund.'

' I cannot conduct you further than Lower Normandy,' said the officer.

So saying, he ordered Candide's irons to be struck off and sent his followers about their business, after which he conducted Candide and Martin to Dieppe, and left them to the care of his brother. There happened just then to be a small Dutch ship in the roads. The Norman, whom the other three diamonds had converted into the most obliging, serviceable being that ever breathed, took care to see Candide and his attendants safe on board the vessel, that was just ready to sail for Portsmouth in England. This was not the nearest way to Venice indeed; but Candide thought himself escaped out of hell, and did not in the least doubt but he should quickly find an opportunity of resuming his voyage to Venice.

CHAPTER XXIII

CANDIDE AND MARTIN TOUCH UPON THE ENGLISH COAST;
WHAT THEY SAW THERE

'Ah Pangloss! Pangloss! Ah, Martin! Martin! Ah, my dear Miss Cunegund! What sort of a world is this?' Thus exclaimed Candide, as soon as he had got on board the Dutch ship.

'Why, something very foolish, and very abominable,' said Martin.

'You are acquainted with England,' said Candide; 'are they as great fools in that country, as in France?'

'Yes, but in a different manner,' answered Martin. 'You know that these two nations are at war about a few acres of snow in the neighbourhood of Canada, and that they have expended much greater sums in the contest than all Canada is worth. To say exactly whether there are a greater number fit to be inhabitants of a mad-house in the one country than the other, exceeds the limits of my imperfect capacity; I know, in general, that the people we are going to visit, are of a very dark and gloomy disposition.'

As they were chatting thus together, they arrived at Portsmouth. The shore, on each side of the harbour, was lined with a multitude of people, whose eyes were steadfastly fixed on a lusty man, who was kneeling down on the deck of one of the men of war, with his eyes bound. Opposite to this personage stood four soldiers, each of whom shot three bullets into his skull, with all the composure imaginable; and when it was done, the whole company went away perfectly well satisfied.

'What the devil is all this for?' said Candide; 'and what demon lords it thus over all the world?'

He then asked who was that lusty man who had been sent out of the world with so much ceremony, and he received for answer, that it was an admiral.

'And, pray,' he said, 'why do you put your admiral to death?'

'Because he did not put a sufficient number of his fellow

creatures to death. You must know, he had an engagement with a French admiral, and it has been proved against
him that he was not near enough to his antagonist.'

'But,' replied Candide, 'the French admiral must have
been as far from him.'

'There is no doubt of that; but in this country it is
found requisite, now and then, to put one admiral to death,
in order to spirit up the others.'

Candide was so shocked at what he saw and heard that he
would not set foot on shore, but made a bargain with
the Dutch skipper (were he even to rob him like the captain
of Surinam) to carry him directly to Venice.

The skipper was ready in two days. They sailed along
the coast of France, and passed within sight of Lisbon,
at which Candide trembled. From thence they proceeded
to the straits, entered the Mediterranean, and at length
arrived at Venice.

'God be praised,' said Candide, embracing Martin,
'this is the place where I am to behold my beloved Cunegund once again. I can rely on Cacambo, like another
self. All is well, all very well, all as well as possible.'

CHAPTER XXIV

OF PACQUETTE AND FRIAR GIROFLÉE

UPON their arrival at Venice, he went in search of Cacambo
at every inn and coffee-house, and among all the ladies of
pleasure; but could hear nothing of him. He sent every
day to inquire of every ship and every vessel that came in:
still no news of Cacambo.

'It is strange!' said he to Martin, 'very strange!
that I should have had time to sail from Surinam to Bordeaux; to travel from thence to Paris, to Dieppe, to
Portsmouth; to sail along the coast of Portugal and Spain,
and up the Mediterranean, to spend some months in Venice;
and that my lovely Cunegund should not have arrived.
Instead of her, I only met with a Parisian impostor, and a
rascally Abbé of Périgord. Cunegund is actually dead,

and I have nothing to do but to follow her. Alas! how much better would it have been for me to have remained in the paradise of El Dorado than to have returned to this cursed Europe! You are in the right, my dear Martin; you are certainly in the right; all is misery and deceit.'

He fell into a deep melancholy, and neither went to the opera in vogue, nor partook of any of the diversions of the Carnival; not a woman caused him even a moment's temptation.

Martin said to him, ' Upon my word, I think you are very simple to imagine that a rascally valet, with five or six millions in his pocket, would go in search of your mistress to the further end of the world, and bring her to Venice to meet you. If he finds her, he will take her for himself; if he does not, he will take another. Let me advise you to forget your valet Cacambo, and your mistress Cunegund.'

Martin's speech was not consoling. Candide's melancholy increased, and Martin never left proving to him that there is very little virtue or happiness in this world; except, perhaps, in El Dorado where hardly anybody can gain admittance.

While they were disputing on this important subject, and still expecting Miss Cunegund, Candide perceived a young Theatine friar in St. Mark's Place, with a girl under his arm. The Theatine looked fresh-coloured, plump, and vigorous; his eyes sparkled; his air and gait were bold and lofty. The girl was very pretty, and was singing a song; and every now and then gave her Theatine an amorous ogle and wantonly pinched his ruddy cheeks.

' You will at least allow,' said Candide to Martin, ' that these two are happy. Hitherto I have met with none but unfortunate people in the whole habitable globe, except in El Dorado; but, as to this couple, I would venture to lay a wager they are happy.'

' Done,' said Martin; ' they are not, for what you will.'

' Well, we have only to ask them to dine with us,' said Candide, ' and you will see whether I am mistaken or not.'

Thereupon he accosted them, and with great politeness invited them to his inn to eat some macaroni, with Lombard partridges and caviare, and to drink a bottle of Montepulciano, Lacrima Christi, Cyprus and Samos wine. The girl blushed; the Theatine accepted the invitation, and she followed him, eyeing Candide every now and then with a mixture of suprise and confusion, while the tears stole down her cheeks. No sooner did she enter his apartment than she cried out:

'How, Mr. Candide, have you quite forgotten poor Pacquette? Do you not know her again?'

Candide, who had not regarded her with any degree of attention before, being wholly occupied with the thoughts of his dear Cunegund, exclaimed:

'Ah! is it you, child? Was it you that reduced Dr. Pangloss to that fine condition I saw him in?'

'Alas! Sir,' answered Pacquette, 'it was I, indeed. I find you are acquainted with everything; and I have been informed of all the misfortunes that happened to the whole family of my lady Baroness and the fair Cunegund. But I can safely swear to you that my lot was no less deplorable; I was innocence itself when you saw me last. A cordelier, who was my confessor, easily seduced me; the consequences proved terrible. I was obliged to leave the castle some time after the Baron kicked you out by the backside from there; and if a famous surgeon had not taken compassion on me, I had been a dead woman. Gratitude obliged me to live with him some time as a mistress: his wife, who was a very devil for jealousy, beat me unmercifully every day. Oh! she was a perfect fury. The doctor himself was the most ugly of all mortals, and I the most wretched creature existing, to be continually beaten for a man whom I did not love. You are sensible, Sir, how dangerous it was for an ill-natured woman to be married to a physician. Incensed at the behaviour of his wife, he one day gave her so affectionate a remedy for a slight cold she had caught, that she died in less than two hours in most dreadful convulsions. Her relations prosecuted the husband, who was obliged to fly, and I was sent to prison. My innocence would not have saved me, if I had not been tolerably handsome. The judge gave me my liberty on condition he should succeed the doctor. However, I was soon supplanted by a rival, turned off without a farthing, and obliged to continue the abominable trade which you men think so pleasing, but which to us unhappy creatures is the most dreadful of all sufferings. At length I came to follow the business at Venice. Ah! Sir, did you but know what it is to be obliged to lie indifferently with old tradesmen, with counsellors, with monks, gon- doliers, and abbés; to be exposed to all their insolence and abuse; to find it often necessary to borrow a petticoat, only that it may be taken up by some disagreeable wretch; to be robbed by one gallant of what we get from another; to be subject to the extortions of civil magistrates; and to have for ever before one's eyes the prospect of old age, a hospital, or a dunghill, you would conclude that I am one of the most unhappy wretches breathing.'

Thus did Pacquette unbosom herself to honest Candide in his closet, in the presence of Martin, who took occasion to say to him:

'You see I have half won the wager already.'

Friar Giroflée was all this time in the parlour refreshing himself with a glass or two of wine till dinner was ready.

'But,' said Candide to Pacquette, 'you looked so gay and content, when I met you, you were singing, and caressing the Theatine with so much fondness that I absolutely thought you as happy as you say you are now miserable.'

'Ah! dear Sir,' said Pacquette, 'this is one of the miseries of the trade; yesterday I was stripped and beaten by an officer; yet to-day I must appear good-humoured and gay to please a friar.'

Candide was convinced, and acknowledged that Martin was in the right. They sat down to table with Pacquette and the Theatine; the entertainment was very agreeable, and towards the end they began to converse together with some freedom.

'Father,' said Candide, to the friar, 'you seem to me to enjoy a state of happiness that even kings might envy; joy and health are painted in your countenance. You have a tight pretty wench to divert you; and you seem to be perfectly well contented with your condition as a Theatine.'

'Faith, Sir,' said Friar Giroflée, 'I wish with all my soul the Theatines were every one of them at the bottom of the sea. I have been tempted a thousand times to set fire to the convent and go and turn Turk. My parents obliged me, at the age of fifteen, to put on this detestable habit only to increase the fortune of an elder brother of mine, whom God confound! Jealousy, discord, and fury reside in our convent. It is true, I have preached some paltry sermons, by which I have got a little money, half of which the prior robs me of, and the remainder helps to pay my girls; but, at night, when I go hence to my convent, I am ready to dash my brains against the walls of the dormitory; and this is the case with all the rest of our fraternity.'

Martin, turning towards Candide, with his usual indifference, said, 'Well, what think you now? Have I won the wager entirely?'

Candide gave two thousand piastres to Pacquette, and a thousand to Friar Giroflée, saying, 'I will answer that this will make them happy.'

'I am not of your opinion,' said Martin; 'perhaps this money will only make them much more wretched.'

'Be that as it may,' said Candide, 'one thing comforts me; I see that one often meets with those whom we expected never to see again; so that, perhaps, as I have found my red sheep and Pacquette, I may be lucky enough to find Miss Cunegund also.'

'I wish,' said Martin, 'she one day may make you happy, but I doubt it much.'

'You are very hard of belief,' said Candide.

'It is because,' said Martin, 'I have seen the world.'

'Observe those gondoliers,' said Candide; 'are they not perpetually singing?'

'You do not see them,' answered Martin, 'at home with their wives and brats. The doge has his chagrin, gondoliers theirs. Nevertheless, in the main, I look upon the gondolier's life as preferable to that of the doge; but the difference is so trifling that it is not worth the trouble of examining into.'

'I have heard great talk,' said Candide, 'of the senator Pococurante, who lives in that fine house at the Brenta, where, they say, he entertains foreigners in the most polite manner. They claim that this man is a perfect stranger to uneasiness.'

'I should be glad to see so extraordinary a being,' said Martin.

Candide thereupon sent a messenger to Signor Pococurante, desiring permission to wait on him the next day.

CHAPTER XXV

CANDIDE AND MARTIN PAY A VISIT TO SIGNOR POCOCURANTE, A NOBLE VENETIAN

CANDIDE and his friend Martin went in a gondola on the Brenta, and arrived at the palace of the noble Pococurante : the gardens were laid out in an elegant taste, and adorned with beautiful marble statues ; his palace was architecturally magnificent. The master of the house, who was a man of sixty, and very rich, received our two travellers with great politeness, but without much ceremony, which somewhat disconcerted Candide, but was not at all displeasing to Martin.

First, two very pretty girls, neatly dressed, brought in chocolate, which was extremely well frothed. Candide could not help praising their beauty and graceful carriage.

'The creatures are well enough,' said the senator ; 'I make them lie with me sometimes, for I am heartily tired of the women of the town, their coquetry, their jealousy, their quarrels, their humours, their meannesses, their pride, and their folly ; I am weary of making sonnets, or of paying for sonnets to be made on them ; but, after all, these two girls begin to grow very indifferent to me.'

After having refreshed himself, Candide walked into a large gallery, where he was struck with the sight of a fine collection of paintings. He asked what master had painted the two first.

'They are Raphael's,' answered the senator. 'I gave a great deal of money for them some years ago, purely out of conceit, as they were said to be the finest pieces in Italy ; but I cannot say they please me : the colouring is dark and heavy ; the figures do not swell nor come out enough, and the drapery has no resemblance to the actual material. In short, notwithstanding the encomiums lavished upon them, they are not, in my opinion, a true representation of nature. I approve of no paintings but where I think I behold nature herself; and there are none of that kind to be met with. I have what is called a fine collection, but I take no manner of delight in them.'

While dinner was getting ready, Pococurante ordered a concert. Candide praised the music to the skies.

'This noise,' said the noble Venetian, 'may amuse one for a little time, but if it was to last above half an hour, it would grow tiresome to everybody, though perhaps no one would care to own it. Music is become the art of executing what is difficult; now, whatever is difficult cannot be long pleasing. I believe I might take more pleasure in an opera, if they had not made such a monster of it as perfectly shocks me; and I am amazed how people can bear to see wretched tragedies set to music; where the scenes are contrived for no other purpose than to lug in, as it were by the ears, three or four ridiculous songs, to give a favourite actress an opportunity of exhibiting her pipe. Let who will, or can, die away in raptures at the trills of an eunuch quavering the majestic part of Cæsar or Cato, and strutting in a foolish manner upon the stage; for my part, I have long ago renounced these paltry entertainments which constitute the glory of modern Italy, and are so dearly purchased by crowned heads.'

Candide opposed these sentiments; but he did it in a discreet manner; as for Martin, he was entirely of the old senator's opinion.

Dinner being served they sat down to table, and after a very hearty repast returned to the library. Candide, observing Homer richly bound, commended the noble Venetian's taste.

'This,' said he, 'is a book that was once the delight of the great Pangloss, the best philosopher in Germany.'

'Homer is no favourite of mine,' answered Pococurante, very coolly : 'I was made to believe once that I took a pleasure in reading him; but his continual repetitions of battles have all such a resemblance with each other; his gods that are for ever in a hurry and bustle, without ever doing anything; his Helen, that is the cause of the war, and yet hardly acts in the whole performance; his Troy, that holds out so long, without being taken: in short, all these things together make the poem very insipid to me. I have asked some learned men, whether they are not in reality as much tired as myself with reading this poet: those who were sincere assured me that he had made them fall asleep; and yet, that they could not well avoid giving him a place in their libraries as a monument of antiquity or like those rusty medals which are of no use in commerce.'

'But your Excellency does not surely form the same opinion of Virgil?' said Candide.

'Why, I grant,' replied Pococurante, 'that the second, third, fourth, and sixth book of his *Æneid* are excellent; but as for his pious Æneas, his strong Cloanthus, his friendly Achates, his boy Ascanius, his silly king Latinus, his ill-bred Amata, his insipid Lavinia, I think there cannot in nature be anything more flat and disagreeable. I must confess, I prefer Tasso far beyond him; nay, even that sleepy tale-teller Ariosto.'

'May I take the liberty to ask if you do not receive great pleasure from reading Horace?' said Candide.

'There are maxims in this writer,' replied Pococurante, 'from whence a man of the world may reap some benefit; and the short and forceful measure of the verse makes them more easily to be retained in the memory. But I see nothing extraordinary in his journey to Brundisium, and his account of his bad dinner; nor in his dirty low quarrel between one Rupilius, whose words, as he expresses it, were full of poisonous filth, and another, whose language was dipped in vinegar. His indelicate verses against old women and witches have frequently given me great offence; nor can I discover the great merit of his telling his friend Mæcenas that if he will but rank him in the class of lyric poets, his lofty head shall touch the stars. Ignorant readers are apt to praise everything by the lump in a writer of reputation. For my part, I read only to please myself. I like nothing but what makes for my purpose.'

Candide, who had been brought up with a notion of never making use of his own judgment, was astonished at what he had heard; but Martin found there was a good deal of reason in the senator's remarks.

'Oh! here is a Cicero,' said Candide: 'this great man, I fancy, you are never tired of reading?'

'Indeed, I never read him at all,' replied Pococurante. 'What a deuce is it to me whether he pleads for Rabirius or Cluentius? I try causes enough myself. I had once some liking for his philosophical works; but when I found he doubted of everything, I thought I knew as much as he, and had no need of a guide to learn ignorance.'

'Ha!' cried Martin, 'here are fourscore volumes of the memoirs of the Academy of Science; perhaps there may be something valuable in them.'

'Yes,' answered Pococurante; 'so there might if any one of the compilers of this rubbish had only invented the art of pin-making: but all these volumes are filled with mere chimerical systems without one single article conducive to real utility.'

'I see a prodigious number of plays,' said Candide, 'in Italian, Spanish, and French.'

'Yes,' replied the Venetian; 'there are I think three thousand, and not three dozen of them good for anything. As to these huge volumes of divinity, and those enormous collections of sermons, they are altogether not worth one single page in Seneca; and I fancy you will readily believe that neither myself, nor any one else, ever looks into them.'

Martin noticed some shelves filled with English books.

'I fancy,' he said, 'that a republican must be highly delighted with those books, which are most of them written with a noble spirit of freedom.'

'It is noble to write as we think,' said Pococurante; 'it is the privilege of humanity. Throughout Italy we write only what we do not think; and the present inhabitants of the country of the Cæsars and Antoninus's dare not acquire a single idea without the permission of a Dominican friar. I should be enamoured of the spirit of the English nation, did it not utterly frustrate the good effects it would produce, by passion and the spirit of party.'

Candide, seeing a Milton, asked the senator if he did not think that author a great man.

'Who?' said Pococurante sharply; 'that barbarian

who writes a tedious commentary in ten books of rumbling verse, on the first chapter of Genesis? that slovenly imitator of the Greeks, who disfigures the creation, by making the Messiah take a pair of compasses from heaven's armoury to plan the world; whereas Moses represented the Deity as producing the whole universe by his fiat? Can I, think you, have any esteem for a writer who has spoiled Tasso's hell and the devil? who transforms Lucifer sometimes into a toad, and, at others, into a pigmy? who makes him say the same thing over again a hundred times? who metamorphoses him into a school-divine? and who, by an absurdly serious imitation of Ariosto's comic invention of fire-arms, represents the devils and angels cannonading each other in heaven? Neither I nor any other Italian can possibly take pleasure in such melancholy reveries; but the marriage of Sin and Death, and snakes issuing from the womb of the former, are enough to make any person sick that is not lost to all sense of delicacy, while his long description of a lazar-house is fit only for a gravedigger. This obscene, whimsical and disagreeable poem met with neglect at its first publication; and I only treat the author now as he was treated in his own country by his contemporaries.'

Candide was sensibly grieved at this speech, as he had a great respect for Homer and was very fond of Milton.

' Alas ! ' said he softly to Martin, ' I am afraid this man holds our German poets in great contempt.'

' There would be no such great harm in that,' said Martin.

' O what a surprising man ! ' said Candide, still to himself ; ' what a prodigious genius is this Pococurante ! nothing can please him.'

After finishing their survey of the library, they went down into the garden, when Candide commended the several beauties that offered themselves to his view.

' I know nothing upon earth laid out in such bad taste,' said Pococurante ; ' everything about it is childish and trifling ; but I shall have another laid out to-morrow upon a nobler plan.'

As soon as our two travellers had taken leave of his Excellency, Candide said to Martin :

'I hope you will own that this man is the happiest of all mortals, for he is above everything he possesses.'

'But do not you see,' answered Martin, 'that he likewise dislikes everything he possesses? It was an observation of Plato, long since, that those are not the best stomachs that reject, without distinction, all sorts of aliments.'

'True,' said Candide, 'but still there must certainly be a pleasure in criticizing everything, and in perceiving faults where others think they see beauties.'

'That is,' replied Martin, 'there is a pleasure in having no pleasure.'

'Well, well,' said Candide, 'I find that I shall be the only happy man at last, when I am blessed with the sight of my dear Cunegund.'

'It is good to hope,' said Martin.

In the meanwhile, days and weeks passed away, and no news of Cacambo. Candide was so overwhelmed with grief, that he did not reflect on the behaviour of Pacquette and Friar Giroflée, who never stayed to return him thanks for the presents he had so generously made them.

CHAPTER XXVI

CANDIDE AND MARTIN SUP WITH SIX STRANGERS; AND WHO THEY WERE

ONE evening when Candide, with his attendant Martin, were going to sit down to supper with some foreigners who lodged in the same inn, a man, with a face the colour of soot, came behind him, and taking him by the arm, said:

'Hold yourself in readiness to go along with us, be sure you do not fail.'

He turned and beheld Cacambo. Nothing but the sight of Cunegund could have given greater joy and surprise. He was almost beside himself with joy. After embracing this dear friend, he said:

'Cunegund must be here? Where, where is she? Carry me to her this instant, that I may die with joy in her presence.'

'Cunegund is not here,' answered Cacambo; 'she is at Constantinople.'

'Good heavens, at Constantinople! but no matter if she was in China, I would fly thither. Let us be gone.'

'We depart after supper,' said Cacambo. 'I cannot at present stay to say anything more to you; I am a slave, and my master waits for me; I must go and attend him at table: but say not a word, only get your supper, and hold yourself in readiness.'

Candide, divided between joy and grief, charmed to have thus met with his faithful agent again, and surprised to hear he was a slave, his heart palpitating, his senses confused, but full of the hopes of recovering his mistress, sat down to table with Martin, who beheld all these scenes with great unconcern, and with six strangers who had come to spend the carnival at Venice.

Cacambo waited at table upon one of these strangers. When supper was nearly over, he drew near to his master, and whispered him in the ear:

'Sire, your Majesty may go when you please, the ship is ready.'

Having said these words, he left the room. The guests, surprised at what they had heard, looked at each other without speaking a word; when another servant drawing near to his master, in like manner said:

'Sire, your Majesty's post-chaise is at Padua, and the bark is ready.'

His master made him a sign, and he instantly withdrew. The company all stared at each other again, and the general astonishment was increased. A third servant then approached another of the strangers, and said:

'Sire, if your Majesty will be advised by me, you will not stay any longer in this place; I will go and get everything ready'—and he instantly disappeared.

Candide and Martin then took it for granted that this was some of the diversions of the carnival, and that these were characters in masquerade. Then a fourth domestic said to the fourth stranger:

'Your Majesty may set out when you please.' Saying this, he went away like the rest.

A fifth valet said the same to a fifth master. But the

sixth domestic spoke in a different style to the person on whom he waited, and who sat next to Candide.

' Troth, Sir,' said he, ' they will trust your Majesty no longer, nor myself neither; and we may both of us chance to be sent to gaol this very night; and therefore I shall take care of myself, and so adieu.'

The servants being all gone, the six strangers, with Candide and Martin, remained in a profound silence. At length Candide broke it by saying :

' Gentlemen, this is a very singular joke, upon my word; why, how came you all to be kings? For my part, I own frankly, that neither my friend Martin here nor myself have any claim to royalty.'

Cacambo's master then began, with great gravity, to deliver himself thus in Italian :

' I am not joking in the least, my name is Achmet III. I was Grand Sultan for many years; I dethroned my brother, my nephew dethroned me, my viziers lost their heads, and I am condemned to end my days in the old seraglio. My nephew, the Grand Sultan Mahmud, gives me permission to travel sometimes for my health, and I am come to spend the carnival at Venice.'

A young man who sat by Achmet spoke next, and said : ' My name is Ivan. I was once Emperor of all the Russias, but was dethroned in my cradle. My parents were confined, and I was brought up in a prison; yet I am sometimes allowed to travel, though always with persons to keep a guard over me, and I am come to spend the carnival at Venice.'

The third said :

' I am Charles Edward, King of England; my father has renounced his right to the throne in my favour. I have fought in defence of my rights, and eight hundred of my followers have had their hearts taken out of their bodies alive and thrown in their faces. I have myself been confined in a prison. I am going to Rome to visit the King my father, who was dethroned as well as myself and my grandfather; and I am come to spend the carnival at Venice.'

The fourth spoke thus :

' I am the King of Poland; the fortune of war has stripped

me of my hereditary dominions. My father experienced the same vicissitudes of fate. I resign myself to the will of Providence, in the same manner as Sultan Achmet, the Emperor Ivan, and King Charles Edward, whom God long preserve; and I am come to spend the carnival at Venice.'

The fifth said:

' I am King of Poland also. I have twice lost my kingdom; but Providence has given me other dominions, where I have done more good than all the Sarmatian kings put together were ever able to do on the banks of the Vistula: I resign myself likewise to Providence; and am come to spend the carnival at Venice.'

It now came to the sixth monarch's turn to speak.

' Gentlemen,' said he, ' I am not so great a prince as the rest of you, it is true; but I am, however, a crowned head. I am Theodore, elected King of Corsica. I have had the title of Majesty, and am now hardly treated with common civility. I have coined money, and am not now worth a single ducat. I have had two secretaries of state, and am now without a valet. I was once seated on a throne, and since that have lain upon a truss of straw in a common gaol in London, and I very much fear I shall meet with the same fate here in Venice, where I come, like your Majesties, to divert myself at the carnival.'

The other five kings listened to this speech with great attention; it excited their compassion; each of them made the unhappy Theodore a present of twenty sequins to get clothes and shirts, and Candide gave him a diamond worth just an hundred times that sum.

' Who can this private person be,' said the five kings, ' who is able to give, and has actually given, a hundred times as much as any of us? Are you, Sir, also a king?'

' No, gentlemen, and I have no wish to be one.'

Just as they rose from table, in came four Serene Highnesses who had also been stripped of their territories by the fortune of war, and were come to spend the remainder of the carnival at Venice. Candide took no manner of notice of them; for his thoughts were wholly employed on his voyage to Constantinople, whither he intended to go in search of his beloved Cunegund.

CHAPTER XXVII

CANDIDE'S VOYAGE TO CONSTANTINOPLE

THE trusty Cacambo had already engaged the captain of the Turkish ship that was to carry Sultan Achmet back to Constantinople, to take Candide and Martin on board. Accordingly, they both embarked, after paying their obeisance to his miserable Highness. As they were going on board, Candide said to Martin :

' You see we supped in company with six dethroned kings, and to one of them I gave charity. Perhaps there may be a great many other princes still more unfortunate. For my part, I have lost only a hundred sheep, and am now going to fly to the arms of Cunegund. My dear Martin, I must insist on it, that Pangloss was in the right. All is for the best.'

' I wish it may be,' said Martin.

' But this was an odd adventure we met with at Venice. I do not think there ever was an instance before, of six dethroned monarchs supping together at a public inn.'

' This is no more extraordinary,' said Martin, ' than most of what has happened to us. It is a very common thing for kings to be dethroned ; and as for our having the honour to sup with six of them, it is a mere accident, not deserving our attention. What does it matter with whom one sups, provided one has good fare ? '

As soon as Candide set his foot on board the vessel, he flew to his old friend and servant Cacambo ; and throwing his arms about his neck, embraced him with transports of joy.

' Well,' said he, ' what news of Cunegund ? Does she still continue the paragon of beauty ? Does she love me still ? How is she ? You have, doubtless, purchased a palace for her at Constantinople ? '

' My dear master,' replied Cacambo, ' Cunegund washes dishes on the banks of the Propontis, in the house of a prince who has very few to wash. She is at present a slave in the family of an ancient sovereign, named Ragotsky, whom the Grand Turk allows three crowns a day to maintain him in his exile; but the most melancholy circumstance of all is, that she has lost her beauty and turned horribly ugly.'

'Ugly or handsome,' said Candide, 'I am a man of honour; and, as such, am obliged to love her still. But how could she possibly have been reduced to so abject a condition, when I sent five or six millions to her by you?'

'Lord bless me,' said Cacambo, 'was not I obliged to give two millions to Senor Don Fernando d'Ibaraa y Figueora y Mascarenas y Lampourdos y Souza, Governor of Buenos Ayres, for liberty to take Miss Cunegund away with me? and then did not a brave fellow of a pirate very gallantly strip us of all the rest? and then did not this same pirate carry us with him to Cape Matapan, to Milo, to Nicaria, to Samos, to Petra, to the Dardanelles, to Marmora, to Scutari? Cunegund and the old woman are now servants to the prince I have told you of; and I myself am slave to the dethroned Sultan.'

'What a chain of terrible calamities!' exclaimed Candide. 'But, after all, I have still some diamonds left, with which I can easily procure Cunegund's liberty. It is a pity she is grown so very ugly.'

Then turning to Martin, 'What think you, friend,' said he, 'whose condition is most to be pitied, the Emperor Achmet's, the Emperor Ivan's, King Charles Edward's, or mine?'

'Faith, I cannot resolve your question,' said Martin, 'unless I had been in the breasts of you all.'

'Ah!' cried Candide, 'was Pangloss here now, he would have known, and satisfied me at once.'

'I know not,' said Martin, 'in what balance your Pangloss could have weighed the misfortunes of mankind, and have set a just estimation on their sufferings. All that I pretend to know of the matter is that there are millions of men on the earth whose conditions are an hundred times more pitiable than those of King Charles Edward, the Emperor Ivan, or Sultan Achmet.'

'Why, that may be,' answered Candide.

In a few days they reached the Bosphorus; and the first thing Candide did was to pay a high ransom for Cacambo: then, without losing time, he and his companions went on board a galley, in order to search for his

Cunegund, on the banks of the Propontis, notwithstanding she was grown so ugly.

There were two slaves among the crew of the galley, who rowed very ill, and to whose bare backs the master of the vessel frequently applied a lash of oxhide. Candide, from natural sympathy, looked at these two slaves more attentively than at any of the rest, and drew near them with a look of pity. Their features, though greatly disfigured, appeared to him to bear a strong resemblance with those of Pangloss and the unhappy Baron Jesuit, Miss Cunegund's brother. This idea affected him with grief and compassion : he examined them more attentively than before.

'In troth,' said he, turning to Martin, 'if I had not seen my master Pangloss fairly hanged, and had not myself been unlucky enough to run the Baron through the body, I could believe these are they rowing in the galley.'

No sooner had Candide uttered the names of the Baron and Pangloss than the two slaves gave a great cry, ceased rowing, and let fall their oars out of their hands. The master of the vessel, seeing this, ran up to them, and redoubled the discipline of the lash.

'Hold, hold,' cried Candide, 'I will give you what money you ask for these two persons.'

'Good heavens ! it is Candide,' said one of the men.

'Candide !' cried the other.

'Do I dream,' said Candide, 'or am I awake? Am I actually on board this galley? Is this my lord Baron, whom I killed? and that my master Pangloss, whom I saw hanged?'

'It is I ! it is I !' cried they both together.

'What ! is this your great philosopher?' said Martin.

'My dear Sir,' said Candide to the master of the galley, 'how much do you ask for the ransom of the Baron of Thunder-ten-tronckh, who is one of the first barons of the empire, and of Mr. Pangloss, the most profound metaphysician in Germany?'

'Why then, Christian cur,' replied the Turkish captain, 'since these two dogs of Christian slaves are barons and metaphysicians, who no doubt are of high rank in their own country, thou shalt give me fifty thousand sequins.'

' You shall have them, Sir : carry me back as quick as thought to Constantinople, and you shall receive the money immediately. No! carry me first to Miss Cunegund.'

The captain, upon Candide's first proposal, had already tacked about, and he made the crew apply their oars so effectively that the vessel flew through the water quicker than a bird cleaves the air.

Candide bestowed a thousand embraces on the Baron and Pangloss.

' And so then, my dear Baron, I did not kill you? and you, my dear Pangloss, are come to life again after your hanging? But how came you slaves on board a Turkish galley? '

' And is it true that my dear sister is in this country? ' said the Baron.

' Yes,' said Cacambo.

' And do I once again behold my dear Candide? ' said Pangloss.

Candide presented Martin and Cacambo to them; they embraced each other, and all spoke together. The galley flew like lightning, and now they were got back to the port. Candide instantly sent for a Jew, to whom he sold for fifty thousand sequins a diamond richly worth one hundred thousand, though the fellow swore to him all the time, by Abraham, that he gave him the most he could possibly afford. He no sooner got the money into his hands than he paid it down for the ransom of the Baron and Pangloss. The latter flung himself at the feet of his deliverer, and bathed him with his tears : the former thanked him with a gracious nod, and promised to return him the money at the first opportunity.

' But is it possible,' said he, ' that my sister should be in Turkey? '

' Nothing is more possible,' answered Cacambo; ' for she scours the dishes in the house of a Transylvanian prince.'

Candide sent directly for two Jews, and sold more diamonds to them; and then he set out with his companions in another galley, to deliver Cunegund from slavery.

CHAPTER XXVIII

WHAT BEFELL CANDIDE, CUNEGUND, PANGLOSS, MARTIN, &c.

' Pardon,' said Candide to the Baron; ' once more let me intreat your pardon, Reverend Father, for running you through the body.'

' Say no more about it,' replied the Baron; ' I was a little too hasty I must own : but as you seem to be anxious to know by what accident I came to be a slave on board the galley where you saw me, I will inform you. After I had been cured of the wound you gave me, by the apothecary of the College, I was attacked and carried off by a party of Spanish troops, who clapped me up in prison in Buenos Ayres, at the very time my sister was setting out from there. I asked leave to return to Rome, to the general of my Order, who appointed me chaplain to the French Ambassador at Constantinople. I had not been a week in my new office, when I happened to meet one evening with a young Icoglan, extremely handsome and well made. The weather was very hot; the young man had an inclination to bathe. I took the opportunity to bathe likewise. I did not know it was a crime for a Christian to be found naked in company with a young Turk. A cadi ordered me to receive a hundred blows on the soles of my feet, and sent me to the galleys. I do not believe that there was ever an act of more flagrant injustice. But I would fain know how my sister came to be a scullion to a Transylvanian prince who has taken refuge among the Turks ? '

' But how happens it that I behold you again, my dear Pangloss ? ' said Candide.

' It is true,' answered Pangloss, ' you saw me hanged, though I ought properly to have been burnt ; but you may remember that it rained extremely hard when they were going to roast me. The storm was so violent that they found it impossible to light the fire ; so they hanged me because they could do no better. A surgeon purchased my body, carried it home, and prepared to dissect me. He began by making a crucial incision from my navel to the clavicle. It is impossible for any one to have been more lamely hanged than I had been. The executioner of the Holy Inquisition was a subdeacon, and knew how to burn people very well, but as for hanging, he was a novice at it, being quite out of the way of his practice; the cord being wet, and not slipping properly, the noose did not join. In short, I still continued to breathe; the crucial incision made me scream to such a degree that my surgeon fell flat upon his back; and imagining it was the devil he was dissecting, ran away, and in his fright tumbled downstairs. His wife hearing the noise flew from the next room, and, seeing me stretched upon the table with my crucial incision, was still more terrified than her husband. She took to her heels and fell over him. When they had a little recovered themselves, I heard her say to her husband, "My dear, how could you think of dissecting an heretic? Don't you know that the devil is always in them? I'll run directly to a priest to come and drive the evil spirit out." I trembled from head to foot at hearing her talk in this manner, and exerted what little strength I had left to cry out, "Have mercy on me!" At length the Portuguese barber took courage, sewed up my wound, and his wife nursed me; and I was upon my legs in a fortnight's time. The barber got me a place as lackey to a Knight of Malta who was going to Venice; but finding my master had no money to pay me my wages, I entered into the service of a Venetian merchant, and went with him to Constantinople.

' One day I happened to enter a mosque, where I saw no one but an old imam and a very pretty young female devotee, who was saying her prayers; her neck was quite bare, and in her bosom she had a beautiful nosegay of tulips, roses, anemones, ranunculuses, hyacinths, and auriculas. She let fall her nosegay. I ran immediately to take it up, and presented it to her with a most respectful bow. I was so long in delivering it, that the imam began to be angry; and, perceiving I was a Christian, he cried out for help; they carried me before the cadi, who ordered me to receive one hundred bastinadoes, and sent me to the galleys. I was chained in the very galley, and to the very same bench with my lord the Baron. On board this galley there were four young men belonging to Marseilles, five Neapolitan priests, and two monks of Corfu, who told us that the like adventures happened every day. The Baron pretended that he had been worse used than myself; and I insisted that there was far less harm in taking up a nosegay, and putting it into a woman's bosom, than to be found stark naked with a young Icoglan. We were continually in dispute, and received twenty lashes a-day with a thong, when the concatenation of sublunary events brought you on board our galley to ransom us from slavery.'

'Well, my dear Pangloss,' said Candide to him, 'when you were hanged, dissected, whipped, and tugging at the oar, did you continue to think that every thing in this world happens for the best?'

'I have always abided by my first opinion,' answered Pangloss; 'for, after all, I am a philosopher; and it would not become me to retract my sentiments; especially, as Leibnitz could not be in the wrong; and that pre-established harmony is the finest thing in the world, as well as the *plenum* and the *materia subtilis*.'

CHAPTER XXIX

IN WHAT MANNER CANDIDE FOUND CUNEGUND AND THE OLD WOMAN AGAIN

WHILE Candide, the Baron, Pangloss, Martin, and Cacambo were relating their several adventures, and reasoning on the contingent or non-contingent events of this world; while they were disputing on causes and effects, on moral and physical evil, on free will and necessity, and on the consolation that may be felt by a person when a slave and chained to an oar in a Turkish galley, they arrived at the house of the Transylvanian prince on the coasts of the Propontis. The first objects they beheld there were Miss Cunegund and the old woman, who were hanging some table-cloths on a line to dry.

The Baron turned pale at the sight. Even the tender

Candide, that affectionate lover, upon seeing his fair Cunegund all sun-burnt, with blear eyes, a withered neck, wrinkled face and arms, all covered with a red scurf, started back with horror; but, recovering himself, he advanced towards her out of good manners. She embraced Candide and her brother; they embraced the old woman, and Candide ransomed them both.

There was a small farm in the neighbourhood, which the old woman proposed to Candide to make a shift with till the company should meet with a more favourable destiny. Cunegund, not knowing that she was grown ugly, as no one had informed her of it, reminded Candide of his promise in so peremptory a manner that the simple lad did not dare to refuse her; he then acquainted the Baron that he was going to marry his sister.

'I will never suffer,' said the Baron, 'my sister to be guilty of an action so derogatory to her birth and family; nor will I bear this insolence on your part: no, I never will be reproached that my nephews are not qualified for the first ecclesiastical dignities in Germany; nor shall a sister of mine ever be the wife of any person below the rank of a baron of the Empire.'

Cunegund flung herself at her brother's feet, and bedewed them with her tears, but he still continued inflexible.

'Thou foolish fellow,' said Candide, 'have I not delivered thee from the galleys, paid thy ransom, and thy sister's too who was a scullion, and is very ugly, and yet I condescend to marry her? and shalt thou make claim to oppose the match? If I were to listen only to the dictates of my anger, I should kill thee again.'

'Thou mayest kill me again,' said the Baron, 'but thou shalt not marry my sister while I am living.'

CHAPTER XXX

CONCLUSION

CANDIDE had, in truth, no great inclination to marry Cunegund; but the extreme impertinence of the baron determined him to conclude the match; and Cunegund pressed him so warmly that he could not recant. He consulted Pangloss, Martin, and the faithful Cacambo. Pangloss composed a fine memorial, by which he proved that the Baron had no right over his sister; and that she might, according to all the laws of the Empire, marry Candide with the left hand. Martin concluded that they should throw the Baron into the sea: Cacambo decided that he must be delivered to the Turkish captain and sent to the galleys; after which he should be conveyed by the first ship to the Father General at Rome. This advice was found to be very good; the old woman approved of it, and not a syllable was said to his sister; the business was executed for a little money: and they had the pleasure of tricking a Jesuit and punishing the pride of a German baron.

It was altogether natural to imagine that after undergoing so many disasters, Candide married to his mistress, and living with the philosopher Pangloss, the philosopher Martin, the prudent Cacambo, and the old woman, having besides brought home so many diamonds from the country of the ancient Incas, would lead the most agreeable life in the world. But he had been so much cheated by the Jews that he had nothing else left but his little farm; his wife, every day growing more and more ugly, became ill-natured and insupportable; the old woman was infirm, and more bad-tempered yet than Cunegund. Cacambo, who worked in the garden, and carried the produce of it to sell at Constantinople, was past his labour, and cursed his fate. Pangloss despaired of making a figure in any of the German universities. And as to Martin, he was firmly persuaded that a person is equally ill-situated everywhere. He took things with patience. Candide, Martin, and Pangloss disputed sometimes about metaphysics and morality. Boats were often seen passing under the windows of the farm fraught with effendis, pashas, and cadis, that were going into banishment to Lemnos, Mytilene, and Erzeroum. And other cadis, pashas, and effendis were seen coming back to succeed the place of the exiles, and were driven out in their turns. They saw several heads very curiously stuffed with straw, being carried as presents to the Sublime Porte. Such sights gave occasion to frequent dissertations; and when no disputes were carried on, the irksomeness was so excessive that the old woman ventured one day to say to them:

' I would be glad to know which is worst, to be ravished a hundred times by negro pirates, to have one buttock cut off, to run the gauntlet among the Bulgarians, to be whipped and hanged at an *auto-da-fé*, to be dissected, to be chained to an oar in a galley, and in short to experience all the miseries through which every one of us hath passed,—or to remain here doing nothing?'

' This,' said Candide, ' is a big question.'

This discourse gave birth to new reflections, and Martin especially concluded that man was born to live in the convulsions of disquiet, or in the lethargy of idleness. Though Candide did not absolutely agree to this; yet he was sure of nothing. Pangloss avowed that he had undergone dreadful sufferings; but having once maintained that everything went on as well as possible, he still maintained it, and at the same time believed nothing of it.

There was one thing which, more than ever, confirmed Martin in his detestable principles, made Candide hesitate, and embarrassed Pangloss. This was the arrival of Pacquette and Friar Giroflée one day at their farm. This couple had been in the utmost distress; they had very speedily made away with their three thousand piastres; they had parted, been reconciled; quarrelled again, been thrown into prison; had made their escape, and at last Brother Giroflée turned Turk. Pacquette still continued to follow her trade wherever she came; but she got little or nothing by it.

' I foresaw very well,' said Martin to Candide, ' that your presents would soon be squandered, and only make them more miserable. You and Cacambo have spent millions of piastres, and yet you are not more happy than Brother Giroflée and Pacquette.'

' Ah ! ' said Pangloss to Pacquette. ' It is heaven who has brought you here among us, my poor child ! Do you know that you have cost me the tip of my nose, one eye, and one ear ? What a handsome shape is here ! and what is this world ! '

This new adventure engaged them more deeply than ever in philosophical disputations.

In the neighbourhood lived a very famous dervish, who passed for the best philosopher in Turkey ; him they went to consult : Pangloss, who was their spokesman, addressed him thus :

' Master, we come to intreat you to tell us why so strange an animal as man has been formed ? '

' Why do you trouble your head about it ? ' said the dervish. ' Is it any business of yours ? '

' But, my Reverend Father,' said Candide, ' there is a horrible deal of evil on the earth.'

' What signifies it,' said the dervish, ' whether there is evil or good ? When his Highness sends a ship to Egypt, does he trouble his head whether the rats in the vessel are at their ease or not ? '

' What must then be done ? ' said Pangloss.

' Be silent,' answered the dervish.

' I flattered myself,' replied Pangloss, ' that we should have the pleasure of arguing with you on causes and effects, on the best of possible worlds, the origin of evil, the nature of the soul, and the pre-established harmony.'

At these words the dervish shut the door in their faces.

During this conversation, news was spread abroad that two viziers of the bench and the mufti had just been strangled at Constantinople, and several of their friends impaled. This catastrophe made a great noise for some hours. Pangloss, Candide, and Martin, as they were returning to the little farm, met with a good-looking old man, who was taking the air at his door, under an alcove formed of orange-trees. Pangloss, who was as inquisitive as he was argumentative, asked him what was the name of the mufti who was lately strangled.

'I cannot tell,' answered the good old man; 'I never knew the name of any mufti or vizier breathing. I am entirely ignorant of the event you speak of; I presume, that in general, such as are concerned in public affairs sometimes come to a miserable end; and that they deserve it : but I never inquire what is happening at Constantinople; I am content with sending thither the produce of the garden which I cultivate.'

After saying these words, he invited the strangers to come into his house. His two daughters and two sons presented them with diverse sorts of iced sherbet of their own making; besides *caymac*, heightened with the peel of candied citrons, oranges, lemons, pine-apples, pistachio-nuts, and Mocha coffee unadulterated with the bad coffee of Batavia or the West Indies. After which the two daughters of this good mussulman perfumed the beards of Candide, Pangloss, and Martin.

'You must certainly have a vast estate,' said Candide to the Turk.

'I have no more than twenty acres of ground,' he replied, 'the whole of which I cultivate myself with the help of my children; and our labour keeps off from us three great evils, idleness, vice, and want.'

Candide, as he was returning home, made profound reflections on the Turk's discourse.

'This good old man,' he said to Pangloss and Martin, 'appears to me to have chosen for himself a lot much preferable to that of the six kings with whom we had the honour to sup.'

'Human grandeur,' said Pangloss, 'is very dangerous, if we believe the testimonies of almost all philosophers; for we find Eglon, King of the Moabites, was assassinated by Ehud; Absalom was hanged by the hair of his head, and run through with three darts; King Nadab, son of Jeroboam, was slain by Baasha; King Elah by Zimri; Ahaziah by Jehu; Athaliah by Jehoiada; the Kings Jehoiakim, Jechoniah, and Zedekiah were led into captivity : I need not tell you what was the fate of Crœsus, Astyages, Darius, Dionysius of Syracuse, Pyrrhus, Perseus, Hannibal, Jugurtha, Ariovistus, Cæsar, Pompey, Nero, Otho, Vitellius, Domitian, Richard II of England, Edward II, Henry VI,

Richard III, Mary Stuart, Charles I, the three Henrys of France, and the Emperor Henry IV.'

'Neither need you tell me,' said Candide, 'that we must take care of our garden.'

'You are in the right,' said Pangloss; 'for when man was put into the Garden of Eden, it was with an intent to dress it : and this proves that man was not born to be idle.'

'Work then without disputing,' said Martin; 'it is the only way to render life supportable.'

The little society, one and all, entered into this laudable design; and set themselves to exert their different talents. The little piece of ground yielded them a plentiful crop. Cunegund indeed was very ugly, but she became an excellent hand at pastry-work; Pacquette embroidered; the old woman had the care of the linen. There was none, down to Brother Giroflée, but did some service; he was a very good carpenter, and became an honest man. Pangloss used now and then to say to Candide :

'There is a concatenation of all events in the best of possible worlds; for, in short, had you not been kicked out of a fine castle by the backside for the love of Miss Cunegund, had you not been put into the Inquisition, had you not travelled over America on foot, had you not run the Baron through the body, and had you not lost all your sheep which you brought from the good country of El Dorado, you would not have been here to eat preserved citrons and pistachio-nuts.'

'Excellently observed,' answered Candide; 'but let us take care of our garden.'

MASTER SIMPLE

CHAPTER I

ONE day, Saint Dunstan, an Irishman by birth, and a saint by profession, left Ireland on a small mountain, which took its route towards the coast of France, and arrived in the bay of St. Malo. When he had dismounted, he gave his blessing to the mountain, which after some profound bows took its leave, and returned to its former place.

Here St. Dunstan laid the foundation of a small priory, and gave it the name of the Priory of the Mountain, which it still keeps, as everybody knows.

In the evening of July 15th, 1689, the Abbé de Kerkabon, Prior of Our Lady of the Mountain, was walking along the shore to take the air with Mlle de Kerkabon his sister. The Prior, who was a little declined in age, was a very good clergyman, beloved by his neighbours as he had been formerly by their wives. What added most to the respect that was paid him, was that among all his clerical neighbours he was the only one that could walk to his bed after supping with his fellows : he was tolerably read in theology ; and when he was tired of reading St. Augustine, he refreshed himself with Rabelais ; so all the world spoke well of him.

Mlle de Kerkabon, who had never been married, notwithstanding her hearty wishes so to be, had preserved a freshness of complexion in her forty-fifth year : her character was that of a good and sensible woman : she was fond of pleasure, and was a devotee.

The Prior, looking on the sea, said to his sister :

' It was here, alas ! that our poor brother embarked with our dear sister-in-law, Madame de Kerkabon, his wife, on board the *Swallow* frigate, in 1669, to see service in Canada. Had he not been killed, probably we might see him again.'

'Do you believe,' said Mlle de Kerkabon, 'that our sister-in-law was eaten by the Iroquois, as we have been told? Certain it is, had she not been eaten, she would have come back; I shall weep for her all my life : she was a charming woman; and our brother, who had a great deal of wit, would no doubt have made a fortune.'

Thus they were going on with mutual tenderness, when they beheld a small vessel enter the bay of Rance with the tide : it was from England, and came to sell provisions : the crew leaped on shore without looking at the Prior, or his sister, who were shocked at the little attention shown them.

Such was not the behaviour, however, of a well-made youth, who, darting himself over the heads of his companions, stood on a sudden before Mlle de Kerkabon. Being unaccustomed to bowing, he made her a sign with his head. His figure and his dress attracted the notice of the brother and sister. His head was uncovered, and his legs bare; his feet were shod in small sandals; from his head his long hair flowed in tresses; a small close doublet displayed the beauty of his shape. He had a sweet and martial air. In one hand he held a small bottle of Barbadoes water, and in the other a bag, in which he had a goblet, and some sea biscuit. He spoke French very intelligibly : he offered some of his Barbadoes to Mlle de Kerkabon and her brother; he drank with them, he made them drink a second time, and all this with an air of such natural simplicity that quite charmed both brother and sister. They offered him their services, and asked him who he was, and where he was going. The young man answered that he did not know; that he had some curiosity; that he had a desire to see how the coast of France was formed; that he had seen it, and was going to return.

The Prior, judging by his accent that he was not an Englishman, took the liberty of asking of what country he was.

'I am a Huron,' answered the youth.

Mlle de Kerkabon, amazed and enchanted to see a Huron who had behaved so politely to her, begged the young man's company to supper : he complied immediately, and all three went together to the Priory of Our Lady of the

Mountain. This short, round lady devoured him with her little eyes, and said from time to time to the Prior :

' This tall lad has a complexion of lilies and roses; what a fine skin he has for a Huron ! '

' Very true, sister,' says the Prior.

She put a hundred questions, one after another, and the traveller answered always pertinently.

The report soon spread that there was a Huron at the Priory : all the genteel company of the country hastened to come and dine. The Abbé de Saint-Yves came with his sister, a handsome, well-educated young Breton girl : the magistrate, the tax-collector, and their wives, came all together. The foreigner was seated between Mlle de Kerkabon and Mlle de Saint-Yves; the company eyed him with admiration; they all talked to him and questioned him together. This did not confuse the Huron; he seemed to have taken Lord Bolingbroke's motto, *Nihil admirari*; but at last, tired out with so much noise, he told them in a sweet, but serious tone :

' Gentlemen, in my country, people talk one after another; how can I answer you, if you will not allow me to hear you ? '

Reasoning always brings people to a momentary reflection; they were all silent. The magistrate, who always made a property of a foreigner wherever he found him, and who was the first man for asking questions in the province, opening a mouth of half a foot, began :

' Sir, what is your name ? '

' I have always been called Master Simple,' answered the Huron; ' and the English have confirmed that name, because I always speak as I think, and act as I like.'

' But being born a Huron, how could you come to England ? '

' I was taken there; I was made prisoner by the English after some resistance, and the English, who love brave people, because they are brave and as honest as ourselves, proposed to me, either to return to my family, or go with them to England. I accepted the latter, having naturally a relish for seeing the world.'

' But, Sir,' said the magistrate with his usual gravity, ' how could you think of abandoning father and mother ? '

' Because I never knew either father or mother,' said the foreigner.

This moved the company; they all repeated, ' Neither *father* nor *mother* ! '

' We will be in their stead,' said the mistress of the house to her brother the Prior : ' how interesting this Huron gentleman is ! '

Master Simple thanked her with a noble and proud cordiality, and gave her to understand that he wanted the assistance of nobody.

' I perceive, Master Simple,' said the huge magistrate, ' that you talk better French than can be expected from a Huron.'

' A Frenchman,' answered he, ' whom they had made prisoner when I was a boy in Huronia, and with whom I contracted a great friendship, taught it me. I very quickly learn what I like to learn. When I came to Plymouth, I met with one of your French refugees, whom you, I know not why, call Huguenots : he improved my knowledge of your language; and as soon as I could express myself intelligibly, I came to see your country, because I like the French well enough if they do not put too many questions.'

Notwithstanding this delicate hint, the Abbé de Saint-Yves asked him, which of the three languages pleased him best, the Huron, English, or French ?

' The Huron, to be sure,' answered Master Simple.

' Is it possible,' cried Mlle de Kerkabon. ' I always thought the French was the most beautiful of all languages, after that of Lower Brittany.'

Then all were eager to know how, in Huron, they said ' tobacco.'

He replied, ' *Taya.*'

' What signifies to eat ? '

' *Essenten.*'

Mlle de Kerkabon was impatient to know how they called ' to make love.'

He informed her, *Trovander*; and insisted, not without reason, that these words were well worth their equivalents in French and English. *Trovander*, especially, seemed very pretty to all the company.

The Prior, who had in his library a Huron grammar,

which had been given by the Rev. Father Sagar Theodat of the Reformed Franciscans, a famous missionary, rose from the table to consult it: he returned quite panting with tenderness and joy; he acknowledged the foreigner for a true Huron. The company speculated a little on the multiplicity of languages; and all agreed that had it not been for the affair of the Tower of Babel, all the world would have spoken French.

The inquisitive magistrate, who till then had some suspicions of the foreigner, conceived the deepest respect for him; he spoke to him with more civility than before, for what reason the Huron could not conceive.

Mlle de Saint-Yves was very curious to know how people made love among the Hurons.

' In performing great actions to please such as resemble you.'

All the company admired and applauded, Mlle de Saint-Yves blushed, and was extremely well pleased. Mlle de Kerkabon blushed likewise, but was not so well pleased; she was a little piqued that this gallantry was not addressed to her; but she was so good-natured that her affection for the Huron was not diminished at all. She asked him, with great complacency, how many mistresses he had had at home.

'I never had more than one,' answered the foreigner; ' Miss Abacaba, the good friend of my dear nurse. The reed is not more straight, ermine is not more white, no lamb meeker, no eagle fiercer, nor a stag swifter than was my Abacaba. One day she pursued a hare not above fifty leagues from our settlement: a base Algonquin, who dwelt a hundred leagues farther, took her hare from her. I was told of it; I ran thither, and with one stroke of my club levelled him with the ground. I brought him to the feet of my mistress bound hand and foot. Abacaba's parents were for eating him, but I always had a disrelish for such kind of dishes; I set him at liberty, I made him my friend. Abacaba was so pleased with my conduct that she preferred me to all her lovers. How she would have continued to love me, had she not been devoured by a bear ! I slew the bear, and wore his hide a long while; but that has not comforted me.'

Mlle de Saint-Yves felt a secret pleasure at hearing that Abacaba had been his only mistress, and that she was no more; yet she did not understand the cause of her own pleasure. All eyes were riveted on the Huron, and he was much applauded for delivering an Algonquin from being eaten by his countrymen.

The merciless magistrate, who could not restrain his thirst for questioning, even asked the Huron what religion he was of; whether he had chosen the English, the French, or that of the Huguenots.

'I am of my own religion,' said he, 'just as you are of yours.'

'Lord!' cried Mlle de Kerkabon, 'I see already that those wretched English have not once thought of baptizing him!'

'Good God,' said Mlle de Saint-Yves, 'how is it possible! How is it possible the Hurons should not be Roman Catholics! Have not those reverend fathers the Jesuits converted all the world?'

Master Simple assured her that in his country nobody was converted, that no true Huron had ever changed his opinion, and that there was not in their language a word to express inconstancy.

These last words pleased Mlle de Saint-Yves extremely.

'Oh! we'll baptize him, we'll baptize him,' said Mlle de Kerkabon to the Prior; 'you shall have that honour, my dear brother, and I will be his godmother; the Abbé de Saint-Yves shall present him at the font; it will be a fine ceremony; it will be talked of all over Brittany, and do us the greatest honour.'

The company were all of the same mind with the mistress of the house; they all cried, 'We'll baptize him.'

The Huron interrupted them, by saying, that in England every one was allowed to live as he pleased. He rather showed some aversion to the proposal which was made, and could not help telling them that the laws of the Hurons were to the full as good as those of Lower Brittany: he finished by saying that he would return the next day. They finished by emptying his bottle of Barbadoes water, and the company went to bed.

After the Huron had been conducted to his room, Mlle de Kerkabon and her friend Mlle de Saint-Yves could not help peeping through the keyhole to see how a Huron went to bed : they saw that he spread the blankets on the floor, and laid himself down upon them in the finest attitude in the world.

CHAPTER II

THE HURON, CALLED MASTER SIMPLE, ACKNOWLEDGED BY HIS RELATIONS

MASTER SIMPLE, according to custom, awoke with the sun, at the crowing of the cock, which is called in England and Huronia, ' the trumpet of the day.' He did not imitate people of fashion who languish on the bed of indolence till the sun has performed half his career, unable to sleep, but not disposed to rise, and lose so many precious hours in that doubtful state, between life and death, and who nevertheless complain that life is too short.

He had already traversed two or three leagues, and killed fifteen brace of game, with ball only, when, upon his return, he found the Prior of Our Lady of the Mountain, with his discreet sister, walking in their nightcaps in their little garden. He presented them with the spoils of his morning labour, and taking from his bosom a kind of little talisman, which he constantly wore about his neck, he intreated them to accept it as an acknowledgment for the kind reception they had given him.

' It is,' said he, ' the most valuable thing I am possessed of : I have been assured that I shall always be happy whilst I carry this little toy about me ; and I give it you that you may always be happy.'

The Prior and his sister smiled with pity at the frankness of the Huron. This present consisted of two little portraits very ill done, tied together with a greasy string.

Mlle de Kerkabon asked him if there were any painters in Huronia.

' No,' replied Master Simple, ' I had this curiosity from my nurse ; her husband had obtained it by conquest, in stripping some of the French of Canada, who had made war upon us ; this is all I know of the matter.'

The Prior looked attentively at these pictures; he changed colour, his hands trembled, and he seemed much affected.

'By our Lady of the Mountain,' he cried out, 'I believe these to be the faces of the captain my brother, and his lady.'

His sister, after having consulted them with the like emotion, thought the same. They were both struck with astonishment and joy blended with grief: they both melted, they both wept, their hearts throbbed, they uttered cries, they snatched the portraits from each other and interchanged them at least twenty times in a second. They seemed to devour the Huron's pictures with their eyes; they asked one after another, and even both at once, at what time, in what place, and how these miniatures fell into the hands of the nurse. They reckoned and computed the time from the captain's departure; they recollected having received advice that he had penetrated as far as the country of the Hurons; and from that time they had never heard anything more of him.

The Huron had told them that he had never known either father or mother. The Prior, who was a man of sense, observed that he had a little beard, and he knew very well that the Hurons never had any. His chin was somewhat hairy; he was therefore the son of a European.

'My brother and sister-in-law,' he said, 'were never seen after the expedition against the Hurons, in 1669. My nephew must then have been sucking at the breast; the Huron nurse has preserved his life, and been a mother to him.'

At length, after a hundred questions and answers, the Prior and his sister concluded that the Huron was their own nephew. They embraced him, whilst tears streamed from their eyes: and Master Simple laughed to think, that a Huron should be nephew to a prior of Lower Brittany.

All the company came downstairs. M. de Saint-Yves, who was a great physiognomist, compared the two pictures with the Huron's countenance: he observed very skilfully that he had the mother's eyes, the forehead and nose of the late Captain de Kerkabon, and the cheeks common to both.

Mlle de Saint-Yves, who had never seen either father or mother, was strenuously of opinion that the young man had a perfect resemblance to them. They all admired Providence and the concatenation of events in this world. In a word, they were so persuaded, so convinced of the birth of the Huron, that he himself consented to be the Prior's nephew, saying that he would as soon have him for his uncle as another.

He went to return thanks in the church of Our Lady of the Mountain; whilst the Huron, with an air of indifference, amused himself in the house drinking.

The Englishmen who had brought him over, and who were ready to set sail, came to tell him that it was time to depart.

' Probably,' said he to them, ' you have not met with any of your uncles or aunts; I shall stay here, go you back to Plymouth. I give you all my clothes, as I have no longer occasion for anything in this world, since I am the nephew of a prior.'

The Englishmen set sail, without being at all concerned whether the Huron had any relations or not in Lower Brittany.

After the uncles, the aunt, and the company had sung *Te Deum*; after the magistrate had once more overwhelmed the Huron with questions; after they had exhausted all their astonishment, joy, and tenderness, the Prior of the Mountain and the Abbé de Saint-Yves, concluded that Master Simple should be baptized with all possible expedition. But the case was very different with a tall robust Huron of twenty-two, and an infant who is regenerated without his knowing anything of the matter. It was necessary to instruct him, and this appeared difficult; for the Abbé de Saint-Yves supposed that a man who was not born in France could not be endued with common sense.

The Prior indeed observed to the company that though, in fact, the ingenuous gentleman his nephew was not so fortunate as to be born in Lower Brittany, he was not, upon that account, in any way deficient in sense, as might be concluded from all his answers; and that, doubtless, nature had greatly favoured him, as well on his father's as on his mother's side.

He then was asked if he had ever read any books. He said he had read Rabelais translated into English, and some passages in Shakespeare, which he knew by heart; that these books belonged to the captain, on board of whose ship he came from America to Plymouth; and that he was very well pleased with them. The magistrate failed not to put many questions to him concerning these books.

'I confess,' said the Huron, 'I thought I understood some things, but not the whole.'

The Abbé de Saint-Yves commented upon this discourse that it was in this manner he himself always read, and that most men read no other way.

'You have,' said he to the Huron, 'doubtless read the Bible.'

'Never, Monsieur Abbé: it was not among the captain's books; I never heard it mentioned.'

'This is the way of those cursed English,' said Mlle de Kerkabon; 'they mind more a play of Shakespeare's, a plum-pudding, or a bottle of rum than they do the Pentateuch. For this reason they have never converted anyone in America. They are certainly cursed by God; and we shall conquer Jamaica and Virginia from them in a very short time.'

Be this as it may, the most skilful tailor in all St. Malo was sent for, to dress the Huron from head to foot. The company separated, and the magistrate went elsewhere to display his inquisitiveness. Mlle de Saint-Yves, in parting, returned several times to observe the young stranger, and he made deeper bows to her than he had ever done to any one in his life.

The magistrate, before he took his leave, presented to Mlle de Saint-Yves a stupid dolt of a son, just come from college; but she scarcely looked at him, so much was she taken up with the politeness of the Huron.

CHAPTER III

THE HURON, CALLED MASTER SIMPLE, CONVERTED

THE Prior, finding that he was somewhat advanced in years, and that God had sent him a nephew for his consolation, took it into his head that he would resign his benefice in his favour, if he succeeded in baptizing him and making him take orders.

The Huron had an excellent memory. The sturdy constitution, inherited from his forbears of Lower Brittany, strengthened by the climate of Canada, had made his head so strong that when he was struck upon it, he scarcely felt it; and when anything was graven in it, nothing could efface it; nothing had ever escaped his memory. His conception was the more sure and lively, by reason that his infancy not having been loaded with useless fooleries, which overwhelm ours, things entered into his head without being clouded. The Prior at length resolved to make him read the New Testament; the Huron devoured it with great pleasure; but not knowing at what time, or in what country, all the adventures related in this book had happened, he did not in the least doubt that the scene of action had been in Lower Brittany; and he swore that he would cut off Caiaphas' and Pontius Pilate's ears if ever he met those scoundrels.

His uncle, charmed with this good disposition, soon made him understand; he applauded his zeal, but, at the same time, acquainted him that it was needless, as these people had been dead upwards of one thousand six hundred and ninety years. The Huron soon got the whole book by heart. He sometimes proposed difficulties that greatly embarrassed the Prior. He was often obliged to consult the Abbé de Saint-Yves, who not knowing what to answer brought a Jesuit of Lower Brittany to perfect the conversion of the Huron.

Grace, at length, operated; and the Huron promised to become a Christian. He did not doubt but that the first step towards it was circumcision.

'For,' said he, 'I do not find in the book that was put into my hands a single person who was not circumcised;

it is therefore evident that I must make a sacrifice of my prepuce, and the sooner the better.'

He sent for the surgeon of the village, and desired him to perform the operation, thinking thereby greatly to rejoice Mlle de Kerkabon, and all the company, when the thing was once done. The surgeon, who had never performed such an operation, acquainted the family, who screamed out. The good lady Kerkabon trembled lest her nephew, whom she knew to be resolute and expeditious, should perform the operation unskilfully himself; and that fatal consequences should ensue, in which ladies, through the goodness of their hearts, are always concerned.

The Prior rectified the Huron's mistake, representing to him that circumcision was no longer in fashion; that baptism was much more gentle and salutary; that the law of grace was not like the law of rigour. The Huron, who had much good sense and was well disposed, disputed, but soon acknowledged his error, which seldom happens in Europe among disputants; in a word, he promised to let himself be baptized whenever they pleased.

It was necessary that he should go previously to confession; and this was the greatest difficulty to surmount. The Huron constantly had in his pocket the book his uncle had given him. He did not there find that a single Apostle had ever been confessed, and this made him very restive. The Prior silenced him, by showing him, in the Epistle of St. James the Less, these words which cause so much trouble to heretics : *Confess your sins to one another*. The Huron was mute, and confessed his sins to a Reformed Franciscan monk. When he had done, he dragged the monk from the confessional chair, and seizing him with a strong arm, placed himself in his seat, making the monk kneel before him.

' Come, my friend, it is said, *we must confess our sins to one another*; I have related to you my sins, and you shall not stir till you recount yours.'

Whilst he said this, he fixed his great knee against his adversary's stomach. The monk roared and groaned, till he made the church re-echo. The noise brought people to his assistance, who found the catechumen cuffing the monk in the name of St. James the Less. The joy of baptizing at once a Low-Breton, a Huron, and an English-man was so great that these singularities were passed over. There were even some theologians of opinion that confession was not necessary, as baptism supplied the place of every-thing.

The Bishop of St. Malo was chosen for the ceremony, who, flattered, as may be believed, at baptizing a Huron, arrived in a pompous equipage, followed by his clergy. Mlle de Saint-Yves put on her best gown to bless God, and sent for a hairdresser from St. Malo so as to shine at the ceremony. The inquisitive magistrate brought the whole country with him. The church was magnificently orna-mented. But when the Huron was summoned to attend the baptismal font, he was not to be found.

His uncle and aunt looked for him everywhere. It was imagined he had gone hunting, according to his usual custom. Every one present at the festival, searched the neighbouring woods and villages; but no intelligence could be obtained of the Huron. They began to fear he had returned to England. Some remembered that he had said he was very fond of that country. The Prior and his sister were persuaded that nobody was baptized there, and were troubled for their nephew's soul. The Bishop was confounded, and ready to return home; the Prior and the Abbé de Saint-Yves were in despair; the magistrate in-terrogated all passers-by with his usual gravity; Mlle de Kerkabon melted into tears; Mlle de Saint-Yves did not weep, but she vented such deep sighs, as seemed to testify her sacramental disposition. They were walking in this melancholy mood, among the willows and reeds upon the banks of the little river Rance, when they perceived, in the middle of the stream, a large figure, tolerably white, with its two arms across its breast. They screamed out and ran away. But, curiosity being stronger than any other consideration, they slipped softly amongst the reeds; and when they were pretty certain they could not be seen, they were willing to see what it was.

CHAPTER IV

THE HURON BAPTIZED

THE Prior and the Abbé, having run to the riverside, asked the Huron what he was doing.

' In faith,' said he, ' gentlemen, I am waiting to be baptized. I have been an hour in the water up to my neck, and I do not think it is civil to let me be quite spent.'

' My dear nephew,' said the Prior to him tenderly, ' this is not the way to be baptized in Lower Brittany; put on your clothes, and come with us.'

Mlle de Saint-Yves, listening to the discourse, said in a whisper to her companion :

' Do you think he will put his clothes on in a hurry? '

The Huron, however, replied to the Prior : ' You will not make me believe now as you did before; I have studied very well since then, and I am very certain there is no other kind of baptism. The eunuch of Queen Candace was baptized in a rivulet. I defy you to show me, in the book you gave me, that people were ever baptized in any other way. I either will not be baptized at all, or the ceremony shall be performed in the river.'

It was in vain to remonstrate to him that customs were altered. He always recurred to the eunuch of Queen Candace. And though Mlle de Saint-Yves and his aunt, who had observed him through the willows, were authorized to tell him that he had no right to quote such a man; they, nevertheless, said nothing—so great was their discretion. The Bishop came himself to speak to him, which was a great thing; but he could not prevail; the Huron disputed with the Bishop.

' Show me,' said he, ' in the book my uncle gave me, one single man that was not baptized in a river, and I will do whatever you please.'

His aunt, in despair, had observed, that the first time her nephew bowed, he made a much lower bow to Mlle de Saint-Yves than to any one in the company; that he had not even saluted the Bishop with so much respect, blended with cordiality, as he did that agreeable young lady. She thought it advisable to appeal to her in this great embar-

rassment; she intreated her to use her influence to engage
the Huron to be baptized according to the custom of Brittany, thinking that her nephew could never be a Christian
if he persisted in being christened in running water.

Mlle de Saint-Yves blushed at the secret joy she felt at
being appointed to execute so important a commission.
She modestly approached the Huron, and squeezing his
hand in quite a noble manner, she said to him :

' What, will you do nothing to please me ? '

As she uttered these words, she cast down her eyes and
raised them with a graceful tenderness.

' Oh ! yes, Miss, everything you require, all that you
command, whether it is to be baptized in water, fire, or
blood—there is nothing I can refuse you.'

Mlle de Saint-Yves had the glory of effecting, in two words,
what neither the importunities of the Prior, the repeated
interrogations of the magistrate, nor the reasoning of the
Bishop, could effect. She was sensible of her triumph;
but she was not yet sensible of its full extent.

Baptism was administered, and received with all the
decency, magnificence, and propriety possible. His uncle
and aunt yielded to the Abbé de Saint-Yves and his sister
the favour of supporting the Huron upon the font. Mlle
de Saint-Yves's eyes sparkled with joy at being a godmother. She was ignorant how much this high title subjected her; she accepted the honour, without being acquainted with its fatal consequences.

As there never was any ceremony that was not followed
by a good dinner, the company took their seats at table after
the christening. The humorists of Lower Brittany said,
they did not choose to have their wine baptized. The
Prior said that wine, according to Solomon, rejoiced the
heart of man. My lord Bishop added, that the patriarch
Judah ought to have tied his ass's colt to the vine, and
steeped his cloak in the blood of the grape; and that he
was sorry the same could not be done in Lower Brittany,
to which God had not allotted vines. Every one endeavoured to say a good thing upon the Huron's christening,
and utter gallantries to the godmother. The magistrate,
ever interrogating, asked the Huron if he was faithful in
keeping his promises.

' How,' said he, ' can I fail keeping them, since I have deposited them in the hands of Mlle de Saint-Yves? '

The Huron grew warm; he had drank his godmother's health many times.

' If,' said he, ' I had been baptized with your hand, I feel that the water which was poured on the nape of my neck would have burnt me.'

The magistrate thought that this was too poetical, being ignorant that allegory is a familiar figure in Canada. But his godmother was very well pleased.

The Huron had, at his baptism, received the name of Hercules. The Bishop of St. Malo frequently inquired, who was this tutelar saint, whom he had never heard mentioned before. The Jesuit, who was very learned, told him, that he was a saint who had wrought twelve miracles. There was a thirteenth, which was well worth the other twelve, but it was not proper for a Jesuit to mention it : this was the transforming of fifty girls into women in one night's time. A wag, who was present, related this miracle very feelingly. The ladies all cast down their eyes, and judged, from the Huron's appearance, that he was worthy of the saint whose name he bore.

CHAPTER V

THE HURON IN LOVE

It must be acknowledged that from the time of this christening and this dinner, Mlle de Saint-Yves passionately wished that the Bishop would make her again an assistant with Master Hercules Simple in some other fine ceremony. However, as she was well brought up, and very modest, she did not dare entirely to own these tender sentiments even to herself; but if a look, a word, a gesture, a thought, escaped from her, she concealed it admirably well under the veil of an infinitely charming modesty. She was tender, lively, and sagacious.

As soon as the Bishop was gone, the Huron and Mlle de Saint-Yves met together, without thinking they were in search of one another. They spoke together, without premeditating what they said. The sincere youth immediately declared that he loved her with all his heart; and that the beauteous Abacaba, with whom he had been desperately in love in his own country, was far inferior to her.

She replied, with her usual modesty, that the Prior his uncle, and the lady his aunt, should be spoken to immediately; and that, on her side, she would say a few words to her dear brother the Abbé de Saint-Yves, and that she flattered herself it would meet with no opposition.

The youth replied that the consent of any one was entirely superfluous, that it appeared to him extremely ridiculous to go and ask others what they were to do; that when two parties were agreed, there was no occasion for a third to accomplish their union.

'I never consult any one,' said he, 'when I have a mind to breakfast, to hunt, or to sleep: I am sensible that in love it is not amiss to have the consent of the person whom we wish for; but as I am in love neither with my uncle nor my aunt, I have no occasion to address myself to them in this affair; and if you will believe me, you may equally dispense with the advice of the Abbé de Saint-Yves.'

It may be supposed that the pretty Breton girl exerted all the delicacy of her wit to bring her Huron to the terms of good breeding. She was even angry, but soon softened. In a word, it cannot be said how this conversation would have ended, if the declining day had not brought the Abbé to conduct his sister home. The Huron left his uncle and aunt to rest, they being somewhat fatigued with the ceremony, and their long dinner. He passed part of the night in writing verses in the Huron language upon his well-beloved; for it should be known, there is no country where love has not rendered lovers poets.

The next day his uncle spoke to him in the following manner, after breakfast, in the presence of Mlle de Kerkabon, who was quite melted at the discourse.

'Heaven be praised, that you have the honour, my dear nephew, to be a Christian of Lower Brittany! But this is not enough; I am somewhat advanced in years: my brother has left only a little bit of ground, which is a very small matter; I have a good priory. If you will only make yourself subdeacon, as I hope you will, I will resign my priory in your favour; and you will live at your ease, after having been the consolation of my old age.'

The Huron replied :

' Uncle, much good may it do you; live as long as you can. I do not know what it is to be a subdeacon, or what it is to resign; but everything will be agreeable to me, provided I have Mlle de Saint-Yves at my disposal.'

' Good God, nephew ! what is it you say ? You love that beautiful young lady to distraction ! '

' Yes, uncle.'

' Alas ! nephew, it is impossible you should ever marry her.'

' It is very possible, uncle; for not only did she squeeze my hand when she left me, but she promised she would ask me in marriage : I certainly shall wed her.'

' It is impossible, I tell you, she is your godmother : it is a dreadful sin for a godmother to squeeze the hand of her godson; it is contrary to all laws, human and divine.'

' The deuce, uncle, you are jesting. Why should it be forbidden to marry one's godmother, when she is young and handsome? I did not find in the book you gave that it was wrong to marry young women who assisted at christenings. I perceive, every day, that an infinite number of things are done here which are not in your book, and nothing is done that is said in it. I must acknowledge to you that this astonishes and displeases me. If I am deprived of the charming Mlle de Saint-Yves on account of my baptism, I give you notice that I will run away with her and un-baptize myself.'

The Prior was confounded; his sister wept.

' My dear brother,' said she, ' our nephew must not damn himself; our Holy Father, the Pope, can give him a dispensation, and then he may be happy, in a Christian-like manner, with the person he loves.'

The ingenuous Hercules embraced his aunt.

' For goodness' sake,' said he, ' who is this charming man, who is so gracious as to promote the amours of girls and boys? I will go and speak to him this instant.'

The dignity and character of the Pope were explained

to him, and the Huron was still more astonished than before.

' My dear uncle,' said he, ' there is not a word of all this in your book; I have travelled, and am acquainted with the sea; we are now upon the coast of the ocean, and I must leave Mlle de Saint-Yves to go and ask leave to have her of a man who lives towards the Mediterranean four hundred leagues from here, and whose language I do not understand ! This is most incomprehensibly ridiculous ! But I will go first to the Abbé de Saint-Yves, who lives only a league from here, and I promise you I will wed my mistress before night.'

Whilst he was yet speaking, the magistrate entered, and, according to his usual custom, asked him where he was going.

' I am going to be married,' replied the ingenuous Hercules, running along; and in less than a quarter of an hour, he was with his charming dear mistress, who was still asleep.

' Ah ! my dear brother,' said Mlle de Kerkabon to the Prior, ' you will never make a subdeacon of our nephew.'

The magistrate was very much displeased at this step; for he laid claim to Mlle de Saint-Yves in favour of his son, who was a still greater and more insupportable fool than his father.

CHAPTER VI

THE HURON FLIES TO HIS MISTRESS, AND BECOMES QUITE FURIOUS

No sooner had the ingenuous Hercules reached the house than having asked the old servant, which was his mistress's apartment, he forced open the door, which was badly fastened, and flew towards the bed.

Mlle de Saint-Yves, startled out of her sleep, cried :

' Ah ! what, is it you? Stop, what are you about ? '

He answered, ' I am going to marry you '; and he would have actually consummated the nuptials, if she had not opposed him with all the decency of a young lady so well educated.

The Huron did not understand raillery, he found all these evasions extremely beside the point.

' Miss Abacaba, my first mistress, did not behave in this manner; you have no honesty; you promised me marriage, and you will not marry; this is being deficient in the first laws of honour; I will teach you to keep your word, and I will set you again in the path of virtue.'

Master Simple possessed an intrepid masculine virtue, worthy of his patron Hercules, whose name was given him at his christening; and he was going to practise it to its full extent, when the alarming outcries of the lady, more discreetly virtuous, brought the sagacious Abbé de Saint-Yves with his housekeeper, an old devoted servant, and the parish priest. The sight of these moderated the courage of the assailant.

' Good God ! ' cried the Abbé, ' my dear neighbour, what are you about ? '

' My duty,' replied the young man; ' I am fulfilling my promises, which are sacred.'

Mlle de Saint-Yves adjusted her dress, but not without blushing. The lover was conducted into another apartment. The Abbé remonstrated to him on the enormity of his conduct. The Huron defended himself upon the privileges of the law of nature, which he understood perfectly well. The Abbé maintained that the law positive should be allowed all its advantages; and that without conventions agreed on between men the law of nature must almost constantly be nothing more than natural felony. Notaries, priests, witnesses, contracts, and dispensations are absolutely necessary. The ingenuous Hercules made answer with the observation constantly adopted by savages :

' You are then very great rogues, since so many precautions are necessary.'

This remark somewhat disconcerted the Abbé.

' There are, I acknowledge, libertines and cheats among us, and there would be as many among the Hurons, if they were united in a great city : but, at the same time, we have discreet, honest, enlightened people; and these are the men who have framed the laws. The more upright we are, the more readily we should submit to them, as we thereby set an example to the vicious, who respect those bounds which virtue has given herself.'

This answer struck the Huron. It has already been observed that his mind was well disposed. He was softened by flattering speeches, which promised him hopes; all the world is caught in these snares; and Mlle de Saint-Yves herself appeared, after having been at her toilet. Everything was now conducted with the utmost good breeding. But notwithstanding this decorum, the sparkling eyes of the ingenuous Hercules constantly made his mistress blush, and the company tremble.

It was with much difficulty he was sent back to his relations. It was again necessary for the charming Mlle de Saint-Yves to interfere; the more she found the influence she had upon him, the more she loved him. She made him depart, and was much afflicted at it : at length, when he was gone, the Abbé, who was not only Mlle de Saint-Yves's elder brother by many years, but was also her guardian, endeavoured to wean his ward from the importunities of this dreadful lover. He went to consult the magistrate, who had always intended his son for the Abbé's sister, and who advised him to place the poor girl in a convent. This was a terrible stroke : such a measure would, to a young lady unaffected with any particular passion, have been inexpressible punishment; but to a love-sick maid, equally thoughtful and tender, it was despair itself.

When the ingenuous Hercules returned to the Prior's house, he related all that had happened with his usual frankness. He met with the same remonstrances, which had some effect upon his mind, though none upon his senses; but the next day, when he wanted to return to his mistress in order to reason with her upon the law of nature and the law of convention, the magistrate acquainted him, with insulting joy, that she was in a convent.

' Very well,' said he, ' I'll go and reason with her in this convent.'

' That cannot be,' said the magistrate; and then entered into a long explanation of the nature of a convent, telling him that this word was derived from *conventus*, in the Latin, which signifies ' an assembly '; and the Huron could not comprehend why he might not be admitted into this assembly. As soon as he was informed that this assembly was a kind of prison in which girls were shut up, a shocking institution, unknown in Huronia and England, he became as furious as was his patron Hercules, when Euritus, King of Œchalia, no less cruel than the Abbé de Saint-Yves, refused him the beauteous Iola, his daughter, not inferior in beauty to the Abbé's sister.   He was on the point of going to set fire to the convent, to carry off his mistress, or be burnt with her.   Mlle de Kerkabon, terrified at such a declaration, gave up all hopes of ever seeing her nephew a subdeacon; and weeping said that the devil had certainly entered into him since he had been christened.

CHAPTER VII

THE HURON REPULSES THE ENGLISH

THE ingenuous Hercules walked towards the sea-shore, wrapped in a deep and gloomy melancholy, with his double-barrelled gun upon his shoulder, and his cutlass by his side, shooting now and then a bird, and often tempted to shoot himself; but he had still some affection for life, for the sake of Mlle de Saint-Yves; by turns execrating his uncle and aunt, all Lower Brittany, and his christening; then blessing them, as they had introduced him to the knowledge of her he loved.   He resolved upon going to burn the convent, but he stopped short for fear of burning his mistress.   The waves of the Channel are not more agitated by the easterly and westerly winds than was his heart by so many contrary emotions.

He was walking along very fast, without knowing whither he was going, when he heard the beat of a drum. He saw, at a great distance, a vast multitude, part of whom ran towards the coast, and the other part flew from it.

A thousand shrieks re-echoed on every side : curiosity and courage hurried him, that instant, towards the spot where the greatest clamour arose, which he attained in a couple of bounds or so.   The commander of the militia, who had dined with him at the Prior's, knew him immediately, and ran to him with open arms.

' Ah ! it is Master Simple : he will fight for us.'

At this the militia, who were almost dead with fear, recovered themselves, crying out with one voice :

' It is the Huron, the ingenuous Huron.'

' Gentlemen,' said he, ' what is the matter? Why are you so scared? Have they shut your mistresses up in convents ? '

Instantly a thousand confused voices cried out :

' Do you not see the English, who are landing ? '

' Very well,' replied the Huron, ' they are a brave people; they never carried off my mistress.'

The commander made him understand that they were coming to pillage the Abbey of the Mountain, drink his uncle's wine, and perhaps carry off Mlle de Saint-Yves; that the little vessel which set him on shore in Brittany had come only to reconnoitre the coast; that they were committing acts of hostility without having declared war against France; and that the province was entirely exposed to them.

' If this be the case,' said he, ' they violate the law of nature : give me leave to act. I lived a good while among them; I am acquainted with their language, and I will speak to them. I do not think they can have so wicked a design.'

During this conversation the English fleet approached; the Huron ran towards it, and having jumped into a little boat, soon rowed to the admiral's ship, and having gone on board, asked whether it was true, that they were come to ravage the coast, without having honestly declared war.

The admiral and all his crew burst out laughing, made him drink some punch, and sent him back.

The ingenuous Hercules, piqued at this reception, thought now of nothing else but beating his old friends for his countrymen and the Prior. The gentlemen of the neighbourhood ran from all quarters, and joined them : they had some cannon, and he discharged them one after the other. The English landed, and he flew towards them, and killed three of them with his own hand : he even wounded the admiral, who had made a joke of him. The whole militia were animated with his prowess; the English returned to their ships, and went on board; and the whole coast re-echoed with the shouts of victory, ' Long live the King ! Long live the ingenuous Hercules ! '

Every one ran to embrace him; every one strove to stop the bleeding of some slight wounds he had received.

'Ah!' said he, 'if Mlle de Saint-Yves were here, she would put on a bandage for me.'

The magistrate, who had hid himself in his cellar during the battle, came to pay his compliments like the rest. But he was greatly surprised, when he heard the ingenuous Hercules say to a dozen young men, who surrounded him, well disposed to serve him :

'My friends, having delivered the Abbey of the Mountain is nothing, we must rescue a maiden.'

The warm blood of these youths were fired by the words alone. He was already followed by crowds, who repaired to the convent. If the magistrate had not immediately acquainted the commandant with their design, and he had not sent a detachment after the joyous troop, the thing would have been done. The Huron was conducted back to his uncle and aunt, who overwhelmed him with tears and tenderness.

'I see very well,' said his uncle, 'that you will never be either a subdeacon or a prior; you will be an officer, and one still braver than my brother the captain, and probably as poor.'

Mlle de Kerkabon could not stop an incessant flood of tears, whilst she embraced him, saying :

'He will be killed too like my brother; it were much better he were a subdeacon.'

The Huron had, during the battle, picked up a large purse full of guineas, which probably the admiral dropped. He did not doubt but that this purse would buy all Lower Brittany, and, above all, make Mlle de Saint-Yves a great lady. Every one persuaded him to repair to Versailles, to receive the recompense due to his services. The commandant, and the principal officers, furnished him with certificates in abundance. The uncle and aunt also approved of this journey. He was to be presented to the King without any difficulty. This alone would give him great weight in the province. These two good folks added to the English purse a considerable present out of their savings. The Huron said to himself :

'When I see the King, I will ask him to give me Mlle de

Saint-Yves in marriage, and certainly he will not refuse me.'

He set out accordingly, amidst the acclamations of the whole district, stifled with embraces, bathed in tears by his aunt, blessed by his uncle, and leaving remembrances for the charming Mlle de Saint-Yves.

CHAPTER VIII

THE HURON GOES TO COURT. HE SUPS UPON THE ROAD WITH SOME HUGUENOTS

THE ingenuous Hercules took the Saumur road in the coach, because there was at that time no other convenience. When he came to Saumur, he was astonished to find the city almost deserted, and to see several families going away. He was told that, six years before, Saumur contained upwards of fifty thousand inhabitants, and that at present there were not six thousand. He mentioned this at the inn, whilst at supper. Several Protestants were at table; some complained bitterly, others trembled with rage, others weeping, said : ' *Nos dulcia linquimus arva, nos patriam fugimus.*'

The Huron, who did not understand Latin, had these words explained to him, which signified, ' We abandon our sweet fields; we fly from our country.'

' And why do you fly from your country, gentlemen? '

' Because we must otherwise acknowledge the Pope.'

' And why not acknowledge him? You have no god-mothers, then, that you want to marry; for I am told it is he that grants this permission.'

' Ah ! Sir, this Pope says that he is master of the domains of kings.'

' But, gentlemen, of what profession are you? '

' Why, Sir, we are for the most part drapers and manu-facturers.'

' If the Pope,' said he, ' claims to be the master of your cloths and manufactures, you do very well not to acknowledge him; but as to kings, it is their business, and why do you trouble yourself with it?'

Here a little man in black took up the argument, and very learnedly set forth the grievances of the company. He talked of the revocation of the Edict of Nantes with so much energy, he deplored in so pathetic a manner the fate of fifty thousand fugitive families, and of fifty thousand others converted by dragoons, that the ingenuous Hercules could not refrain from shedding tears.

'Whence arises it,' said he, 'that so great a king, whose renown extends even to the Hurons, should thus deprive himself of so many hearts that would have loved him, and so many arms that would have served him?'

'Because he has been imposed upon, like other great kings,' replied the little orator. 'He has been made to believe that, as soon as he utters a word, all people think as he does; and that he can make us change our religion, just as his musician Lulli, in a moment, changes the decorations of his opera. He has not only already lost five or six hundred thousand very useful subjects, but he has turned many of them into enemies; and King William, who is at this time master of England, has composed several regiments of these identical Frenchmen, who would otherwise have fought for their monarch.

'Such a disaster is the more astonishing, as the present Pope, to whom Louis XIV sacrifices a part of his people, is his declared enemy. A violent quarrel has subsisted between them for near nine years; it has been carried so far that France was in hopes of at length casting off the yoke, by which it has been kept in subjection for so many ages to this foreigner, and, more particularly, of not giving him any more money, which is the prime mover of the affairs of this world. It, therefore, appears evident that this great king has been imposed on, as well with respect to his interest, as to the extent of his power, and that even the magnanimity of his heart has been struck at.'

The Huron, more and more touched, asked who were the Frenchmen who thus deceived a monarch so dear to the Hurons.

'They are the Jesuits,' he was answered; 'and particularly Father de la Chaise, His Majesty's Confessor. It is to be hoped that God will one day punish them for it, and that they will be driven out, as they now drive us. Can any misfortune equal ours? Monsieur de Louvois besets us on all sides with Jesuits and dragoons.'

' Well, gentlemen,' replied the Huron, who could contain himself no longer, ' I am going to Versailles to receive the reward due to my services; I will speak to Monsieur de Louvois; I am told it is he who makes war from his closet. I shall see the King, and I will acquaint him with the truth; it is impossible not to yield to this truth, when it is felt. I shall return very soon to marry Mlle de Saint-Yves, and I beg you will be present at our nuptials.'

These good people now took him for some great lord, who travelled *incognito* in the coach. Some took him for the King's fool.

There was at table a disguised Jesuit, who acted as a spy to the Reverend Father de la Chaise. He gave him an account of everything that passed, and Father de la Chaise reported it to M. de Louvois. The spy wrote. The Huron and the letter arrived almost at the same time at Versailles.

CHAPTER IX

THE ARRIVAL OF THE HURON AT VERSAILLES. HIS RE-CEPTION AT COURT

THE ingenuous Hercules was set down from a *pot-de-chambre*,* in the court of the kitchens. He asked the chair men, what hour the King could be seen? The chair men laughed in his face, just as the English admiral had done. He treated them in the same manner, he beat them : they were for retaliation, and the scene was like to have proved bloody, if a life-guardsman, who was a gentleman of Brittany, had not passed by, and dispersed the mob.

' Sir,' said the traveller to him, ' you appear to me to be a brave man. I am nephew to the Prior of our Lady of

---

* A vehicle that goes from Paris to Versailles, which resembles a little covered tumbrel.

the Mountain. I have killed Englishmen, and I am come to speak to the King. I beg you will conduct me to his chamber.'

The soldier, delighted to find a man of courage from his province, who did not seem acquainted with the customs of the Court, told him that this was not the manner of speaking to the King, and that it was necessary to be presented by M. de Louvois.

'Very well, then, conduct me to M. de Louvois, who will, doubtless, conduct me to his Majesty.'

'It is even more difficult,' resumed the soldier, 'to speak to M. de Louvois than to his Majesty. But I will conduct you to M. Alexander, first commissioner of war, and this will be just the same as if you spoke to the minister.'

They accordingly repaired to M. Alexander's, who was first clerk; but they could not be introduced, he being closely engaged in business with a lady of the Court, and no person was allowed admittance.

'Well,' said the lifeguardsman, 'there is no harm done, let us go to M. Alexander's first clerk; this will be just the same as if you spoke to M. Alexander himself.'

The Huron, quite astonished, followed him; they remained together half an hour in a little antechamber.

'What is all this?' said the ingenuous Hercules. 'Is all the world invisible in this country? It is much easier to fight in Lower Brittany against Englishmen than to meet with people at Versailles, with whom one has business.'

He amused himself for some time with relating his amours to his countryman; but the clock striking recalled the soldier to his post, when a mutual promise was given of meeting on the morrow. The Huron remained another half an hour in the antechamber, ruminating upon Mlle de Saint-Yves, and the difficulty of speaking to kings and first clerks.

At length the official appeared.

'Sir,' said the ingenuous Hercules, 'if I had waited to repulse the English as long as you have made me wait for my audience, they would certainly have ravaged all Lower Brittany without opposition.'

These words struck the clerk. He at length said to the inhabitant of Brittany :

' What is your request ? '

' A reward,' said the other, showing his certificates ı ' these are my titles.'

The clerk read, and told him that probably he might obtain leave to purchase a lieutenancy.

' Me ! what, must I pay money for having repulsed the English ? Must I pay a tax to be killed for you, whilst you are peaceably giving your audiences here ? You are certainly jesting. I require a company of cavalry for nothing. I require that the king shall set Mlle de Saint-Yves at liberty from the convent, and that he give her me in marriage. I want to speak to the King in favour of fifty thousand families, whom I propose restoring to him. In a word, I want to be useful; let me be employed and advanced.'

' What is your name, Sir, who talk in such a lordly way.'

' Oh ! oh ! ' answered the Huron; ' you have not then read my certificates ? This is the way one is treated ! My name is Hercules de Kerkabon ; I have been christened, and I lodge at the Blue Dial.'

The clerk concluded, like the people at Saumur, that his head was turned, and did not pay him much attention.

The same day, the Reverend Father de la Chaise, Confessor to Louis XIV, received his spy's letter, which accused the Breton Kerkabon of favouring in his heart the Huguenots, and condemning the conduct of the Jesuits. M. de Louvois had, on his side, received a letter from the inquisitive magistrate, which depicted the Huron as a wicked, lewd fellow, inclined to burn convents and carry off the nuns.

Hercules, after having walked in the gardens of Versailles, which became irksome to him, and after having dined like a native of Huronia and Lower Brittany, had gone to rest, in the pleasant hope of seeing the King the next day; obtaining Mlle de Saint-Yves in marriage; having, at least, a company of cavalry; and of setting aside the persecution against the Huguenots. He was rocking himself asleep with these flattering ideas, when the police entered his chamber, and seized upon his double-barrelled gun and his great cutlass.

They took an inventory of his ready money, and then

conducted him to the castle erected by King Charles V, son to John II, near the street of St. Antoine, at the Porte des Tournelles.

What was the Huron's astonishment on his way thither, the reader is left to imagine. He at first fancied it was all a dream; and remained for some time in a state of stupefaction: presently transported with rage, that gave him more than common strength, he collared two of his guards who were with him in the coach, flung them out of the door, cast himself after them, and then dragged the third, who tried to hold him. He fell in the attempt, when they tied him, and replaced him in the carriage.

'This then,' said he, 'is what one gets by driving the English out of Lower Brittany! What wouldst thou say, charming Mlle de Saint-Yves, if thou didst see me in this situation!'

They at length arrived at their destination. He was carried in silence into the chamber in which he was to be locked up, like a corpse going to the grave. This room was already occupied by an old solitary student of Port Royal, named Gordon, who had been languishing there for two years.

'See,' said the head turnkey, 'here is company I bring you'; and immediately the enormous bolts of this strong door, secured with large iron bars, were fastened upon them. These two captives were thus separated from all the world.

CHAPTER X

THE HURON IS SHUT UP IN THE BASTILLE WITH A JANSENIST

M. GORDON was a healthy old man, of a serene disposition, who was acquainted with two great things; the one was, to bear adversity; the other, to console the afflicted. He approached his companion with an open sympathizing air, and said to him, whilst he embraced him:

'Whoever you are that is come to partake of my grave, be assured that I shall constantly forget myself in softening your torments in the infernal pit where we are plunged. Let us adore Providence that has conducted us here. Let us suffer in peace, and trust in hope.'

These words had the same effect upon the simple youth as English drops, which recall a dying person to life and show to his astonished eyes a glimpse of light.

After the first compliments were over, Gordon, without urging him to relate the cause of his misfortune, by the sweetness of his discourse, and by that interest which two unfortunate persons share with each other, inspired him with a desire to open his heart, and to disburden himself of the weight which oppressed him; but he could not guess the cause of his misfortune, and the good man Gordon was as much astonished as himself.

'God must, doubtless,' said the Jansenist to the Huron, 'have great designs for you, since he conducted you from Lake Ontario into England, from there to France; caused you to be baptized in Lower Brittany, and has now lodged you here for your salvation.'

'I' faith,' replied Hercules, 'I believe the devil alone has interfered in my destiny. My countrymen in America would never have treated me with the barbarity that I have experienced; they have not the least idea of it. They are called savages—they are good people, but rustic; and the men of this country are refined villains. I am indeed greatly surprised to have come from another world, to be shut up in this, under four bolts, with a priest; but I consider what an infinite number of men set out from one hemisphere to go and get killed in the other, or are wrecked on the voyage, and are eaten by the fishes. I cannot discover the gracious designs of God over all these people.'

Their dinner was brought them through a grating. The conversation turned upon Providence, *lettres de cachet*, and upon the art of not succumbing to the disgrace to which all men in this world are exposed.

'It is two years that I have been here,' said the old man, 'without any other consolation than myself and books; and yet I have never been a single moment out of temper.'

'Ah! Monsieur Gordon,' cried Hercules, 'you are not then in love with your godmother: if you were as well acquainted with Mlle de Saint-Yves as I am, you would be in a state of desperation.'

At these words he could not refrain from tears, which greatly relieved him from his oppression.

' How is it, then, that tears solace us? It seems to me that they should have a quite opposite effect.'

' My son,' said the good old man, ' everything is physical about us; all secretions are useful to the body, and all that comforts it, comforts the soul: we are the machines of Providence.'

The ingenuous Huron, who, as we have already observed more than once, had a great share of understanding, entered deeply into the consideration of this idea, the seeds whereof appeared to be in himself. After this he asked his companion why his person had for two years been confined by four bolts.

' By effectual grace,' answered Gordon : ' I pass for a Jansenist; I know Arnaud and Nicole; the Jesuits have persecuted us. We believe that the Pope is nothing more than a bishop like another, and therefore Father de la Chaise has obtained from the King his penitent an order for robbing me, without any form of justice, of the most precious inheritance of man, liberty.'

' This is very strange,' said the Huron, ' all the unhappy people I have met with have been made so solely by the Pope. With respect to your effectual grace, I acknowledge, I do not understand what you mean; but I consider it as a very great favour that God has let me in my misfortunes meet with a man such as you, who pours into my heart such consolation as I thought myself incapable of receiving.'

The conversation became every day more interesting and instructive. The souls of the two captives became linked together. The old man knew a great deal, and the young man was willing to learn. At the end of the first month, he applied himself eagerly to the study of geometry. Gordon made him read Rohault's *Physics*, which book was still in fashion; and he had good sense enough to find in it nothing but doubts and uncertainties.

He afterwards read the first volume of the *Enquiry after Truth*. This instructive work gave him new light.

' What ! ' said he, ' does our imagination and our senses

deceive us to that degree? What, are not our ideas formed by objects, and can we not acquire them by ourselves?'

When he had gone through the second volume, he was not so well satisfied; and he concluded it was much easier to destroy than to build.

His colleague, astonished that a young ignoramus should make such a remark only to be expected from men of high intellect, conceived a very high opinion of his understanding, and was more strongly attached to him.

'Your Malebranche,' said he to Gordon one day, 'seems to have written half his book whilst he was in possession of his reason, and the other half with the assistance only of imagination and prejudice.'

Some days after, Gordon asked him:

'What do you think of the soul, and the manner in which we receive our ideas? of volition, grace, and free agency?'

'Nothing,' replied the Huron. 'If I think sometimes, it is that we are under the power of the Eternal Being, like the stars and the elements; that he operates everything in us; that we are small wheels of the immense machine, of which he is the soul; that he acts according to general laws, and not from particular views: this is all that appears to me intelligible; all the rest is to me a dark abyss.'

'But this, my son, would be making God the author of sin!'

'But, father, your effectual grace would equally make him the author of sin; for certainly all those to whom this grace was refused, would sin; and is not he who gives us up to evil, the author of evil?'

This sincerity greatly embarrassed the good man; he found that all his endeavours to extricate himself from this quagmire were ineffectual; and he heaped such quantities of words upon one another, which seemed to have meaning, but which in fact had none (in the style of physical pre-motion), that the Huron could not help pitying him. This question evidently determined the origin of good and evil; and poor Gordon was reduced to the necessity of recurring to Pandora's box, the egg of Ormuzd pierced by Ahriman, the enmity between Typhon and Osiris, and, at last, original sin; and these he huddled together in profound darkness, without their throwing the least glimmering light upon one another. However, this romance of the soul diverted their thoughts from the contemplation of their own misery; and, by a strange magic, the multitude of calamities dispersed throughout the world diminished the sensation of their own miseries : they did not dare complain, when all mankind was in a state of suffering.

But in the repose of night the image of the charming Mlle de Saint-Yves effaced from the mind of her lover every metaphysical and moral idea. He awoke with his eyes bathed in tears; and the old Jansenist forgot his effectual grace, and the Abbé de Saint-Cyran, and Jansenius himself, to give consolation to a youth whom he judged guilty of a mortal sin.

After these lectures and their reasonings were over, their adventures furnished them with subjects of conversation; after this store was exhausted, they read together, or separately. The young man's understanding daily increased; and he would certainly have made great progress in mathematics had not the thought of Mlle de Saint-Yves frequently distracted him.

He read histories; they made him melancholy. The world appeared to him too wicked and too miserable. In fact, history is nothing more than a picture of crimes and misfortunes. The crowd of innocent and peaceable men are always invisible upon this vast theatre. The characters are but ambitious, perverse men. The pleasure which history affords is derived from the same source as tragedy, which would languish and become insipid, were it not inspired with strong passions, great crimes, and piteous misfortunes. Clio must be armed with a dagger as well as Melpomene.

Though the history of France is not less filled with horror than those of other nations, it nevertheless appeared to him so disgusting in the beginning, so dry in the continuation, so trifling in the end, even in the time of Henry IV, and ever destitute of grand monuments, or foreign to those fine discoveries which have illustrated other nations, that he was obliged to fight against distaste in order to go through all the particulars of obscure calamities confined to one little corner of the world.

Gordon thought like him. They both laughed with pity

when they read of the sovereigns of Fezensacs, Fesansaquet, and Astarac. Such a study could be relished only by their heirs, if they had any. The brilliant ages of the Roman Republic made him sometimes quite indifferent as to any other part of the globe. The spectacle of victorious Rome, the law-giver of nations, engrossed his whole soul. He glowed in contemplating a people who were governed for seven hundred years by enthusiasm for liberty and glory.

Thus days, weeks, and months rolled by; and he would have thought himself happy in the sanctuary of despair, if he had not been in love.

The natural goodness of his heart was softened still more when he reflected upon the Prior of Our Lady of the Mountain, and the affectionate Mlle de Kerkabon.

' What must they think,' he would often repeat, ' when they can get no tidings of me ? They must think me an ungrateful wretch.'

This idea rendered him inconsolable; he pitied those who loved him much more than he pitied himself.

CHAPTER XI

HOW THE HURON DEVELOPED HIS GENIUS

READING ennobles the soul, and an enlightened friend affords consolation. Our captive had these two advantages in his favour, which he had never expected.

' I shall begin to believe in metamorphosis, for I have been transformed from a brute into a man.'

He formed a library with part of the money which he was allowed to dispose of. His friend encouraged him to commit to writing such observations as occurred to him. These are his notes upon ancient history :

' I imagine that nations were for a long time like myself; that they did not become enlightened till very late; that for many ages they were occupied with nothing but the passing moment; that they thought very little of what was past, and never of the future. I have travelled five or six hundred leagues across Canada, and I did not meet

with a single monument : no one is in any way acquainted
with the actions of his predecessors. Is not this the natural
state of man ? The human species of this continent appear
to me superior to that of the other. They have extended
their being for many ages by arts and knowledge. Is this
because they have beards upon their chins, and God has
refused this ornament to the Americans ? I do not believe
it ; for I find the Chinese have very little beard, and that
they have cultivated arts for upwards of five thousand
years. In effect, if their annals go back upwards of four
thousand years, the nation must necessarily have been united,
and in a flourishing state, for more than fifty centuries.

' One thing particularly strikes me in this ancient history
of China, which is, that almost everything is probable
and natural. I admire it because it is not tinctured with
anything of the marvellous.

' Why have all other nations adopted fabulous origins ?
The ancient chroniclers of the history of France, who, by
the by, are not very ancient, make the French descend
from one Francus, the son of Hector. The Romans said
they were the issue of a Phrygian, though there was not in
their whole language a single word that had the least con-
nection with the language of Phrygia. The gods had
inhabited Egypt for ten thousand years, and the devils
Scythia, where they engendered the Huns. I meet with
nothing before Thucydides but romances similar to those
of Amadis, and far less amusing. Apparitions, oracles,
prodigies, sorcery, metamorphoses are interspersed throughout with the explanation of dreams, which are the bases
of the destiny of the greatest empires and the smallest
states. Here are speaking beasts, there brutes that are
adored, gods transformed into men, and men into gods. If
we must have fables, let us at least have such as appear
the emblem of truth. I admire the fables of philosophers,
but I laugh at those of children, and I hate those of
impostors.'

He one day hit upon a history of the Emperor Justinian.
It was there related that some ignoramuses of Constantinople had delivered, in very bad Greek, an edict against
the greatest captain of the age, because this hero had
uttered the following words in the warmth of conversation :

'Truth shines forth with its proper light, and people's minds are not illumined with flaming piles.' The ignoramuses declared that this proposition was heretical, smelling of heresy; and that the contrary action was catholic, universal, and Grecian : ' The minds of the people are not enlightened but with flaming piles, and truth cannot shine forth with its own light.'

These Linostolians thus condemned several discourses of the captain and published an edict.

' What ! ' said the Huron with much emotion, ' shall such people publish edicts? '

' They are not edicts,' replied Gordon ; ' they are counter-edicts, which all the world laughed at in Constantinople, and the Emperor the first. He was a wise prince, who knew how to reduce the Linostolian ignoramuses to a state incapable of doing anything but good. He knew that these gentlemen—and several other Pastophores—had tired the patience of the emperors, his predecessors, with counter-edicts in more serious matters.'

' He did very right,' said the Huron ; ' the Pastophores should be maintained and kept within bounds.'

He committed several other observations to paper, which astonished old Gordon.

' What ! ' said he to himself, ' have I consumed fifty years in instruction, and I fear I have not attained to the natural good sense of this child, who is almost a savage ! I tremble to think I have so arduously strengthened prejudices, and he listens to simple Nature alone.'

The good man had some little books of criticism, some of those periodical pamphlets, wherein men, incapable of producing anything themselves, blacken the productions of others; where a Visé insults a Racine, and a Faydit a Fénelon. The Huron ran over some of them.

' I compare them,' he said, ' to certain gnats that lodge their eggs in the posteriors of the finest horses, which do not, however, prevent their running.'

The two philosophers scarcely deigned to cast their eyes upon these excrements of literature.

They soon after went through the elements of astronomy. The Huron sent for a globe of the heavens : he was delighted at this great spectacle.

'How hard it is,' said he, 'that I should only begin to be acquainted with heaven, when the power of contemplating it is taken from me! Jupiter and Saturn revolve in these immense spaces; millions of suns illumine myriads of worlds; and, in this corner of the earth on which I am cast, there are beings that deprive me, a creature possessed of sight and powers of thought, of those worlds whither my eye might reach, and even that in which God created me! The light created for the whole universe is lost to me. It was not hidden from me in the northern horizon, where I passed my infancy and youth. Without you, my dear Gordon, I should be annihilated here.'

CHAPTER XII

THE HURON'S SENTIMENTS UPON THEATRICAL PIECES

THE young Huron resembled one of those hardy trees which, planted in an ungrateful soil, in a little time extend their roots and branches, when transplanted to a more favourable spot; and it was very extraordinary that this favourable spot should be a prison.

Among the books which employed the leisure of the two captives were some poems, the translations of Greek tragedies, and some dramatic pieces in French. Those passages that dwelt on love communicated at once pleasure and pain to the soul of the Huron. They were but so many images of his beloved. The fable of the two pigeons rent his heart; he was so far estranged from his tender dove.

Molière enchanted him. He taught him the manners of Paris and of human nature.

'To which of his comedies do you give the preference?'

'Without any doubt, to *Tartufe*.'

'I am of your opinion,' said Gordon; 'it was a Tartufe that flung me into this dungeon, and perhaps they are Tartufes who have been the cause of your misfortunes.'

'What do you think of these Greek tragedies?'

'They are very good for the Greeks.'

But when he read the modern *Iphigénie, Phèdre, Andro-*

maque, Athalie, he was in ecstasy, he sighed, he wept,—and he learnt them by heart, without meaning to do so.

'Read *Rodogune,*' said Gordon. 'It is said to be a capital production; the other pieces which have given you so much pleasure are trifles compared with this.'

The young man had scarce got through the first page, before he said :

'This is not written by the same author.'

'How do you know that? '

'I know nothing yet; but these lines touch neither my ear nor my heart.'

'O ! ' said Gordon, 'the versification is not important.'

The Huron asked, 'What must I judge by then? '

After having read the piece very attentively, without any other design than being pleased, he looked steadfastly at his friend with dry eyes and was astonished, not knowing what to say. At length, being urged to give his opinion, with respect to what he felt, this was the answer he made :

'I understood very little of the beginning; the middle disgusted me; but the last scene greatly moved me, though there appears to me but little probability in it. I am interested in none of the characters, and I do not remember twenty lines, I who recollect them all when they please me.'

'This piece, nevertheless, passes for the best upon our stage.'

'If that be the case,' said he, 'it is perhaps like many people who are not worthy of the places they hold. After all, this is a matter of taste, and mine cannot yet be formed. I may be mistaken; but you know I am accustomed to say what I think, or rather what I feel. I suspect that illusion, fashion, caprice, often warp the judgments of men. I have spoken in accordance with Nature; and it may be that in me Nature greatly lacks perfection; but perhaps also it is often too little considered by the majority of men.'

Here he repeated some lines from *Iphigénie,* which he was full of; and though he declaimed but indifferently, he uttered them with such truth and feeling that he made the old Jansenist weep. He then read *Cinna,* which did not excite his tears, but his admiration.

CHAPTER XIII

THE BEAUTIFUL MLLE DE SAINT-YVES GOES TO VERSAILLES

WHILST the unfortunate young man was more enlightened than consoled, whilst his genius, so long stifled, unfolded itself with so much rapidity and strength, whilst Nature, which was attaining a degree of perfection in him, avenged herself of the outrages of fortune, what became of the Prior, his good sister, and the beautiful recluse Mlle de Saint-Yves? The first month they were uneasy, and the third they were immersed in sorrow. False conjectures and ill-grounded reports alarmed them. At the end of six months, it was concluded he was dead. At length, the Prior and Mlle de Kerkabon learned by a letter of ancient date, which one of the King's guards had written to Brittany, that a young man resembling the Huron arrived one night at Versailles, but that since that time no one had heard him spoken of.

'Alas!' said Mlle de Kerkabon, 'our nephew has done some ridiculous thing, which has brought on some terrible consequences. He is young, a Low Breton, and cannot know how to behave at Court. My dear brother, I never saw Versailles nor Paris; here is a fine opportunity. We shall, perhaps, find our poor nephew: he is our brother's son, and it is our duty to assist him. Who knows, we may perhaps at length prevail upon him to become a subdeacon, when the fire of youth is somewhat abated. He was much inclined to the sciences. Do you remember how he reasoned upon the Old and New Testament? We are answerable for his soul; he was baptized at our instigation. His dear mistress Mlle de Saint-Yves does nothing but weep incessantly. Indeed we must go to Paris. If he is concealed in any of those infamous houses of pleasure which I have often heard of, we will get him out.'

The Prior was touched by his sister's words. He went in search of the Bishop of St. Malo, who had baptized the Huron, and requested his protection and advice. The prelate approved of the journey. He gave the Prior letters of recommendation to Father de la Chaise, the King's

Confessor, who was invested with the first dignity in the kingdom; to Harlay, Archbishop of Paris; and to Bossuet, Bishop of Meaux.

At length, the brother and sister set out; but when they came to Paris, they found themselves bewildered in a great labyrinth without clue or end. Their means were small, and they had occasion every day for carriages to pursue their search, and they discovered nothing.

The Prior waited upon the Reverend Father de la Chaise : he was with Mademoiselle du Thron, and could not give audience to priors. He went to the Archbishop's door : the prelate was shut up with the beautiful Mademoiselle de Lesdiguières about church matters. He flew to the country house of the Bishop of Meaux : he was upon a close examination, with Mademoiselle de Mauléon, of the mystical amour of Madame Guyon. At length, however, he gained access to these two prelates; they both declared they could not interfere with regard to his nephew, as he was not a subdeacon.

He, at length, saw the Jesuit, who received him with open arms, protesting he had always entertained the greatest private esteem for him, though he had never known him. He swore that his Society had always been attached to the inhabitants of Lower Brittany.

' But,' said he, ' has not your nephew the misfortune of being a Huguenot ? '

' Certainly not, Reverend Father.'

' May he not be a Jansenist ? '

' I can assure your Reverence that he is scarcely a Christian. It is only about eleven months since he was christened.'

' This is very well;—we will take care of him. Is your benefice considerable ? '

' No, a mere trifle, and our nephew costs us a great deal.'

' Are there any Jansenists in your neighbourhood ? Take great care, my dear Prior, they are more dangerous than Huguenots, or even Atheists.'

' My Reverend Father, we have none; it is not even known at our Lady of the Mountain what Jansenism is.'

' So much the better; go, there is nothing I will not do for you.'

He dismissed the Prior in this affectionate manner, but thought no more about him.

Time slipped away, and the Prior and his good sister were almost in despair.

In the meanwhile, the cursed magistrate urged very strenuously the marriage of his great booby son with the beautiful Mlle de Saint-Yves, who was taken purposely out of the convent. She always entertained a passion for her godson in proportion as she detested the husband who was designed for her. The insult that had been offered her by shutting her up in a convent increased her affection; and the mandate for wedding the magistrate's son completed her antipathy for him. Chagrin, tenderness, and terror racked her soul. Love, we know, is much more inventive and more daring in a young woman than friendship in an aged Prior and an aunt upwards of forty-five. Besides, she had received good instruction in her convent, with the assistance of romances, which she read by stealth.

The beautiful Mlle de Saint-Yves remembered the letter that had been written by a life-guardsman to Lower Brittany, and which had been spoken of in the province. She resolved to go herself and gain information at Versailles; to throw herself at the minister's feet, if her husband should be in prison, as it was said, and obtain justice for him. I know not what secret intelligence she had gained that at Court nothing is refused to a pretty woman; but she knew not the price of these boons.

Having taken this resolution she was comforted, and was at peace. She no longer repulsed her boorish suitor. She received her detestable father-in-law, she paid fond attention to her brother, and spread happiness throughout the house. On the day appointed for the ceremony, she secretly departed at four o'clock in the morning, with the little nuptial presents she had received, and all she could gather. Her plan was so well laid that she was about ten leagues upon her journey, when, about noon, her absence was discovered, and when every one's consternation and surprise was inexpressible. The inquisitive magistrate asked more questions that day than he had done for a week before; the intended bridegroom was more stupefied than ever. The Abbé de Saint-Yves resolved in his rage to pursue his sister. The magistrate and his son were disposed to accompany him. Destiny led almost the whole canton of Lower Brittany to Paris.

The beautiful Mlle de Saint-Yves was not without apprehensions that she should be pursued. She rode on horseback, and she got all the intelligence she could, without being suspected, from the couriers, if they had not met a fat abbé, an enormous magistrate, and a young booby, galloping as fast as they could to Paris. Learning, on the third day, that they were not far behind, she took a quite different road, and was skilful and lucky enough to arrive at Versailles, while they were in a fruitless pursuit after her, at Paris. But how was she to behave at Versailles? Young, handsome, untutored, unsupported, unknown, exposed to every danger, how could she dare go in search of one of the King's guards? She had some thoughts of applying to a Jesuit of low rank, for there were some for every station of life; as God, they say, has given different aliments to every species of animals, so had he given the King his confessor, who was called, by all solicitors of benefices, the Head of the Gallican Church. Then came the princesses' confessors; the ministers had none, they were not such dupes. There were Jesuits for the genteel mob, and particularly those for chambermaids, by whom were known the secrets of their mistresses; and this was no small vocation. The beautiful Mlle de Saint-Yves addressed herself to one of these last, who was called Father Tout-à-tous (All-things-to-all-men). She confessed to him, set forth her adventure, her situation, her danger, and conjured him to get her a lodging with some good devotee, who might shelter her from temptations.

Father Tout-à-tous introduced her to one of his most trusty penitents—the wife of a court cupbearer. From the moment Mlle de Saint-Yves became her lodger, she did her utmost to obtain the confidence and friendship of this woman. She gained intelligence of the Breton guardsman, and invited him to visit her. Having learned from him that her lover had been carried off after having had a conference with one of the first clerks, she hurried to this clerk. The sight of a fine woman softened him, for it must be allowed God created woman only to tame mankind.

The scribe, thus mollified, acknowledged to her everything.

'Your lover has been in the Bastille almost a year, and without your intercession he would, perhaps, have ended his days there.'

The tender Mlle de Saint-Yves swooned. When she had recovered herself, the penman told her :

'I have no power to do good; all my influence extends to doing harm sometimes. Take my advice, wait upon Monsieur de Saint-Pouange, who has the power of doing both good and ill; he is Monsieur de Louvois's cousin and favourite. This minister has two souls : the one is Monsieur de Saint-Pouange, and Madame Dufresnoy is the other, but she is at present absent from Versailles; so that you have nothing to do but captivate the protector I have pointed out to you.'

The beautiful Mlle de Saint-Yves, divided between some trifling joy and excessive grief, between a glimmering of hope and dreadful apprehensions ;—pursued by her brother, idolizing her lover, wiping her tears, which flowed in torrents; trembling and feeble, yet summoning all her courage ;—in this situation, she flew swiftly to the house of Monsieur de Saint-Pouange.

CHAPTER XIV

THE PROGRESS OF THE HURON'S INTELLECT

THE ingenuous youth was making a rapid progress in the sciences, and particularly in the science of man. The cause of this sudden disclosure of his understanding was as much owing to his savage education, as to the disposition of his soul; for having learned nothing in his infancy, he had not imbibed any prejudices. His mind not having been warped by error had retained all its primitive rectitude. He saw things as they were; whereas the ideas that are communicated to us in our infancy make us see them all our life in a false light.

'Your persecutors are abominable wretches,' said he

to his friend Gordon. 'I pity you for being oppressed, but I condemn you for being a Jansenist. All sects appear to me to be founded in error; tell me if there are any sectaries in geometry?'

'No, my child,' said the good old Gordon, heaving a deep sigh; 'all men are agreed concerning truth, when demonstrated; but they are too much divided about latent truths.'

'Say rather, about latent falsehood. If there were but one single hidden truth in your load of arguments, which have been so often sifted for such a number of ages, it would doubtless have been discovered, and the universe would certainly have been unanimous, at least, in that respect. If this truth had been necessary, as the sun is to the earth, it would have been as brilliant as that planet. It is an absurdity, an insult to human nature; it is an attack upon the Infinite and Supreme Being to say there is a truth essential to the happiness of man which God has concealed.'

All that this ignorant youth said, instructed only by Nature, made a very deep impression upon the mind of the old unhappy scholar.

'Is it really certain,' he cried, 'that I should have made myself truly miserable for mere chimeras? I am much more certain of my misery than of effectual grace.—I have spent my time in reasoning about the liberty of God and human nature, but I have lost my own; neither St. Augustine nor St. Prosper will ever draw me out of the pit where I am.'

The ingenuous Huron, who gave way to his natural characteristic, at length said :

'Will you give me leave to speak to you boldly and frankly? Those who bring upon themselves persecution for such idle disputes seem to me to have very little sense; those who persecute, appear to me monsters.'

The two captives entirely coincided with respect to the injustice of their captivity.

'I am a hundred times more to be pitied than you,' said the Huron; 'I was born free as the air : I had two lives—liberty and the object of my love; and I am deprived of both. We are both in fetters, without knowing who

put them on us, or without being able to inquire. I lived
a Huron for twenty years. It is said they are barbarians,
because they avenge themselves of their enemies; but
they never oppress their friends. I had scarcely set foot
in France before I shed my blood for this country : I
have, perhaps, preserved a whole province, and my reward
is to be swallowed up in this sepulchre of the living, where
I should have died with rage, had it not been for you.
There must then be no laws in this country. Men are
condemned without being heard. This is not the case in
England. Alas ! it was not against the English I should
have fought.'

Thus his growing philosophy could not brook Nature
being insulted in the first of her rights, and he gave vent
to his just anger.

His companion did not contradict him. Absence ever
increases ungratified love, and philosophy does not diminish
it. He as frequently spoke of his beloved as he did of
morality or metaphysics. The more he purified his sentiments, the more he loved. He read some new romances;
but he met with few that depicted to him the real state
of his soul. He always felt that his heart stretched beyond
the bounds of his author.

' Alas ! ' said he, ' almost all these writers have nothing
but wit and art.'

At length, the good Jansenist priest became, insensibly,
the confidant of his tenderness. He was hitherto acquainted with love as a sin, with which a penitent accuses
himself at confession. He now learned to know it as a
sentiment equally noble and tender, which can elevate
the soul as well as soften it, and can produce, sometimes,
virtues. In fine, for the last miracle, a Huron converted a
Jansenist.

CHAPTER XV

THE BEAUTIFUL MLLE DE SAINT-YVES RESISTS SOME DELICATE PROPOSALS

THE charming Mlle de Saint-Yves, still more afflicted than
her lover, waited accordingly upon M. de Saint-Pouange,

accompanied by her friend with whom she lodged, each having their faces covered with their hoods. The first thing she saw at the door was the Abbé de Saint-Yves, her brother, coming out. She was terrified, but her pious friend supported her spirits.

' For the very reason,' said she, ' that people have been speaking against you, speak to him for yourself. You may be assured that the accusers in this part of the world are always in the right, unless they are immediately detected. Besides, your presence will have greater effect, or else I am much mistaken, than the words of your brother.'

Ever so little encouragement to a passionate lover makes her intrepid. Mlle de Saint-Yves appeared at the audience. Her youth, her charms, her languishing eyes, moistened with some involuntary tears, attracted every one's attention. Every sycophant to the deputy minister forgot, for an instant, the idol of power, to contemplate that of beauty. Saint-Pouange conducted her into a closet; she spoke with an affecting grace; Saint-Pouange felt some emotion. She trembled, but he told her not to be afraid.

' Return to-night,' said he; ' your business requires some reflection, and it must be discussed at leisure. There are too many people here at present. Audiences are rapidly dispatched. I must get to the bottom of all that concerns you.'

He then paid her some compliments upon her beauty and manner of thinking, and advised her to come at seven in the evening.

She did not fail, and her pious friend again accompanied her; but she kept in the hall, where she was reading the *Christian Pedagogue*, whilst Saint-Pouange and the beautiful Mlle de Saint-Yves were in the back room. He began by saying :

' Would you believe it, Mademoiselle, that your brother has been to request me to grant him a *lettre de cachet* against you; but, indeed, I would sooner grant one to send him back to Lower Brittany.'

' Alas ! Sir,' said she, ' *lettres de cachet* are granted very liberally in your offices, since people come from the extremity of the kingdom to solicit them like pensions. I

am very far from requesting one against my brother; I
have much reason to complain of him; but I respect the
liberty of mankind; and therefore supplicate for that of a
man, whom I want to make my husband; of a man, to
whom the King is indebted for the preservation of a
province; who can beneficially serve him; and who is the
son of an officer killed in his service. What is he accused
of? How could he be treated so cruelly without being
heard?'

The deputy minister then showed her the letter of the
spy Jesuit, and that of the perfidious magistrate.

'What!' said she with astonishment, 'are there such
monsters upon earth? And would they force me to marry
the stupid son of a ridiculous wicked man? And is it
upon such evidence that the fate of citizens is determined?'

She threw herself upon her knees, and, with a flood of
tears, solicited the freedom of the brave man who adored
her. Her charms appeared to the greatest advantage in
such a situation. She was so beautiful that Saint-Pouange,
bereft of all shame, insinuated to her that she would
succeed, if she began by yielding him the first fruits of
what she reserved for her lover. Mlle de Saint-Yves,
shocked and confused, pretended for some time not to
understand him; and he was obliged to explain himself
more clearly. One word, used with some reserve, brought
on another less delicate, which was succeeded by one still
more expressive. The revocation of the *lettre de cachet* was
not only proposed, but pecuniary recompenses, honours,
and places; and the more he promised, the greater was
his desire not to be refused.

Mlle de Saint-Yves wept, whilst her anguish almost
choked her, half resting upon a sofa, scarcely able to
believe what she saw and heard. Saint-Pouange, in turn,
threw himself upon his knees. He was not unattractive,
and might not so much have shocked a heart less pre-
possessed; but Mlle de Saint-Yves adored her lover, and
thought it the greatest of crimes to betray him in order to
serve him. Saint-Pouange renewed with greater fervency
his prayers and entreaties. He, at length, went so far as
to say that this was the only means of obtaining the liberty
of the man whose interest she had so violently and affec-

tionately at heart. This uncommon conversation continued for a long time. The devotee in the antechamber, in reading her *Christian Pedagogue,* said to herself :

' Good heavens ! What can they be doing there for these two hours ? My Lord Saint-Pouange never before gave so long an audience; perhaps he has refused everything to this poor girl, and she is still entreating him.'

At length her companion came out of the inner room in the greatest confusion, without being able to speak, wrapped in meditation upon the character of the great and the half great, who so slightly sacrifice the liberty of men and the honour of women.

She did not utter a syllable all the way back. But being returned to her friends, she burst out, and told all that had happened. Her pious friend made frequent signs of the cross.

' My dear friend,' said she, ' you must consult to-morrow Father Tout-à-tous, our director; he has much influence over Monsieur de Saint-Pouange; he is confessor to many of the female servants of the house; he is a pious accommodating man, who also has the direction of some women of fashion. Yield to him; this is my way; and I always found myself right. We weak women stand in need of a man to lead us : and so, my dear friend, I'll go to-morrow in search of Father Tout-à-tous.'

CHAPTER XVI

SHE CONSULTS A JESUIT

No sooner was the beautiful and disconsolate Mlle de Saint-Yves with her holy confessor than she told him that a powerful, voluptuous man had proposed to her to set at liberty the man whom she intended making her lawful husband, and that he required a great price for his service; that she held such infidelity in the highest detestation; and that if her life only had been required, she would much sooner have sacrificed it than have submitted.

' What an abominable sinner,' said Father Tout-à-tous.

'You should tell me the name of this vile man; he must certainly be some Jensenist; I will inform against him to his Reverence Father de la Chaise, who will place him in the situation in which your dear beloved intended bridegroom now is.'

The poor girl, after much struggle and embarrassment, at length named Saint-Pouange.

'My Lord Saint-Pouange!' cried the Jesuit. 'Ah! my child, the case is quite different; he is cousin to the greatest minister we have ever had; a man of worth, a protector of the good cause, a good Christian: he could not possibly entertain such a thought; you certainly must have misunderstood him.'

'Oh! Father, I did but understand him too well. I am lost on whichever side I turn: the only alternative I have to choose is misery or shame; either my lover must remain buried alive, or I must make myself unworthy of living. I cannot let him perish, nor can I save him.'

Father Tout-à-tous endeavoured to console her with these gentle expressions:

'In the first place, my child, never use the word *lover*; it intimates something worldly, which may offend God: say my *husband*; for although he is not yet your husband, you consider him as such, and nothing can be more decent.

'Secondly, though he be ideally your husband, and you are in hopes he will be such, he is not so in effect; consequently, you will not commit adultery—an enormous sin, that should always be avoided as much as possible.

'Thirdly, actions are not maliciously culpable, when the intention is virtuous; and nothing can be more virtuous than to procure your husband his liberty.

'Fourthly, you have examples in holy antiquity that may miraculously serve you for a guide. St. Augustine relates that under the proconsulate of Septimius Acidinus, in the year of our salvation 340, a poor man could not pay unto Cæsar what belonged to Cæsar, and was justly condemned to die, notwithstanding the maxim, *Where there is nothing, the king must lose his right*. The object in question was a pound of gold. The culprit had a wife, in whom God had united beauty and prudence. An old miser promised to give a pound of gold, and even more, to the lady, upon condition that he committed with her the sin of uncleanness. The lady thought she did not act wrong to save her husband's life. St. Augustine highly approves of her generous resignation. It is true that the old miser cheated her, and, perhaps, her husband was nevertheless hanged; but she did all that was in her power to save his life.

' You may assure yourself, my child, that when a Jesuit quotes St. Augustine, that saint must certainly have been in the right. I advise you to nothing; you are prudent, and it is to be presumed that you will do your husband a service. My Lord Saint-Pouange is an honest man; he will not deceive you; this is all I can say; I will pray to God for you; and I hope everything will take place for his glory.'

The beautiful Mlle de Saint-Yves, who was no less terrified with the Jesuit's discourse than with the proposals of the deputy minister, returned in despair to her friend. She was tempted to deliver herself by death from the horror of leaving in a shocking captivity the lover she adored, and the shame of releasing him at the dearest of all prices, which was the sole property of this unfortunate lover.

CHAPTER XVII

SHE YIELDS THROUGH VIRTUE

She entreated her friend to kill her; but this lady, who was fully as indulgent as the Jesuit, spoke to her still more clearly.

' Alas ! ' said she, ' business is seldom carried on at this agreeable, gallant, and famous court upon any other terms. The most considerable, as well as the most indifferent, places are seldom given away, but at the price required of you. Hearken, you have inspired me with friendship and confidence; I will own to you that if I had been as contrary as you are, my husband would not be enjoying the post upon which he lives; he knows it, and so far from being displeased, he considers me as his benefactress; and

K 33

himself as my creature. Do you think that all those who
have been at the head of provinces, or even armies, have
been indebted for their honours and fortune solely to their
services? There are some who are beholden to the ladies
their wives. The dignities of war are solicited by love;
and a place is given to him who has got the handsomest
wife.

'You are in a situation that is still more critical; the
object is to let your lover see daylight, and to marry him;
it is a sacred duty that you are to fulfil. No one has ever
censured the great and beautiful ladies I mention to you;
the world will applaud you : it will be said that you only
allowed yourself to be guilty of a weakness, through an
excess of virtue.'

'Heavens!' cried Mlle de Saint-Yves. 'What kind of
virtue is this? What a labyrinth of distress! What a
world! What experiences I have had of men! A Father
de la Chaise and a ridiculous magistrate imprison my
lover; I am persecuted by my family; assistance is offered
me, only that I may be dishonoured! A Jesuit has ruined
a brave man, another Jesuit wants to ruin me : on every
side snares are laid for me, and I am upon the very brink
of destruction! I must either kill myself or speak to the
King; I will throw myself at his feet as he goes to mass
or the playhouse.'

'His attendants will not let you approach him,' said her
good friend; 'and if you should be so unfortunate as to
speak to him, Monsieur de Louvois, or the Reverend Father
de la Chaise, might bury you in a convent for the rest of your
days.'

Whilst this generous friend thus increased the perplexities
of Mlle de Saint-Yves's tortured soul, and plunged the
dagger deeper in her heart, a messenger arrived from M. de
Saint-Pouange with a letter, and two fine pendant earrings. Mlle de Saint-Yves, with tears, refused accepting
of any part of the contents of the packet; but her friend
took charge of them herself.

As soon as the messenger was gone, our confidante read
the letter, in which a little supper was proposed to the two
friends for that night. Mlle de Saint-Yves protested she
would not go, whilst her pious friend endeavoured to make

her try on the diamond earrings; but Mlle de Saint-Yves could not endure them, and opposed it all the day long. At length, being entirely wrapped up in the contemplation of her lover, overcome and dragged along, not knowing whether she was carried, she let herself be led to the fatal supper. She had remained inexorable to all entreaties of putting on the earrings; so that her confidante took them with her, and placed them in her ears, against her will, before they sat down to supper. Mlle de Saint-Yves was so confused and agitated that she underwent this torment, and her patron considered it as a very favourable prognostic. Towards the end of the repast, her friend very prudently retired. Her patron then showed her the revocation of the *lettre de cachet*, the grant of a considerable recompense, and a captain's commission, which were accompanied with unlimited promises.

' Ah ! ' said Mlle de Saint-Yves, with a deep sigh, ' how much should I love you, if you did not desire to be loved so much ! '

In a word, after a long resistance, shrieks, cries, and torrents of tears, weakened with the conflict, overwhelmed and languishing, she was compelled to yield; and the only consolation now left her was that she resolved to think of nothing but the ingenuous Huron, whilst her cruel ravisher relentlessly enjoyed the advantage of that necessity to which she was reduced.

CHAPTER XVIII

SHE DELIVERS HER LOVER AND A JANSENIST

AT daybreak she flew to Paris with the minister's mandate. It would be difficult to depict the agitations of her mind in this journey. Imagine a virtuous and noble soul, humbled by its own reproaches, intoxicated with tenderness, distracted with the remorse of having betrayed her lover, and elated with the pleasure of releasing the object of her adoration. Her torments, her conflicts, her success by turns engaged her reflections. She was no longer that inno-

cent girl whose ideas were confined to a provincial education. Love and misfortunes had united to mould her
anew. Sentiment had made as rapid a progress in her
mind as reason had in that of her unfortunate lover. Girls
learn to feel more easily than men learn to think. Her
adventure afforded her more instruction than four years
confinement in a convent.

Her dress was dictated by the greatest simplicity. She
viewed with horror the trappings with which she had
appeared before her fatal benefactor. She had left her
friend her earrings without having looked at them. Charmed
and confused, idolizing the Huron and detesting herself,
she at length arrived at the gate of ' that dreadful castle,
the palace of vengeance, where oft crimes and innocence
are alike immured.' *

When she was upon the point of getting out of the
coach her strength failed her; some people came to her
assistance : she entered, whilst her heart was in the greatest
palpitation, her eyes streaming, and her whole frame
bespoke the greatest consternation. She was presented to
the Governor; she made to speak to him, but she had
lost all power of expression; she showed her order, whilst
with great difficulty she articulated some accents. The
Governor entertained a great esteem for his prisoner, and
he was greatly pleased at his being released. His heart
was not callous, like those of most of his brethren, who
think of nothing but the wages gained from guarding their
captives; extort their revenues from their victims; and
living by the misery of others, conceive a horrid joy at the
lamentations of the unfortunate.

He sent for the prisoner into his apartment. The two
lovers swooned at the sight of each other. The beautiful
Mlle de Saint-Yves remained for a long time motionless,
without any symptoms of life; the other soon recalled his
fortitude.

' This,' said the Governor, ' is probably the lady your
wife; you did not tell me you were married. I am in-

* De cet affreux chateau, palais de la vengeance,
    Qui renferme souvent le crime et l'innocence.
                        —Voltaire : *Henriade*, ch. iv. 456–7.

formed that it is through her generous solicitude that you have obtained your liberty.'

' Alas ! ' said the beautiful woman, in a faltering voice, ' I am not worthy of being his wife '; and swooned again.

When she recovered her senses, she presented, with a trembling hand, the grant and written promise of a company. The Huron, equally astonished and affected, awoke from one dream to fall into another.

' Why was I shut up here? How could you deliver me? Where are the monsters who thrust me here? You are a divinity sent from heaven to succour me.'

The beautiful Mlle de Saint-Yves lowered her eyes, then looked at her lover, blushed, and instantly turned away her streaming eyes. In a word, she told him all she knew, and all she had undergone, except what she was willing to conceal for ever, but which any other except the Huron, more accustomed to the world and better acquainted with the customs of courts, would easily have guessed.

' Is it possible that a wretch like the magistrate can have deprived me of my liberty? Alas ! I find that men like the vilest of animals, can all hurt. But is it possible that a monk, a Jesuit, the King's Confessor, should have contributed to my misfortunes as much as the magistrate, without my being able to imagine under what pretence this detestable knave has persecuted me ? Did he make me pass for a Jansenist? In fine, how came you to remember me? I did not deserve it; I was then only a savage. What ! could you, without advice, without assistance, undertake a journey to Versailles? You appeared there, and my fetters were broken ! There must then be in beauty and virtue an invincible charm, that opens gates of iron, and softens hearts of steel.'

At the word ' virtue ' a flood of tears issued from the eyes of the beautiful Mlle de Saint-Yves. She did not know how far she had been virtuous in the crime with which she reproached herself.

Her lover thus continued :

' Thou angel, who hast broken my chains, if thou hast had sufficient influence (which I cannot yet comprehend) to obtain justice for me, obtain it likewise for an old man who first taught me to think, as thou didst to love. Misfortunes have united us; I love him as a father; I can neither live without thee nor him.'

' I ! Shall I ask a favour of the same man who . . .'

' Yes, I will be beholden to you for everything, and I will owe nothing to any one but yourself.—Write to this man in power, overwhelm me with kindnesses, complete what you have begun, perfect your miracles.'

She was sensible she ought to do everything her lover desired. She wanted to write, but her hand refused its office. She began her letter three times, and tore it up as often; at length she got to the end, and the two lovers left the prison, after having embraced the old martyr to effectual grace.

The happy, yet disconsolate Mlle de Saint-Yves knew where her brother lodged; thither she repaired; and her lover took an apartment at the same house.

They had scarcely reached their lodging before her protector sent the order for releasing the good old Gordon, at the same time making an appointment with her for the next day.

Thus was every generous and laudable action of hers performed at the price of her honour. She considered with detestation this practice of selling at once the happiness and misery of man. She gave the order of release to her lover, and refused the appointment of a benefactor, whom she could no more see without expiring with shame and grief. Her lover could not have left her upon any other errand than to release his friend. He flew to the place of his confinement, and fulfilled this duty in reflecting upon the strange vicissitudes of this world, and admiring the courageous virtue of a young lady, to whom two unfortunate men owed more than their life.

CHAPTER XIX

THE HURON, THE BEAUTIFUL MLLE DE SAINT-YVES, AND THEIR RELATIONS ARE REASSEMBLED

THE generous and respectable, but faithless girl, was with her brother the Abbé de Saint-Yves, the good Prior of the

Mountain, and Mlle de Kerkabon. They were equally
astonished, but their situations and sentiments were very
different. The Abbé de Saint-Yves was expiating the
wrongs he had done his sister at her feet, and she pardoned
him. The Prior and his sympathizing sister likewise wept,
but it was for joy. The filthy magistrate and his insupportable son did not trouble this affecting scene. They
had set out upon the first report of their antagonist's being
released; they hastened to bury in their own province
their folly and fear.

The four characters in this drama, variously agitated,
were waiting for the return of the young man, who had
gone to deliver his friend. The Abbé de Saint-Yves did
not dare to raise his eyes to meet those of his sister : the
good Mlle de Kerkabon said :

' I shall then see once more my dear nephew.'

' You will see him again,' said the charming Mlle de
Saint-Yves, ' but he is no longer the same man; his
behaviour, his manners, his ideas, his sense, all have undergone a complete change; he is become as respectable as
he was ignorant and strange to everything. He will be
the honour and consolation of your family. Would that
I could also be the honour of mine ! '

' What, are you not the same as you were ? ' said the
Prior. ' What then has happened to work so great a
change ? '

During this conversation the Huron returned holding
the Jansenist by the hand. The scene now was changed,
and became more interesting. It began by the uncle and
aunt's tender embraces. The Abbé de Saint-Yves almost
flung himself at the knees of the ingenuous Huron, who was
no longer ingenuous. The language of the eyes formed all
the discourse of the two lovers, who, nevertheless, expressed
every sentiment with which they were penetrated. Satisfaction and acknowledgment sparkled in the countenance
of the one, whilst embarrassment was depicted in Mlle de
Saint-Yves' melting, but half-averted eyes. Every one was
astonished that she should mingle grief with so much joy.

The venerable Gordon soon endeared himself to the
whole family. He had shared the unhappiness of the
young prisoner, and this was a sufficient title. He owed

his deliverance to the two lovers, and this alone reconciled him to love : the acrimony of his former sentiments was dismissed from his heart; he, as well as the Huron, was converted into a man. Every one related his adventures before supper. The two abbés and the aunt listened as children do to stories of ghosts, and like men all interested in so many calamities.

'Alas!' said Gordon, 'there are perhaps upwards of five hundred virtuous people in the same fetters as Mlle de Saint-Yves has broken; their misfortunes are unknown. Many hands are found to strike the unhappy multitude, but seldom one to succour them.'

This very just reflection increased his sensibility and gratitude; everything heightened the triumph of the beautiful Mlle de Saint-Yves; the grandeur and intrepidity of her soul were the subjects of each one's admiration. This admiration was blended with that respect which we feel in despite of ourselves for a person who we think has some influence at court. But the Abbé de Saint-Yves sometimes said :

'What could my sister have done, to obtain this influence so soon?'

Supper was ready, and every one seated very early; when, lo! the worthy confidante of Versailles arrived, without being acquainted with anything that had passed; she was in a coach and six, and it was easily seen to whom the equipage belonged. She entered with that air of authority assumed by people in power who have a great deal of business, saluted the company with much indifference, and pulling the beautiful Mlle de Saint-Yves on one side said :

'Why do you make people wait so long? Follow me; here are the diamonds you forgot.'

However softly she uttered these expressions, the Huron, nevertheless, overheard them; he saw the diamonds; the brother was speechless; the uncle and aunt testified that kind of surprise common to good people who have never before beheld such magnificence. The young man, whose mind was now formed by a year's reflection, could not help making some against his will, and was for a moment in anxiety. His mistress perceived it, and a mortal paleness spread itself over her countenance; a tremor seized her, and it was only with difficulty she could support herself.

'Ah, madam,' said she to her fatal friend, 'you have ruined me, you have given me a mortal blow.'

These words pierced the heart of the Huron; but he had already learned to possess himself; he did not dwell upon them, lest he should make his mistress uneasy before her brother; but he turned pale as well as she.

Mlle de Saint-Yves, distracted at the change she perceived in her lover's countenance, pulled the woman out of the room into the passage, and there threw the jewels at her feet, saying:

'Ah! these were not my seducers, you well know; but he that gave them shall never set eyes on me again.'

Her friend took them up, whilst the girl added:

'He may either take them back again, or give them to you; begone, and do not make me still more odious to myself.'

The ambassadress at length returned, not being able to understand the remorse to which she had been witness.

The beautiful Mlle de Saint-Yves, greatly oppressed, and feeling a revolution in her body that almost suffocated her, was compelled to go to bed; but that she might not alarm any one, she kept her pains and sufferings to herself: and, under pretence of only being weary, she asked leave to take a little rest: this, however, she did not do, till she had reassured the company with consolatory and flattering expressions, and cast such a kind look upon her lover as darted fire into his soul.

The supper, without her to animate it, was in the beginning gloomy; but this gloominess was of that interesting kind that affords attractive and useful conversation, so superior to that frivolous joy which is sought after, and which is usually nothing more than a troublesome noise.

Gordon, in a few words, gave the history of Jansenism and Molinism; of those persecutions with which one party hampered the other; and of the obstinacy of both. The Huron entered into a criticism thereupon, pitying those men who, not satisfied with all the confusion occasioned by these opposite interests, create evils by imaginary

*K 936

interests and unintelligible absurdities. Gordon related,
the other judged; the guests listened with emotion, and
gained new light. The length of misfortune, and the
shortness of life, then became the topics. It was remarked
that all professions have peculiar vices and dangers annexed
to them; and that from the prince down to the lowest
beggar, all seem alike to accuse Nature. How happens it
that so many men, for so little money, perform the office
of persecutors, serjeants, and executioners of others?
With what inhuman indifference does a man in place sign
the destruction of a family; and with what joy, still more
barbarous, do mercenaries execute them?

'I saw in my youth,' said the good old Gordon, 'a
relation of the Marshal de Marillac, who, being prosecuted
in his own province on account of that illustrious but
unfortunate man, concealed himself under a borrowed
name in Paris. He was an old man near seventy-two
years of age. His wife, who accompanied him, was nearly
the same age. They had a libertine son, who, at fourteen
years of age, absconded from his father's house, turned
soldier, and deserted; he had gone through every stage of
debauchery and misery : at length, having changed his
name, he was in the guards of Cardinal Richelieu (for this
priest, as well as Mazarin, had guards), and had obtained
a constable's staff in their company of satellites.

'This adventurer was appointed to arrest the old man
and his wife, and acquitted himself with all the obduracy
of a man who was willing to please his master. As he
was conducting them, he heard these two victims deplore
the long succession of miseries which had befallen them
from their cradle. This aged couple reckoned as one of
their greatest misfortunes the wildness and loss of their
son. He recognized them, but he nevertheless led them
to prison; assuring them, that his Eminence was to be
served in preference to everybody else. His Eminence
rewarded his zeal.

'I have seen a spy of Father de la Chaise betray his
own brother, in hopes of a little benefice, which he did not
obtain; and I saw him die, not of remorse, but of grief at
having been cheated by the Jesuit.

'The vocation of confessor, which I for a long while

exercised, made me acquainted with the secrets of families. I have known very few, who, though immersed in the greatest distress, did not externally wear the mask of felicity, and every appearance of joy; and I have always observed that great grief was the fruit of our unconstrained desires.'

' For my part,' said the Huron, ' I imagine that a noble, grateful, sensible man may always be happy; and I doubt not but to enjoy an unchequered felicity with the charming, generous Mlle de Saint-Yves. For I flatter myself,' added he, addressing himself to her brother with a friendly smile, ' that you will not now refuse me as you did last year : besides, I shall pursue a more decent method.'

The Abbé in confusion apologized for the past, and protested an unalterable attachment.

His uncle said this would be the most glorious day of his whole life. His good aunt, delighted and weeping for joy, cried out :

' I always said you would never be a subdeacon; this sacrament is preferable to the other; would to God I had been honoured with it ! but I will serve you for a mother.'

And now every one vied with each other in applauding the gentle Mlle de Saint-Yves.

Her lover's heart was too full of what she had done for him, and he loved her too much, for the affair of the jewels to make any lasting impression on him. But those words, which he too well heard—' You have given me a mortal blow '—still secretly terrified him, and interrupted all his joy, whilst the eulogiums paid his beautiful mistress still increased his love. In a word, nothing was thought of but her, nothing was mentioned but the happiness those two lovers deserved. A plan was set on foot to live altogether at Paris, and schemes of grandeur and fortune succeeded : they gave themselves up to those hopes which the smallest ray of happiness engenders. But the Huron felt, in the secret recesses of his heart, a sentiment that exploded this illusion. He read over the promises signed Saint-Pouange, and the commission signed Louvois : these men were described to him such as they were, or such as they were thought to be. Every one spoke of the ministers and administration with the freedom of convivial conversation, which is considered in France as the most precious liberty to be obtained on earth.

'If I were King of France,' said the Huron, 'this is the kind of minister that I would choose for the war department. I would have a man of the highest birth, as he has to give orders to the nobility. I would require that he should himself have been an officer, and have passed through the various ranks; or, at least, that he attained the rank of Lieutenant-General, and was worthy of being a Marshal of France. For is it not essential that he should have served himself and be acquainted with the details of the service? And will not officers obey with a hundred times more alacrity a military man, who like themselves has been signalized by his courage, than a mere man of the cabinet, who, at most, can only guess at the operations of a campaign, let him have ever so great a share of sense? I should not be displeased at my minister's generosity, even though it might sometimes embarrass a little the keeper of the royal treasury. I should like him to have a facility in business, and to be able to distinguish himself by that kind of gaiety of mind, which is the lot of a man superior to business, so agreeable to the nation, and which renders the performance of every duty less irksome.' This is the character he would have chosen for a minister, as he had constantly observed that such an amiable disposition is incompatible with cruelty.

Monsieur de Louvois would not, perhaps, have been satisfied with the Huron's wishes; his merit lay in a different walk.

But whilst they were still at table, the disorder of the unhappy girl took a fatal turn; her blood was on fire, the symptoms of a malignant fever had appeared; she suffered, but did not complain, unwilling to disturb the pleasure of the guests.

Her brother, knowing that she was not asleep, went to the foot of her bed: he was astonished at the condition he found her in. Everybody flew to her; her lover immediately followed her brother. He was certainly the most alarmed, and the most affected of any one; but he had learned to unite discretion to all the happy gifts

Nature had bestowed upon him, and a quick sense of what was fitting came over him.

A neighbouring physician was immediately sent for. He was one of those itinerant doctors, who confound the last disorder they were consulted upon with the present; who follow a blind practice in a science from which the most mature investigation and justest observations do not preclude uncertainty and danger. He greatly increased the disorder, by prescribing a fashionable nostrum.—Can fashion extend to medicine? This folly was then too prevalent in Paris.

Her grief contributed still more than her physician to render her disorder fatal. Her body suffered martyrdom in the torments of her mind. The crowd of thoughts which agitated her breast, communicated to her veins a more dangerous poison than that of the most burning fever.

CHAPTER XX

THE DEATH OF THE BEAUTIFUL MLLE DE SAINT-YVES, AND ITS CONSEQUENCES

ANOTHER physician was called in, but he, instead of assisting Nature and leaving her to act in a young body, the organs of which were calling life back, applied himself solely to counteract the effects of his brother's prescription. The disorder, in two days, became mortal. The brain, which is thought to be the seat of the mind, was as violently afflicted as the heart, which, we are told, is the seat of the passions.

By what incomprehensible mechanism are the organs in subjection to sentiment and thought? How is it that a single melancholy idea shall disturb the whole course of the blood; and that the blood should in turn communicate irregularities to the human understanding? What is that unknown fluid, which certainly exists, and, quicker and more active than light, flies in less than the twinkling of an eye into all the channels of life, produces sensations, memory, joy or grief, reason or madness; recalls with horror what we would choose to forget; and renders a thinking animal, either a subject of admiration, or an object of pity and compassion?

These were the reflections of the good old Gordon; and these observations, so natural, which men seldom make, did not prevent his sympathy; for he was not of the number of those gloomy philosophers, who pique themselves upon being insensitive. He was affected at the fate of this young woman, like a father who sees his dear child yielding to a slow death. The Abbé de Saint-Yves was desperate; the Prior and his sister shed floods of tears; but who could describe the situation of her lover? All expression falls far short of the summit of his affliction, and language here proves its imperfection.

His aunt, almost lifeless, supported the head of the dying girl in her feeble arms; her brother was upon his knees at the foot of her bed; her lover squeezed her hand, which he bathed in tears; his groans rent the air, whilst he called her his guardian angel, his life, his hope, the half of himself, his mistress, his wife. At the word 'wife,' a sigh escaped her, whilst she looked upon him with inexpressible tenderness, and then abruptly gave a horrid scream. Presently, in one of those intervals when grief, the oppression of the senses, and pain subside, and leave the soul its liberty and powers, she cried out :

' I, your wife !—Ah ! dear lover, this name, this happiness, this felicity were not for me !—I die, and I deserve it. O God of my heart !—O you, whom I sacrificed to infernal demons—it is done—I am punished—live and be happy.'

These tender, but dreadful expressions were incomprehensible;—yet they melted and terrified every heart. She had the courage to explain herself, and her auditors shook with astonishment, grief, and pity. They, with one voice, detested the man in power, who repaired a shocking act of injustice only by his crimes, and who had forced the most amiable innocence to be his accomplice.

' Who? You guilty ! ' said her lover, ' no, you are not; guilt can only be in the heart ;—yours is devoted solely to virtue and to me.'

This opinion he corroborated by such expressions as

seemed to recall the beautiful Mlle de Saint-Yves back to life. She felt some consolation from them, and was astonished at being still beloved. The aged Gordon would have condemned her at the time he was only a Jansenist; but having attained wisdom, he esteemed her, and wept.

In the midst of these lamentations and fears, whilst the dangerous situation of this worthy girl engrossed every breast, and all were in the greatest concern, a courier arrived from Court.

'A courier! from whom? And upon what account?'

He was sent by the King's Confessor to the Prior of the Mountain; it was not Father de la Chaise who wrote, but Brother Vadbled, his valet-de-chambre, a man of great consequence at that time, who acquainted the archbishops with the Reverend Father's pleasure, who gave audience, promised benefices, and sometimes issued *lettres de cachet.* He wrote to the Abbé of the Mountain that his Reverence had been informed of his nephew's exploits; that his being sent to prison was through a mistake; that such little disgraces frequently happened, and should therefore not be attended to; and, in fine, it behoved him, the Prior, to come and present his nephew the next day : that he was to bring with him that good man Gordon; and that he, Brother Vadbled, would introduce them to his Reverence and M. de Louvois, who would say a word to them in his antechamber.

He added that the history of the Huron, and his combat against the English, had been related to the King; that doubtless the King would deign to take notice of him in passing through the gallery, and perhaps he might even nod his head to him. The letter concluded by flattering him with hopes that all the ladies of the Court would show their eagerness to send for his nephew to their levees; and that several among them would bid him good-day, and that he would certainly be talked of at the King's supper. The letter was signed, 'Your affectionate brother Jesuit, Vadbled.'

The Prior having read the letter aloud, his furious nephew for a moment suppressed his rage, and said nothing to the bearer : but turning towards the companion of his misfortunes, asked him what he thought of that style? Gordon replied :

' This, then, is the way that men are treated like monkeys ! They are first beaten, and then they dance.'

The Huron recovering his proper character, which always returned in the great emotions of his soul, tore the letter to bits, and threw them in the courier's face :

' There is my answer,' said he.

His uncle in terror, fancying he saw thunderbolts and twenty *lettres de cachet* at once fall upon him, immediately wrote the best excuse he could for these transports of passion in a young man, which he considered as the ebullition of a great soul.

But a sadder care now seized every heart. The beautiful and unfortunate Mlle de Saint-Yves was already sensible of her approaching end; she was serene, but it was that kind of shocking serenity, the effect of exhausted nature, no longer able to withstand the conflict.

' Oh, my dear lover ! ' said she, in a faltering voice, ' death punishes me for my weakness; but I die with the consolation of knowing you are free. I adored you whilst I betrayed you, and I adore you in bidding you farewell for ever.'

She did not make a parade of a ridiculous fortitude; she did not understand that miserable glory of having some of her neighbours say, ' She died with courage.' Who, at twenty, can be at once torn from her lover, from life, and what is called honour, without regret, without pang? She felt all the horror of her situation, and made it felt by those expiring looks and accents which speak with so much force. In a word, she shed tears like other people, at those intervals that she had the strength to weep.

Let others strive to celebrate the pompous deaths of those who insensibly rush into destruction. This is the lot of all animals; we die like them only when age or disorders make us resemble them by the stupidity of our organs. Whoever suffers a great loss, must feel great regret; if they are stifled, it is nothing but vanity that is pursued, even in the arms of death.

When the fatal moment came, all around her wept

and cried aloud. The Huron lost the use of his senses. Great souls feel more violent sensations than those of less tender dispositions. The good old Gordon knew enough of him to make him dread that when he came to himself, he would be guilty of suicide. All kinds of arms were put out of his way, and this the unfortunate young man perceived : he said to his relations and Gordon, without shedding any tears, without a groan, or the least emotion :

'Do you then think that any one upon earth hath the right and power to prevent my putting an end to my life?'

Gordon took care to avoid making a parade of those commonplace declamations, whereby it is endeavoured to be proved that we are not allowed to exercise our liberty in ceasing to be, when we are in a shocking situation; that we may not leave the house, when we can no longer remain in it; that a man is on earth like a soldier at his post : as if it signified to the Being of beings whether the conjunction of the particles of matter were in one spot or another : impotent reasons, to which a firm and resolute despair disdains to listen, and to which Cato replied only with the use of a dagger.

The Huron's sombre and dreadful silence, his doleful aspect, his trembling lips, and the shivering of his whole frame, to every spectator's soul communicated that mixture of compassion and terror, which fetters all its powers, precludes discourse, and is only uttered by faltering accents. The hostess and her family came running; they trembled to behold the state of his desperation, yet all kept their eyes upon him, and attended to all his movements. The ice-cold corpse of the beautiful Mlle de Saint-Yves had already been carried into a lower hall, out of the sight of her lover, who seemed still in search of it, though incapable of observing any object.

In the midst of this spectacle of death, while the dead body was exposed at the door of the house; while two priests by the side of a holy water-pot were repeating prayers with an air of distraction; while some passengers, through idleness, sprinkled the bier with some drops of holy water, and others went their ways indifferent; while her relations were drowned in tears, and every one thought the lover would not survive his loss;—in this situation Saint-Pouange arrived with his friend, the lady of Versailles.

His transitory taste having been but once gratified became a fixed passion. The refusal of his generous gifts had piqued his pride. Father de la Chaise would never have suggested the thought of coming into this house; but Saint-Pouange, having constantly before his eyes the image of the beautiful Mlle de Saint-Yves and burning to satisfy a passion, which by a single enjoyment had fixed in his heart the poignancy of desire, did not hesitate to come himself in search of her, whom he would not, perhaps, have been inclined to see a third time, had she gone to him of her own accord.

He alighted from his coach; and the first object that presented itself was a bier : he turned away his eyes with that simple distaste of a man bred up in pleasures, and who thinks he should avoid a sight which might recall him to the contemplation of human misery. He wished to go upstairs. The woman from Versailles inquired through curiosity whose funeral it was. The name of Mlle de Saint-Yves was pronounced. At this name she turned pale, and gave a shocking shriek. Saint-Pouange now returned, while surprise and grief possessed his soul. The good old Gordon stood with streaming eyes : he, for a moment, ceased his lamentations to acquaint the courtier with all the circumstances of this melancholy catastrophe. He spoke with that authority which is the companion to sorrow and virtue. Saint-Pouange was not naturally wicked : the torrent of business and amusements had hurried away his soul, which was not yet acquainted with itself. He did not border upon that grey age, which usually hardens the hearts of ministers; he listened to Gordon with a downcast look, and some tears escaped him which he was surprised to shed; he learned what repentance was.

' I will,' said he, ' see this extraordinary man you have mentioned to me; he touches me almost as much as this innocent victim, whose death I have been the occasion of.'

Gordon followed him as far as the chamber, where were the Prior de Kerkabon, the Abbé de Saint-Yves, and some neighbours, who were recalling to life the young man, who had again fainted.

' I have been the cause of your misfortunes,' said this deputy minister, ' and my whole life shall be employed in making reparation.'

The first idea that struck the Huron was to kill him, and then destroy himself. Nothing was more suitable to the circumstances; but he was without arms, and closely watched. Saint-Pouange was not repulsed by refusals, accompanied with reproach, contempt, and the insults which he deserved and which were lavished upon him. Time softens everything. M. de Louvois at length succeeded in making an excellent officer of the Huron, who has appeared under another name at Paris and in the army, applauded by all honest men, being at once a warrior and an intrepid philosopher.

He never spoke of what had happened to him, without being greatly moved; and yet his greatest consolation was to speak of it. He cherished the memory of his beloved to the last moment of his life. The Abbé de Saint-Yves and the Prior were each provided with good livings; the good Kerkabon rather chose to see his nephew invested with military honours than in the subdeaconry. The devotee of Versailles kept the diamond earrings, and received besides a handsome present. Father Tout-à-tous had presents of chocolate, coffee, and confectionery, with the *Meditations* of the Reverend Father Croiset, and the *Flower of the Saints*, bound in morocco. The good Gordon lived with the Huron till his death, in the most friendly intimacy; he had also a benefice, and forgot, for ever, effectual grace, and the concomitant concurrence. He took for his motto, *Misfortunes are of some use.* How many worthy people are there in the world who may justly say, *Misfortunes are good for nothing !*

PRINCESS OF BABYLON

The aged Belus, King of Babylon, thought himself the first man upon earth; for all his courtiers told him so, and his historiographers proved it. What might excuse this ridiculous vanity in him was that, in fact, his predecessors had built Babylon upwards of thirty thousand years before him, and he had embellished it. We know that his palace and his park, situated a few parasangs from Babylon, extended between the Euphrates and the Tigris, which washed those enchanted banks. His vast house, three thousand feet in front, almost reached to the clouds. The platform was surrounded with a balustrade of white marble, fifty feet high, which supported colossal statues of all the kings and great men of the empire. This platform, composed of two rows of bricks, covered with a thick surface of lead from one extremity to the other, bore twelve feet of earth; and upon this earth were raised groves of olive, orange, citron, palm, clove, cocoa, and cinnamon trees, which formed alleys that the rays of the sun could not penetrate.

In this garden the waters of the Euphrates, pumped into a hundred conduits, filled several huge marble basins, and then, carried by canals, flowed through the park, forming cascades of six thousand feet in length as well as a hundred thousand fountains, whose height was scarcely perceptible. Afterwards the waters returned to the Euphrates, of which they were part. The gardens of Semiramis, which astonished Asia several ages after, were only a feeble imitation of these ancient prodigies; for in the time of Semiramis everything began to degenerate amongst men and women.

But what was more admirable in Babylon, and eclipsed everything else, was the only daughter of the King, named Formosanta. It was from her pictures and statues that in succeeding times Praxiteles sculptured his Aphrodite,

and the one called the 'Venus of the Lovely Hips.'
Heavens, what a difference between the original and the
copies! So Belus was prouder of his daughter than of his
kingdom. She was eighteen years old: it was necessary
she should have a husband worthy of her; but where was
he to be found? An ancient oracle had ordained that
Formosanta could not belong to any but him who could
bend the bow of Nimrod.

This Nimrod, the strong hunter before the Lord, had
left a bow seven Babylonian feet in length, made of ebony,
harder than the iron of Mount Caucasus, which is wrought in
the forges of Derbent; and no mortal since Nimrod could
bend this astonishing bow.

It was again said that the arm which should bend this
bow would kill the most terrible and ferocious lion that
should be let loose in the Circus of Babylon. This was not
all; the bender of the bow, and the conqueror of the lion,
should overthrow all his rivals: but he was above all things
to be very sagacious, the most magnificent and most
virtuous of men, and possess the rarest object in the whole
universe.

Three kings appeared, who were bold enough to claim
Formosanta: Pharaoh of Egypt, the Shah of India, and
the great Khan of the Scythians. Belus appointed the day
and place of combat, which was to be at the extremity of
his park, in the vast expanse surrounded by the joint
waters of the Euphrates and the Tigris. Round the lists a
marble amphitheatre was erected, which would contain
five hundred thousand spectators. Opposite the amphitheatre was placed the King's throne; he was to appear
with Formosanta, accompanied by the whole Court; and
on the right and left between the throne and the amphitheatre, there were other thrones and seats for the three
kings, and for all the other sovereigns who were anxious to
be present at this august ceremony.

The King of Egypt arrived first, mounted upon the bull
Apis, and holding in his hand the cithern of Isis. He was
followed by two thousand priests clad in linen vestments
whiter than snow, two thousand eunuchs, two thousand
magicians, and two thousand warriors.

The King of India came soon after in a chariot drawn by

twelve elephants. He had a train still more numerous and more brilliant than Pharaoh of Egypt.

The last who appeared was the King of the Scythians. He had none with him but chosen warriors, armed with bows and arrows. He was mounted upon a superb tiger, which he had tamed, and which was as tall as any of the finest Persian horses. The majestic and important mien of this king effaced the appearance of his rivals; his naked arms, as sinewy as they were white, seemed already to bend the bow of Nimrod.

These three princes immediately prostrated themselves before Belus and Formosanta. The King of Egypt presented the Princess with two of the finest crocodiles of the Nile, two hippopotami, two zebras, two Egyptian rats, and two mummies, with the books of the great Hermes, which he judged to be the rarest things upon earth.

The King of India offered her a hundred elephants, each bearing a wooden gilt tower, and laid at her feet the Veda written by the hand of Xaca himself.

The King of the Scythians, who could neither write nor read, presented a hundred warlike horses with black fox-skin trappings.

The Princess lowered her eyes before her lovers, and bowed with such a grace as was at once modest and noble.

Belus ordered the kings to be conducted to the thrones that were prepared for them.

' Would I had three daughters,' said he to them, ' I should make six people this day happy ! '

He then made the competitors cast lots which should try Nimrod's bow first. Their names were inscribed and put into a golden casque. That of the King of Egypt came out first; then the name of the King of India appeared. The King of Scythia, viewing the bow and his rivals, did not complain at being the third.

While these brilliant trials were preparing, twenty thousand pages and twenty thousand youthful maidens distributed, without any disorder, refreshments to the spectators between the rows of the seats. Every one acknowledged, that the gods had instituted kings for no other cause than every day to give festivals, upon condition they should be diversified; that life is too short to be made

any other use of; that lawsuits, intrigues, wars, the alterca-
tions of theologians, which consume human life, are horrible
and absurd; that man is born only for happiness; that he
would not passionately and incessantly pursue pleasure,
were he not designed for it; that the essence of human
nature is to enjoy oneself, and all the rest is folly. This
excellent moral was never controverted but by facts.

While preparations were being made for determining
the fate of Formosanta, a young stranger, mounted upon
a unicorn, accompanied by his valet, mounted on a like
animal, and bearing upon his hand a large bird, appeared
at the barrier. The guards were surprised to observe in
this equipage a figure that had an air of divinity. He had,
as hath been since related, the face of Adonis upon the
body of Hercules; it was majesty accompanied by the
graces. His black eyebrows and flowing fair tresses were
a mixture of beauty unknown at Babylon, and charmed all
observers. The whole amphitheatre rose up, the better to
see the stranger: all the ladies of the court viewed him
with looks of astonishment. Formosanta herself, who had
hitherto kept her eyes fixed upon the ground, raised them
and blushed; the three kings turned pale; all the spectators, in comparing Formosanta with the stranger, cried
out:

'There is no other in the world but this young man who
can be so handsome as the Princess.'

The ushers, struck with astonishment, asked him if he
was a king. The stranger replied that he had not that
honour, but that he had come from a great distance,
excited by curiosity, to see if there were any king worthy
of Formosanta. He was introduced into the first row of the
amphitheatre, with his valet, his two unicorns, and his bird.
He saluted with great respect Belus, his daughter, the three
kings, and all the assembly. He then took his seat, not
without blushing. His two unicorns lay down at his feet,
his bird perched upon his shoulder; and his valet, who
carried a little bag, placed himself by his side.

The trials began. The bow of Nimrod was taken out of
its golden case. The first master of the ceremonies,
followed by fifty pages, and preceded by twenty trumpets,
presented it to the King of Egypt, who made his priests

bless it; and supporting it upon the head of the bull Apis, he did not question his gaining the first victory. He dismounted, and came into the middle of the Circus; he tried, exerted all his strength, and made such ridiculous contortions, that the whole amphitheatre re-echoed with laughter, and Formosanta herself could not help smiling.

His High Almoner approached him :

' Let your Majesty give up this idle honour, which depends solely upon the nerves and muscles; you will triumph in everything else. You will conquer the lion, as you are possessed of the sabre of Osiris. The Princess of Babylon is to belong to the prince who is most sagacious, and you have solved enigmas. She is to wed the most virtuous : you are such, since you have been educated by the priests of Egypt. The most generous is to carry her off, and you have presented her with two of the handsomest crocodiles, and two of the finest rats in the Delta. You are possessed of the bull Apis and the books of Hermes, which are the scarcest things in the universe. No one can dispute Formosanta with you.'

' You are in the right,' said the King of Egypt, and resumed his throne.

The bow was then put into the hands of the King of India. It blistered his hands for a fortnight; but he consoled himself in presuming that the King of Scythia would not be more fortunate than himself.

The Scythian handled the bow in his turn. He united skill with strength : the bow seemed to have some elasticity in his hands; he bent it a little, but he could never bring it anything near a curve. The spectators, who had been prejudiced in his favour by his agreeable aspect, lamented his ill success, and concluded that the beautiful Princess would never be married.

The unknown youth leaped into the area, and addressing himself to the King of Scythia said :

' Your Majesty need not be surprised at not having entirely succeeded. These ebony bows are made in my country; there is only one peculiar twist to give them. Your merit is greater in having bent it than if I were to curve it.'

He then took an arrow, and placing it upon the string,

bent the bow of Nimrod, and made the arrow fly beyond the gates. A million hands at once applauded the prodigy. Babylon re-echoed with acclamations, and all the women agreed how happy it was for so handsome a youth to be so strong.

He then took out of his pocket a small ivory tablet, and wrote upon it with a golden pencil, fixed the tablet to the bow, and presented it all together to the Princess with such a grace as charmed every spectator. He then modestly returned to his place between his bird and his valet. All Babylon was in astonishment, the three kings were confounded whilst the stranger did not seem to pay the least attention to what had happened.

Formosanta was still more surprised to read upon the ivory tablet tied to the bow, these verses written in good Chaldean :

> L'arc de Nembrod est celui de la guerre;
> L'arc de l'Amour est celui du bonheur;
> Vous le portez. Par vous ce dieu vainqueur
> Est devenu le maître de la terre.
> Trois rois puissants, trois rivaux aujourd'hui,
> Osent prétendre à l'honneur de vous plaire:
> Je ne fais pas qui votre cœur préfère,
> Mais l'univers sera jaloux de lui.*

This little madrigal did not displease the Princess. It was criticized by some of the lords of the ancient Court, who said that formerly, in the good old times, Belus would have been compared to the sun, and Formosanta to the moon; his neck to a tower, and her throat to a bushel of wheat. They said the stranger had no sort of imagination, and that he had lost sight of the rules of true poetry, but all the ladies thought the verses very gallant. They were astonished that a man, who handled a bow so well, should have so much wit. The lady of honour to the Princess said to her :

' Madam, what numerous talents are here entirely lost !

---

* Nimrod's is the warlike bow :—The bow of love is that of happiness :—This you bear. Through you the victorious god is become master of the earth. Three powerful kings, rivals of the day, have dared pretend to the honour of pleasing you. I know not which your heart prefers, but the whole universe must be jealous of him.

What benefit will this young man derive from his wit and Belus's bow? '

' Being admired,' said Formosanta.

' Ah ! ' said the lady, ' one more madrigal, and he might very well be beloved ! '

Nevertheless, Belus, having consulted his sages, declared, that though none of these kings could bend the bow of Nimrod, his daughter was nevertheless to be married, and that she should belong to him who could conquer the great lion, which was purposely in training in his great menagerie. The King of Egypt, upon whose education all the wisdom of Egypt had been exhausted, judged it very ridiculous to expose a king to the ferocity of wild beasts in order to be married. He acknowledged he considered the possession of Formosanta of inestimable value; but he imagined that if the lion should strangle him, he could never wed this fair Babylonian. The King of India was of the same way of thinking with the Egyptian; they both concluded that the King of Babylon was laughing at them, and that they should send for armies to punish him; that they had many subjects, who would think themselves highly honoured to die in the service of their masters, without its costing them a single hair of their sacred heads; that they could easily dethrone the King of Babylon, and then they would draw lots for the fair Formosanta.

This agreement being made, the two kings each sent an express messenger into his respective country, with orders to assemble three hundred thousand men to carry off Formosanta.

However, the King of Scythia descended alone into the area with his scimitar in hand. He was not distractedly enamoured with Formosanta's charms; glory till then had been his only passion, and it had led him to Babylon. He was willing to show that if the Kings of India and Egypt were so prudent as not to tilt with lions, he was courageous enough not to decline the combat, and he would restore the dignity of the crown. His uncommon valour would not even allow him to avail himself of the assistance of his tiger. He advanced singly, slightly armed with a steel casque ornamented with gold, shaded with three horses' tails as white as snow.

One of the most enormous and ferocious lions that fed upon the Antilibanian mountains, was let loose upon him. His tremendous talons appeared capable of tearing the three kings to pieces at once, and his gullet to devour them; his roaring made the amphitheatre resound. The two proud champions flew with the utmost precipitancy and in the most rapid manner at each other. The courageous Scythian plunged his sword into the lion's throat; but the point meeting with one of those thick teeth that nothing can penetrate, was broken into splinters; and the monster of the woods, more furious from his wound, had already impressed his bloody claws into the monarch's sides.

The unknown youth, touched with the peril of so brave a prince, leapt into the arena as swift as lightning; and cut off the lion's head with as much dexterity, as we have lately seen, in our carousals, youthful knights knock off the heads of Moors, or catch up the rings.

Then drawing out a small box, he presented it to the Scythian king, saying to him :

' Your Majesty will there find the genuine dittany, which grows in my country. Your glorious wounds will be healed in a moment. Accident alone prevented your triumph over the lion; your valour is not the less to be admired.'

The King of Scythia, animated more with gratitude than jealousy, thanked his benefactor; and after having tenderly embraced him, returned to his seat to apply the dittany to his wounds.

The stranger gave the lion's head to his valet, who having washed it at the great fountain which was beneath the amphitheatre, and drained all the blood, took an iron instrument out of his little bag, with which having drawn the lion's forty teeth, he supplied their place with forty diamonds of equal size.

His master, with his usual modesty, returned to his place; he gave the lion's head to his bird.

' Beauteous bird,' said he, ' carry this small homage, and lay it at the feet of Formosanta.'

The bird winged his way with the dreadful spoil in one of his talons, and presented it to the Princess, bending his neck with humility and crouching before her. The sparkling diamonds dazzled the eyes of every beholder. Such magnificence was unknown even in superb Babylon; the emerald, the topaz, the sapphire, and the pyrope were as yet considered the most precious ornaments. Belus and the whole court were struck with admiration. The bird which presented this gift surprised them still more. It was of the size of an eagle, but its eyes were as soft and tender as those of the eagle are fierce and threatening. Its bill was rose-colour, and seemed somewhat to resemble Formosanta's handsome mouth. Its neck represented all the colours of the rainbow, but still more lively and brilliant; gold, in a thousand shades, glittered upon its plumage; its feet resembled a mixture of silver and purple; and the tails of those beautiful birds which have since drawn Juno's car, did not come up to the splendour of this bird's tail.

The attention, curiosity, astonishment, and delight of the whole Court were divided between the jewels and the bird. He had perched upon the balustrade between Belus and his daughter Formosanta; she flattered it, caressed it, and kissed it. It seemed to receive her embraces with a mixture of pleasure and respect. When the Princess gave the bird a kiss, it retruned to the embrace, and then looked upon her with languishing eyes. She gave it biscuits and pistachios, which it received in its purple-silvered claw, and carried them to its bill with inexpressible grace.

Belus, who had attentively considered the diamonds, concluded that scarce any one of his provinces could repay so valuable a present. He ordered that more magnificent gifts should be prepared for the stranger than those that were destined for the three monarchs. This young man, said he, is doubtless son to the King of China, or of that part of the world called Europe, which I have heard spoken of; or of Africa, which, it is said, is in the neighbourhood of the kingdom of Egypt.

He immediately sent his first equerry to compliment the stranger, and ask him whether he was himself the sovereign, or son to the sovereign of one of those empires; and why, being possessed of such surprising treasures, he had come with nothing but the valet and a little bag?

Whilst the equerry advanced towards the amphitheatre to execute his commission, another valet arrived upon a unicorn. This valet, addressing himself to the young man, said :

'Ormar, your father is approaching the end of his life : I am come to tell you.'

The stranger raised his eyes to heaven, whilst tears streamed from them, and answered only by saying, 'Let us depart.'

The equerry, after having paid Belus's compliments to the conqueror of the lion, to the giver of the forty diamonds, and to the master of the beautiful bird, asked the valet of what kingdom was the father of this young hero sovereign. The valet replied :

'His father is an old shepherd, who is much beloved in the district.'

During this conversation, the stranger had already mounted his unicorn. He said to the equerry, 'My lord, pay homage for me at the feet of Belus and his daughter. I must entreat her to take particular care of the bird I leave with her, as it is matchless like herself.'

In uttering these last words he set off, and flew like lightning; the two valets followed him, and he was in an instant out of sight.

Formosanta could not refrain from crying out. The bird turning towards the amphitheatre, where his master had been seated, seemed greatly afflicted to find him gone; then looking steadfastly at the Princess, and gently rubbing her beautiful hand with his bill, he seemed to betroth himself to her service.

Belus, more astonished than ever at hearing that this very extraordinary young man was the son of a shepherd, could not believe it. He dispatched messengers after him; but they soon returned with word that the three unicorns, upon which these men were mounted, could not be caught up; and that according to the rate they went, they must go a hundred leagues a day.

§ 2

Every one reasoned upon this strange adventure, and wearied themselves with conjectures. How can the son of a shepherd make a present of forty large diamonds? How comes it that he is mounted upon a unicorn? This bewildered them, and Formosanta, whilst she caressed her bird, was sunk into a profound reverie.

Princess Aldea, her cousin-germane, who had a beautiful figure, and who was almost as handsome as Formosanta, said to her:

'Cousin, I know not whether this demigod be the son of a shepherd; but methinks he has fulfilled all the conditions stipulated for your marriage. He has bent Nimrod's bow, he has conquered the lion, he has a great share of sense, having written for you a very pretty extempore verse; and after having presented you with forty large diamonds, you cannot deny that he is the most generous of men. In his bird he possessed the most curious thing upon earth. His virtue cannot be equalled, since though he might have stayed with you, he departed without hesitation, as soon as he heard his father was ill. The oracle is fulfilled in every particular, except that wherein he is to overcome his rivals; but he has done more, he has saved the life of the only competitor he had to fear; and when the object is beating the other two, I believe you cannot doubt that he will easily succeed.'

'All that you say is very true,' replied Formosanta: 'but is it possible that the greatest of men, and perhaps the most lovable too, should be the son of a shepherd?'

The lady of honour, joining in the conversation, said that the title of Shepherd was frequently given to kings; that they were called Shepherds, because they attended their flocks very closely; that this was doubtless a piece of ill-timed pleasantry in his valet; that this young hero had come so badly equipped only to show how much his personal merit alone was above the fastidious parade of kings. The Princess made no answer but in giving her bird a thousand tender kisses.

A great festival was nevertheless prepared for the three kings, and for all the princes who had come to the feast. The King's daughter and niece were to do the honours. The King received presents worthy of the magnificence of Babylon. Belus, during the time the repast was being served, assembled his Council upon the marriage of the beautiful Formosanta, and this is the way he delivered himself as a great politician :

' I am old : I know not what further to do with my daughter, or upon whom to bestow her. He who deserved her is nothing but a mean shepherd; the Kings of India and Egypt are cowards; the King of the Scythians would be very agreeable to me, but he has not performed any one of the conditions imposed. I will again consult the oracle. In the meanwhile, deliberate among you, and we will conclude in accordance with what the oracle says; for a king should follow nothing but the dictates of the immortal gods.'

He then repaired to the temple : the oracle answered in few words according to custom : ' Thy daughter shall not be married till she has traversed the globe.'

Belus returned in astonishment to the Council, and related this answer.

All the ministers had a profound respect for oracles; they therefore all agreed, or at least appeared to agree, that they were the foundation of religion; that reason should be mute before them; that it was by their means that kings reigned over their people; that without oracles there would be neither virtue nor repose upon earth.

At length, after having testified the most profound veneration for them, they almost all concluded that this oracle was impertinent, and that it should not be obeyed; that nothing could be more indecent for a young woman, and particularly the daughter of the great King of Babylon, than to run about, without any particular destination; that this was the most certain method to prevent her marriage, or on the other hand it would bring about her engagement in a clandestine, shameful, and ridiculous one; that, in a word, this oracle had no common sense.

The youngest of the ministers named Onadasus, who had more sense than the rest, said that the oracle doubtless meant some pilgrimage of devotion, and offered to be the Princess's guide. The Council approved of his opinion, but every one was for being her equerry. The King determined that the Princess might go three hundred parasangs upon the road to Arabia, to the temple, whose saint had the reputation of procuring young women happy marriages,

and that the doyen of the Council should accompany her.
After this determination they went to supper.

§ 3

In the centre of the gardens, between two cascades, an
oval saloon was erected, three hundred feet in diameter,
whose azure roof, intersected with golden stars, represented
all the constellations and planets, each in its proper station;
and this ceiling turned about, as well as the canopy, by
machines as invisible as those which direct the celestial
motions. A hundred thousand flambeaux, inclosed in
rich crystal cylinders, illuminated the outside and inside
of the dining-hall. A buffet with steps contained twenty
thousand vases and golden dishes; and opposite the buffet,
upon other steps, were seated a great number of musicians.
Two other amphitheatres were decked out; the one with
the fruits of each season, the other with crystal decanters,
in which sparkled every kind of wine upon earth.

The guests took their seats round a table divided into
compartments, which resembled flowers and fruits, all in
precious stones. The beautiful Formosanta was placed
between the Kings of India and Egypt; the amiable Aldea
next the King of Scythia. There were about thirty princes,
and each was seated next one of the handsomest ladies of
the Court. The King of Babylon, who was in the middle,
opposite his daughter, seemed divided between the chagrin
of being yet unable to marry her, and the pleasure of still
beholding her. Formosanta asked leave to place her bird
upon the table next her; the King approved.

The music, which played, furnished every prince with an
opportunity of conversing with his female neighbour. The
festival was as agreeable as it was magnificent. A ragout
was served before Formosanta, which her father was very
fond of. The Princess said it should be carried to his
Majesty; the bird immediately took hold of it, and carried
it in a miraculous manner to the King. Never had anything more astonishing been seen at supper. Belus caressed
it as much as his daughter had done. The bird afterwards

took its flight to return to her. It displayed in flying so
fine a tail, and its extended wings set forth such a variety
of brilliant colours, the gold of its plumage shot forth such
a dazzling brilliance that all eyes were fixed upon him. All
the musicians were struck motionless, and their instruments
afforded harmony no longer. No one ate, no one spoke,
nothing but a buzzing of admiration was to be heard. The
Princess of Babylon kissed it during the whole supper,
without considering whether there were any kings in the
world. Those of India and Egypt felt their spite and
indignation rekindle with double force, and they resolved
speedily to set their three hundred thousand men in motion
to obtain revenge.

As for the King of Scythia, he was engaged in entertaining
the beautiful Aldea : his haughty soul despising, without
malice, Formosanta's inattention, had conceived for her
more indifference than resentment.

' She is handsome,' said he; ' I acknowledge it; but she
appears to me one of those women who are entirely taken
up with their own beauty, and who fancy that mankind
are greatly obliged to them when they deign to appear in
public. I should prefer an ugly complaisant woman that
showed some regard, to that beautiful statue. You have,
Madam, as many charms as she possesses, and you condescend
to converse, at least, with strangers. I acknowledge to
you with the sincerity of a Scythian that I prefer you to
your cousin.'

He was, however, mistaken in regard to the character
of Formosanta; she was not so disdainful as she appeared;
but his compliments were very well received by Princess
Aldea. Their conversation became very interesting; they
were very well contented, and already certain of one another
before they left table.

After supper the guests walked in the groves. The King
of Scythia and Aldea did not fail to seek for a place of
retreat. Aldea, who was sincerity itself, thus declared
herself to the Prince :

' I do not hate my cousin though she is handsomer than
myself, and is destined for the throne of Babylon; the
honour of pleasing you may very well stand in the stead of
charms. I prefer Scythia with you, to the crown of Babylon

without you. But this crown belongs to me by right, if there be any right in the world; for I am of the elder branch of Nimrod, and Formosanta is only of the younger. Her grandfather dethroned mine, and put him to death.'

'Such, then, is the force of blood in the House of Babylon!' said the Scythian. 'What was your grandfather's name?'

'He was called Aldea like me; my father bore the same name; he was banished to the extremity of the empire with my mother; and Belus, after their death, having nothing to fear from me, was willing to bring me up with his daughter. But he has resolved that I shall never marry.'

'I will avenge the cause of your father, of your grandfather, and your cause,' said the King of Scythia. 'I am responsible for your being married: I will carry you off the day after to-morrow by daybreak; for we must dine to-morrow with the King of Babylon; and I will return and support your rights with three hundred thousand men.'

'I agree to it,' said the beauteous Aldea; and after having exchanged their words of honour, they separated.

The incomparable Formosanta had a long time since retired to rest. She had ordered a little orange tree, in a silver case, to be placed by the side of her bed that her bird might perch upon it. Her curtains were drawn, but she was not in the least disposed to sleep; her heart and her imagination were too much awake. The charming stranger was ever before her sight; she fancied she saw him shooting an arrow with Nimrod's bow; she contemplated him in the act of cutting off the lion's head; she repeated his madrigal; at length, she saw him returning from the crowd upon his unicorn. Tears, sighs, and lamentations overwhelmed her at this reflection. At intervals she cried out:

'Shall I then never see him more? Will he never return?'

'He will return, Madam,' replied the bird from the top of the orange tree. 'Can one once have seen you, and not desire to see you again?'

'Heavens! Eternal Powers! My bird speaks the purest Chaldean.'

In uttering these words she drew back the curtain, put out her hand to him, and knelt upon her bed, saying, ' Art thou a god descended upon earth? Art thou the great Ormuzd concealed under this beautiful plumage? If thou art, restore me this charming young man.'

' I am nothing but a winged animal,' replied the bird; ' but I was born at the time when all animals still spoke; when birds, serpents, asses, horses, and griffins conversed familiarly with man. I would not speak before company, lest your ladies of honour should have taken me for a sorcerer; I would not discover myself to any but you.'

Formosanta was speechless, bewildered, and intoxicated with so many wonders: desirous of putting a hundred questions to him at once, she at length asked him how old he was.

' Twenty-seven thousand nine hundred years and six months, Madam; I date my age from the little revolution of heaven which your magi call the precession of the equinoxes, and which is accomplished in about twenty-eight thousand of your years. There are revolutions of a much greater extent, so are there beings much older than I. It is twenty-two thousand years since I learnt Chaldean in one of my travels. I have always had a very great taste for the Chaldean language, but my brethren, the other animals, have renounced speaking in your climate.'

' And why so, my divine bird? '

' Alas! because men have accustomed themselves to eat us instead of conversing and instructing themselves with us. Barbarians! should they not have been convinced that having the same organs with them, the same sentiments, the same wants, the same desires, we had what is called a soul, the same as they; that we were their brothers, and that none should be dressed and ate but the wicked? We are so far your brothers that the Supreme Being, the Omnipotent and Eternal Being, having made a compact with men, expressly comprehended us in the treaty. He forbade you to nourish yourselves with our blood, and we to suck yours.

' The fables of your ancient Locman, translated into so many languages, will be a testimony eternally subsisting of the happy commerce you formerly carried on with us.

They all begin with these words : *In the time when beasts spoke*. It is true, there are many ladies among you who keep up an incessant conversation with their dogs; but they have resolved not to answer, since they have been compelled by whipping to go hunting, and become accomplices in the murder of our ancient and common friends, stags, deers, hares, and partridges.

'You have still some ancient poems in which horses speak, and your coachmen daily address them in words, but in so barbarous a manner, and uttering such infamous expressions, that horses, which formerly entertained so great a kindness for you, now detest you.

'The country which is the residence of your charming stranger, the most perfect of men, is the only one in which your species has continued to love ours, to converse with us; and this is the only country of the world where men are just.'

'And where is this country of my dear stranger? What is the name of his empire? For I will no more believe he is a shepherd than that you are a bat.'

'His country, Madam, is that of the Gangarides, a virtuous and invincible people, who inhabit the eastern shore of the Ganges. The name of my friend is Amazan. He is no king; and I know not whether he would so much humble himself as to be one; he has too great a love for his fellow-countrymen; he is a shepherd like them. But do not imagine that those shepherds resemble yours; who, covered with rags and tatters, watch their sheep, far better clad than themselves; who groan under the burden of poverty, and who pay to an extortioner half the miserable stipend of wages which they receive from their masters. The Gangaridian shepherds are all born equal and are the masters of innumerable herds, which cover their fields in constant verdure. They are never killed; it is a horrid crime beside the Ganges to kill and eat one's fellow creature. Their wool is finer and more brilliant than the finest silk, and constitutes the greatest traffic of the East. Besides, the land of the Gangarides produces all that can flatter the desires of man. Those large diamonds which Amazan had the honour of presenting you with are from a mine which belongs to him. A unicorn, on which you saw him mounted, is the usual animal the Gangarides ride upon. It is the finest, the proudest, most terrible, and at the same time most gentle animal, that ornaments the earth. A hundred Gangarides, with as many unicorns, would be sufficient to disperse innumerable armies. About two centuries ago, a King of India was mad enough to want to conquer this nation : he appeared, followed by ten thousand elephants and a million of warriors. The unicorns pierced the elephants, just as I have seen upon your table beads pierced in golden brooches. The warriors fell under the sabres of the Gangarides, like crops of rice mowed by the people of the East. The King was taken prisoner, with upwards of six thousand men. He was bathed in the salutary water of the Ganges, followed the regimen of the country, which consists only of vegetables, and in which Nature there hath been amazingly liberal in order to nourish every breathing creature. Men who are fed with carnivorous aliments, and drenched with spirituous liquors, have sharp adult blood, which turns their brains a hundred different ways. Their chief rage is a fury to spill their brother's blood, and lay waste fertile plains to reign over church-yards. Six full months were taken up in curing the King of India of his disorder; when the physicians judged that his pulse was in a greater state of tranquillity, they certified this to the Council of the Gangarides. The Council, having followed the advice of the unicorns, humanely sent back the King of India, his silly Court, and impotent warriors, to their own country. This lesson made them wise, and from that time the Indians respected the Gangarides, as ignorant men, willing to be instructed, revere the Chaldean philosophers they cannot equal.'

' By the by, my dear bird,' said the Princess to him, ' do the Gangarides profess any religion? Have they one? '

' Madam, we meet to return thanks to God on the days of the full moon : the men in a great temple made of cedar, and the women in another, to prevent their devotion being diverted : all the birds assemble in a grove, and the quad-rupeds on a fine green-sward. We thank God for all the benefits He has bestowed upon us. We have in particular some parrots that preach wonderfully well.

'Such is the country of my dear Amazan; there I reside; my friendship for him is as great as the love with which he has inspired you. If you will credit me, we will set out together, and you shall pay him a visit.'

'Really, my dear bird, this is a very pretty profession of yours,' replied the Princess, smiling. She burned with desire to undertake the journey, but did not dare say so.

'I serve my friend,' said the bird; 'and, after the happiness of loving you, the greatest is to be an assistant in your amours.'

Formosanta was quite fascinated; she fancied herself transported from earth. All she had seen that day, all she then saw, all she heard, and particularly all that she felt now in her heart, so ravished her as far to surpass what those fortunate Mussulmans now feel, who disencumbered from their terrestrial ties, find themselves in the ninth heaven in the arms of their houris, surrounded and penetrated with glory and celestial felicity.

§ 4

She passed the whole night in speaking of Amazan. She no longer called him anything but her shepherd; and from this time it was that the names of *shepherd* and *lover* were indiscriminately used throughout certain nations.

Sometimes she asked the bird whether Amazan had had any other mistresses. He answered 'No'; and she was at the summit of felicity. Sometimes she asked how he passed his life; and she, with delight, learnt that it was employed in doing good, in cultivating arts, in penetrating into the secrets of nature, and improving himself. She at times wanted to know if the soul of her lover was of the same nature as that of her bird; how it happened that he had lived twenty thousand years, when her lover was not above eighteen or nineteen. She put a hundred such questions, to which the bird replied with such discretion as excited her curiosity. At length sleep closed their eyes, and yielded up Formosanta to the sweet delusion of dreams sent by the gods, which sometimes surpass reality itself, and which all the philosophy of the Chaldeans can scarcely explain.

Formosanta did not wake till very late. The day was far advanced, when the King her father entered her chamber. The bird received his Majesty with respectful politeness, went before him, fluttered his wings, stretched his neck, and then replaced himself upon his orange tree. The King seated himself upon his daughter's bed. Her dreams had made her still more beautiful. His large beard approached her lovely face, and after having twice embraced her, he spoke to her in these words :

' My dear daughter, you could not yesterday find a husband agreeable to my wishes ; you nevertheless must marry ; the prosperity of my empire requires it. I have consulted the oracle, which you know never errs, and which directs all my conduct. His commands are that you should traverse the globe. You must therefore begin your journey.'

' Ah ! doubtless, to the Gangarides,' said the Princess ; and in uttering these words, which escaped her, she was sensible of her indiscretion. The King, who was utterly ignorant of geography, asked her what she meant by the Gangarides. She easily evaded the question. The King told her she must go upon a pilgrimage, that he had appointed the persons who were to attend her, the doyen of the Counsellors of State, the High Almoner, a lady of honour, a physician, an apothecary, her bird, and all necessary domestics.

Formosanta, who had never been out of her father's palace, and who till the arrival of the three kings and Amazan had led a very insipid life, according to the etiquette of rank and the parade of pleasure, was charmed at setting out upon a pilgrimage.

' Who knows,' said she, whispering to her heart, ' if the gods may not inspire Amazan with the like desire of going to the same chapel, and I may have the happiness of again seeing the pilgrim ? '

She affectionately thanked her father, saying she had always entertained a secret devotion for the saint she was going to visit.

Belus gave an excellent dinner to his guests, who were

all men. They formed a very ill-assorted company; kings, princes, ministers, pontiffs, all jealous of each other; all weighing their words, and equally embarrassed with their neighbours and themselves. The repast was very gloomy, though they drank pretty freely. The Princesses remained in their apartments, each meditating upon their respective journeys. They dined at their little cover. Formosanta afterwards walked in the gardens with her dear bird, who, to amuse her, flew from tree to tree, displaying his superb tail and divine plumage.

The King of Egypt, who was heated with wine, not to say drunk, asked one of his pages for a bow and arrow. This Prince was, in truth, the most unskilful archer in his whole kingdom. When he aimed at a mark, the place of the greatest safety was the spot he hoped to hit. But the beautiful bird, flying as swiftly as the arrow, seemed to court it, and fell bleeding in the arms of Formosanta. The Egyptian, bursting into a foolish laugh, retired to his place. The Princess rent the skies with her moans, melted into tears, tore her hair and beat her breast. The dying bird said to her in a low voice :

' Burn me, and fail not to carry my ashes to Arabia Felix, to the east of the ancient city of Aden or Eden, and expose them to the sun upon a little pile of cloves and cinnamon.'

After having uttered these words he expired. Formosanta was for a long time in a swoon, and saw the light again only to burst into sighs and groans. Her father partaking of her grief, and cursing the King of Egypt, did not doubt but that this accident foretold some fatal event. He went hastily to consult the oracle of his chapel.

The oracle replied, ' A mixture of everything; life and death, infidelity and constancy, loss and gain, calamities and good fortune.'

Neither he nor his Council could comprehend any meaning in this reply; but, at length, he was satisfied with having fulfilled the duties of devotion.

His daughter was bathed in tears, whilst he consulted the oracle; she paid the funeral obsequies to the bird which he had directed, and resolved to carry its remains into Arabia at the risk of her life. He was burnt in incombustible flax, with the orange tree on which he used to perch. She gathered up the ashes in a little golden vase, set with rubies, and the diamonds taken from the lion's mouth. Oh! that she could, instead of fulfilling this melancholy duty, have burnt alive the detestable King of Egypt! This was her sole wish. She, in spite, put to death the two crocodiles, his two hippopotami, his two zebras, his two rats, and had his two mummies thrown into the Euphrates. Had she been possessed of his bull Apis, she would not have spared him.

The King of Egypt, enraged at this affront, set out immediately to forward his three hundred thousand men. The King of India, seeing his ally depart, set off also upon his return the same day, with a firm intention of combining his three hundred thousand Indians with the Egyptian army. The King of Scythia decamped in the night with the Princess Aldea, fully resolved to fight for her at the head of three hundred thousand Scythians, and to restore her the inheritance of Babylon, which was her right, as she was descended from the elder branch.

As for the beautiful Formosanta, she set out at three in the morning with her caravan of pilgrims, flattering herself that she might go into Arabia, and execute the last will of her bird; and that the justice of the gods would restore her the dear Amazan, without whom life was become insupportable.

Thus when the King of Babylon awoke, he found all his company gone. 'How mighty festivals terminate!' said he; 'and what a surprising vacuum they leave in the soul, when the hurry is over!' But he was transported with a rage truly royal, when he found that Princess Aldea was carried off. He ordered all his ministers to be called up, and the Council to be convened. Whilst they were dressing, he failed not to consult the oracle; but he could never get from it any other than these words, so celebrated since throughout the universe: 'When girls are not married by their relations, they marry themselves.'

Orders were immediately issued to march three hundred thousand men against the King of Scythia. Thus was the torch of the most dreadful war lighted up, which was produced by the amusements of the finest festival ever given upon earth. Asia was upon the point of being overrun by four armies of three hundred thousand men each. It is plain that the war of Troy, which astonished the world some ages after, was mere child's play in comparison with this; but it should also be considered that in the Trojans' quarrel, the object was nothing more than a very libidinous old woman, who had contrived to be twice run away with; whereas, in this case, the cause was threefold—two girls and a bird.

The King of India went to meet his army upon the large fine road which then led straight to Babylon, at Kashmir. The King of Scythia flew with Aldea by the fine road which led to Mount Immaus. All these fine roads have disappeared in course of time, by reason of bad government. The King of Egypt had marched to the west, along the coast of the little Mediterranean Sea, which the ignorant Hebrews have since called the Great Sea.

As to the charming Formosanta, she followed the road to Bassora, planted with lofty palm trees, which furnished a perpetual shade, and fruits at all seasons. The temple, in which she was to perform her pilgrimage, was in Bassora itself. The saint, to whom this temple had been dedicated, was pretty nearly in the style of him who was afterwards adored at Lampsacus. He not only procured young women husbands, but he often supplied the husband's place. He was the holiest saint in all Asia.

Formosanta had no sort of inclination for the saint of Bassora; she only invoked her dear Gangaridian shepherd, her charming Amazan. She proposed embarking at Bassora, and making her way into Arabia Felix to perform what her deceased bird had commanded.

At the third stage, scarcely had she entered into a fine inn, where her harbingers had made all the necessary preparations for her, when she learnt that the King of Egypt was arrived there also. Informed by his emissaries of the Princess's route, he immediately altered his course, followed by a numerous escort. Having alighted, he placed sentinels at all the doors; then repaired to the beautiful Formosanta's apartment, when he addressed her by saying :

' Madam, you are the lady I was in quest of; you paid me very little attention when I was at Babylon; it is just to punish scornful capricious women : you will, if you please, be kind enough to dine with me to-night; you will have no other bed than mine, and I shall behave to you according to my pleasure.'

Formosanta saw very well that she was not the stronger; she judged that good sense consisted in knowing how to conform to one's situation; she resolved to get rid of the King of Egypt by an innocent stratagem : she looked at him from the corners of her eyes, which after-ages have called ogling; and thus she spoke to him, with a modesty, grace, and sweetness, a confusion, and a thousand other charms, which would have made the wisest man a fool, and deceived the most discerning :

' I acknowledge, Sir, I always appeared with a downcast look when you did the King my father the honour of visiting him. I had some apprehensions for my heart, I dreaded my too great simplicity; I trembled lest my father and your rivals should observe the preference I gave you, and which you so highly deserved. I can now declare my sentiments. I swear by the bull Apis, which after you is the thing I respect the most in the world, that your proposals have enchanted me. I have already dined with you at my father's, and I will dine again here with you, without his being of the party; all that I request of you is that your High Almoner should drink with us : he appeared to me at Babylon to be an excellent guest; I have some remarkably good Chiras wine, I will make you both taste it. As to your second proposition, it is very engaging; but a girl well brought up should not dwell upon it; satisfy yourself with being informed, that I consider you as the greatest of kings, and the most amiable of men.'

This discourse turned the King of Egypt's head; he agreed to have the almoner's company.

' I have another favour to ask you,' said the Princess, ' which is to allow me to speak to my apothecary : women have always some little ails that require attention, such as vapours in the head, palpitations of the heart, colics, and the like, which at particular times require some assistance; in a word, I at present stand in need of my apothecary, and I hope you will not refuse me this slight testimony of love.'

'Madam,' replied the King of Egypt, 'though the designs of an apothecary are directly opposite to mine, and the objects of his art are directly contrary to those of mine, I know life too well to refuse you so just a demand; I will order him to attend you whilst supper is preparing. I imagine you must be somewhat fatigued by the journey; you will also have occasion for a chamber-maid, you may order her whom you like best to attend you; I will afterwards wait your commands and conveniency.'

He retired, and the apothecary, and a chamber-maid named Irla, entered. The Princess had an entire confidence in her; she ordered her to bring six bottles of Chiras wine for supper, and to make all the sentinels, who had her officers under arrest, drink the same; then she recommended her apothecary to infuse in all the bottles certain pharmaceutic drugs, which made those who took them sleep twenty-four hours, and with which he was always provided : She was punctually obeyed. The King returned with his High Almoner in about half an hour's time; the conversation at supper was very gay; the King and the priest emptied the six bottles, and acknowledged there was no such good wine in Egypt : the chamber-maid was careful to make the servants-in-waiting drink. As for the Princess, she took great care not to drink any herself, saying that she was ordered by her physician a particular regimen. They were all presently asleep.

The King of Egypt's almoner had one of the finest beards that a man of his rank could wear. Formosanta cut it off very skilfully; then sewing it to a ribbon, she put it on her own chin. She then dressed herself in the priest's robes, and decked herself in all the marks of his dignity, and her waiting-maid clad herself like the sacristan of the goddess Isis; at length, having furnished herself with his urn and jewels, she set out from the inn amidst the sentinels, who were asleep like their master. Her attendant had taken care to have two horses ready at the door. The Princess could not take with her any of the officers of her train; they would have been stopped by the guards.

Formosanta and Irla passed through several ranks of soldiers, who, taking the Princess for the high-priest, called her, 'My most Reverend Father in God,' and asked his blessing. The two fugitives arrived in twenty-four hours at Bassora, before the King awoke. They then threw off their disguise, which might have created some suspicion. They fitted out with all possible expedition a ship, which carried them by the Straits of Ormus, to the beautiful banks of Eden in Arabia Felix. This was that Eden, whose gardens were so famous that they have since been the residence of the justest of mankind; they were the model of the Elysian Fields, the Gardens of the Hesperides, and those of the Fortunate Islands; for in those warm climates men imagined there could be no greater felicity than shades and murmuring brooks. To live eternally in Heaven with the Supreme Being, or to walk in the garden of paradise, was the same thing to those who incessantly spoke without understanding one another, and who could scarce have any distinct ideas or just expressions.

As soon as the Princess found herself in this land, her first care was to pay her dear bird the funeral obsequies he had required of her. Her beautiful hands prepared a small pile of cloves and cinnamon. What was her surprise when, having spread the ashes of the bird upon this pile, she saw it blaze of itself! They were all presently consumed. In the place of the ashes there appeared nothing but a large egg, from whence she saw her bird issue more brilliant than ever. This was one of the most happy moments the Princess had ever experienced in her whole life; there was but another that could ever be dearer to her; it was the object of her wishes, but almost beyond her hopes.

' I plainly see,' said she to the bird, ' you are the phœnix which I have heard so much spoken of. I am almost ready to expire with joy and astonishment. I did not believe in your resurrection; but it is my good fortune to be convinced of it.'

' Resurrection, Madam,' said the phœnix to her, ' is one of the most simple things in the world. There is nothing more astonishing in being born twice than once. Everything in this world is the effect of resurrection; caterpillars are regenerated into butterflies; a kernel put into the earth is regenerated into a tree. All animals buried in the earth regenerate into vegetations, herbs, and plants, and nourish other animals, of which they speedily compose part of the substance; all particles which composed bodies are transformed into different beings. It is true that I am the only one to whom Ormuzd has granted the favour of regenerating in my own form.'

Formosanta, who from the moment she first saw Amazan and the phœnix, had passed all her time in a round of astonishment, said to him :

' I can easily conceive that the Supreme Being may form out of your ashes a phœnix nearly resembling yourself; but that you should be precisely the same person, that you should have the same soul, is a thing, I acknowledge, I cannot very clearly comprehend. What became of your soul when I carried you in my pocket after your death ? '

' Good heavens, Madam ! is it not as easy for the great Ormuzd to continue action upon a single atom of my being, as to begin afresh this action ? He had before granted me sensation, memory, and thought; he grants them to me again; whether he united this favour to an atom of elementary fire latent within me, or the assemblage of my organs, is, in reality, of no consequence; men, as well as phœnixes, are equally ignorant how things come to pass; but the greatest favour the Supreme Being has bestowed upon me, is to regenerate me for you. Oh ! that I may pass the twenty-eight thousand years which I have still to live before my next resurrection, with you and my dear Amazan ! '

' My dear phœnix, remember what you first told me at Babylon, which I shall never forget, and which flattered me with the hope of again seeing my dear shepherd, whom I idolize; we must indeed pay the Gangarides a visit together, and I must take him back with me to Babylon.'

' This is precisely my design,' said the phœnix; ' there is not a moment to lose. We must go in search of Amazan by the shortest road, that is, through the air. There are in Arabia Felix two griffins, who are my particular friends, who live only a hundred and fifty thousand leagues from here; I am going to write to them by the pigeons' post, and they will be here before night. We shall have time to work you a little convenient couch with drawers in which you may place your provisions. You will be quite at your

ease in this vehicle, with your maid.   These two griffins are
the most vigorous of their kind; each of them will support
one of the poles of the canopy between their claws.   But,
once again, time is very precious.'

He immediately went with Formosanta to order the
couch at an upholsterer's of his acquaintance.   It was
made complete in four hours.   In the drawers were placed
small fine loaves, biscuits superior to those of Babylon,
large lemons, pineapples, cocoanuts and pistachios, Eden
wine, which is as superior to that of Chiras as Chiras is to
that of Surinam.

The canopy was as light as it was commodious and solid.
The two griffins arrived at Eden by the appointed time.
Formosanta and Irla placed themselves in the vehicle.
The two griffins carried it off like a feather.   The phœnix
sometimes flew after it, and sometimes perched upon its
back.   The two griffins winged their way towards the
Ganges with the velocity of an arrow which rends the air.
They never stopped but a moment at night, for the travellers
to have some refreshment, and the carriers to take a
draught of water.

They at length reached the country of the Gangarides.
The Princess's heart palpitated with hope, love, and joy.
The phœnix stopped the vehicle before Amazan's house;
he desired to speak with him; but he had been absent
from home three hours, without any one knowing whither
he was gone.

There are no words, even in the Gangaridian language,
that could express Formosanta's extreme despair.

' Alas ! this is what I dreaded,' said the phœnix : ' the
three hours which you passed at the inn upon the road to
Bassora with that wretched King of Egypt have perhaps
been at the price of the happiness of your whole life;   I
very much fear we have lost Amazan, without the possibility
of recovering him.'

He then asked the servants, if they could greet the
lady his mother.   She answered that her husband had
died only two days before, and she could speak to no one.
The phœnix, who was not without influence in the house,
introduced the Princess of Babylon into a saloon, the walls
of which were covered with orange-tree wood inlaid with

ivory. The inferior shepherds and shepherdesses, who were
dressed in long white garments with gold-coloured trim-
mings, served her up, in a hundred plain porcelain baskets,
a hundred various delicious meats, amongst which no
disguised carcasses were to be seen; they consisted of rice,
sago, vermicelli, macaroni, omelets, milk, eggs, cream,
cheese, pastry of every kind, vegetables, and fruit of a
smell and taste of which no idea can be formed in other
climates; and they were accompanied with a profusion of
refreshing liquors superior to the finest wine.

Whilst the Princess regaled herself, seated upon a bed
of roses, four peacocks, who were luckily mute, fanned her
with their brilliant wings; two hundred birds, two hundred
shepherds and shepherdesses, warbled a concert in two
different choirs; the nightingales, canaries, linnets, chaf-
finches sang the higher notes with the shepherdesses, and
the shepherds sang the tenor and the bass. In everything
there was nature, simple and beautiful. The Princess
acknowledged that if there was more magnificence at
Babylon, Nature was infinitely more agreeable among the
Gangarides; but whilst this consolatory and voluptuous
music was being played, tears flowed from her eyes, whilst
she said to the damsel Irla :

'These shepherds and shepherdesses, these nightingales,
these linnets, are making love; and for my part, I am
deprived of the Gangaridian hero, the worthy object of my
most tender and impatient desires.'

Whilst she was taking this collation, and tears and admiration kept pace with each other, the phœnix addressed
himself to Amazan's mother, saying :

'Madam, you cannot avoid seeing the Princess of
Babylon; you know . . .'

'I know everything,' said she, 'even her adventure at
the inn upon the road to Bassora; a blackbird related the
whole to me this morning; and this cruel blackbird is the
cause of my son's going mad, and leaving his paternal
abode.'

'You do not know, then, that the Princess regenerated
me?'

'No, my dear child, the blackbird told me that you were
dead, and this made me inconsolable. I was so afflicted

at this loss, the death of my husband, and the precipitate flight of my son, that I ordered my door to be shut to every one. But since the Princess of Babyon has done me the honour of paying me a visit, I beg she may be immediately introduced; I have matters of the last importance to acquaint her with, and I choose you should be present.'

She then went to meet the Princess in another saloon. She could not walk very well; this lady was about three hundred years old; but she had still some agreeable vestiges of beauty; it might be discovered that about her two hundred and thirtieth, or two hundred and fortieth year, she must have been a most charming woman. She received Formosanta with a respectful nobleness, blended with an air of interest and chagrin, which made a very lively impression upon the Princess.

Formosanta immediately paid her the compliments of condolence upon her husband's death.

' Alas ! ' said the widow, ' you have more reason to lament his death than you imagine.'

' I am, doubtless, greatly afflicted,' said Formosanta, ' he was father to——,' here a flood of tears prevented her from going on. ' For his sake only I undertook this journey, amidst many perils, and narrowly escaped many dangers. For him I left my father, and the most splendid Court in the universe. I was detained by the King of Egypt, whom I detest. Having escaped from this ravisher, I have traversed the air, in search of the only man I love. When I arrive, he flies from me ! ' Here sighs and tears prevented her from saying more.

His mother then said to her :

' Madam, when the King of Egypt carried you off when you dined with him at an inn upon the road to Bassora, when your beautiful hands filled him bumpers of Chiras wine, did you observe a blackbird that flew about the room ? '

' Yes, indeed,' said the Princess, ' I do now recollect there was such a bird, though I did not then pay it any kind of attention; but in collecting my ideas, I now remember well that at the instant when the King of Egypt got up from table to give me a kiss, the blackbird flew out at the window giving a loud cry, and never appeared after.'

' Alas ! Madam,' resumed Amazan's mother, ' this is precisely the cause of all our misfortunes : my son had dispatched this blackbird to gain intelligence of your health, and all that passed at Babylon. He proposed speedily to return, throw himself at your feet, and consecrate to you the remainder of his life. You know not to what a pitch he adores you. All the Gangarides are both loving and faithful; but my son is the most passionate and constant of them all. The blackbird found you at an inn, drinking very cheerfully with the King of Egypt and a vile priest; he afterwards saw you give this monarch, who had killed the phœnix, a fond embrace;—the man my son holds in utter detestation. The blackbird, at the sight of this, was seized with a just indignation; he flew away cursing your fatal amours : he returned this day, and has related everything; but, just Heaven, at what a juncture ! at the very time that my son was deploring with me the loss of his father, and that of the phœnix, the very instant I had informed him he was your cousin-germane ! '

' Oh heavens ! my cousin, Madam, is it possible? By what chance? How can this be? What, am I so happy as to be thus allied ! and yet so miserable as to have offended him ! '

' My son is, I tell you,' said his mother, ' your cousin, and I shall presently convince you of it; but in becoming my relation, you rob me of my son; he cannot survive the grief which the embrace you gave to the King of Egypt has occasioned him.'

' Ah ! my dear aunt,' cried the beautiful Formosanta, ' I swear, by him and the all-powerful Ormuzd, that this embrace, so far from being criminal, was the strongest proof of love your son could receive from me. I disobeyed my father for his sake. For him I went from the Euphrates to the Ganges. Fallen into the hands of the worthless Pharaoh of Egypt, I could not escape his clutches but by artifice. I call the ashes and soul of the phœnix, which were then in my pocket, to witness; he can do me justice. But how can your son, born upon the banks of the Ganges, be my cousin? I, whose family have reigned upon the banks of the Euphrates for so many centuries? '

' You know,' said the venerable Gangaridian lady to her,

'that your grand-uncle, Aldea, was King of Babylon, and that he was dethroned by Belus's father?'

'Yes, Madam.'

'You know that this Aldea had in marriage a daughter named Aldea, brought up in your Court. It was this prince, who, being persecuted by your father, took refuge in our happy country under another name : he married me : by him I bore young Prince Aldea Amazan, the most beautiful, the most courageous, the strongest, and most virtuous of mortals—and at this hour the maddest. He went to the Babylonian festival upon the credit of your beauty; since that time he has idolized you, and, perhaps, I shall never again set eyes upon my dear son.'

She then displayed to the Princess all the titles of the House of the Aldeas. Formosanta scarce deigned to look at them.

'Ah! Madam, do we examine what is the object of our desire? My heart sufficiently believes you. But where is Aldea Amazan? Where is my kinsman, my lover, my king? Where is my life? What road has he taken? I will seek for him in every sphere the Eternal Being has framed, and of which he is the greatest ornament. I will go to the star Canope, to Sheath, to Aldebaran; I will go and convince him of my love and my innocence.'

The phœnix absolved the Princess of the crime that was imputed to her by the blackbird, of fondly embracing the King of Egypt; but it was necessary to undeceive Amazan and recall him. Birds were dispatched on every side, unicorns set forward on every road : news at length arrived that Amazan took the road towards China.

'Well, then,' said the Princess, 'let us set out for China; the journey is not long, and I hope I shall bring you back your son in a fortnight at the latest.'

At these words the mother of Amazan and the Princess both shed tears of love; they most tenderly embraced in the great effusion of their hearts.

The phœnix immediately ordered a coach with six unicorns. Amazan's mother furnished two thousand horsemen, and made the Princess her niece a present of some thousands of the finest diamonds of her country. The phœnix, afflicted at the evil occasioned by the blackbird's indiscretion, ordered all the blackbirds to quit the country; and from that time none have been met with upon the banks of the Ganges.

§ 5

The unicorns, in less than eight days, carried Formosanta, Irla, and the phœnix, to Cambalu, the capital of China. This city was larger than that of Babylon, and its magnificence very different. These fresh objects, these new manners, would have amused Formosanta could anything but Amazan have engaged her attention.

As soon as the Emperor of China learnt that the Princess of Babylon was at one of the city gates, he dispatched to her four thousand mandarins in ceremonial robes : they all prostrated themselves before her, and presented her with a compliment written in golden letters upon a sheet of purple silk. Formosanta told them that if she were possessed of four thousand tongues, she would not omit replying immediately to every mandarin ; but that having only one, she hoped they would be satisfied with her general thanks. They conducted her, in a respectful manner, to the Emperor.

He was the most just, the politest, and wisest monarch upon earth. It was he who first tilled a small field with his own imperial hands, to make agriculture respectable to his people. He first allotted premiums to virtue : laws in all other countries were shamefully confined to the punishment of crimes. This Emperor had just banished from his dominions a gang of foreign *bonzes*, who had come from the extremities of the West, with the frantic hope of compelling all China to think like themselves; and who, under pretence of teaching truths, had already acquired honours and riches. In expelling them, he delivered himself in these words, which are recorded in the annals of the empire :

' You may here do as much harm as you have elsewhere; you are come to preach dogmas of intolerance, in the most tolerant nation upon earth. I send you back that I may never be compelled to punish you. You will be honourably conducted to my frontiers; you will be furnished with everything necessary to return to the confines of the hemisphere from whence you came. Depart in peace, if you can be at peace, and never return.'

The Princess of Babylon learnt with pleasure this resolution and this speech; she was the more certain of being well received at Court, as she was very far from entertaining any dogmas of intolerance. The Emperor of China, in dining with her tête-à-tête, had the politeness to banish all disagreeable etiquette : she presented the phœnix to him, who was greatly caressed by the Emperor, and who perched upon his chair. Formosanta, towards the end of the repast, ingenuously acquainted him with the cause of her journey, and entreated him to search for the beautiful Amazan in the city of Cambalu; and in the meanwhile she acquainted the Emperor with her adventures, without concealing the fatal passion with which her heart burnt for this youthful hero.

' To whom are you speaking of him ? ' said the Emperor of China; ' he did me the pleasure of coming to my court; I was enchanted with this amiable Amazan. It is true that he is deeply afflicted; but his graces are thereby the more affecting. No one of my favourites has more wit than he, there is not a gowned mandarin who has more knowledge, nor a military one who has a more martial or heroic air. His extreme youth adds an additional value to all his talents. If I were so unfortunate, so abandoned by the Tien and Changti, as to desire to be a conqueror, I would desire Amazan to put himself at the head of my armies, and I should be sure of conquering the whole universe. It is a great pity that his melancholy sometimes causes a distemper of his spirit.'

' Ah ! Sir,' said Formosanta, with much agitation and grief, blended with an air of reproach, ' why did you not make me dine with him? This is a mortal stroke you have given me !—send for him immediately.'

' Madam,' replied the Emperor, ' he set out this very morning, without acquainting me with his destination.'

Formosanta, turning towards the phœnix, said to him, ' Did you ever know so unfortunate a damsel as myself? ' But, resuming, she said, ' Sir, how came he to quit so polite a court, and in which, methinks, one might pass one's life, in so abrupt a manner? '

' This was the case, Madam,' said he. ' One of the most amiable of the princesses of the blood, falling desperately in love with him, fixed a rendez-vous to meet him at noon; he set out at daybreak, leaving this billet for my kinswoman, whom it hath cost a deluge of tears.

' " Beautiful princess of the blood of China, you are deserving of a heart that was never offered up to any other altar; I have sworn to the immortal gods never to love any other than Formosanta Princess of Babylon, and to teach her how to conquer one's desires in travelling. She has had the misfortune to yield to a worthless King of Egypt: I am the most unfortunate of men; I have lost my father and the phœnix, and the hope of being loved by Formosanta. I left my mother in affliction, and my country, unable to live a moment in that spot where I learnt that Formosanta loved another than me. I swore to traverse the earth, and be faithful. You would despise me, and the gods punish me, if I violated my oath : choose another lover, Madam, and be as faithful as I am.'

' Ah ! give me that miraculous letter,' said the beautiful Formosanta, ' it will afford me some consolation : I am happy in the midst of my misfortunes. Amazan loves me; Amazan for me renounces the embraces of princesses of China; there is no one upon earth but himself endowed with so much fortitude; he sets me a most brilliant example; the phœnix knows I did not stand in need of it : how cruel it is to be deprived of one's lover for the most innocent embrace given through pure fidelity ! But, in fine, whither is he gone? What road has he taken? Deign to inform me, and I will set out.'

The Emperor of China told her that, according to the reports he had received, her lover had taken the road towards Scythia. The unicorns were immediately harnessed, and the Princess, after the most tender compliments, took leave of the Emperor, with the phœnix, her chambermaid Irla, and all her train.

As soon as she arrived in Scythia, she was more convinced than ever how much men and governments differed,
and would differ, till such time as some more enlightened
people should by degrees remove that cloud of darkness
which had covered the earth for so many ages; and till
there should be found, in barbarous climes, heroic souls who
would have strength and perseverance enough to trans-
form brutes into men.   There are no cities in Scythia,
consequently no agreeable arts; nothing was to be seen but
extensive fields, and whole nations whose sole habitations
were tents and chariots.   Such an appearance struck her
with terror.   Formosanta inquired in what tent or wagon
the King was lodged.   She was informed that he had set
out eight days before with three hundred thousand cavalry
to attack the King of Babylon, whose niece, the beautiful
Princess Aldea, he had carried off.

' What ! hath he run away with my cousin ? ' cried
Formosanta.   ' I could not have imagined such an incident.
What ! is my cousin, who was too happy in paying her
court to me, become a queen, and I am not yet married ? '

She was immediately conducted, by her desire, to the
Queen's tent.

Their unexpected meeting in such distant climes; the
uncommon occurrences they mutually had to impart to
each other, gave such charms to this interview as made
them forget they never loved one another : they saw each
other with transport; and a soft illusion supplied the
place of real tenderness : they embraced with tears; and
there was a cordiality and frankness on each side that
could not have taken place in a palace.

Aldea remembered the phœnix and the waiting-maid
Irla. She presented her cousin with sable skins, who in
return gave her diamonds.   The war between the two kings
was spoken of.   They deplored the state of men, whom
capricious monarchs despatch to cut each others' throats
for a difference of policy which two honest men might easily
settle in an hour.   But the principal topic was the handsome
stranger, who had conquered lions, given the largest diamonds in the universe, the writer of madrigals, now become
the most miserable of men from the intelligence of a blackbird.

' He is my dear brother,' said Aldea.

' He is my lover,' cried Formosanta : ' you have, doubtless, seen him; is he still here? For, cousin, he knows he is your brother; he cannot have left you so abruptly as he did the King of China.'

' Have I seen him? Good heavens ! Yes, he passed four whole days with me. Ah ! cousin, how much my brother is to be pitied ! A false report has absolutely turned his brain; he roams about the world, without knowing whither he is destined. Imagine to yourself that his frenzy is so great that he has refused the favours of the handsomest Scythian lady in all Scythia. He set out yesterday, after writing her a letter which has thrown her into despair. As for him, he is gone to visit the Cimmerians.'

' God be thanked ! ' cried Formosanta ; ' another refusal in my favour ! My good fortune is beyond my hope, as my misfortunes have surpassed my greatest apprehensions. Procure me this charming letter that I may set out and follow him, loaded with his sacrifices. Farewell, cousin ! Amazan is among the Cimmerians, and I fly to meet him.'

Aldea judged that the Princess her cousin was still more frantic than her brother Amazan. But as she had herself been sensible of the effects of this epidemic contagion, having given up the delights and magnificence of Babylon for a King of Scythia ; and as the women are always interested in those follies that are the effects of love, she sympathized with Formosanta's affliction, wished her a happy journey, and promised to assist her passion, if ever she was so fortunate as to see her brother again.

§ 6

The Princess of Babylon with her phœnix arrived soon at the empire of the Cimmerians, a country indeed much less populous than China, but of twice the extent ; in former times like Scythia, but, long ages since, become as flourishing as those kingdoms which boast of setting a model for other states.

After a few days' journey, she entered a very large city, which had of late been greatly improved by the reigning empress : she herself was not there at that time, but was making a tour through her dominions, from the frontiers of Europe to those of Asia, in order to judge of their state and condition with her own eyes, to inquire into their grievances, and to provide the proper remedies for them, to increase their advantages and to disseminate knowledge.

One of the principal magistrates of that ancient capital, as soon as he was informed of the arrival of the Babylonian lady and the phœnix, lost no time in paying her all the honours of the country; being certain that his mistress, the most polite and generous princess in the world, would be extremely well pleased to find that he had received so illustrious a lady with all that respect which she herself would have shown her.

The Princess was lodged in the palace, whence they dispersed an intruding throng of people, and entertained her with great splendour and elegance. The Cimmerian lord, who was an excellent natural philosopher, diverted himself in conversing with the phœnix, at such times as the Princess chose to retire to her own apartment. The phœnix told him that he had formerly travelled among the Cimmerians, but that he would not have known the country again.

'How comes it,' said he, 'that such prodigious changes have been brought about in so short a time? Formerly, when I was here, about three hundred years ago, I saw nothing but savage Nature in all her horrors; at present, I perceive industry, arts, splendour, and politeness.'

'This mighty revolution,' replied the Cimmerian, 'was begun by one man, and is now carried to perfection by one woman; a woman who is a greater legislator than the Isis of the Egyptians, or the Ceres of the Greeks. Most law-givers have been unhappy owing to a narrow genius and an arbitrary disposition, which confined their views to the countries they governed : each of them looked upon his own, as the only people existing upon the earth, or as if they ought to be at enmity with all the rest : they formed institutions, introduced customs, and established a religion for them alone. Thus the Egyptians, so famous for those heaps of stones, have dishonoured and besotted themselves with their barbarous superstitions. They despise all other nations as profane; refuse all manner of intercourse with them; and, excepting those conversant in the Court, who now and then rise above the prejudices of the vulgar, there is not an Egyptian who will eat off a plate that had ever been used by a stranger. Their priests are equally cruel and absurd. It were better to have no laws at all, and to follow those notions of right and wrong engraved on our hearts by Nature, than to subject society to institutions so inhospitable.

' Our Empress has adopted a quite different system; she considers her vast dominions, under which all the meridians on the globe are united, as under an obligation of correspondence with all the nations dwelling under those meridians. The first and most fundamental of her laws is a universal toleration of all religions, and an unbounded compassion for every error. Her penetrating genius perceives that though the modes of religious worship differ, yet morality is everywhere the same : by this principle, she has united her people to all the nations on earth, and the Cimmerians will soon consider the Scandinavians and the Chinese as their brethren. Not satisfied with this, she has resolved to establish this invaluable toleration, the strongest link of society, among her neighbours : by these means, she has obtained the title of the " Parent of her country "; and, if she perseveres, will acquire that of the " Benefactress of mankind."

' Before her time, the men, who were unhappily possessed of power, sent out legions of murderers to ravage unknown countries, and to water with their blood the inheritance of their fathers. Those assassins were called *heroes*, and their robberies accounted glorious achievements. But our sovereign courts another sort of glory; she has sent forth her armies to be the messengers of peace; not only to prevent men from being the destroyers, but to oblige them to be the benefactors, of one another. Her standards are the ensigns of public tranquillity.'

The phœnix was quite charmed with what he heard from this nobleman; he told him that though he had lived twenty-seven thousand nine hundred years and seven months in this

world, he had never seen anything like it.   He then inquired
after his friend Amazan.   The Cimmerian gave the same
account of him that the Princess had already heard from
the Chinese and the Scythians.   It was Amazan's constant
practice to run away from all the Courts he visited, the
instant any lady made him an assignation, at which he
might be prevailed upon to give some proofs of human
frailty.   The phœnix soon acquainted Formosanta with
this fresh instance of Amazan's fidelity, a fidelity so much
the more surprising, since he could not imagine his Princess
would ever hear of it.

Amazan had set out for Scandinavia, where he was
entertained with sights still more surprising.   In this
place, he beheld monarchy and liberty subsisting together
in a manner thought incompatible in other states; the
labourers of the ground shared in the legislature with the
grandees of the realm and a young prince gave his people
most urgent hopes of his worthiness to reign over a free
nation.   That was the most extraordinary thing there :
that a prince equally remarkable for his extreme youth
and uprightness possessed a sovereign authority over his
country, acquired by a solemn contract with his people.

Amazan beheld a philosopher on the throne of Sarmatia,
who might be called a King of Anarchy; for he was the
chief of a hundred thousand petty kings, one of whom
with his single voice could render ineffectual the resolu-
tions of all the rest.   Æolus had not more difficulty to keep
the warring winds within their proper bounds than this
monarch to reconcile the spirits of his subjects.   He was
the master of a ship surrounded with eternal storms; but
the vessel did not founder, for he was an excellent pilot.

In traversing those various countries, so different from
his own, Amazan persevered in rejecting all the favourable
advances made to him, though incessantly distracted with
the embrace given by Formosanta to the King of Egypt,
being resolved to set Formosanta an amazing example of an
unshaken and unparalleled fidelity.

The Princess of Babylon with the phœnix was ever close
at his heels, and scarcely ever missed him but by a day or
two, without the one being tired of roaming, or the other
losing a moment in pursuing him.

Thus they traversed the immense continent of Germany, where they beheld with wonder, the progress which reason and philosophy had made in the North; even their princes were enlightened, and were become the patrons of freedom of thought. Their education had not been trusted to men who had an interest in deceiving them, or who were themselves deceived; they were brought up in the knowledge of universal morality, and in the contempt of superstition; they had banished from all their estates a senseless custom which had enervated and depopulated the southern countries; this was to bury alive, in immense dungeons, infinite numbers of both sexes who were eternally separated from one another, and sworn to have no communication together. This madness had contributed as much as the most cruel wars in laying waste the earth.

The princes of the North had at last found out that if they wanted a good breed of horses, they must not separate the finest stallions from the mares. They had likewise exploded other errors equally absurd and pernicious; in short, men had at last ventured to make use of their reason in those immense regions; whereas it was still believed almost everywhere else that they could not be governed but in proportion to their ignorance.

§ 7

From Germany, Amazan arrived at Batavia: where his perpetual grief was in a good measure alleviated, by observing among the inhabitants a faint resemblance to his happy countrymen the Gangarides. There he saw liberty, property, equality, plenty, and toleration; but the ladies were so indifferent that not one made him any amorous advances: a thing he had never met with before. It is true, had he been inclined to address them, they would have yielded one after another; though, at the same time, not one would have been the least in love; but he was far from any thoughts of making conquests.

Formosanta had nearly caught him in this insipid nation: he had set out but a moment before her arrival.

Amazan had heard so much among the Batavians in praise of a certain island called Albion, that he was determined to embark with his unicorns on board a ship, which, with a favourable easterly wind, carried him in four hours to that celebrated country, more famous than Tyre, or the island of Atlantis.

The beautiful Formosanta, who had followed him to the banks of the Volga, the Vistula, the Elbe, and the Weser, arrived finally at the mouths of the Rhine, where it discharges its waters into the German Ocean.

Here she learned that her beloved Amazan had just set sail for Albion. She thought she saw the vessel on board of which he was, and could not help crying out for joy : at which the Batavian ladies were greatly surprised, not imagining that a young man could possibly occasion so violent a transport. They took, indeed, but little notice of the phœnix, as they reckoned his feathers would not fetch near so good a price as those of their own ducks, and other water-fowl. The Princess of Babylon hired or chartered two vessels to carry herself and her retinue to that happy island, which was soon to possess the only object of her desires, the soul of her life, and the god of her heart.

An unpropitious wind from the west arose of a sudden, just as the faithful and unhappy Amazan landed on the Albion shore, and detained the ships of the Babylonian princess, just as they were going to put to sea. Seized with anguish of heart, bitter grief and deep melancholy, she betook herself to bed, determined to remain there till the wind should change; but it blew for the space of eight days, with an unremitting violence. The Princess, during this age of eight days, employed her maid of honour Irla in reading romances; which were not indeed written by the Batavians; but as they were the carriers of the universe, they trafficked in the wit as well as commodities of other nations. The Princess purchased from Mark Michael Rey, the bookseller, all the novels which had been written by the Ausonians and the Welches, the sale of which had been wisely prohibited among those nations, to enrich their neighbours the Batavians. She expected to find in those histories some adventure similar to her own, which might alleviate her grief. The maid of honour read, the phœnix gave his advice, and the princess, finding nothing in the *Fortunate Country Maid*, in the *Sofa*, or in the *Four Facardins*, that had the least resemblance to her own affairs, interrupted the reader every moment, by asking how the wind stood.

§ 8

In the meantime Amazan was on the road to the capital of Albion, in his coach and six unicorns, all his thoughts employed on his dear Princess : at a small distance he perceived a carriage overturned in a ditch; the servants had gone different ways in quest of assistance, but the owner kept his seat, smoking his pipe with great tranquillity, since smoking was the habit then, without testifying the smallest impatience : his name was My Lord What-then, in the language from which I translate these memoirs.

Amazan made all the haste possible to help him, and with his simple arm set the carriage to rights, so much was his strength superior to that of other men. My Lord What-then took no other notice of him than to say, ' A stout fellow, by G—d ! '

Meanwhile the country people, being come up, flew into a great passion at being called out to no purpose, and fell upon the stranger. They abused him, called him dog of a foreigner, and challenged him to fight.

Amazan seized a brace of them in each hand, and threw them twenty paces from him; the rest seeing this, pulled off their hats, and bowing with great respect, asked his Honour for something to drink. He gave them more money than they had ever seen in their lives before. My Lord What-then now expressed great esteem for him, and asked him to dinner at his country house, about three miles off. His invitation being accepted, he went into Amazan's coach, his own being out of order by the accident.

After a quarter of an hour's silence, My Lord What-then, looking upon Amazan for a moment, said, ' How d'ye do? ' which, by the way, is a phrase without any meaning; adding, ' You have got six fine unicorns there.' With this he continued smoking as usual.

M 936

The traveller told him his unicorns were at his service, and that he had brought them from the country of the Gangarides : thereupon he took occasion to inform him of his affair with the Princess of Babylon, and the unlucky kiss she had given the King of Egypt : to this the other made no reply, being very indifferent whether there were any such people in the world as a King of Egypt or a Princess of Babylon. He remained dumb for another quarter of an hour; then he asked his companion a second time how he did, and whether they had any good roast beef among the Gangarides. Amazan answered with his wonted politeness that they did not eat their brethren on the banks of the Ganges; he then explained to him that system which many ages afterwards was named the Pythagorean philosophy. But My Lord fell asleep in the meantime, and made but one nap of it till he came to his own house.

He was married to a young and charming woman, on whom Nature had bestowed a soul as lively and sensible as her husband's was dull and stupid. Several gentlemen of Albion had that day come to dine with her; among whom there were characters of all sorts; for that country having been almost always under the government of foreigners, the families that had come over with these princes had imported their different manners. There were in this company some persons of a very amiable disposition, others of a superior genius, and a few of very profound learning.

The mistress of the house had none of that awkward affected stiffness, that false modesty, with which the young Albion ladies were then reproached; she did not conceal, by a scornful look and an affected taciturnity, her lack of ideas; and the embarrassing humility of having nothing to say. Never was a woman more engaging. She received Amazan with a grace and politeness that were quite natural to her. The extreme beauty of this young stranger, and the sudden comparison she could not help making between him and her husband, immediately struck her in a most sensible manner.

Dinner being served, she placed Amazan at her side, and helped him to all sort of puddings, having learned from himself that the Gangarides never fed upon anything which had received from the gods the celestial gift of life. His beauty and strength, the manners of the Gangarides, the progress of arts, religion, and government, were the subjects of a conversation equally agreeable and instructive all the time of the entertainment, which lasted till night : during which My Lord What-then drank a good deal and said nothing.

After dinner, while my lady was pouring out the tea, still feeding her eyes on the young stranger, he entered into a long conversation with a Member of Parliament; for every one knows that there was, even then, a parliament called Wittenagemot, or the Assembly of Wise Men. Amazan inquired into the constitution, laws, manners, customs, forces, usages, and arts, which made this country so respectable; and the Member of Parliament answered him in the following manner :

' For a long time we went stark naked, though our climate is none of the hottest. We were likewise for a long time enslaved by a people come from the ancient country of Saturn, watered by the Tiber. But the mischiefs we have done one another have greatly exceeded all that we ever suffered from our first conquerors. One of our princes carried his dastardliness to such a pitch, as to declare himself the subject of a priest, who dwells also on the banks of the Tiber, and is called the Old Man of the Seven Mountains : it has been the fate of these seven mountains to domineer over the greater part of Europe, then inhabited by brutes in human shape.

' To those times of infamy and debasement succeeded the ages of barbarity and confusion. Our country, more tempestuous than the surrounding ocean, has been ravaged and drenched in blood by our civil discords; many of our crowned heads have perished by a violent death : above a hundred princes of the royal blood have ended their days on the scaffold, whilst the hearts of their adherents have been torn from their breasts, and thrown in their faces. In short, it is the province of the hangman to write the history of our island, seeing this personage has finally determined all our affairs of moment.

' But to crown these horrors, it is not very long since some fellows wearing black mantles, and others who cast white shirts over their jackets, having been bitten by mad dogs, communicated their madness to the whole nation. Our country was then divided into two parties, the murderers and the murdered, the executioners and the sufferers, plunderers and slaves; and all in the name of God, and whilst they were seeking the Lord.

'Who would have imagined that from this horrible abyss, this chaos of dissension, cruelty, ignorance, and fanaticism, a government should at last spring up, the most perfect, it may be said, now in the world; yet such has been the event. A prince, honoured and wealthy, all-powerful to do good, without any power to do evil, is at the head of a free, warlike, commercial, and enlightened nation. The nobles on one hand and the representatives of the people on the other share the legislature with the monarch.

'We have seen, by a singular fatality of events, disorder, civil wars, anarchy and wretchedness lay waste the country, when our kings aimed at arbitrary power: whereas tranquillity, riches, and universal happiness have only reigned among us, when the prince has remained satisfied with a limited authority. All order has been subverted whilst we were disputing about mysteries, but was re-established the moment we grew wise enough to despise them. Our victorious fleets carry our glory over all the ocean; our laws place our lives and fortunes in security; no judge can explain them in an arbitrary manner, and no decision is ever given without the reasons assigned for it. We should punish a judge as an assassin, who should condemn a citizen to death without declaring the evidence which accused him, and the law upon which he was convicted.

'It is true, there are always two parties among us, who are continually writing and intriguing against each other; but they constantly reunite, whenever it is needful to arm in defence of liberty and our country. These two parties watch over one another, and mutually prevent the violation of the sacred trust of the laws: they hate one another, but they love the State; they are like those jealous lovers, who pay court to the same mistress with a spirit of emulation.

'From the same fund of genius by which we discovered and supported the natural rights of mankind, we have carried the sciences to the highest pitch to which they can attain among men. Your Egyptians, who pass for such great mechanics; your Indians, who are believed to be such great philosophers; your Babylonians, who boast of having observed the stars for the course of four hundred and thirty thousand years; the Greeks, who have written so much, and said so little, know in reality nothing in comparison with our shallowest scholars, who have studied the discoveries of our great masters. We have ravished more secrets from Nature in the space of a hundred years than the human species has been able to discover in as many ages.

'This is a true account of our present state. I have concealed from you neither the good nor the bad; neither our shame nor our glory; and I have exaggerated nothing.'

At this discourse Amazan felt a strong desire to be instructed in those sublime sciences his friend spoke of; and if his passion for the Princess of Babylon, his filial duty to his mother whom he had quitted, and his love for his native country had not made strong remonstrances to his distempered heart, he would willingly have spent the remainder of his life in Albion. But that unfortunate kiss his Princess had given the King of Egypt did not leave his mind at sufficient ease to study the abstruse sciences.

'I confess,' said he, ' to having made a solemn vow to roam about the world, and to escape from myself. I have a curiosity to see that ancient land of Saturn, that people of the Tiber and of the Seven Mountains, who have been heretofore your masters; they must undoubtedly be the first people on earth.'

'I advise you by all means,' answered the other, ' to take that journey, if you have the smallest taste for music or painting. Even we ourselves frequently carry our spleen and melancholy to the Seven Mountains. But you will be greatly surprised when you see the descendants of our conquerors.'

This was a long conversation, and although Amazan was a little touched in the head he spoke in so agreeable a manner, his voice was so charming, his whole behaviour so noble and engaging, that the mistress of the house could not resist the pleasure of having a little private chat with

him in her turn. She tenderly squeezed his hand as she
spoke, and darted such looks at him from her wary and
sparkling eyes, that they shot desire through every movement of the soul. She kept him to supper, and to sleep
there that night. Every moment, every word, every look,
inflamed her passion. When all were retired to rest, she
sent him a little *billet-doux*, not doubting he would come to
entertain her in bed, whilst My Lord What-then was asleep
in his. Amazan had once more the courage to resist;
such marvellous effects does a grain of folly produce in an
exalted and deeply-wounded mind !

Amazan, according to custom, wrote the lady an answer
full of respect, representing to her the sacredness of his oath,
and the strict obligation he was under to teach the Princess
of Babylon to conquer her passions; after which he harnessed his unicorns and departed for Batavia, leaving all
the company in deep admiration of him, and the lady in
profound despair. In the agonies of her grief she dropped
Amazan's letter. My Lord What-then read it next morning.

' Damn it,' said he, shrugging up his shoulders, ' what
stuff and nonsense have we got here? ' and then rode out
fox-hunting with some of his drunken neighbours.

Amazan was already sailing upon the sea, possessed of a
geographical chart, with which he had been presented by
the learned Albion he had conversed with at Lord What-
then's. He was extremely astonished to find the greater
part of the earth upon a single sheet of paper.

His eyes and imagination wandered over this little space;
he observed the Rhine, the Danube, the Alps of Tyrol,
there specified under different names, and all the countries
through which he was to pass before he arrived at the city
of the Seven Mountains; but he more particularly fixed
his eyes upon the country of the Gangarides, upon Babylon,
where he had seen his dear princess, and upon the fatal
country of Bassora, where she had given a kiss to the King
of Egypt. He sighed, and tears streamed from his eyes;
but he agreed with the Albion who had presented him with
the universe in epitome, when he averred that the inhabitants of the banks of the Thames were a thousand times
better instructed than those upon the banks of the Nile,
the Euphrates, and the Ganges.

As he returned into Batavia, Formosanta flew towards Albion with her two ships that went at full sail. Amazan's ship and the Princess's crossed one another, and almost touched; the two lovers were close to each other, which they could not doubt of.

Ah ! had they but known it ! but tyrannic destiny would not allow it.

§ 9

No sooner had Amazan landed on the flat muddy shore of Batavia than he flew like lightning towards the city of the Seven Mountains. He was obliged to traverse the southern part of Germany. At every four miles he met with a prince and princess, maids of honour and beggars. He was astonished everywhere at the coquetries of these ladies and maids of honour, which they displayed with German good faith; and he only answered with modest refusals. After having cleared the Alps he embarked upon the Sea of Dalmatia, and landed in a city that had no resemblance to anything he had heretofore seen. The sea formed the streets, and the houses were erected in the water. The few public places with which this city was ornamented were filled with men and women with double faces; that which Nature had bestowed upon them, and a pasteboard one, ill painted, with which they covered their natural visage; so that this people seemed to consist of spectres. Upon arriving in this country, strangers immediately purchase these visages, in the same manner as people elsewhere furnish themselves with hats and shoes. Amazan despised a fashion so contrary to nature; he appeared just as he was. There were in the city twelve thousand girls registered in the great book of the Republic; these girls were useful to the State, being appointed to carry on the most advantageous and agreeable trade that ever enriched a nation. Common traders usually send, at great risk and expense, merchandises of various kinds to the East; but these beautiful merchants carried on a constant traffic without risk, which constantly sprang from their charms. They all came to present themselves to the handsome

Amazan, and offer him his choice.   He fled with the utmost
precipitancy, uttering the name of the incomparable
Princess of Babylon, and swearing by the immortal gods
that she was far handsomer than all the twelve thousand
Venetian girls.

'Sublime traitress,' he cried in his transports, 'I will
teach you to be faithful ! '

Now, the yellow surges of the Tiber, pestiferous fens, a
few pale emaciated inhabitants, clothed in tatters which
displayed their dry tanned hides, appeared to his sight,
and bespoke his arrival at the gate of the city of the Seven
Mountains, that city of heroes and legislators who conquered and policed a great part of the globe.

He expected to have seen at the triumphal gate five
hundred battalions commanded by heroes, and in the
senate an assembly of demigods giving laws to the earth;
but the only army he found consisted of about thirty
tatterdemalions, mounting guard with umbrellas for fear
of the sun.   Being arrived at a temple which appeared to
him very fine, but not so magnificent as that of Babylon,
he was greatly astonished to hear a concert performed by
men with female voices.

'This,' said he, 'is a mighty pleasant country, which
was formerly the land of Saturn.   I have been in a city
where no one showed his own face;   here is another where
men have neither their own voices nor beards.'

He was told that these singers were no longer men;
that they had been divested of their virility that they might
sing the more agreeably the praises of a great number of
persons of merit.   Amazan could not comprehend the
meaning of this.   These gentlemen desired him to sing;
he sung a Gangaridian air with his usual grace.   His
voice was a fine alto.

'Ah, Signor,' said they, 'what a delightful soprano
you would have, if——'

'If what ? ' said he.   'What do you mean ? '

'Ah ! Signor, if you were——'

'If I were what ? '

'If you were—without a beard ! '

They then explained to him very pleasantly, and with the
most comic gesticulations, according to the custom of their

country, the point in question. Amazan was quite confounded.

' I have travelled a great way,' said he, ' but I never before heard such a whim.'

After they had sung a good while, the Old Man of the Seven Mountains went with great ceremony to the gate of the temple; he cut the air in four parts with his thumb raised, two fingers extended and two bent, in uttering these words in a language no longer spoken : ' To the city and to the universe.'

The Gangarid could not comprehend how two fingers could extend so far.

He presently saw the whole Court of the master of the world file off. This Court consisted of grave personages, some in scarlet, and others in violet robes : they almost all eyed the handsome Amazan with a tender look; they bowed to him, and said to one another, ' *San Martino, che bel ragazzo ! San Pancratio, che bel fanciullo !* '

The zealots, whose vocation was to show the curiosities of the city to strangers, very eagerly offered to conduct him to several ruins, in which a muleteer would not choose to pass a night, but which were formerly worthy monuments of the grandeur of a royal people. He moreover saw pictures two hundred years old, and statues that had remained twenty ages, which appeared to him master-pieces in their kind.

' Can you still produce such works ? '

' No, your Excellency,' replied one of the zealots; ' but we despise the rest of the earth, because we preserve these rarities. We are a kind of old-clothes men, who derive our glory from the cast-off garb in our warehouses.'

Amazan desired to see the Prince's palace, and he was accordingly conducted thither. He saw men dressed in violet-coloured robes, who were reckoning the money of the revenues of the domains of lands, so much from one situated upon the Danube, another upon the Loire, others upon the Guadalquivir, or the Vistula.

' Oh ! oh ! ' said Amazan, after having consulted his geographical map, ' your master, then, possesses all Europe, like those ancient heroes of the Seven Mountains ? '

' He should possess the whole universe by divine right,'

*ₘ 936

replied a violet-liveried man; 'and there was even a time when his predecessors nearly compassed universal monarchy; but their successors are so good as to content themselves at present with some moneys which the kings their subjects pay to them in the form of a tribute.'

'Your master is, then, in fact, the King of kings; is that his title?' said Amazan.

'No, your Excellency, his title is the *servant of servants*; he was originally a fisherman and porter, wherefore the emblems of his dignity consist of keys and nets; but he at present issues orders to every king in Christendom. It is not a long while since he sent one hundred and one mandates to a King of the Celts, and the king obeyed.'

'Your fisherman must then have sent five or six hundred thousand men to put these hundred and one orders into execution?'

'Not at all, your Excellency; our holy master is not rich enough to keep ten thousand soldiers on foot; but he has five or six hundred thousand divine prophets dispersed in other countries. Those prophets of various colours are, as they ought to be, supported at the expense of the people; they proclaim from heaven that my master may, with his keys, open and shut all locks, and particularly those of strong boxes. A Norman priest, who held the post of confidant of this king's thoughts, convinced him he ought to obey, without replying, the hundred and one thoughts of my master; for you must know that one of the prerogatives of the Old Man of the Seven Mountains is never to err, whether he deigns to speak or deigns to write.'

'In faith,' said Amazan, 'this is a very singular man; I should be curious to dine with him.'

'Were your Excellency even a king, you could not eat at his table; all that he could do for you would be to allow you to have one served by the side of his, but smaller and lower. But if you are inclined to have the honour of speaking to him, I will ask an audience for you on condition of the *buona mancia*, which you will be kind enough to give me.'

'Very readily,' said the Gangarid.

The violet-liveried man bowed.

'I will introduce you to-morrow,' said he; 'you must

make three very low bows, and you must kiss the Old Man of the Seven Mountains' feet.' At this information Amazan burst into so violent a fit of laughing that he was almost choked; he went out, holding his sides, and laughed till the tears ran down his cheeks, till he reached the inn, where the fit still continued upon him for a long time.

At dinner, twenty beardless men and twenty violins produced a concert. He received the compliments of the greatest lords of the city during the remainder of the day; these made him proposals still more extravagant than that of kissing the Old Man of the Seven Mountains' feet. As he was extremely polite, he at first imagined that these gentlemen took him for a lady, and informed them of their mistake with great decency and circumspection; but being somewhat closely pressed by two or three of those violet-coloured gentry, who were the most forward, he threw them out of the window, without fancying he had made any great sacrifice to the beautiful Formosanta. With the greatest precipitation he left this city of the masters of the world, where he found himself necessitated to kiss an old man's toe, as if his cheek were at the end of his foot, and where young men are accosted in a more whimsical manner.

§ 10

In all the provinces through which he passed, having constantly repulsed every amorous overture of every species, being ever faithful to the Princess of Babylon, though incessantly enraged at the King of Egypt, this model of constancy at length arrived at the new capital of the Gauls. This city, like many others, had alternately submitted to barbarity, ignorance, folly, and misery. The first name it bore was Dirt and Mire; it then took that of Isis, from the worship of Isis, which had reached even here. Its first senate consisted of a company of watermen. It had long been in bondage, and submitted to the ravages of the heroes of the Seven Mountains; and some ages after, some other heroic thieves, who came from the farther banks of the Rhine, had seized upon its little lands.

Time, which changes all things, had formed it into a city, half of which was very noble and very agreeable, the other half somewhat barbarous and ridiculous : this was the emblem of its inhabitants. There were within its walls at least a hundred thousand people, who had no other employment than play and diversion. These idlers were the judges of those arts which the others cultivated. They were ignorant of all that passed at Court ; though they were only four short miles distant from it :—but it seemed to be at least six hundred thousand miles off. Agreeableness in company, gaiety, and frivolity formed the most important and sole consideration of their lives : they were governed like children, who are extravagantly supplied with gewgaws to prevent their crying. If the horrors which had, two centuries before, laid waste their country, or those dreadful periods when one half of the nation massacred the other for sophisms, were mentioned, they, indeed, said, ' This was not well done '; then they fell to laughing, or singing catches.

In proportion as the leisured classes were polished, agreeable, and amiable, it was observed there was a greater and more shocking contrast between them and those who were engaged in business.

Among the latter, or such as pretended so to be, there was a gang of melancholy fanatics, whose absurdity and knavery divided their character, whose appearance alone diffused misery, and who would have overturned the world, had they been able to gain a little credit. But the nation of idlers, by dancing and singing, forced them into obscurity in their caverns, as the warbling birds drive the creaking bats back to their holes and ruins.

A smaller number of these busybodies were the preservers of ancient barbarous customs, against which Nature terrified loudly exclaimed. They consulted nothing but their worm-eaten registers. If they there discovered a foolish horrid custom, they considered it a sacred law. It was from this vile practice of not daring to think for themselves, but of always extracting their ideas from the ruins of those times when no one thought at all, that in the metropolis of pleasure there still remained some shocking manners. Hence it was that there was no proportion between crime and punishment. A thousand deaths were sometimes inflicted upon an innocent victim, to make him acknowledge a crime he had not committed.

The extravagancies of youth were punished with the same severity as poisoning or parricide. The leisured classes screamed loudly at these exhibitions, and the next day thought no more about them, but were buried in the contemplation of some new fashion.

This people saw a whole age elapse in which the fine arts attained a degree of perfection that far surpassed the most sanguine hopes : foreigners then repaired thither, as they did to Babylon, to admire the great monuments of architecture, the wonders of gardening, the sublime efforts of sculpture and painting. They were charmed with a species of music that reached the heart without astonishing the ears.

True poetry, that is to say, such as is natural and harmonious, that which addresses the heart as well as the mind, was unknown to this nation before this happy period. New kinds of eloquence displayed sublime beauties. The theatres in particular re-echoed with masterpieces that no other nation ever approached. In a word, good taste prevailed in every profession, to such a degree that there were even good writers among the Druids.

So many laurels, that had branched even to the skies, soon withered in an exhausted soil. There remained but a very small number, whose leaves were of a pale dying verdure. This decay was occasioned by the facility of producing, by a laziness which prevented good productions, by a satiety of the brilliant, and by a taste for the bizarre. Vanity protected arts that brought back times of barbarity; and this same vanity, in persecuting real talents, forced them to quit their country; the hornets banished the bees.

There was scarcely any real arts, scarcely any real genius; merit now consisted in reasoning at random upon the merit of the last age. The dauber of an inn sign-post criticized with an air of sagacity the works of the greatest painters; and the blotters of paper disfigured the works of the greatest writers. Ignorance and bad taste had other daubers in their pay; the same things were repeated in a hundred volumes, under different titles. Every work was either a dictionary or a pamphlet. A Druid gazetteer wrote twice a week the obscure annals of an unknown people possessed with the devil and of celestial prodigies operated in garrets by little beggars of both sexes : other ex-Druids, dressed in black, ready to die with rage and hunger, set forth their complaint, in a hundred different writings, that they were no longer allowed to cheat mankind, this privilege being conferred on some goats clad in grey ; and some Arch-Druids were employed in printing defamatory libels.

Amazan was quite ignorant of all this, and even if he had been acquainted with it, he would have given himself very little concern about it, having his head filled with nothing but the Princess of Babylon, the King of Egypt, and the inviolable vow he had made to despise all female coquetry, in whatever country his despair should drive him.

The gaping ignorant mob, whose curiosity exceeds all the bounds of nature and reason, for a long time thronged about his unicorns ; the more sensible women forced open the doors of his lodging to contemplate his person.

He at first testified some desire of visiting the Court ; but some of the idle who constituted good society, and casually went thither, informed him that it was quite out of fashion, that times were greatly changed, and that all amusements were confined to the city. He was invited that very night to sup with a lady, whose sense and talents had reached foreign climes, and who had travelled in some countries through which Amazan had passed. This lady gave him great pleasure, as well as the society he met at her house. Here reigned a decent liberty, gaiety without tumult, science without pedantry, and wit without asperity. He found that the phrase *good society* was not altogether meaningless, though the title was frequently usurped by pretenders. The next day he dined in a society far less amiable, but much more voluptuous. The more he was satisfied with the guests, the more they were pleased with him. He found his soul soften and dissolve, like the aromatics of his country, which gradually melt in a moderate heat and exhale in delicious perfumes.

After dinner he was conducted to a place of public entertainment which was enchanting, but condemned, by the Druids, because it deprived them of their auditors, which excited their jealousy the more. The entertainment here consisted of pleasing verses, delightful songs, dances which expressed the movements of the soul, and scenes that charmed the eye while deceiving it. This kind of pastime, which included so many kinds, was known only under a foreign name; it was called an *Opera*, which formerly signified, in the language of the Seven Mountains, work, care, occupation, industry, enterprise, task, business. This business enchanted him. A female singer, in particular, charmed him by her melodious voice, and the graces that accompanied her : this girl of *business*, after the performance, was introduced to him by his new friends. He presented her with a handful of diamonds; for this she was so grateful that she could not leave him all the rest of the day. He dined with her, and during the repast he forgot his sobriety; and after the repast he also forgot his vow of being ever insensible to beauty, and all the blandishments of coquetry. What an instance of human frailty !

The beautiful Princess of Babylon arrived at this juncture, with her phœnix, her chamber-maid Irla, and her two hundred Gangaridian cavaliers mounted on their unicorns. It was a long while before the gates were opened. She immediately asked if the handsomest, the most courageous, the most sensible, and the most faithful of men was still in that city. The magistrates readily concluded that she meant Amazan. She was conducted to his lodging. She entered, her heart beating. Her whole soul was penetrated with inexpressible joy at seeing once more in her lover the model of constancy. Nothing could prevent her entering his chamber; the curtains were open; and she saw the beautiful Amazan sleeping in the arms of a handsome brunette. They both stood in great need of rest.

Formosanta expressed her grief with such screams as made the house echo, but which could wake neither her cousin nor the girl of *business*. She swooned into the arms of Irla. As soon as she had recovered her senses, she retired from this fatal chamber with grief blended with rage. Irla gained intelligence of the young lady who passed such sweet hours with the handsome Amazan. Irla was told she was a girl of *business*, very complaisant, who united to her other talents that of singing very gracefully.

'O just Heaven! O powerful Ormuzd!' cried the beautiful Princess of Babylon, bathed in tears, 'by whom, and for whom am I thus betrayed? He that could reject for my sake so many princesses, to abandon me for a strolling Gaul! No—I can never survive this affront.'

'Madam,' said Irla to her, 'this is the disposition of all young people, from one end of the world to the other; were they enamoured with a beauty descended from heaven, they would at certain moments be unfaithful to her for the sake of an ale-house girl.'

'It is done,' said the Princess, 'I will never see him again whilst I live: let us depart this instant, and let the unicorns be harnessed.'

The phœnix conjured her to stay at least till Amazan awoke, and he might speak to him.

'He does not deserve it,' said the Princess; 'you would cruelly offend me; he would think that I had desired you to reproach him, and that I am willing to be reconciled to him: if you love me do not add this injury to the insult he has offered me.'

The phœnix, who after all owed his life to the daughter of the King of Babylon, could not disobey her. She set out with all her attendants.

'Whither are you going, Madam?' said Irla to her.

'I do not know,' replied the Princess; 'we will take the first road we find; provided I fly from Amazan for ever I am content.'

The phœnix, who was wiser than Formosanta, because he was divested of passion, consoled her upon the road. He gently remonstrated to her that it was shocking to punish oneself for the faults of another; that Amazan had given her proofs sufficiently striking and numerous of his fidelity, so that she should forgive him for having forgot himself for one moment; that this was the only occasion on which he had been wanting of the grace of Ormuzd; that it would render him only the more constant in love and virtue for the future; that the desire of expiating his fault would raise him beyond himself; that it would be the means of increasing her happiness; that many great princesses before her had forgiven such slips, and had no reason to be sorry afterwards : and he was so thoroughly possessed of the art of persuasion that Formosanta's mind grew more calm and peaceable; she was now sorry she had set out so soon; she thought her unicorns went too fast, but she did not dare return : great was the conflict between her desire of forgiving and that of showing her rage, between her love and vanity. However, her unicorns pursued their pace; and she traversed the world, according to the prediction of her father's oracle.

When Amazan awoke, he was informed of the arrival and departure of Formosanta and the phœnix. He was told of the rage and distraction of the Princess; how she had sworn never to forgive him.

' Then,' said he, ' there is nothing left for me to do, but follow her and kill myself at her feet.'

The report of this adventure drew together his festive companions, who all remonstrated to him that he had much better stay with them; that nothing could equal the pleasant life they led in the centre of arts and peaceable delicate voluptuousness; that many strangers, and even kings, had preferred such an agreeable enchanting repose, to their country and their thrones : moreover, his vehicle was broke, and that a saddler was making another for him according to the newest fashion; that the best tailor of the whole city had already cut out for him a dozen suits in the latest fashion; that the most vivacious and most amiable ladies in the whole city, at whose houses dramatic performances were represented, had each appointed a day to give him a regale. The girl of *business* was in the meanwhile drinking her chocolate at her toilet, laughing, singing, and ogling the beautiful Amazan, who by this time perceived she had no more sense than a goose.

A sincerity, cordiality, and frankness as well as magnanimity and courage constituted the character of this great Prince; he related his travels and misfortunes to his friends. They learnt that he was cousin-germane to the Princess; they were informed of the fatal kiss she had given the King of Egypt.

' Such little tricks,' said they, ' are forgiven between

relations, otherwise one's whole life would pass in perpetual uneasiness.'

Nothing could shake his design of pursuing Formosanta; but his carriage was not ready, and he was compelled to remain three days among the idle, in feasting and pastimes : he, at length, took his leave of them, embracing them, and making them accept of the diamonds of his country that were the best mounted, and recommending to them a constant pursuit of frivolity and pleasure, since they were thereby more agreeable and happy.

' The Germans,' said he, ' are the grey-beards of Europe; the people of Albion are grown men; the inhabitants of Gaul are children, and I love to play with children.'

§ 11

His guides had no difficulty in following the route the Princess had taken; there was nothing else talked of but her and her large bird. All the inhabitants were still in a state of fascination. The people of Dalmatia and the Marches of Ancona were lately surprised in a manner less agreeable, when they saw a house fly in the air; the banks of the Loire, of the Dordogne, the Garonne, and the Gironde, still echoed with acclamations.

When Amazan reached the foot of the Pyrenees, the magistrates and Druids of the country made him dance whether he would or not, a *Tambourin*; but as soon as he cleared the Pyrenees, nothing presented itself that was either gay or joyous. If he here and there heard a peasant sing, it was a doleful ditty : the inhabitants stalked with much gravity, having a few strung beads and a poniard at their waist. The nation, clothed in black, appeared to be in mourning. If Amazan's servants asked passengers any questions, they were answered by signs; if they went into an inn, the host acquainted his guests in three words that there was nothing in the house; but that the things they so pressingly wanted might be fetched a few miles off.

When those votaries to taciturnity were asked if they

had seen the beautiful Princess of Babylon pass, they answered with less brevity than usual :

' We have seen her; she is not so handsome; there are no beauties that are not tawny; she displays a throat of alabaster, which is the most disgusting thing in the world, and which is scarcely known in our climate.'

Amazan advanced towards the province watered by the Betis. The Tyrians had not discovered this country above twelve thousand years, about the time they discovered the great island of Atlantis, inundated so many centuries after. The Tyrians cultivated Betica, which the natives of the country had never done, being of opinion that it was not their place to meddle with anything, and that their neighbours the Gauls should come and cultivate their lands. The Tyrians had brought with them some Hebrews, who, from that time, wandered through every clime where money was to be got. The Hebrews, by extraordinary usury at fifty per cent, had possessed themselves of almost all the riches of the country. This made the people of Betica imagine the Hebrews were sorcerers; and all those who were accused of witchcraft were burnt without mercy by a company of Druids, who were called the Inquisitors, or the *Anthropokaies*. These priests immediately put them in a masquerade habit, seized upon their effects, and devoutly repeated the Hebrews' own prayers, whilst they were baking by a slow fire, *por amor de Dios*.

The Princess of Babylon alighted in that city which has since been called Seville. Her design was to embark upon the Betis to return by Tyre to Babylon, and see again King Belus her father; and forget, if possible, her perfidious lover; or at least to ask him in marriage. She sent for two Hebrews, who transacted all the business of the Court. They were to furnish her with three ships. The phœnix made all the necessary contracts with them, and settled the price after some little dispute.

The hostess was a great devotee, and her husband, who was no less religious, was a Familiar; that is to say, a spy of the Druid Inquisitors *Anthropokaies*. He failed not to inform them that in his house was a sorceress and two Hebrews, who were entering into a compact with the devil, disguised like a large gilt bird. The Inquisitors

having learned that the lady was possessed of a large
quantity of diamonds, swore point blank that she was a
sorceress : they waited till night to imprison the two
hundred cavaliers and the unicorns, which slept in very
extensive stables; for the Inquisitors are cowards.

Having strongly barricaded the gates, they seized
the Princess and Irla; but they could not catch the phœnix,
who flew away with great swiftness; he did not doubt
of meeting with Amazan upon the road from Gaul to
Seville.

He met him upon the frontiers of Betica, and acquainted
him with the disaster that had befallen the Princess.
Amazan was struck speechless with rage; he armed himself
with a steel cuirass damascened with gold, a lance twelve
feet long, two javelins, and an edged sword called the
Thunderer, which at one single stroke would rend trees,
rocks, and Druids : he covered his beautiful head with a
golden casque, shaded with heron and ostrich feathers.
This was the ancient armour of Magog, which his sister
Aldea gave him when upon his journey in Scythia. The
few attendants he had with him all mounted their unicorns.

Amazan, in embracing his dear phœnix, uttered only
these melancholy expressions : ' I am guilty ! Had I
not slept with a girl of *business* in the city of the idle,
the Princess of Babylon would not have been in this
alarming situation; let us fly to the Inquisitors.'

He presently entered Seville. Fifteen hundred alguazils
guarded the gates of the enclosure in which the two hundred
Gangarides and their unicorns were shut up, without being
allowed anything to eat : all the necessary preparations
were being made for the sacrifice of the Princess of Babylon,
her chamber-maid Irla, and the two rich Hebrews.

The high Inquisitor, surrounded by his subaltern
Inquisitors, was already seated upon his sacred tribunal :
a crowd of Sevillians, wearing strung beads at their girdles,
joined their two hands without uttering a syllable; when
the beautiful Princess, Irla, and the two Hebrews, were
brought forth with their hands tied behind their backs, and
dressed in masquerade habits.

The phœnix entered the prison by a dormer window,
while the Gangarides began to break open the doors. The

invincible Amazan shattered them without. They sallied forth all armed upon their unicorns, and Amazan put himself at their head. He had no difficulty in overthrowing the alguazils, the Familiars, or the priests called *Anthropokaies*; each unicorn pierced dozens at a time. The thundering Amazan cut to pieces all he met; the people flew away in black cloaks and dirty ruffs, always keeping fast hold of their blest beads *por amor de Dios*.

Amazan collared the high Inquisitor upon his tribunal, and threw him upon the pile, which was prepared about forty paces distant; and he also cast upon it the other lesser Inquisitors, one after the other. He then prostrated himself at Formosanta's feet.

' Ah! how lovable you are,' said she; ' and how I should adore you, if you had not been faithless to me with a girl of *business* ! '

Whilst Amazan was making his peace with the Princess, whilst his Gangarides cast upon the pile the bodies of all the Inquisitors, and the flames ascended to the clouds, Amazan saw an army that approached him at a distance. An aged monarch with a crown upon his head advanced upon a car, drawn by eight mules, harnessed with ropes; a hundred other cars followed. They were accompanied by grave-looking men in black cloaks and ruffs, mounted upon very fine horses; a multitude of people, with greasy hair, followed silently on foot.

Amazan immediately drew up his Gangarides about him, and advanced with his lance couched. As soon as the King perceived him, he took off his crown, alighted from his car, and embraced Amazan's stirrup, saying to him :

' Man, sent by the gods, you are the avenger of human kind, the deliverer of my country, my protector. These holy monsters, of which you have purged the earth, were my masters, in the name of the Old Man of the Seven Mountains : I was forced to suffer their criminal power. My people would have deserted me, if I had tried even to moderate their abominable crimes. From this moment I breathe, I reign, and I am indebted to you for it.'

He afterwards respectfully kissed Formosanta's hand, and entreated her to get into his coach drawn by eight mules with Amazan, Irla, and the phœnix. The two

Hebrew bankers, who still remained prostrate on the ground through fear and gratitude, now raised their heads; and the troop of unicorns followed the King of Betica into his palace.

As the dignity of a king who reigned over a serious people required that his mules should go at a very slow pace, Amazan and Formosanta had time to relate to him their adventures. He also conversed with the phœnix, admiring and frequently embracing him. He easily comprehended how brutal and barbarous the people of the West should be considered, who ate animals, and did not understand their language; that the Gangarides alone had preserved the nature and dignity of primitive man; but he particularly agreed that the most barbarous of mortals were the Inquisitors, of whom Amazan had just purged the earth. He incessantly blessed and thanked him. The beautiful Formosanta had already forgotten the girl of *business*, and had her soul filled with nothing but the valour of the hero who had preserved her life. Amazan being acquainted with the innocence of the embrace she had given the King of Egypt, and the resurrection of the phœnix, tasted the purest joy, and was intoxicated with the most violent love.

They dined at the palace, but had a very indifferent repast. The cooks of Betica were the worst in Europe. Amazan advised the King to send for some from Gaul. The King's musicians performed, during the repast, that celebrated air which has since been called the *Follies of Spain*. After dinner matters of business were discussed.

The King inquired of the handsome Amazan, the beautiful Formosanta, and the charming phœnix, what they proposed doing.

'For my part,' said Amazan, 'my intention is to return to Babylon, of which I am the heir presumptive, and to request of my uncle Belus my cousin-germane, the incomparable Formosanta, unless she would rather choose to live with me among the Gangarides.'

'My design certainly is,' said the Princess, 'never to separate from my cousin-germane. But I imagine he will agree with me that I should return first to my father, because he only gave me leave to go upon a pilgrimage to Bassora, and I have wandered all over the world.'

' For my part,' said the phœnix, ' I will follow everywhere these two tender generous lovers.'

' You are right,' said the King of Betica; ' but your return to Babylon is not so easy as you may imagine. I receive daily intelligence from that country by Tyrian ships, and my Hebrew bankers, who keep a correspondence with all the people of the earth. The people are up in arms towards the Euphrates and the Nile. The King of Scythia claims the inheritance of his wife, at the head of three hundred thousand warriors on horseback. The Kings of Egypt and India are also laying waste the banks of the Tigris and the Euphrates, each at the head of three hundred thousand men, to revenge themselves for being laughed at. Whilst the King of Egypt is absent from his country, his foe the King of Ethiopia is ravaging Egypt with three hundred thousand men; and the King of Babylon has as yet only six hundred thousand men to defend himself.

' I acknowledge to you,' continued the King, ' when I hear of those prodigious armies which are vomited forth from the East, and their astonishing magnificence; when I compare them to my trifling bodies of twenty or thirty thousand soldiers, which it is so difficult to clothe and nourish; I am inclined to think the eastern subsisted long before the western hemisphere. It should seem that we sprang only yesterday from chaos and barbarity.'

' Sire,' said Amazan, ' the last comers frequently outstrip those who first began the course. It is thought in my country that man was first created in India; but this I am not certain of.

' And,' said the King of Betica to the phœnix, ' what do you think ? '

' Sire,' replied the phœnix, ' I am as yet too young to have any knowledge concerning antiquity. I have lived only about twenty-seven thousand years; but my father, who had lived five times that age, told me he had learnt from his father that the countries of the East had always been more populous and richer than the others. It had been transmitted to him from his ancestors that the generation of all animals had begun upon the banks of the Ganges. For my part,' said he, ' I have not the vanity to be of this opinion. I cannot believe that the foxes of

Albion, the marmots of the Alps, and the wolves of Gaul
are descended from my country : in like manner, I do not
believe that the firs and oaks of your country descended
from the palm and cocoa trees of India.'

' But whence are we descended, then ? ' said the King.

' I do not know,' said the phœnix ; ' all I want to know
is, whither the beautiful Princess of Babylon and my dear
Amazan may go.'

' I very much question,' said the King, ' whether with
his two hundred unicorns he will be able to destroy so many
armies of three hundred thousand men each.'

' Why not ? ' said Amazan.

The King of Betica felt the force of this sublime question,
' Why not ? ' but he imagined sublimity alone was not
sufficient against innumerable armies.

' I advise you,' said he, ' to seek the King of Ethiopia ;
I have connections with that black prince through my
Hebrews. I will give you letters of recommendation to
him : as he is at enmity with the King of Egypt, he will be
only too happy to be strengthened by your alliance. I can
assist you with two thousand sober brave men ; and it will
depend upon yourself to engage as many more of the people
who reside, or rather skip about the foot of the Pyrenees,
and who are called Basques. Send one of your warriors
upon a unicorn with a few diamonds, there is not a Basque
that will not quit the castle, that is, the thatched cottage of
his father—to serve you. They are indefatigable, courageous, and agreeable ; and whilst you wait their arrival, we
will give you festivals, and prepare your ships. I cannot
too much acknowledge the service you have done me.'

Amazan was enjoying the happiness of having recovered
Formosanta, and in conversing with her he tasted in tranquillity all the charms of reconciled love, which are almost
equal to growing passion.

A troop of proud joyous Basques soon arrived, dancing a
tambourin. The other haughty grave troop of Beticans
were ready. The old sunburnt King tenderly embraced
the two lovers ; he sent great quantities of arms, beds,
chess-boards, black clothes, onions, sheep, fowls, flour, and
particularly garlic, on board the ships, in wishing them a
happy voyage, invariable love, and many victories.

The fleet approached the shore, where it is said that, many ages after, the Phœnician lady Dido, sister to one Pygmalion, and wife to one Sichæus, having left the city of Tyre, came and founded the superb city of Carthage, in cutting a bull's hide into thongs, according to the testimony of the gravest authors of antiquity, who never related fables, and according to the professors who have written for young boys; though, after all, there never was a person at Tyre named Pygmalion, Dido, or Sichæus, which names are entirely Greek; and though, in fine, there was no king in Tyre in those times.

Proud Carthage was not then a sea-port; there were at that time only a few Numidians there, who dried fish in the sun. They coasted along Bizacenes, the Syrtes, the fertile banks where since arose Cyrene and the great Chersonese.

They at length arrived towards the first mouth of the sacred Nile. It was at the extremity of this fertile land that the ships of all commercial nations were already received in the port of Canopus without knowing whether the god Canopus had founded this port, or whether the inhabitants had manufactured the god; whether the star Canopus had given its name to the city, or whether the city had bestowed it upon the star : all that was known of this matter was that the city and the star were both very ancient; and this is all that can be known of the origin of things, of what nature soever they may be.

It was here that the King of Ethiopia, having ravaged all Egypt, saw the invincible Amazan and the adorable Formosanta come on shore. He took one for the god of war, and the other for the goddess of beauty. Amazan presented to him the letter of recommendation from the King of Betica. The King of Ethiopia immediately entertained them with some admirable festivals, according to the indispensable custom of heroic times. They then conferred about their expedition to exterminate the three hundred thousand men of the King of Egypt, the three hundred thousand of the Emperor of the Indies, and the three hundred thousand of the great Khan of the Scythians, who laid siege to the immense, proud, voluptuous city of Babylon.

The two hundred Spaniards whom Amazan had brought

with him said that they had nothing to do with the King of Ethiopia's relieving Babylon; that it was sufficient their king had ordered them to go and deliver it; and that they were formidable enough for this expedition.

The Basques said that they had performed many other exploits, that they would alone defeat the Egyptians, the Indians, and the Scythians, and that they would not march with the Spaniards unless these were in the rear-guard.

The two hundred Gangarides could not refrain from laughing at the pretensions of their allies, and they maintained that with only one hundred unicorns they could put to flight all the kings of the earth. The beautiful Formosanta appeased them by her prudence, and by her enchanting discourse. Amazan presented to the black monarch his Gangarides, his unicorns, his Spaniards, his Basques, and his beautiful bird.

Everything was soon ready to march by Memphis, Heliopolis, Arsinoe, Petra, Artemita, Sora, and Apameia, to attack the three kings, and to prosecute this memorable war, in comparison with which all the wars ever waged by man were nothing more than mere cock-fights.

Every one knows how the King of Ethiopia became enamoured with the beautiful Formosanta, and how he surprised her in bed when a gentle sleep closed her long eye lashes. We remember that Amazan, a witness of this spectacle, thought he saw day and night in bed together. It is no secret that Amazan, enraged at the insult, drew his thundering sword, with which he cut off the perverse head of the insolent negro, and drove all the Ethiopians out of Egypt. Are not these prodigies written in the book of the Chronicles of Egypt? Fame has with her hundred tongues proclaimed the victories he gained over the three kings with his Spaniards, his Basques, and his unicorns. He restored the beautiful Formosanta to her father. He set at liberty all his mistress's train, whom the King of Egypt had reduced to slavery. The great Khan of the Scythians declared himself his vassal; and his marriage was confirmed with Princess Aldea. The invincible and generous Amazan, acknowledged heir of the kingdom of Babylon, entered the city in triumph with the phœnix, in the presence of a hundred tributary kings. The festival of his marriage far surpassed that which King Belus had given. The bull Apis was served up roasted at table. The Kings of Egypt and India were cup-bearers to the married pair; and these nuptials were celebrated by five hundred capital poets of Babylon.

Oh! Muses, who are constantly invoked at the beginning of a work, I only implore you at the end. It is needless to reproach me with saying grace, without having said *benedicite*. But, Muses! you will not be less my patronesses. Prevent, I beseech you, any supplemental scribblers spoiling, by their fables, the truths which I have taught mortals in this faithful narrative; in the manner they have falsified *Candide, Master Simple*, and the chaste adventures of the chaste Jane, which have been disfigured by an ex-Capuchin, in verses worthy of Capuchins, in the Batavian editions. May they not do this injury to my typographer, who has a numerous family, and who is scarcely capable to obtain types, paper, and ink.

Oh! Muses, impose silence upon the detestable Cogé, chattering professor of the College of Mazarin, who, not contented with the moral discourses of Belisarius and the Emperor Justinian, has written vile defamatory libels against these two great men.

Gag that pedant Larcher, who, though entirely ignorant of the ancient Babylonian tongue, without ever having travelled, as I have, upon the banks of the Euphrates and the Tigris, has had the impudence to maintain, that the beautiful Formosanta, daughter to the greatest king in the world, and Princess Aldea, and all the women of this respectable Court, prostituted themselves to the grooms of Asia, for money in the great temple of Babylon. This college libertine, the declared foe of you and modesty, accuses the beautiful Egyptians of Mendes, of being enamoured with nothing but goats; secretly proposing to himself, from this example, to make a tour to Egypt, and have some agreeable intrigues.

Being as little acquainted with modern history as antiquity, he insinuates, in order to ingratiate himself with some old dowager, that our incomparable Ninon lay at the age of fourscore, with the Abbé Gedouin, member of the French Academy, and of the Academy of Inscriptions and Belle

Lettres. He never heard of the Abbé Chateauneuf, whom he takes for the Abbé Gedouin. He is as little acquainted with Ninon as he is with the ladies of Babylon.

Muses, daughters of heaven, your foe Larcher goes still further; he pens long eulogiums in favour of pederasty, and has the insolence to say, that all the bambinos of my country are addicted to this infamous practice. He thinks to escape by increasing the number of the guilty.

Chaste and noble Muses, who equally detest pedantry and pederasty, protect me against Mr. Larcher !

And you, Mr. Aliboron, who call yourself Fréron, at one time called a Jesuit; you, whose Parnassus is sometimes at the Bedlam, and sometimes at the corner ale-house; you, who have received so much justice upon all the stages of Europe, in the decent comedy of the *Écossaise*; you, the worthy son of the priest Desfontaines, the offspring of his amours with those beautiful children who carry an iron, and are blindfolded like the son of Venus, and who, like him, fly into the air, though they never go beyond the tops of chimneys; my dear Aliboron, for whom I always entertained so much affection, and who made me laugh for a month incessantly at the time of the performance of the *Écossaise*; I recommend to you my Princess of Babylon : say everything you can against her, so that she may be read.

I shall not here forget you, Ecclessiastical Gazetteer, illustrious orator of the *Convulsionnaires*, Father of the Church founded by the Abbé Bécherand and Abraham Chaumeix; fail not to say in your writings, equally pious, eloquent, and sensible, that the Princess of Babylon is a heretic, a deist, and an atheist. But above all, endeavour to prevail upon the Sieur Riballier to have the Princess of Babylon condemned by the Sorbonne : you will, thereby, afford my bookseller much pleasure, to whom I have given this little history for his new year's gift.